Readers Love LEE PINI

When We Finally Kiss Good Night
"Such a sweet short story of finding a possible HEA and embracing the Miracle of Christmas."

—Paranormal Romance Guild

As Long As You Love Me So
"An adorable young adult/new adult love story, this romance is as sweet as the cover."

—Rainbow Book Reviews

The Boyfriend Fix
"Surprises, secrets, lies and sex."

—Paranormal Romance Guild

By LEE PINI

The Boyfriend Fix
Good at People
Owl You Need is Love
Six Places to Fall in Love
Strangers to Husbands

CAMP LAKE BAY HOLIDAY
As Long As You Love Me So
When We Finally Kiss Good Night

Published by DREAMSPINNER PRESS
www.dreamspinnerpress.com

OWL YOU
NEED IS LOVE

LEE PINI

REAMSPINNER
PRESS

Published by

DREAMSPINNER PRESS

8219 Woodville Hwy #1245
Woodville, FL 32362 USA
www.dreamspinnerpress.com

Owl You Need is Love
© 2025 Lee Pini

Cover Art
© 2025 Reece Notley
reece@vitaenoir.com
Cover content is for illustrative purposes only and any person depicted on the cover is a model.

Trade Paperback ISBN: 978-1-64108-814-5
Digital ISBN: 978-1-64108-813-8
Trade Paperback published April 2025
v. 1.0

To everyone who didn't figure things out right away.

Chapter One

GORDON HATES this drive.

It's been a warm, perfect fall, which means the road is jammed with cabin traffic: Twin Cities suburbanites looking for that last beautiful weekend on the lake before they take in the boat and dock. After he blares his horn and tailgates the fourth person sitting in the left lane doing seventy (the speed limit, when the left lane is for speeders!), he gives up with a vehement "Fucking tourists," and turns off the cruise control.

He has so many better things he could be doing this weekend, but instead he's driving north, Spotify playlist at rock concert decibels, because his grandfather had to go and die.

People die, obviously. Old people, especially. What they do not do, in Gordon's experience, is leave massive undeveloped parcels of land and old houses to their estranged grandsons.

His did, though. Gordon didn't even know his grandfather had died. He didn't know the man, because even though his parents raised him in Sawmill Lake, Minnesota, where his grandfather also lived, his mom never spoke to her own father. Some falling out years ago. Gordon carried on the tradition and never had a relationship with him. He never missed what he never had.

He doesn't miss Sawmill Lake, either. Nothing ever happened there when he was growing up, and he can't imagine anything's happened since he left twenty years ago. It's a typical northern Minnesota small town.

God, he's supposed to be packing up Becky's things that somehow made their way to his new apartment. Including the potato masher. Which means he's going to have to buy a potato masher.

Maybe he'll pick one up this weekend in Sawmill Lake. That is, if he can find one that doesn't have a bear or a loon on it. Yeah, right. Who is he kidding? Sawmill Lake's main industry is selling northern Minnesota kitsch to all the cabin people from the Cities. It's not much of an industry, from what Gordon remembers. No one from the Cities has a cabin in Sawmill Lake—they only drive through on the way to more picturesque places.

He almost misses his exit because he's passing another idiot too busy messing around on their phone to pay attention to driving. There's a lot less traffic on the state highway that leads to town, though. By the time he rolls up on Water Street, he's more on the disgruntled side of Bad Mood than outright pissed.

He parks in front of Edna's Diner. God, this place is still here? It was one of his high school hangouts. How old is Edna? She seemed ancient back then.

Gordon grimaces. He probably would seem ancient to his teenage self. Thirty-six years old, engaged and de-engaged? He's a fossil.

Thinking of himself as a fossil probably makes him seem even older. Kids probably don't say that anymore.

Even though this town is the last place he wants to be, the sight of Edna's makes nostalgia bite at him. And he's hungry after the drive. *And*, most importantly, he's putting off seeing his grandfather's lawyer (aka the only lawyer in town) as long as possible. "Oh, what the hell," Gordon mutters, getting out of the car and going inside.

There's still a bell on the door, which tinkles as it swings inward. Gordon stops for a second to take in the place. It looks exactly the same. Same green vinyl booths, same Formica counter, same glass case by the register filled with pies. Hopefully the pies aren't the same, but he wouldn't be surprised if all the old standards were in there. Cherry, apple, peach, rum raisin, lemon meringue. The place smells the same too—like grease and stale cigarette smoke.

At least there aren't ashtrays on the tables anymore like there were when he was a kid. No blue haze of cigarette smoke, either, which is also an improvement.

He seats himself and within a minute a middle-aged woman in yoga pants and a department store blouse is at the table, menu in hand. Gordon scans her face, wondering if he knows her. Knew her. She's blond and her mascara is a little clumpy. Her skin has that leathery look that too much time outside without sunscreen gives you.

Her name tag says Steph, and his mind comes up empty on any Stephs from his childhood. She doesn't look much older than him, though, in which case she would have been an unattainable older woman.

"Can I get'cha something to drink, hon?" Steph asks.

"Coffee?" Gordon hates himself for the rise in inflection. "Coffee," he repeats definitively.

"Sure. I'll give you a minute with the menu and be right back with that."

The menu is huge, one of those extra-long sheets, edged in vinyl with tarnished metal corners and laminated in what seems like an old shower liner. Grease, grease, grease, house salad, grease. Also just like the way it used to be. He decides on a chicken sandwich because it seems the least unhealthy.

Steph returns with coffee and takes his order. The coffee goes down like battery acid; Gordon winces and doctors it with several packets of sugar and powdered creamer. How long can he justify sitting here, rotting his stomach by drinking this crap, before he goes to meet the lawyer?

The last few weeks feel unreal. They started with him finally, after years of handwringing and soul-searching, coming out as bi to his fiancée, Becky. It went perfectly. She was super supportive, and he felt... lighter. Weightless. Like he could finally take a full breath now that he was embracing his full self.

Then Becky broke up with him. Their shared life had to be detangled—they'd lived together for years before Gordon had proposed—and they had an entire house to divide and pack up. In the course of that, Becky revealed that the reason she broke off the engagement wasn't, like she'd said, because she "wasn't ready for marriage after all." During a huge fight over a bunch of stupid things, she threw in his face that the reason she broke up with him was because she couldn't be married to a bi man.

"Everyone knows," she'd said, "that bi guys are really just gay guys who haven't figured it out yet."

Obviously, he dealt with that in a really healthy way: by getting drunk on a Sunday night at a mall Applebee's and stumbling home to his new apartment. The next morning, he got the call from his grandfather's lawyer. Hungover and miserable, he listened as the lawyer informed him that his grandfather had died recently and that the will named Gordon as beneficiary of the house and the three hundred and four acres it sat on.

The chicken sandwich arrives, along with a refill on his coffee. Gordon wasn't even aware he was drinking it.

He's almost done with the sandwich when a voice above him exclaims, "Holy shit, is that Gordy Schumacher?"

A man stands in front of his table, hands out like he's ready to stop traffic, a comically agape expression on his face. His sandy hair is thinning, and he has a bit of a gut. Midwestern Dude Gone To Seed.

"Yeah…," Gordon says slowly in his best *do I know you?* voice.

The man grins and thumps himself on the chest. "It's Jason! Jason Miller!"

Gordon's brain spins uselessly until it manages to access the rarely used files where his memories of this place are stored. It finally clicks. "Jason! Oh my god!"

Oh my god is right. Jason Miller is the same age as him. They were in the same grade. Friends, kind of. Does Gordon look like he does?

Okay, maybe he could stand to drop a few pounds. Maybe more than a few. He'd like to think of himself as *cuddly*, but he's kind of worried people look at him and just see *fat*. Or maybe he can qualify as a bear? At least his hair is as thick as always. Last time he checked, there wasn't any gray hiding in the black, and no gray in his body hair. Now that he's starting all over on the dating market, this stuff matters again.

Jason Miller looks thrilled, and Gordon tries to remember if they were better friends than he thinks. Didn't they just smoke behind the school together sometimes? "Are you back in town?" Jason asks.

"No," Gordon says immediately. Because he's not.

"Just in town for a visit?"

Gordon hesitates. While getting into the whole thing isn't something he wants to do, sharing some of it would maybe get a little bit of the weight off his chest. "My grandfather died a few weeks ago," he says.

With a stoic grimace of sympathy, Jason says, "Sorry to hear that, man."

"No, it's okay—I mean, thanks. But I didn't really know him." Picking at a chip on the edge of the table, Gordon adds, "I guess I'm mentioned in the will, so I came up to meet with the lawyer."

At that moment, Steph comes by with the check. "Whenever you're ready, hon," she says. Maybe she heard about him being in a will and is hoping for a good tip.

"Well, I should probably…," Gordon says, motioning vaguely between the bill and the door.

"Sure, sure, I don't want to keep you." Jason steps back so Gordon can get out of the booth to pay, then follows him out of the diner to the sidewalk. "Listen, are you going to be in town a couple days? We should grab a few beers, catch up. Where've you been living, anyway?"

"Minneapolis." Not anymore, of course—not since he moved out of the house he owned with Becky in Northeast. Now he's in one of the suburbs, because apartments are cheaper. "You're still around here?"

Proudly, Jason says, "Yep. I work over at my cousin's real estate company in Hibbing. Trying to move from payroll to selling."

"Oh." C'mon, Gordon, do better. "That's cool."

"Pays the bills. So, what do you say about those beers?" There's a kind of goading look on Jason's face, like he knows he's suggesting something fun and maybe a little transgressive.

Of course, it's not, because they're men in their mid-thirties now, not kids drinking PBRs in a field, but what the hell. Gordon could do worse than have a few beers with a friendly face from the past. "Yeah, I'm staying for a week to get everything in order." At his grandfather's old house, which is now *his* house. He's assuming he can get the internet hooked up again so he can work from here next week instead of taking more PTO. "We could get drinks later?"

"Get drinks!" Jason slaps him on the back. "You sound like my ex making plans with her girlfriends."

Gordon finds himself smiling weakly and reflexively, even though it was a gross comment. Before he figures out how to respond, a loud engine rumble fills the air. It's annoying, but also not unexpected in a small northern Minnesota town. He looks for the source of the sound, expecting a souped-up pickup.

Instead, he sees an old Crown Vic rolling down Water Street, windows down despite the crisp bite in the September air. Music is blasting from the open windows, which Gordon recognizes after a second—"Loser" by Beck. The Crown Vic obviously has a past as a police car. It still has the black-and-white paint job and a grill on the front fender.

The Crown Vic turns sharply into a parking place on the other side of the street, tires squealing. "Speaking of girlfriends," Jason says with a chuckle.

The comment doesn't make much sense to Gordon, especially not when a tall, just-this-side-of-gangly man unfolds himself from the driver's seat. He's Minnesota pale, with unkempt, shaggy blond hair. For a second after getting out of his car, he stands there, glancing around, until his eyes fall on Gordon and Jason.

Jason gives the man an exaggerated wave and yells across the street, "Hey, Charlie! Pull the wings off any flies lately?"

Even from across the street, Gordon sees how the guy's face shutters. He yanks his denim shearling jacket tighter and hurries into the Ben Franklin store he's parked in front of.

Gordon frowns and looks at Jason. There's definitely a dynamic between Jason and that guy that he doesn't understand, but shouting mean comments at your neighbors isn't cool. "What was that all about?" he asks.

Still chuckling, Jason says, "What, Charlie Manson over there?" When Gordon doesn't say anything, Jason adds incredulously, "You remember, don't you? He was such a freak when we were in high school! He's still a weird little guy."

Granted, Gordon has tried to block out most of his high school memories, but he doesn't remember a Charlie Manson. "I don't think I knew him."

"Sure you did! C'mon, remember, he looked like Fall Out Boy, dyed his hair black and wore all that black eye makeup. It was gay as hell." Jason slaps Gordon on the back. "Careful if you're alone in a dark room with him, is all I'm saying."

There *was* a group of kids in high school who slouched around all in black. Gordon has a bad feeling he made fun of them, and an even worse feeling that if the people he was hanging out with called anyone gay (or worse), Gordon probably went right along with it.

Now, he replies, "I'm not sure what you *are* saying, actually."

The chill in his voice makes Jason's smile fade. "Hey, I don't have any problem with gay people. Nothing wrong with it. I mean, unless some dude tries to cop a feel or something."

Gordon grits his teeth. Same old Sawmill Lake. Suddenly, the meeting with the lawyer is looking a lot more tolerable.

"Well, I better get going," Gordon says, taking a step backward toward his car.

"Right, right! Hope there's something good for you in the will." Jason's face lights up. "And hey! Let me give you my number. I know a great place to get a couple beers."

There's no polite way to say he doesn't want Jason's number or to renege on the plans to meet later. Well, maybe there is, but Gordon doesn't know it. He's too Minnesotan, plus there's some weird, nagging

Arab urge toward hospitality from his mom. So instead of saying what he'd like to, he gives Jason his phone number and agrees again that it will be great to catch up at the bar.

When Gordon sets off down the sidewalk toward the lawyer's office two blocks away, he's scowling again. He's only been back in this dumb town for half an hour, and he's already added one more thing to the list of stuff he doesn't need in his life—an old house, a bunch of land, and a shitty acquaintance from his youth.

One week. He'll get all the paperwork in order, and then he'll put the house and land up for sale. He doesn't care what happens to it. If a developer wants to come in, knock down the house, and put up a Walmart, good for them. After he unloads the place, it won't be his problem anymore.

Chapter Two

YOU WOULD think that sixteen years out of high school, you wouldn't still get called the same nasty nicknames. Maybe Charlie's special, though. Maybe he just doesn't appreciate how witty and hilarious a nickname "Charlie Manson" is.

Charlie lingers at the back of the Ben Franklin for longer than he needs to, just to make sure Jason Miller isn't still standing outside. He only came in for some sewing supplies and more shoelaces, and he's really taking his time matching the colors of the thread to the shoelaces. Which doesn't matter. Like. At all. Except he really doesn't want Jason Miller shouting at him again.

At least the guy with him didn't join in. Charlie did a double take when he looked across the street, because for a second, he was sure that the unfamiliar man with Jason wasn't actually unfamiliar. He thought, for a *second*, that it was Gordon Schumacher.

But that's impossible, because Gordon Schumacher didn't come back to town for his grandfather's funeral, so why would he be here now? No, it was just someone who looked strikingly like him. Some friend of Jason's, which meant he was no one Charlie wanted to know.

Charlie adds another spool of thread and another pack of sewing needles to his basket. It's been at least fifteen minutes now, so he chances going to the front of the store. His shoulders sag in relief as he sees through the window that the sidewalk across the street is empty. He brings his basket to the register, beaming when he sees that Donna is there.

"Charlie!" she greets. "When did you sneak in?"

"Um, a little b-bit ago." Stupid stutter. His ears go red, too, even though he's known Donna for years and really doesn't feel shy around her. She's an older lady, probably in her seventies? Charlie's not great with judging people's ages, but her hair is white, and she has wrinkles from a lifetime of smiling and laughing.

"I must have been on my break," Donna says, smiling. "I'm glad you came in today! That special thread you ordered came in."

"Really?" Charlie brightens. "That was fast!"

She chuckles. "I think they expect the order by now. This little old Ben Franklin store in the middle of nowhere's been ordering spools of nylon thread for decades now. First Ibrahim, now you." His face must fall at the mention of Ibrahim. His heart does, so why wouldn't his face? Donna reaches for his hand and clasps it tightly in hers. Her skin is dry and papery but comforting. "I'll get the thread from the back."

"Thanks," he mumbles, embarrassed. There's a lump in his throat suddenly, and his eyes are stinging, and he hates showing that kind of emotion in front of anyone. He's already the town's favorite target of mockery. Showing the wrong kind of emotion will just give them something new to jeer about.

His sister, if they talked more than once a year, would tell him to just leave this ass-backward town, already. Maybe he should. She did. Except he has roots here that matter, even if they only matter to him and all the strangers he shares his research with.

Donna bustles back to the front with the thread he had the store order. It's several types of black nylon: a heavy duty one, a super heavy duty one, and a fine one. He needs it to repair his mist nets, the long nets used to catch birds, mostly, but people use them for bats too.

One time when Charlie was out with Ibrahim, they caught a bat. Charlie was terrified about extracting it from the net—he knew how to get birds out, even the teeny songbirds that sometimes get confused and fly into the net at night. But the bat might as well have been an alien species for all Charlie knew what to do with it, and he was so scared he was going to hurt it.

Ibrahim didn't blink, though. He held the bat gently while he untangled it, and when he had to cut one of the thicker trammel lines that buttress each pocket of the net, he said, "The health of the animal first, Charlie. Always. Nets can be mended, but we can't undo any hurt we cause an animal."

The lump comes back to Charlie's throat and he has to look down at the counter and blink back tears. Donna scans his purchases and bags up everything, pretending she doesn't notice him crying. Normally he would have already made the repairs to his nets instead of waiting practically until his research season starts, but Ibrahim's health deteriorated so fast, and— they'd normally done it together, sewing up holes, knitting together loose or saggy spots. A very stupid, very childish part of Charlie had insisted that if he repaired his nets on his own, it was like giving up on Ibrahim.

Ibrahim died anyway.

"Oh, honey," Donna says. Charlie still can't look at her. "I know he meant a lot to you."

Charlie clears his throat and waits for the tears to subside. Another customer walking in through the door helps with that. His shoulders tighten and he hardens himself, just in case it's someone who's made a professional sport out of mocking him.

They don't, but the knot of tension between his shoulders stays right where it is. He takes a swift breath and manages to meet Donna's eyes. She smiles at him and taps the spot on the cash register that shows the total. Charlie pays and Donna slides the paper bag across the counter. In a whisper, she says, "Threw in a little treat for you. Look once you're outside."

"I don't want you to get in trouble," he whispers back.

"Oh, psh." She waves a dismissive hand. "Just show me some pictures of those cute little owls."

He smiles. "Of course."

Motioning, she says, "Now get going. Have your treat. Not while you drive!"

That gets a laugh out of him. "Promise."

When he gets outside, he peeks into the bag. There's a Pearson's Salted Nut Roll sitting on top of all his other purchases. He huffs out another quiet laugh. Donna's always doing stuff like this. He guesses with Ibrahim gone, she's his only friend in Sawmill Lake. She's definitely the only one who knows that every October and November, he goes out and sits in the woods, trying to catch migrating owls in nets.

As he goes back to his car, he sees someone hurrying down the sidewalk. It's the man who was standing with Jason when Charlie got here, he realizes, which makes him hunch his shoulders, trying to be as inconspicuous as possible. But the man doesn't glance his way, instead flinging the front passenger door of his car open and grabbing something from the seat.

When he straightens and locks the car again (which marks him as an outsider even more clearly than the Bloomington Toyota license plate frame), Charlie gets another look at him. Light brown skin, thick, curly black hair, full lips, short beard, nose with a slight hook to the end of it.

Charlie freezes like a deer caught in headlights. It's been years—sixteen of them, to be exact—but now that he's paying more attention, there's no mistaking it. The husky build and short beard make him look grown up, but that's definitely Gordon Schumacher, back in town after leaving and not looking back.

Gordon Schumacher, who is Ibrahim's estranged grandson. Why is he here? He didn't come for the funeral. Charlie knows they haven't—*hadn't*—spoken in decades, but he never knew why. Some fight between Ibrahim and his daughter, Gordon's mother, that left such a rift that it never healed.

Which Charlie always felt bad about, and then a little guilty, because maybe Gordon's loss was Charlie's gain. Maybe Ibrahim never would have become his mentor and his friend if Gordon was around.

Instead, there was Charlie, alone and angry about... well, about everything, from his deadbeat father to his mom's illness, from the state of the world to the ignorance of the people around him, from the way he was bullied at school to the fact that school was boring and stupid, from the hope things would get better when he graduated to the reality that they didn't. The same bullies were still there, making fun of Charlie's clothes and his hair and the way he stutters and calling him slurs.

And then Ibrahim had taken him under his wing. So to speak.

Gordon hurries away from his car again, clutching a thick manila envelope to his chest. Charlie breaks out in a sweat. He doesn't really care if Gordon comes back or not, but there's one thing that might be a problem. Charlie was still planning on setting his nets up on Ibrahim's land.

It's a perfect spot—isolated, quiet, with a nice stand of cedars that the owls prefer. He already trimmed back all the undergrowth and branches that take over his net lanes through the spring and summer. Yesterday after logging off work, Charlie paced out the length of the nets and hammered the ground poles into place. He just has to repair his nets this afternoon; then he's ready to set up tonight and start his research season.

Absently, he tears open the wrapper of the Salted Nut Roll and takes a big bite of peanuts, caramel, and nougat while his eyes follow Gordon's rapid progress down the sidewalk and into Kristofferson & Klein Law.

The only lawyer in town probably means Ibrahim's will. At least, Charlie assumes Ibrahim had one, though he doesn't know for sure. It doesn't bode well for Charlie continuing to use Ibrahim's land. Land goes to family, not the town weirdo, even if the town weirdo was the one who stayed. The only one who cared.

He's glad he spent a little extra time tidying Ibrahim's house this week, finally tucking away the old photo albums and the children's book Ibrahim was looking at, that he left out before he—

That last day. Before the ambulance came. At least, Charlie assumes Ibrahim was looking at the photo albums and the kid book, since obviously he wasn't there. The book is in Arabic, so Charlie doesn't know what it's called, but there's a young Middle Eastern boy on the cover with a falcon, so he can take a wild guess that it's about falconry.

He didn't have the emotional fortitude to look at either the albums or the book. He's finally getting to the point where he can be in the house without bursting into huge wracking sobs that hurt his rib cage. Ibrahim can't be gone, and yet he obviously is. Charlie put the photo albums and the book in Ibrahim's bedside table, as though he's going to come back and pick up where he left off looking at them.

The house is tidy for Gordon now. That's a good thing, probably.

Charlie finishes his candy bar and tosses the wrapper in a garbage can. There's nothing he can do about the ownership of Ibrahim's land, and he doesn't plan on giving up his net lanes. He'll just keep using them, and if Gordon has a problem with it, well, then… then Charlie will figure that out later.

Chapter Three

GORDON LEARNS several useful facts during the two hours he spends at Lakeside Tavern. One, Jason thankfully improves with alcohol. Two, Gordon has to continue to endure him, because the cousin Jason works for in Hibbing is in commercial real estate, and Jason's going to put him in touch with Gordon about the three hundred and four acres he suddenly finds himself in possession of.

Three, said three hundred and four acres are apparently widely believed to be haunted.

"Haunted?" Gordon laughs. He hasn't had anywhere near enough shitty beer to believe that. "Haunted by what? Wait, don't tell me, the house is built on a Native American burial mound. Or no, an Ojibwe maiden threw herself off a cliff on the land?"

There's no cliff on the land. There's no cliff anywhere in Sawmill Lake.

"You're laughing now, man, but I'm telling you." Jason points the neck of his bottle at Gordon. "People see shit in there. Lights. Something moving around in the trees. Always in the fall too… right around Halloween…."

"Ooooooh, spooky," Gordon says. "And it couldn't be, I don't know, kids?"

"Kids get chased out." Jason pauses, presumably for dramatic effect. "By something."

"*Something*," Gordon snorts. "Probably my grandfather. I get the sense he didn't like people much."

That feels like maybe a bit of an understatement after the meeting with the lawyer. Mr. Klein was polite and did a lot of Minnesota talking-around an awkward topic, but it sounded like Gordon's grandfather was unpleasant every time he had an appointment at the office.

That fits, right? He and Mom had such a huge, earth-shattering fight that they never spoke again. He had no presence in Gordon's life. He didn't come to Mom's funeral. He probably wasn't a great guy.

"Bet you twenty bucks you see something creepy out there this week." Jason swigs his Michelob, smirking.

"I don't want to take your money," Gordon says, smirking right back.

Jason clunks his beer down and leans forward across the high top. "Worried there's actually something out there?"

"One hundred percent no." Gordon swallows a mouthful of Surly, which is the closest thing to craft beer he could get at Lakeside. "Just not interested in boring bets."

"Chicken." Jason lets out a yeasty belch. "'Scuse me. What if we make it less boring, then? Fifty?" When Gordon chuckles, Jason adds, "A hundred?"

Gordon leans back in his chair and glances around the bar. Dim and a little dingy, all knotted-pine log construction, like he's in a damn voyageur cabin. There's a cardboard six-pack carrier on the table holding napkins, water-spotted cutlery, and bottles of ketchup and mustard that make Gordon's hands feel sticky even though he hasn't touched them. A paper menu listing a selection of greasy appetizers is taped on the front of the cardboard.

"Well?" Jason prompts.

Gordon shakes his head. "Pretty sure I've seen this movie. I take the bet, foolishly overconfident in my city-dwelling science ways, and you and some of your buddies sneak onto the land tonight dressed up as ghosts or something, scaring the shit out of me and making yourself a cool hundred."

Jason looks guilty. Gordon folds his arms over his chest and says, "I should've bet on *that*."

To Jason's credit, he laughs and gives Gordon a good-natured smile. "Okay, okay. The idea crossed my mind. But I'm not pulling your leg about it being haunted out there. That's true."

After draining the rest of his beer, Gordon says, "Maybe I'll get one of those ghost hunter shows out there before I sell off the place. If they find ghosts, your cousin can sell the land to a hotel and turn it into a big thing. Haunted hotel packages. Full cooked breakfast and ghosts! Goldmine."

It's really not that funny, but Jason's kind of drunk, so he laughs loudly. Gordon will take it. He actually can't really remember the last time he made someone laugh. Definitely not Becky, and the one time in the last month he had time to meet a friend, all Gordon did was get in his feels about Becky leaving. He was too scared to even come out to Jennifer, even though she's his best friend, because he was too afraid she'd say the same thing that Becky had about him just being in denial about being gay. She'd have been nicer about it, but... what if she dismissed him like that?

Anyway, it goes without saying that Gordon won't be coming out to Jason. It hadn't been in his plans to come out to anyone in this town, but after Jason's casual homophobia about that Charlie guy, it's definitely off the table.

"You were always funny, Gordy. That's what I liked about you in high school," Jason says.

Gordon shrugs and gets to his feet. "I'd say *I'll be here all night...* but I won't. I better get over to my grandfather's house to see what kind of shape it's in. For all I know the guy was a hoarder and I'll have to clear a path to a couch."

Raising his bottle, Jason says, "Good luck, man. Text me if you need a hand clearing shit out this weekend."

Gordon pauses. "Really?" Maybe Jason isn't so bad after all.

"Sure." Jason smiles. "What are friends for, right?"

"Right...." Maybe Jason's drunker than he seems. Maybe *Gordon* is drunker than he thinks, and he's hallucinating this. Clearing out the house that belonged to the dead grandfather of a high school acquaintance has to rank even higher on the Worst Things to Get Dragged Into list than helping someone move. "Well, thanks. I'll let you know."

When Gordon steps outside, the last of the September daylight has nearly faded and the hint of chill in the air from earlier has thickened to a damp bite. So much for that perfect fall. Above the horizon of pines, the sky is a clear, washed lavender. A few bright stars shine in the gauzy gloaming. Or maybe they're planets. Gordon's never been good at that stuff.

He has to flip through the folder he brought back from the lawyer's office, where he scribbled down his grandfather's address. He punches it into his phone and turns the volume up all the way so he can hear the turn-by-turn instructions. His Corolla doesn't have one of those built-in displays that connects to your phone. Too old. Maybe when he sells this property, he can get a new car. And pay off his student loans. And have enough left over for a down payment on a house so he doesn't have to live in an apartment building across the parking lot from one of the Cities' dumpiest malls.

Despite the fact that Sawmill Lake is a small town (population: 3,346), it still takes almost ten minutes to get from Lakeside Tavern to the house.

At least, Gordon hopes that's where he is. It's almost fully dark when his phone announces, "Your destination is on the right," but somehow it doesn't just feel dark, it feels... lightless. He doesn't see a house at all, just a gravel driveway with a mailbox at the end of it. Cautiously, he eases off the road and into the driveway, reading the reflective stick-on numbers on the mailbox—14614, which matches what he wrote down.

Well, good. It's the right place. He aims the car down the driveway and follows it for what feels like half a mile but is probably more like two hundred feet. His headlights cut through the dark to illuminate a two-story farmhouse. Stairs lead up to a front porch and a door. It's hard to tell in the anemic light from his headlights, but the house looks like it's painted green. There aren't any glaringly obvious horror movie red flags, like huge strips of paint peeling from the outside or the front porch sagging so much that a stiff breeze could knock it down.

Taking a deep breath, Gordon fishes the key from the envelope that was included with everything the lawyer gave him. Gravel crunches under his shoes as he gets out of the car. The sound of the door slamming is too loud—or maybe it's just that there's no other noise. It's eerily silent. No loud music, no buses. No road noise at all. No planes.

He forgot how quiet it gets at night up here. Never quite *this* quiet in town, where Gordon's childhood home was, but still quiet. When he moved down to Minneapolis, the constant background noise of a metropolitan area was a big adjustment. Now he's doing it in reverse.

Not that he's going to get used to it. He's here for a week. Just enough time to get stuff in order, then he can do everything else from a distance. He doesn't need to be around to sell the property.

As he walks up the steps to the front porch, he remembers Jason's insistence that this place is haunted. It's kind of creepy out here, sure. Quiet. Isolated. Dark as fuck. So like, sure, Gordon can see where a rumor like that might get started, that it's haunted. Obviously, it isn't.

The back of Gordon's neck prickles like someone's watching him from the dark.

He fumbles to get the key in the lock, missing a few times. The prickling on the back of his neck gets worse, crawling down his shoulders and into his chest. His heart rate picks up each time he doesn't fit the key into the lock, and he tells himself to just *not look back*—

The key finally slides home and Gordon turns it with a rush of air, stumbling over the threshold. He whirls, eyes darting across the driveway, from the tree on one side, to his car, to a wooden fence on the other side. There is, of course, nothing there.

Jesus. This property isn't haunted. Jason was messing with him.

Still, Gordon is really, *really* hoping the electric company got out here to turn on the power after he called.

With the aid of his phone flashlight, he finds a light switch. The light blazes on and Gordon finds himself in a large, neat kitchen. Copper-bottomed pots and pans hang from pegs on one wall. There's a double-basin sink with a drying rack next to it, empty of dishes. The cabinets look old but well-maintained, as do the appliances.

Gordon approaches the counter. There's a puzzle book sitting there with mail stacked tidily next to it, including several magazines. Gordon picks up the one on the top. It's about birds. He flips through it, a weird, dizzy feeling coming over him. This is a thing he knows about his grandfather now. His grandfather liked birds. It's the *only* thing he knows about his grandfather, at least until he starts going through more things in the house.

Even seeing his grandfather's name on the mail is a jolt. Ibrahim Yassin. Gordon hasn't really been thinking of him as a real person who had a real life. A name, interests, hobbies. A job? He has no idea what his grandfather did for a living or if he was still working when he died.

For the first time, a tiny tendril of regret creeps through him. But there's no point in that now—Ibrahim Yassin is dead and gone. Gordon had no relationship with him and now he never will. He can't even ask anyone *why*. His mother is dead too, killed in a car accident six years ago.

Maybe his dad knows, but Gordon isn't close to his dad. After his parents got divorced, it kind of seemed like his dad wasn't interested in more than a call, and later a text, on major holidays and birthdays.

Gordon nudges another bird magazine out of the pile. There's a fierce-looking bird on the cover with bright orange eyes and a wicked, curved beak. Some kind of hawk, Gordon thinks. Probably not the same ones he sees sitting on streetlights along the freeway in the Cities. The magazine is called *North American Falconry*.

That pings something in the back of his brain. Didn't he read some book when he was a kid about people catching falcons and like… training them, or something?

He stops and stares blankly into the distance, the memory picking at the edges of solidity. How weird—he hasn't thought about that book in a million years. He can't remember what it was about, just that the cover was a brown kid in a thawb with a desert-y landscape in the background and a bird like the one on the cover of the magazine flying at his shoulder.

He can't remember where it went. Maybe he got bored with it and his parents tossed it. That's two questions he could ask his dad, now. Maybe he should actually break the only-texting-on-birthdays-and-holidays unofficial rule.

Later. Just because the kitchen is tidy doesn't mean the rest of the house will be. With a deep breath, Gordon walks through the open door in the kitchen to the next room. When he turns the light on, he's pleasantly surprised again. This must be the living room. Couch—old but clean, armchair, coffee table. There's a potted palm by one window, surprisingly green and healthy considering no one's been watering it.

The rest of the house is the same. Well-kept, clean, and full of little hints as to the person his grandfather was. Gordon can't bring himself to examine the bedroom, other than flipping the light on and off. He hasn't seen any evidence of ghosts yet, but he has a feeling they'll find him if he makes himself at home in his dead grandfather's bedroom tonight.

In the closet nearest to the bathroom, Gordon finds some sheets and blankets, which he brings downstairs to make a bed up for himself on the couch. They smell a tiny bit musty, but clean.

With that done, Gordon stops and stands in the quiet, still house. It's early, too early to go to bed, but he's not sure what to do. There's a TV in the living room—an *ancient* TV. Whoa. Gordon goes closer just to marvel at it. It's one of the huge ones they had when he was a kid. It must work or it wouldn't be here, but it definitely can't stream anything.

Gordon finds a remote on the coffee table and turns the TV on experimentally. It flickers to life and a laugh track blares from the speaker.

He jumps, heart pounding, and laughs at himself before turning the volume down. It's just an old sitcom from the nineties. Looks like his grandfather had cable, and apparently it hasn't been shut off yet. That gives him hope for the internet, but he doesn't feel like checking for a Wi-Fi signal right now.

Instead, he settles on the couch, leaning back into the soft, unsupportive cushions. The sitcom isn't very funny, or maybe didn't age well, but it's comforting. Gordon didn't even know he needed something comforting right now.

The TV station plays a few more episodes before the local news comes on. Gordon turns off the TV. He doesn't care about the local news.

The total silence returns. Maybe he should keep the TV on just for some background noise.

Wait, no—it's not total silence. There's a faint sound coming from outside. Something high-pitched. It almost sounds like a truck backing up, but that doesn't make any sense. There aren't any trucks out here. Are there?

He has to get his duffel bag out of the car anyway, so he can try to figure it out.

Outside, the noise is louder and sounds even more like a truck backing up. Gordon looks around, mystified. There's no telltale red glow from a truck's taillights. Plus, the sound seems to be coming not from the direction of the road, but from somewhere in the dark of the property.

The back of Gordon's neck does that prickly thing again. There's no moon tonight, and with very little light pollution, it means he can't see more than a few feet in front of him. The light from inside the house casts diffuse squares on the ground; the silver of his car gleams as it picks up the glow. Beyond that, it's just shadows and blackness.

And a weird, unexplainable noise coming from somewhere on the property.

Gordon is absolutely not thinking about Jason's stories about this place being haunted.

He takes a step toward the car and suddenly sees a small, faint light floating in front of him. His heart jumps into his throat and he scrambles backward.

Then he realizes it's not floating in front of him. It's in the distance—it's small and faint because it's far away. He takes a few deep breaths to slow his pounding heart.

Since he refuses to believe there are ghosts out there, that leaves only one other possibility—it's people. And he'd put money on it being Jason. Asshole. And after Gordon was kind of starting to like him too.

Irritated now, Gordon opens the car and breaks out the emergency kit. There's a flashlight, better than the one on his phone. He grabs it and flicks it on. For good measure, he shrugs on the puffer vest that's in the back seat.

Annoyance powers him across the dark field, the light from the house fading behind him. Dry yellow grass rustles against his jeans, and dusty particles float like snow in the beam of his flashlight. The beeping gets steadily louder as he walks, but the closer he gets to the source, the more his certainty that it's Jason ebbs.

He doesn't believe for a second that this land is haunted. But what if he's stumbling on some kind of weird cult? Or like… a satanic ritual?

The trees loom darker the nearer he gets, their shadows bleeding out and seeming to blot out his flashlight. Gordon stops at the edge of them. The beeping is definitely coming from in here, and he's close to it. It's loud now.

Maybe it was a bad idea to come out here. Who knows what the hell he's about to stumble into? He should have brought a knife. Not that he has a knife. A kitchen knife, then. Or even a key, so he could make a fist around it and have something to jab with.

He stands there, shifting from foot to foot, trying to decide what to do. There's always the police… but Gordon's been living in Minneapolis for too many years now to trust the police.

Cautiously, Gordon takes a step forward, moving a branch aside so he can shine his flashlight into the trees. Soft needles brush his hand. He doesn't see anything, so he takes another careful step.

A light turns on to his left, bathing him in bright white. Gordon shouts in panic, turns to flee, and gets a branch across the face. He stumbles backward, trips, and falls flat on his back.

He can't breathe. He's dying. He's going to be sacrificed or chopped up into tiny pieces or *something*—

The bright light bounces, getting bigger, and says, "Shit, are you okay? What the hell are you doing out here? Ugh. Can you get up? You don't have a concussion, do you? Please don't have a concussion."

Gordon's ribs expand again in a heaving breath, and he coughs a few times before pushing himself into a sitting position. His flashlight landed at his side, so he grabs it and points it at the light.

A man in a shearling coat throws up his hands over his eyes. The light is a headlamp strapped around his forehead. "Oh," Gordon says. "I know you. Charlie Manson, right?"

The man drops his hands away from his face and scowls. "It's Charlie Gustafson. And you're interrupting a USGS research project."

Chapter Four

CHARLIE HOLDS his ground but inside he's freaking out. He didn't even get three full hours of banding before Gordon showed up. This is it. Gordon's here to kick him off the land, and then where is Charlie going to do his research? It's not like he's swimming in friends who would be happy to have him tramping around in the middle of the night for a month and a half every fall.

Gordon squints up at him, bits of dead leaves and cedar needles stuck in his black curls. "Your last name's not Manson?" he asks, sounding baffled.

It's so earnest that Charlie knows he's not just being a jerk. "Gustafson," Charlie repeats.

The squinting doesn't stop. Charlie guesses he could aim his headlamp away from Gordon's eyes. "Are you researching that noise?" Gordon asks.

"That n-noise is for my research." Charlie's trying really hard not to lose his grip on this situation, but Gordon's making him so *nervous*. Obviously the next thing out of his mouth is going to be *Get off my land*.

"You're the one making it?" Gordon sounds affronted. "It's really annoying!"

One of the obvious benefits to banding on Ibrahim's land was the lack of neighbors. Yes, the sound is annoying, but it's never been an issue because there's no one around to complain. Charlie knows other owl banders online who have been hounded off their banding sites by people in surrounding neighborhoods who get mad about the sound, and he's always been happy he doesn't have to deal with that.

"I c-can't help it. That's what they sound l-like," he says, aware that this is distinctly unhelpful and likely to make Gordon think he's insane.

And indeed, Gordon asks, "They? Who are *they?*"

From the look on his face, you'd think Charlie just revealed he's researching aliens. "Northern saw-whet owls," he clarifies, only it obviously doesn't clarify anything, because Gordon looks just as confused. At least Charlie got the name out without stuttering. His heart is beating fast and he's sweating.

Gordon's mouth opens, then closes. He seems like he's having trouble deciding what to say. "You know you're trespassing, right?"

Charlie swallows hard. Somehow Gordon Schumacher makes even those dreaded words sound lovely. Even back in high school, Charlie liked hearing Gordon talk. He has a nice voice, warm and baritone. He even sounds warm telling Charlie to get out.

"I...," he begins, searching for the words to defend himself. But Gordon didn't even come back for Ibrahim's funeral. He only came back to—it's obvious now—collect on Ibrahim's will. The house and land went to Gordon, just like Charlie thought.

A sick pit of betrayal that he knows he shouldn't feel lodges in his throat. He wasn't Ibrahim's family. Of course the house and land would go to family. Family who never came to visit Ibrahim, not once, not even when he got sick, so why would they care that Ibrahim gave Charlie the run of this property?

Gordon winces and gets to his feet. "So what's with the owls?"

Huh?

Charlie stares at Gordon, eyes wide, heart rabbiting. "Uh," he says. It's still maybe better than stuttering.

Rubbing his backside, Gordon adds, "Northern sawmill owls? Is that what you said? USGS research project on owl sounds?"

"It's on their migratory patterns," Charlie says. "And it's northern saw-*whet* owls."

"What did I say?"

"Sawmill."

"Did you explain what the noise is?"

Charlie feels a faintly hysterical urge to laugh. "D-Do you maybe want to just... see?"

What is he doing? His mouth is saying things his brain hasn't had a chance to fully vet. Or maybe his mouth is acting on survival instinct. Maybe if Gordon sees that Charlie isn't causing any harm out here, he won't make him leave.

Gordon blinks. "See? Like... see owls?"

"Yeah." The alarm on Charlie's phone goes off and his mouth says some more words he didn't think about before letting them tumble out: "I have to do a net check right now. You can come, if you want?"

This is expressly against the rules. Members of the public can*not* come if they want. The agency that oversees bird banding operations in the United States is very clear on that point. But Charlie doesn't take it back.

He doesn't take it back because he wants to keep banding here... and maybe also, just a little, because seeing Gordon again after all these years is bringing back more and more forcefully what a huge crush Charlie had on him in high school.

Clearly Gordon never even knew who he was—but plus side, that means he never was one of the people who mocked or bullied Charlie.

"You don't need help catching them, do you?" Gordon sounds nervous. "They have like... sharp claws, right?"

Charlie shakes his head. "I don't need help."

"Well... okay. Sure. It seems interesting?" Gordon's uncertainty is endearing. Hopefully he's not one of those people who's afraid of birds. Charlie doesn't trust those people. Then again, Charlie doesn't really trust anyone, so that's not saying much.

Motioning for Gordon to follow, Charlie walks through the woods to where his banding station is set up. Years ago Charlie found someone online giving away an old picnic table in Hibbing. He borrowed Ibrahim's pickup and hauled it back here, and then with Ibrahim's help, brought it to this stand of trees. Before that, they used a collapsible table. The picnic table is sturdier. Plus it's one less thing to put up and take down at two in the morning.

From the picnic table, he scoops up the remote for the audio lure and his messenger bag full of... well, bags. He slings it across his chest and continues through the trees, glancing over his shoulder once to make sure Gordon is still following him.

It's only a minute to get to the net lanes. Charlie will be surprised if there are any birds in the nets with the commotion of Gordon bursting in and Charlie sneaking up on him. Actually, he feels bad about that now. But he didn't know who was coming across the field! It could have been a serial killer or something.

He pushes the mute button on the remote for the lure and the piping saw-whet call cuts off. "Wait, what did you do?" Gordon asks.

Charlie holds up the remote to show him. "It's an audio lure. It plays different calls to lure animals. I set it to the northern saw-whet owl call, and then it lures the owls here." He pauses, unsure if any of this makes sense. He's never had to explain to anyone.

At least he hasn't stuttered since Gordon said he wanted to come see what Charlie's doing out here. That's... interesting. Charlie doesn't know what to make of it.

He ducks under a branch, muscle memory keeping him from snagging his jacket on anything. Leaves and grass rustle as Gordon follows significantly less smoothly.

The nets stretch out in front of Charlie, though he knows Gordon probably can't see them. They're practically invisible unless you know they're there. They have to be for birds to fly into them.

Each net is strung up between aluminum poles, usually reaching about ten feet off the ground. They're made of thin, black mesh and have five "pockets" each. Charlie's nets are two different lengths, six meter and nine meter. He has two of each, set in varying positions in this cedar grove. The audio lure is stuck on a branch in the middle of the net lanes to increase the chances of an owl flying into a net on its way toward the sound.

"Walk where I do," Charlie instructs Gordon. "And be careful where you step. If the owls go into pocket one, they can be on the ground, and they're hard to see."

"Okay," Gordon says. He looks like he has no idea what he's agreeing to.

Nevertheless, he does what Charlie says, keeping to exactly the same spots Charlie puts his feet. Charlie starts at Net Two, a nine-meter net. It's obvious at a glance that there's no owl in it, but as he walks it, he tugs up on the thicker trammel line that separates each net pocket. Six-meter Net Four extends perpendicular from Net Two into the trees, and that one is empty too. Then there's Net One, another nine-meter, placed along the same line as Net Two. Empty.

He gets lucky at Net Three, the farthest back net, six-meter and on another perpendicular. About halfway down the net, there's the telltale sag of an owl caught.

Charlie's heart leaps. It does every single time he catches an owl, even though he's banded hundreds of them at this point. It never gets old. And this is his first one of the season!

"Is that… an owl?" Gordon whispers.

Charlie almost forgot he was there. "Yeah!" he says quietly but brightly. "I have to get it out." He hesitates. "You can come closer to watch."

Gordon nods, his eyes wide.

Right away, Charlie can tell it's going to be an easy extraction. He makes a mental note of the direction the owl flew into the net from and which pocket it's caught in. Then he reaches in and takes gentle hold of the legs, staying away from the four wicked, needle-sharp talons.

"Is it okay?" Gordon asks in a small voice. "It's so still."

"It's fine," Charlie assures him. "Its instinct is to stay still." The owl is clutching some of the net in its talons, so Charlie untangles that first. From there, it's an easy matter of easing a couple loops of net over the joint of each wing, then gently pulling the net over the saw-whet's head. It always makes him smile how ruffled all the feathers look on their little faces as the net comes off.

Charlie keeps a secure hold on the legs and holds the owl upright to show Gordon. "Oh wow," Gordon breathes, which makes Charlie swell with pride. People aren't impressed with him very often. Or like. Ever. Not that he tries. He stays away from most people.

The owl stares at Charlie, big golden eyes looking vaguely affronted. It always makes him laugh that saw-whets are so small but manage to look *so* aggrieved. They're about as tall as a person's hand, and most of that is feathers, which are brown on the back and tops of the wings, streaky white and brown on the breast, and mostly white on the undersides of the wings.

"It's small," Gordon says, craning to get a closer look. "Is it a baby?"

"No, this is as big as they get." Just from the way it felt in his hand when he was getting it out of the net, Charlie is already pretty sure this is a female, but measurements will tell him for sure.

He reaches into his messenger bag with his free hand and pulls out a roughly owl-sized bag made of an old pillowcase. Carefully, he puts the owl inside the bag and ties it closed securely.

"Now I band it," Charlie says, just in case Gordon thinks he's collecting cute owls in bags to bring home with him or something.

"Can I watch that part too?" Gordon asks uncertainly. "Or is that, like, the science-y stuff and I'm not allowed to see?"

"It's the science-y stuff, but you're allowed to see."

After Charlie leads Gordon out of the net lanes, he turns the lure back on. Gordon jumps and laughs sheepishly. "I can't believe owls actually fly toward that. It's so *loud*."

"Yeah," Charlie says, searching for something to add. Now that they're just walking through the dark and Charlie doesn't have the owl to focus on, he feels shy. What if he tries to talk and he starts stuttering?

Luckily, it's a short walk back to the banding site. Charlie gets his things ready one-handed while holding the owl bag in the other. Now and then, the owl shifts inside the bag.

Once he has his tools out, he pulls the three-ring binder containing his data closer and angles his headlamp down. He uses a small portable scale to get a weight, scribbles it down, and carefully removes the owl from the bag.

Again, he stays away from the talons, holding the owl in the bird-bander's grip—index and middle fingers loosely trapping the neck while he keeps the wings closed against his palm. He also keeps his pinkie and ring fingers locked on the legs to make sure the owl can't sink one of those talons into his hand.

Quickly, he takes his measurements to determine the sex—the weight of the empty bag, which he subtracts from the weight he took before, giving him the owl's weight, then the length of the tail. He doesn't even need to consult his saw-whet sexing cheat sheet—she's way too heavy to be a male, and the tail is too long.

Based on her size, he uses the larger of the two bands he has. Putting the actual band on the owl is always the nerve-wracking part of this. All bird banders have special pliers made to open and close the small, aluminum bands that are engraved with a unique, nine-digit number. The pliers have a gap in them that's exactly the size of the band, so they never touch the bird's leg.

Still nerve-wracking, though. Saw-whet owls' legs are also covered in feathers, so sometimes it's hard to get a good fit on the band. This one is easy, though, so Charlie is able to move on to taking more measurements. He makes a note of each data point in his binder.

The final one is age. For that, he turns his headlamp off and grabs a blacklight flashlight, wedging the base in his mouth and opening the owl's wings one at a time. The undersides fluoresce bright pink under the blacklight. Gordon makes a delighted little gasping sound. Charlie has to concentrate on not smiling, because if he smiles, his mouth will lose its grip on the flashlight.

Based on the pink pattern that shows up under the blacklight, Charlie knows it's a bird that was hatched earlier this year. He takes the blacklight out of his mouth, wincing at the metallic taste it leaves behind, and says softly, "Okay, sweetie, all done. You get to go soon."

He puts her carefully into a small wooden box and closes the lid, then sets a timer on his phone. She'll stay in the box long enough so her eyes can adjust back to darkness, and then he'll let her go.

Charlie releases a breath, tension he wasn't fully aware of leaving with it. Even though he knows he's good at this, the first owl of the year is still stressful. What if somehow he forgot everything he thought he knew in the past ten months?

He realizes he hasn't said a word to Gordon since they left the nets. With his headlamp off, he can't see Gordon's reflection, only the vague form of him sitting on the other side of the picnic table.

Clearing his throat, Charlie says, "So, um. That's what I, um, d-do."

"I have," Gordon says, "no idea what I just watched."

Heat rises up Charlie's neck into his face. At least Gordon can't see him. But he'll still be able to hear Charlie stuttering, because all Charlie's confidence flees as he realizes he didn't do the *one thing* he needed to accomplish here: make Gordon see that Charlie's doing something out here that he should be allowed to keep doing.

"Oh! I. Um. I sh-sh-sh-should h-have—sorry, I d-d-d-didn't mean t-to—"

FUCK.

Charlie grips the edge of the table so hard it hurts. Once again, he's grateful to the darkness so he doesn't have to see the way Gordon's staring. People look one of two ways when he starts stuttering. Either they get a terrified expression on their face, like he has an intellectual disability and they don't know how to handle that now that it's being sprung on them, or they stare like he's a freak.

"Oh—sorry, no, I didn't mean to sound like a jerk!" Even though Gordon's face isn't clear, the way he's leaning forward across the table is. "I just didn't know people did... all of *this*." His arm waves vaguely in the air. "*What* are you doing, again?"

Before he answers, Charlie closes his eyes and pays attention to his breathing. It's one of the simplest ways he can combat his stutter, though mindfulness is hard when he's stressed or anxious.

Slowly, he says, "Northern saw-whet owl b-banding." Better. "I'm... I'm banding them to study their migration. And... p-population. And some other, um... specific things."

The pauses aren't a huge improvement over the stuttering, but they're less frustrating to him. From experience, he knows they're mildly less frustrating to the listener too.

There's a silence. "So this is like, an environmentalist thing?" Gordon asks.

Oh no. What's the best answer here? Gordon isn't the sort of person to use *tree-hugger* as an epithet, is he?

"More like... conservation," Charlie says. Yeah right, they're functionally the same, but "conservation" sounds more scientific and less protesters handcuffed to bulldozers.

"Oh, okay. Cool." Gordon pauses. "Dumb question, but are you going to let the owl go?"

Charlie lets out a surprised snort of laughter. "Yeah. I put the owls in a box to let their eyes adjust to the dark again."

Sounding relieved, Gordon says, "Oh! Okay, yeah, that does make sense, now that you say it. You put it in the box, and I was like.... Actually I don't know, I thought you said you were studying them, but then I wondered if you sell them or something? Like for people to keep as pets. And then you just said conservation, so that definitely didn't seem right."

The urge to laugh keeps bubbling up in Charlie's chest. "No, no— oh my god, no. Owls make such bad pets. Not to mention that's super illegal."

"Is it?"

"Yeah, you have to be licensed and stuff to keep an owl. Like for rehabbing it or for education. Oh, except with great horned owls, Minnesota lets you take them as a falconry bird. But they're still not pets! Ibrahim was always really clear on that. Not that he ever took owls, he always said they made bad falconry birds, but—"

"Wait," Gordon says.

Charlie shuts up, his brain whirring back over what he just said.

"Ibrahim," Gordon says. "Do you mean my grandfather?"

"Oh," Charlie says. "Um."

He hadn't actually meant to bring up Ibrahim. Obviously at some point he was going to play that card, the good old *your grandfather was cool with me conducting my research here* card, but the right time didn't seem to have arrived.

"Yes?" he says.

"You knew my grandfather," Gordon says, like he's grappling with something. "I mean, I guess you did, since this is his land. You must have gotten his permission to do your research here, right?"

"Well, um." Charlie's heart starts pounding again. He hadn't even realized it had calmed until it rocketed right back up again. This is way more fraught than environmentalist vs. conservation. Charlie knows next to nothing about the relationship between Gordon and Ibrahim. He knows Gordon left; he knows Ibrahim never got to see him. He knows Gordon didn't come to the funeral.

So maybe he should gloss over the facts. Maybe he should be vague. Not *lying*, obviously. But leaving some information out that might not land the best way in this specific situation.

But he's Charlie Gustafson, so he says, "Your grandfather taught me everything I know. He's the reason I'm an owl bander."

Chapter Five

AN ALARM goes off on Charlie's phone. He scrambles off the picnic table bench, backing away like Gordon's an angry bear. Gordon can't decide if that feels fair or not. He's frozen, a weird trickling sort of… betrayal? dripping through him, the way water finds its way through tiny cracks in stone until it eventually forms gaping crevasses. Or just splits the rock in half.

"Owl," Charlie says, darting forward to, Gordon assumes, grab the box he put the owl in. A minute ago, Gordon was excited to watch the owl fly away. Now he can't move, and Charlie seems perfectly happy to let him sit there, immobile, while he hurries away into the dark.

Gordon's mind whirls and he feels…. He doesn't know. Hurt and angry. And betrayed. Yeah. He's ready to say he feels betrayed. And it's stupid, because he had no relationship with his grandfather. So who cares if his grandfather had, like, a protégé, or whatever? It was literally none of Gordon's business or concern, and it changes nothing. His grandfather is dead, Gordon got the house. Gordon got the land. Who cares if some guy studying owls is the person who his grandfather actually liked enough to spend time with?

Soft footsteps crinkle in the leaf litter and pine needles on the ground. "She f-flew away," Charlie says in a small voice. "Took off… south."

Gordon clenches his fists and turns toward Charlie. After sitting in the dark for ten minutes along with the owl, his own eyes are better adjusted to the lack of light. One of Charlie's owl boxes is clutched to his midsection, the light wood standing out against the night. It's the same color as Charlie's hair, which is a shaggy mess hanging unevenly around his ears and on the back of his neck.

"Cool," Gordon says flatly. Charlie's shoulders cringe inward. "So you just, what, cozied up to my grandfather because you knew he had all this land?"

Charlie's mouth opens but nothing comes out.

Somewhere deep in his brain, Gordon knows he's being a complete asshole. It doesn't stop him adding, "You were probably hoping he'd leave it to you, right? Since he didn't give a shit about his actual family?"

Chin dropping toward the ground, Charlie says softly, "No. Th- that's not...."

Without waiting for Charlie to finish whatever he's going to say, Gordon grabs his flashlight from the picnic table and turns it on. Charlie winces against the sudden light, hair falling over his face and into his eyes, which he doesn't brush away. In the flashlight beam, his pale skin is ice-white.

"You can stay out here for tonight," Gordon says, a harsh note grating between his molars. "After that, I don't know. I'll have to see."

He doesn't wait for Charlie to respond before stalking off through the trees.

THE OWL sound is still going when Gordon falls asleep sometime after midnight. At first listening to it pisses him off, and he decides he's definitely going to tell Charlie Gustafson that he can't do his owl research here. Here on *Gordon's land.* Which his grandfather left *him*, not Charlie. If he liked Charlie so much that he taught him all the bird stuff, he should have just left everything to Charlie. And obviously the fact that he *didn't* means he didn't want Charlie to have it.

Secure in the knowledge that he's definitely going to win, he finally falls asleep.

When he wakes up in the morning, he can't remember where he is. The light is coming in at the wrong angle for both the house in Minneapolis that he doesn't live in anymore and the soulless new apartment that he wishes he didn't.

The rush of realization hits him like a sucker punch. He's in his dead grandfather's house. The living room looks different in the light. Homier, more lived-in and comfortable. The worn-out old couch he slept on looks less worn-out and more well-loved.

He pushes himself upright, trying to figure out why he feels like something's wrong.

Oh. Wait.

Last night rushes back to him—the trek through the woods, Charlie, watching Charlie with the owl. Flipping out at Charlie for having a relationship with Gordon's estranged grandfather, which seemed reasonable and correct at the time.

His stomach twists and he feels sick. Shit. He was a huge prick, wasn't he? Did he threaten to kick him out of his owl research place?

Shit.

Gordon scrubs his hands over his face, then gets up. He doesn't actually want to kick Charlie off his land, but there's nothing he can do to fix it right now. He doesn't know anything about Charlie. Without a phone number or an address, there's no way to get in touch with him. Hopefully he'll come back tonight, and Gordon can straighten stuff out.

Since his plan for today was to start getting the house ready to put on the market, he concentrates on that. Except he was expecting the house to be a huge mess, and it's not. If he doesn't have to clean, then he has to start throwing stuff out. Which he wasn't counting on doing until mid-week. He was going to call one of those companies that will bring a dumpster to your house.

He gives the bathroom and kitchen a clean just because, but they really don't need it. They're spotless.

It's actually kind of weird. Gordon didn't know people could live in a house and keep it this clean.

The good news on the internet is that there *is* Wi-Fi. The bad news is that it's password protected, and obviously Gordon doesn't know the password. He calls the internet provider and they suggest he use a wired connection until he can find his password. At first he tries to clarify that no, it's not *his* password, but what's the point?

So he goes hunting for an ethernet cable, which feels like hunting for a pot of gold in this town. The nearest "city" is Hibbing, which has some computer repair stores, but they aren't open on weekends.

After a fruitless morning of calling around to stores within a fifty-mile radius, Gordon gives up and goes to get lunch at Edna's.

Steph from yesterday drops a menu at his table again. "Hey, hon. Food that good yesterday?"

When he looks up at her, there's a little sparkle to her eyes and a slightly crooked cant to her lips. "Best meal I've had in years," he says, raising an invisible glass to her.

She laughs. "I'll let Sean know. He always says his culinary genius is underappreciated. Coffee for you again?"

"Please." While Gordon sits in his booth alone, folding an empty sugar packet into a smaller and smaller square, he thinks about what he's going to do with the property. Sell it still, obviously. But he feels kind of bad knowing that Charlie is using it for research. If Gordon talks to Jason's cousin, the commercial real estate guy, they'll probably put a big box store there. There isn't anything like that around here and, as his fruitless hunt for an ethernet cable proved, the town needs one. Then Charlie wouldn't be able to do his research, and that's totally pulling out the rug from underneath him.

Plus there was the whole... thing last night. That thing where Gordon kind of threw a tantrum because he got his feelings hurt. He needs to find some way to get in touch with Charlie to let him know it's okay for him to keep studying owls in that spot. And maybe Gordon can hold off selling the property until Charlie doesn't need it anymore.

Steph stops by the booth to refill his coffee. "You're Mr. Yassin's grandkid, right?" she asks.

Gordon stiffens. "Yeah," he says. "Were you buddy-buddy with him too?"

She gives him a weird look. "Nooo...."

Waving, Gordon says, "Never mind. Why do you ask?"

She leans a hip against the table. "I heard he passed, that's all. My family was sorry to hear that."

"Oh. Thanks." Gordon unfolds the sugar packet just so he can fold it again. "I, uh, couldn't make it to the funeral. I heard it was nice, though." Lies. He hasn't been told about a funeral, let alone if it was nice.

But he finds himself on the receiving end of a funny look again. "Where'd you hear that?"

"Er...." Gordon fumbles. "Was it not nice?"

With a shrug, she says, "Don't know. I don't think anyone in town went. He kept to himself. Didn't have many friends." Maybe he looks confused, because her expression softens a little. "He bought meat from my parents' farm for years. Well, my brothers run the place now with our parents getting up there."

Gordon's sure he looks completely clueless, but she's looking at him like he should understand what she means by "bought meat." Is that like… some kind of gay innuendo? Hell, why not find out his grandfather was gay on top of everything else!

"Meat…?" he tries.

"Yeah, like beef? Lamb?" She gives him a funny look again. "We were already doing kosher meat, and he asked if we'd be willing to do halal too. So I'd see him a few times a year when he came by the farm to pick up the cuts he ordered."

What's the bigger mindfuck here, the fact that his grandfather kept halal when Gordon's mom, and thus, Gordon, never bothered, or the fact that his podunk hometown has a place that supplies kosher and halal meat? At least gay innuendo is off the table for now.

"He seemed like an interesting guy," she adds.

For the first time, Gordon is embarrassed at how little he knows about his grandfather. He's also embarrassed at how shocked he was to hear Steph say *halal* and obviously know what it means.

"He left me his property," Gordon says without exactly meaning to.

"Oh yeah?" Steph looks pleased. "Are you gonna stick around, you think?"

"Oh, well… I mean, I don't know. Probably not." Why is he waffling? He's not going to stick around, and he knows it.

Nodding, she says, "We're kind of in the middle of nowhere."

No kidding. "Yeah, and my job…." Is totally remote. But she doesn't need to know that. "It's just kind of far away from everything up here." Wanting to get away from the subject of why he's going to cut and run from Sawmill Lake for a second time in his life the minute he can swing it, he asks, "How did your family get into doing kosher meat?"

She laughs. "My dad. He talks to everybody. One day it turned out the guy he was talking the ear off of owned a kosher deli in Duluth. My dad convinced him to start buying from us."

Crinkling his forehead, Gordon says, "You'd just started doing it?"

"Nope! My dad had to figure everything out." Steph laughs again. "He's like that. Definitely leaps before he looks."

With an answering smile, Gordon says, "Sounds like it paid off."

Her expression gets wistful. "Yeah. But Mr. Yassin was the only customer we had for the halal meat. I'm not sure if we'll keep doing it. Unless you…?"

"Sorry, no. I'm not religious."

She looks unbothered. "Well, listen, I better check on my other tables."

"Oh! Yeah, no, sorry, I didn't mean to keep you."

Flashing a smile at him, she says, "You're all good, hon."

When she walks away, Gordon goes back to folding and unfolding the empty sugar packet and drinking his coffee. It's as bad as it was yesterday, and he can't bring himself to finish a second cup.

As he gets up to pay his check at the front, Steph stops by again and hands him a piece of paper with an address scribbled on it. "I don't know how long you'll be in town, but if you need any eggs or cheese, stop by the farm and tell them I sent you. They'll give you some for cheap. Just so you have something in the fridge."

Before he has the chance to thank her, she bustles off again.

Huh.

With the afternoon trickling away, Gordon tells himself when he gets back to the house, he's going to start sorting through the personal effects his grandfather left behind. The lawyer made it sound like that while the cancer was a surprise, there was still time for his grandfather to get things in order.

Still, it strikes him just *how* in order things are once he's back in the house. Gordon finds a staircase that leads down to a basement, and even though it takes a lot of psyching himself up to go down there, when he gets to the bottom of the creaking wooden staircase and fumbles for the pull string to turn the bare bulb on, everything is neat and clean. The washing machine and dryer are down here, plus the furnace. There's a workbench with tools mounted on pegboard above it.

Gordon moves farther into the unfinished space. He was expecting spiderwebs and musty damp, and while there's an unmistakable earthy smell, it's not overpowering or bad. A set of neatly organized metal shelves draws his attention, and he goes to inspect them.

There are plastic tote bins slotted into each shelf, so Gordon pulls out one of them. This is a strange place to start going through his grandfather's stuff, but he's doing it, he guesses. When he pops the lid off the tote, he finds several canvas bags. Inside are masses of black string. Gordon dumps one out and holds up the strands. Not string—it's a net.

Realization hits him. This is the same kind of net that Charlie was using last night to catch owls. Are all these totes full of his grandfather's bird stuff?

A bolt of regret goes through him, an echo of the hurt and betrayal he felt last night. Now that his grandfather has the vaguest shape of a person, Gordon wishes…. He's not sure. He wishes things hadn't gone the way they did, with him never knowing anything about this man, including *why* he didn't know anything about him.

Pushing all that aside, Gordon tries going through the plastic totes on the shelf. Most of it seems to be related to the same kind of research that Charlie is doing. One tote contains nothing but three-ring binders with sheets of paper full of inscrutable codes. Another tote has a fishing tackle box in it, but there's no fishing stuff inside. It's organized carefully, but full of stuff Gordon doesn't know what to make of.

Actually, that's not exactly true, is it? Some of it looks familiar. Charlie was using some of these things last night, Gordon's sure of it.

Guilt crawls through him. The way he acted last night was out of line. Seeing all these tools, all this stuff that Gordon never knew existed, really brings it home. His grandfather had a passion for birds and this research, which he obviously shared with Charlie. And yeah, it feels shitty to know that his grandfather could and did have close relationships with people—just not him. But that's not Charlie's fault.

Carefully, Gordon puts the lid on the tote and replaces the ones he took down on the shelf again. His determination to look through the rest of the house at his grandfather's belongings fades. Somehow, he finds himself sitting in front of the ancient TV again, half his attention on the fading daylight.

What time does Charlie set his nets up? What time does he arrive out there? Is he going to be willing to talk to Gordon again? What is Gordon's plan, even? Why is everything in him, suddenly, focused on talking to Charlie tonight?

Well, duh. It's because Charlie's a link to his grandfather, whom he never knew. And Gordon's, like… looking for a link to that. Or whatever. And also, the stuff Charlie was doing was genuinely interesting.

And… so was Charlie. The intensity and concentration on his face as he wrote down all his data about the owl—something about that is lodged in Gordon's mind and won't go anywhere. He keeps seeing the notch between Charlie's pale eyebrows and the way he caught his bottom lip with his teeth.

The skin on Gordon's arm prickles at the thought.

He figured he'd wait until around the same time as last night to trek across the field and into the woods, but as the sun dips low over the tree line and the sky turns the color of faded, washed-out denim, he abruptly decides he should go now. Sneaking up on Charlie in the dark is a bad idea. He'll just head out there now and wait for Charlie to get there, and no one has to surprise anyone else. In the dark, at least. Charlie will probably still be surprised to see Gordon out there after everything Gordon said last night.

It's a plan. Gordon pulls on a hoodie (the only one he brought), grabs his flashlight and keys, and goes to wait for Charlie.

Chapter Six

CHARLIE TIES himself in knots trying to figure out if he should go back out to his banding site again. *We'll have to see,* Gordon said about Charlie continuing to band there. All day, Charlie keeps expecting his phone to ring with a call telling him he's banned, or there's a restraining order against him. Or something. He doesn't even have a clear idea of who would make the call, but every notification makes him jump and feel sick to his stomach.

No one calls, though. And by midafternoon, Charlie decides he's going to go back and band tonight. All the poles for the nets are out there, anyway. If Gordon wants him gone, he'll have to come out and tell Charlie to leave.

With evening coming on swiftly, Charlie pulls his Crown Vic off the old farm road that's closest to his site. Using Ibrahim's driveway to drive across the field and park right at the site is easier and closer for hauling his gear, but for obvious reasons, he can't park there anymore.

He can't carry everything in one trip, so he grabs as much as he can and tramps into the woods. It takes forever to walk back and forth—at least twenty minutes. He's never going to be anything but skinny, but at least he gets his exercise hauling his stuff all this way every night for two months of the fall.

Walking through the woods always centers him. Whatever's happened during the day, the quiet and the thin light filtering through the trees allows him to put it in perspective. Stress at his day job, weird looks in town, grief, loneliness. Some of the stuff falls away and some of it just recedes. It's like taking a deep breath and letting it out to find yourself ten pounds lighter.

Then he walks into his clearing, and Gordon is sitting at the picnic table.

So much for feeling ten pounds lighter.

Charlie stops dead in his tracks. His stomach twists hard with fear and his heart pounds. When Gordon stands, Charlie clutches his tote closer to his chest.

"Hey," Gordon says. His facial expression is guilty and awkward. Oh god. He's going to tell Charlie to leave. This is it.

"I n-never thought I was g-going to get anything in the will!" Charlie bursts out. Gordon looks perplexed. Gulping a lungful of air, Charlie adds, "That wasn't why I... why I... why I worked with Ibrahim. Your g-grandfather, I mean. I just... I liked him. And working with him."

"Oh." Gordon's face reddens and he looks at the ground, rubbing a hand through his hair. "Um. So last night, I was... an asshole. This is just, like, a lot, the last few weeks. But yeah, I shouldn't have said all that stuff. I don't really think you were trying to take advantage of my grandfather."

It takes a second for all of that to sink in. An apology. Gordon is apologizing to him. Saying he was wrong. "So...." Charlie ventures, "are you... making me leave?"

Gordon winces. "No. I shouldn't have.... No. No, it's cool if you do your owl research out here. I don't mind. It's not like I'm using it for anything."

This is Charlie's cue to say something. *Thank you* would be a good start. But he's so surprised—he was so prepared to hear the opposite—that all he can do is gape. Just like the freak everyone thinks he is.

Gordon's eyes dart from Charlie's face to the tote he's still holding, which is getting heavy. "Do you need some help with that?" Gordon asks.

It's an olive branch, Charlie thinks. He may not be good at interacting with people, but he's pretty good at reading them from years of watching from the sidelines.

Walking past Gordon to set the tote on the picnic table, Charlie struggles to find some words. Any words. "I'm just carrying my gear from the car."

"I can help with that!" Gordon says eagerly.

Actually, Charlie was trying to say that he *doesn't* need help. It's just carrying stuff from the car. But Gordon's giving him a tentative smile, and he's so... beautiful. His skin looks so smooth and perfect. Golden. Somehow his hair looks even curlier and more luscious in the fading daylight. What would it feel like to run his fingers through it? To catch them on those curls and to rasp his palm over that beard?

"Okay," Charlie hears himself say.

Gordon's smile gets surer. It's lopsided. And there's a dimple. Charlie remembers that dimple from high school and how devastating it was to his little gay heart. Presumably scores of women have fallen victim to it since then. Possibly more. Probably more. Is Gordon wearing a ring?

As they head back to Charlie's car, he sneaks a look at Gordon's left hand. No ring. It gives him a stupid thrill, because apparently you're never too old to pine for a straight guy. Straightness aside, there's no way a man like Gordon would ever go for a guy like Charlie.

Once they get back to Charlie's car, that point is illustrated by the way Gordon looks hefting another tote out of the trunk. It's the heavier one, which he grabs before Charlie can. His maroon University of Minnesota sweatshirt tightens across his shoulders, chest, and stomach, and *that's* new since high school. Gordon's got bulk to him now—thick body, solid muscles, and a belly that Charlie wouldn't mind pressing himself up against.

Since Gordon has the heavy stuff, that leaves Charlie carrying nothing but the plastic bag of snacks he bought from the gas station convenience store on the way over. He clears his throat and forces himself to speak. "Thank you. For not… making me leave."

"You really don't have to thank me."

"No, I d-do. You own all this now?"

"Yeah." Gordon huffs out a breath. "I got a call last week saying my grandfather died and left his house and property to me. I don't even remember the man. There was some big family rift when I was young." Glancing at Charlie, Gordon adds, "You probably know all about this."

Uncomfortably, Charlie says, "N-not really. I, um. Knew there was something." He pauses, and without thinking, blurts out, "Is that why you didn't come to the funeral?"

"Yeah." Gordon's tone is hard to read. Not happy. Not sad, exactly, either. Resigned, maybe, and a little disillusioned.

Charlie tightens his fingers around the handles of the plastic bag. "Sorry. That wasn't any of my business."

With a small, humorless laugh, Gordon says, "It sounds like it kind of is. You were close to my grandfather. Man, you must have thought

I was the biggest asshole on the planet. I skip my own grandfather's funeral, then stroll into town to claim my inheritance. And then I threaten to screw up your research."

Shaking his head, Charlie assures him, "No." It's not even a lie, because there are way bigger assholes in Sawmill Lake.

Gordon offers that tentative smile again. The dimple peeks out. Even if it's not the full dimple, it still makes Charlie's heart stutter.

When they get back to the picnic table, Charlie says, "Thanks for the help carrying everything."

"I mean, least I could do." Hands stuck in his pockets, Gordon looks around the clearing. "Do you come out here every night by yourself?"

Charlie gets to work unpacking everything and setting it up the way he needs it. Unlatching his tackle box with his tools and bands gives him something to do with his hands, which helps with his stutter. "Yeah. In the fall. Sometimes Ibrahim—your grandfather, sorry—came out with me. But owls weren't his project. So not every night."

He pops open the tote containing the nets and the audio lure, but once he's holding them, he's not sure what he's supposed to do about Gordon, who's still standing there with his hands in his pockets. "Oh," he says, realizing. "You're worried about the noise?"

Gordon looks surprised. "No. I mean, it's annoying, but I'm sure I'll get used to it. No, I guess I just wondered if you want some help tonight? Since I'm already out here."

For a second, all Charlie can do is blink at him. Is he hallucinating? Did he fall and hit his head on a rock?

"You want to… help?" he says uncertainly. Maybe he heard wrong. Or misunderstood somehow.

"If you don't want any help, that's fine," Gordon says quickly. He looks disappointed, though, so Charlie knows it's not fine. "It's just, this is something my grandfather did, and… I don't know. Being in his house, it's like, I feel like I should try to get to know him a little? Stupid, I know. It's not like it changes how things were."

"It's not stupid," Charlie says feelingly. Gordon's eyes shoot to his, and then Charlie's afraid he was too strong. "You can stay and help."

Gordon smiles and Charlie's heart trips over itself. If Gordon's sticking around, Charlie will have to get that under control.

"So um, I'm going to set up the nets now." Charlie gestures vaguely with his full hands, figuring Gordon won't care about that part.

But Gordon follows, trailing him like an enthusiastic puppy. As Charlie puts up the nets, Gordon watches carefully, like he's really interested. It's funny to think back on the first time Charlie put up a net by himself. He felt so clumsy and it took him forever. Ibrahim's patience was infinite, and it didn't take long for Charlie to get faster. Now he could do it in his sleep.

Once the nets are up, he turns the audio lure on, nestles it in its spot, and says, "Okay. Now we wait. I do net checks every half an hour."

"Want me to set a timer?" Gordon asks.

Charlie's eyebrows rise. Is Gordon just trying to be helpful because he feels bad about last night? And is that patronizing or actually kind of nice?

"Sure," Charlie says. No harm in letting Gordon help out. Obviously he'll get bored in an hour or two. It takes a particular kind of person to sit out in the cold and dark until the wee hours of the morning, and it's hard to imagine that Gordon is that kind of person, simply because most people aren't.

As Gordon sets his alarm, Charlie turns on the lure. The high, piping call of the male northern saw-whet rings through the woods. Gordon jumps. Charlie tries not to smile. There. That's his revenge for Gordon being a jerk yesterday.

And then… they sit next to each other at the picnic table. In silence. Uncomfortable silence. Five minutes go by, then ten. Charlie doesn't need to talk. He's used to sitting out here alone. He's used to being alone in general. Not in like, a sad way. Okay, well, maybe sometimes in a sad way. But being alone isn't something he dreads, even if it's also not something he relishes.

Still, this is awkward. Maybe Gordon won't make it more than one net check.

After ten minutes of listening to the lure, Gordon clears his throat and whispers, "Is it okay if we talk? Or do we have to be quiet?"

"Oh! No, we can… we can talk. I thought you didn't want to."

"No, I just didn't know if it wasn't allowed or something."

"It's allowed."

"Cool." Gordon folds his hands together on his lap. Maybe Charlie should tell him about Ibrahim? But he doesn't know where to start.

Before Charlie can figure out what to do, Gordon says, "I don't know if I ever actually came out and said it, but my grandfather left the house and land to me."

Charlie jiggles his foot before he tucks it behind one ankle. "I figured."

Gordon stares off into the darkness. "I honestly never thought I'd come back to this town."

"You never wondered about him?" Charlie asks without thinking. As usual. Staying quiet is like bubble wrap for himself. If he's talking, he'll probably blurt out something inappropriate.

With a shrug, Gordon says, "I don't know. No, sorry, that's not true. I didn't. Ever." He kicks a heel against the ground, which shakes the bench of the picnic table. "Which sounds really bad now. But I was super young when he and my mom fell out. I probably asked about him when I was a little kid? But I got older and he just wasn't part of my life. And after I left, my parents left here too."

"I can't believe your parents and you avoided Ibrahim," Charlie says. "It's such a small town."

Gordon looks at him. It's mostly dark, but still light enough that his flummoxed facial expression is clear. "Huh. Yeah, I never thought about that. Man." He shakes his head. "The lengths people will go to when they don't want to admit they screwed up."

Over the years Charlie knew Ibrahim, he got the sense that Ibrahim felt he was to blame for what happened—and that, yeah, he was too proud to apologize. Or maybe too scared. Pride keeps people from apologizing, but fear is just as much to blame. If you haven't apologized yet, you haven't been rebuffed yet, either.

"You only came up here to l-look at the house?" Charlie asks, not knowing what else to say.

"Yeah. I wanted to clean it up. Apparently the guy was a neat freak, though. Everything's spotless."

"Oh." Charlie coughs to cover the way he cringes. "No, I... I didn't know anyone was coming. I cleaned it up. I've been getting his mail too."

Now Gordon's staring. "You've been in the house?"

The heavy lead ball of mortification and anxiety rises up Charlie's throat, but he manages to get out, "I h-had a k-key."

Far from looking angry, Gordon looks hopeful. "Do you happen to know the Wi-Fi password?"

The question takes a second to process. "The Wi-Fi? Yeah, I set up the password for Ibrahim because he just left it open. Do you need it?"

Nodding, Gordon says, "I'm spending the week up here getting stuff in order, so I need to get on the Wi-Fi for work."

The lead ball sinks back to its home in Charlie's intestines and relief takes its place. "Remind me before you go, I'll give it to you."

Gordon pats him on the back and the touch jolts Charlie. "Thanks."

The touch means nothing. Gordon is straight. He's just being friendly. Guys pat their bros on the back. Though it wasn't that back slap thing guys do, it was just... nice. Just a nice back pat.

He's overthinking this.

Gordon is staring into the distance again, and now it's dark, so Charlie can't see his face very well. Abruptly, Gordon faces him and says, "Hey, I'm sorry about Jason Miller yesterday."

With a shrug, Charlie says, "I'm used to it."

There's no mistaking the unhappiness on Gordon's face, even in the dark. "Well, he said some shitty stuff, and I didn't like it."

"Did he call me a fag?" Charlie asks.

Gordon looks horrified. "No!"

"Oh. I guess that's good. He used to."

"I would have said something if he had." Gordon doesn't sound so sure, though, which makes Charlie think Jason said *something* homophobic, even if it wasn't that.

With another shrug, Charlie says, "I've heard it all before. Ever since high school. It's okay." Gordon keeps looking at him and Charlie wracks his brain for what liberal straight people want to hear so they'll stop with the performative guilt. "I'm sure you're a g-good, um, ally. Or whatever."

"Ally." Gordon seems like he's turning the word over. Surely he knows what that means? "Yeah, I don't... I don't think I'm an ally."

That's... maybe not what a gay man wants to hear when he's alone in the dark with another man. Charlie wonders if he needs to get out the Swiss Army knife he uses to cut out badly tangled birds from the nets.

"Because I'm bi," Gordon says.

There's a more silent silence. The lure seems incredibly loud.

Gordon lets out a huge, gusty breath. "Whoa. You're only the second person I've come out to."

Very deliberately, Charlie discards his first two responses ("You *are?*" and "I really would have loved to know that twenty years ago."). Unfortunately, what comes out of his mouth is, "Welcome to the queer club."

Mortifying. Why is he like this?

Somehow, Gordon laughs, sounding relieved. "Thanks. That went way better than the first person I told."

Even though there's a breeziness to his tone, there's hurt lurking underneath. Charlie can hear it throbbing like a fresh wound, and he wants to put an arm around Gordon and tell him it's okay, there will always be shitty people who won't accept you, but you just have to let them go. Except he's not the kind of person who puts his arm around other people to comfort them. Or a person who gets called on to comfort people. Or a person who even knows what to say to be comforting.

"Are you...?" Gordon asks.

Charlie's brow furrows. "Am I what?"

"Queer."

Oh god, wasn't that obvious? "Yeah, I thought I…. Yeah. I'm gay. Sorry. I'm used to everyone knowing."

Shifting on the bench, Gordon asks, "Is it hard being gay up here?"

"You mean am I getting hate-crimed?" Charlie asks. When Gordon makes a noise that sounds like both assent and embarrassment, Charlie says, "No. I mean, people like Jason say stuff, but I l-learned how to ignore that a long time ago."

"That's good. I mean, not that he says stuff. It's shitty he says stuff. But it's good you're not getting hate-crimed." Gordon fiddles with the hem of his sweatshirt. "So you're able to meet people?"

Charlie can't help but laugh. "God, no." Something clunks dully in his chest that has no right being there as a possibility occurs to him. "Oh. Do you… want to hook up w-with someone while you're h-here?"

None of his business. Just because Charlie has swiped left on every gay, bi, or bicurious guy within a fifty-mile radius doesn't mean Gordon won't want to fuck any of them. Especially if he just came out. He'll probably want to make up for lost time.

Of course, if Gordon wanted to hook up with *him*…. Well, Charlie would very much not be opposed to that.

Still fiddling with his shirt, Gordon says, "No, it's not that. I just don't really know how to meet guys."

"In the Cities?" Charlie asks incredulously. He wants to kick himself. Now he's the one being shitty. "Sorry. Just. From up here, the Cities are like…."

"Queer friendly?" Gordon offers.

"I was going to say teeming with men who like dick. But. Yeah."

Gordon laughs so hard he snorts. A dangerous feeling fizzes in Charlie's stomach and sends warmth tingling all the way to his fingertips. "So you're funny, huh?"

Charlie ducks his head. Usually, he's not. At least, not out loud. Usually, all the funny things he wants to say stay trapped inside. He doesn't understand why they're coming out around Gordon.

And of course, he doesn't know what to say now. *Freak accident*, he considers and discards. Instead, he says, "Just go on Grindr to meet guys."

Somehow, even though Charlie can't really see Gordon's face, he can feel the waves of discomfort coming off him. "Isn't Grindr not, um. Super friendly to guys like me?"

As much as Charlie wants to act like he doesn't know what Gordon's talking about, he does. "You mean c-can it be a cesspool of shallow bigots who'll block you if you have more than ten percent body fat?"

"Uggghhh." Gordon folds at the waist, his face in his hands. "I'm too fat to be bi, aren't I?"

For a second, Charlie is too stunned to say anything. Finally, he manages, "You… are *not*… fat. And it wouldn't matter if you were."

"Right." No one has ever sounded more unconvinced of something in the history of the planet, Charlie's pretty sure.

Which is probably why he blurts out what he does: "If I saw you on Grindr I'd DM you."

And thank fuck, Gordon's net check alarm goes off right at that moment.

Chapter Seven

GORDON'S ALARM startles him. He fumbles for his phone to shut it off, Charlie's words ping-ponging around inside his skull. Unfortunately, Charlie's already on his feet, snatching his messenger bag full of owl bags off the picnic table. Gordon has to hurry to catch up with him as he darts into the woods.

While Gordon may not be the smartest guy around, he can tell when someone's embarrassed. Obviously Charlie was just trying to reassure him about his body not being totally horrific and off-putting to other men, and he's worried Gordon's going to take it wrong.

Yeah right. There's no chance of Gordon thinking he has a shot with someone like Charlie, who's smart and handsome. Even though social stuff seems to make him nervous, he's also self-assured. Obviously confident about who he is. So, yeah, the idea of Charlie ever being interested in Gordon in a million years is laughable.

When Gordon catches up with Charlie, he's breathing heavily. Charlie just adjusts his bag across his chest and begins his careful walk along each net. Should Gordon say something?

He's going to say something. "Hey, didn't mean to make things awkward. Thanks for being nice about all of"—he gestures at his midsection, then realizes Charlie isn't looking at him—"this."

Charlie makes a noise that sounds like, "Mrrggmph," which doesn't provide a ton of clarity about what he's thinking. Though that's probably for the best, since what he's probably thinking is, *Wow, this Gordon guy is really clueless. Doesn't figure out he's bi until his thirties, doesn't know how to meet a guy in one of the gayest cities in the country, and now probably thinks I want to jump his bones when I was just being nice.*

Maybe Gordon shouldn't have impulsively come out to him. It definitely wasn't on his list of things to do in Sawmill Lake. But something came over him and he just… wanted to. Charlie felt safe.

There are two owls in the last net. Gordon moves close to watch, half expecting Charlie to tell him to back up. Charlie doesn't, though. In the illumination from the headlamp strapped around Charlie's head, Gordon sees his eyes flick up to take in Gordon's attention. He shifts slightly, which gives Gordon a better view. Did he do it on purpose?

Just like last night, the owl is still and unmoving in the net. And just like last night, Gordon finds it a little unnerving. The black net tangled around the little owl's wings and head just looks really sad. Gordon feels bad for them.

Charlie does something that looks simultaneously really easy and really complicated, deftly pulling net out of the owl's claws, over its wings, and off its head. When he flips it right side up, the owl bursts into motion, flapping its wings rapidly.

Gordon jumps but Charlie doesn't even flinch. "Shh, I know, sweetie, I know," Charlie murmurs. "You're okay. I'm just going to put you in this bag, okay?"

Which is… adorable. Last night, Charlie talked to the owl too. And Gordon also thought it was adorable then—he just forgot about it with all the drama, which was of his own making. And now he's caused some more, so he's two for two.

The owl calms as Charlie carefully puts it into the little cloth bag he pulls from his satchel. After he ties it shut, he starts to hang the bag on a nearby branch. "I can hold it," Gordon offers.

Charlie looks him in the eyes for the first time in the past few minutes. His front teeth catch on his bottom lip. "Are you sure?" he asks.

Gordon holds out a hand. Apparently Charlie trusts him enough not to drop the owl, because he hands over the bag. "Hold it up here, above the knot," Charlie says. "She might foot you, otherwise."

"Foot me?"

"Stick her talons into you," Charlie says over his shoulder as he goes to get the other owl out of the net.

So footing sounds terrible. Gordon determinedly holds the bag where Charlie told him to. The bag bounces a few times as the owl moves around inside. "Um, Charlie? It's moving."

"That's okay," comes Charlie's response, floating in the darkness. Gordon looks at him, a bright, concentrated pool of light, hands busy and nimble as they work the owl free of the net tangled around it. Something funny twists in Gordon's stomach.

In a minute, Charlie has the second owl in a bag. His shoulders cringe inward a little as he passes Gordon, which Gordon finds, quite unexpectedly, that he hates. Not the cringing, but the fact that Charlie thinks Gordon might mock him. Or… something. Gordon doesn't really know Charlie, let alone how he thinks, but something's different.

They go back to the banding site in silence. Charlie bands the owls in silence. Gordon hates that they're not talking. The owl stuff, though… that's really cool. It almost makes up for the silence. And there's something to be said for Charlie's intensity as he's banding—the way he focuses all his attention on what he's doing, every single one of his movements spare and precise.

After the second owl is all banded and measured and chilling in its dark box, Gordon has a little bit of a feel for the process. He waits for Charlie to release the first owl, and when he returns to the picnic table, Gordon asks, "So my grandfather taught you how to do all this?"

Charlie stills for a moment and Gordon's afraid he said the wrong thing. But then Charlie sits. The same economy of movement he displays with the owls is present as he lowers himself to the bench and crosses one leg over the other.

"Yeah," he says. The grief in his voice is unmistakable. Weird turn of events for Gordon to roll into town after his grandfather's death, only to find himself in a position to comfort a man that his grandfather had looked on as… a protégé? Or something more? A son? A grandson?

It strikes him as strange, though, that if Charlie and his grandfather were so close, that Charlie didn't get anything in the will.

"Yeah?" Gordon prompts.

There's a long moment where Gordon thinks Charlie isn't going to say anything else, which Gordon fills by telling himself silently not to push if Charlie doesn't want to talk about it.

Slowly, Charlie says, "I went through some… stuff. After high school. Sometimes I just had to get away, so I came out here." He looks at his boots. Maybe Gordon's imagining it, but it seems like there's a tiny smile threatening one corner of his mouth. "One day when I was out here, there was this pigeon on the ground. It looked like it was hurt or something, so I went to see if I could help. I walked straight into Ibrahim's nets and got myself ridiculously tangled up. Then this man appeared out of nowhere, running straight at me and yelling, and I kind of freaked out."

Gordon can't help laughing. "Okay, but—fair. I would've freaked out too."

Charlie darts a glance at him, and Gordon's sure there's a smile on his face. "After he got me untangled, he chewed me out for interrupting his work and said I could've wrecked his nets. I kept trying to get a word in to explain, and when he finally let me talk, I said I was just trying to help the pigeon, because it was hurt, and he gave me the most, like... assessing look. Like he was measuring me up." He pauses. "You don't remember your grandfather at all?"

Even though it's pointless, Gordon really tries for a second. There's nothing, though, not a face, not any feeling of warmth or anything. That book with the kid and the bird on the cover pops into his head, but there's no connection to his grandfather that he can remember.

When he shakes his head, Charlie goes on, "Well, he had this way he looked at things, sometimes. Like he was cataloging everything you'd ever done and all the things you were still going to do, and then he was going to decide if you were worth his time."

"He must have decided you were worth it."

"I guess so." Charlie interlaces his fingers in his lap. "Anyway, he did that cataloging thing, and then he said he needed help catching birds for research, and I looked like I'd be good at it. I think he liked that I was worried about the pigeon. It wasn't hurt, it was just a lure."

Regret sloshes in Gordon's stomach yet again. Is he wrong about the reason he had no relationship with his grandfather? Maybe it wasn't the fight between his grandfather and his mom. Maybe it was the fact that Ibrahim could see from afar that Gordon didn't really have anything special to recommend him.

Story of his life.

Their elbows brush and Gordon pulls back instinctively, which he regrets. Charlie draws his arms closer to his body, too. "So, yeah. After that I helped him out. I got my own banding license eventually but I worked with Ibrahim really closely for years."

"That's cool," Gordon says, though something thick is in his throat.

There's a pause, and then Charlie says uncertainly, "Thanks?"

Neither of them speak for a second. Then, mortifyingly, Gordon lets out a giggle. Charlie snaps his head around to look at him, faint light shining on his wide eyes. Something about that just makes Gordon laugh again, before he manages to get out, "I'm sorry! I'm sorry, I'm not laughing at you." He barely knows what he's laughing at. "Just—'here's the story of how your grandfather basically adopted me and passed on all of this knowledge,' and all I can say is *that's cool.*"

Charlie lets out a snort of laughter too. Which sets Gordon off again, which makes Charlie laugh harder. That's how the two of them spend the remaining minutes before the alarm goes off to release the second owl.

"Do you want to let this one go?" Charlie asks.

Gordon sits up straight. "Really? I'm allowed to do that?"

"Sure. If you want."

"Yeah, I want." It surprises him how excited he is. Until last night, he never thought much about birds, but here he is, thrilled to let an owl out of a box, interested in all the measurements Charlie takes and records in his three-ring binder.

They walk closer to the trees, Charlie carrying the box. When the deeper gloom seems ready to wrap around them, Charlie hands the box to Gordon. Inside, the owl moves, talons scratching against the wood.

"What do I do?" Gordon asks, suddenly panicked he's going to do something wrong.

Gently but deliberately, Charlie situates the box in Gordon's hands, then guides his arms so Gordon is holding the box with outstretched arms. "Now you just have to pull the top toward you," Charlie murmurs.

Knowing full well he's treating this like he's doing surgery and probably looks stupid, Gordon does what Charlie says. The hinge on the lid squeaks.

Nothing happens. Then there's a rustle and a flutter of wings. A small, dark shape materializes on the edge of the box. Gordon's breath stops and the world narrows to just this space. Soundlessly, the owl turns its head and regards him with huge eyes.

The box dips a tiny bit as the owl launches itself into the air. It happens so fast, and it's so dark, and the owl is so small and silent, that Gordon loses track of it immediately.

"She flew east," Charlie says, sounding satisfied.

Air fills Gordon's lungs again, but he can't think of what to say. He pulls his arms in, tucking the box under one, and stands there.

"Are you okay?" Charlie asks, a concerned note in his voice. "She didn't foot you, did she?"

Shaking himself, Gordon turns to Charlie, still holding the box. "No, I'm fine. I just—I was wondering… I mean, I don't want to step on your toes or get in your way or anything. And I'm only in town through next weekend. But could I maybe help you while you're out here?"

Chapter Eight

SOMEHOW, CHARLIE ends the night driving Gordon back to Ibrahim's house. No, Gordon's house. Charlie has to get used to that. After tonight, that actually seems possible. Even though it's just past two in the morning and they only got two more owls, Gordon stuck it out.

As Charlie pulls up to the house, warm light spills from the kitchen window, illuminating a fuzzy circle of grass. The world at 2:00 a.m. is his favorite. It's quiet and still and everything's possible. It's liminal in a different way than dawn and dusk, the darkness and the silence stretching forever. Under cover of that darkness, you have the freedom to remake yourself the same way the world remakes itself overnight.

"So I w-was thinking," Charlie says, cursing the return of the stutter. He did so well tonight, even when he wasn't talking about owls and banding, but being in his car has changed part of the dynamic between Gordon and him. Seeing Gordon in the passenger seat, the way his solid body fills the space, and being close enough to get the faint smell of him, is making attraction jitter in Charlie's veins.

He clears his throat and tries again. "I was thinking, if you want to help me, I sh-should give you a primer. During the day, so you can see."

"Sure," Gordon says, easy and unconcerned. "Want to swing by for lunch? I picked up some stuff today, so I actually have food in the house."

"Oh! Um." Charlie's face gets hot. Stupid. Gordon isn't asking him out, he's just being nice. "Y-yeah, I can do that."

"Cool." Gordon opens the door, which clunks alarmingly. When Charlie waves a hand to indicate it's okay—as long as the door doesn't fall off, he doesn't care how much it complains—Gordon smiles. "It's a date."

Charlie gets halfway home before he realizes he has a big, stupid smile on his face.

PARKING IN Gordon's driveway feels weird, even though Charlie has been coming here regularly to keep an eye on the house. Ibrahim died three weeks ago, and the past feels like it's broken completely away from the present.

He grabs one of his totes from the back, slams the trunk shut, and thumps up the familiar wooden steps to the door. As he's shifting the tote in his arms to get a hand free so he can knock, the door flies open.

"Hi!" Gordon sounds breathless. His hair is damp like he just got out of the shower, flopping in loose curls over his forehead. The T-shirt he's wearing (Prince: *Purple Rain*) is a size too small, and it looks like he just pulled it on, because there's a slice of brown skin showing above the waistband of his gray joggers. Black hair spreads across his belly, thickest right below his navel.

"Hi," Charlie replies, the tote only half moved into a stable position. He has to prop it on his thigh before he loses his grip on it.

Also, he needs to stop staring at Gordon's hairy stomach before he loses his grip on appropriate behavior. There's a hot stirring low in his gut that's nothing but trouble.

"Sorry—here, let me get that," Gordon says, reaching for the tote before Charlie can protest. The tote isn't heavy, but Gordon's arms still bulge against the sleeves of the T-shirt as he hefts it. "Come in. I guess you know your way around...."

Charlie follows Gordon to the living room, where he puts the tote in the middle of the floor. He does know his way around, and the house looks exactly the way it did the last time Charlie came in to check on things. The palm by the window might need to be watered. Maybe Charlie should have taken it home with him last time he was here. It just felt so *final* to do it.

"Hey, I totally forgot to get the Wi-Fi password from you last night," Gordon says, brandishing his phone with a note-taking app open.

"Shit, sorry." Charlie winces. "You didn't n-need it today, did you?"

"No, it's fine, not until tomorrow." There's an easy smile on Gordon's face. "And you're saving me a huge amount of fucking around with the cable company, so don't worry about it."

Charlie tries to internalize the idea of not worrying about it, but the problem is that in the light of day, Gordon is so much more attractive than Charlie was ready for. The feelings sparking along Charlie's nerves make his teenage feelings look like puppy love.

Teenage Gordon was cute. Mid-thirties Gordon is hot. The strong line of his jaw, chin covered in that short, neat beard; the jut of his Adam's apple and the shelf of his collarbone; the thick, meaty solidity of his body.

Charlie fumbles for his phone so he stops staring, even though he remembers the password. Ibrahim always managed to get himself kicked off his Wi-Fi, so Charlie has plenty of practice reciting it. "Ready for it?" he asks.

"Yup."

"It's zero-two-two-four-one-nine-eight-nine." Charlie looks up from his phone at Gordon, who's staring at him, a strange look on his face. "Got it?" Charlie asks. "Or do you need me to repeat it?"

"Oh-two, twenty-four, nineteen eighty-nine?" Gordon asks. "Like, February twenty-fourth, nineteen eighty-nine?"

"I... guess." Charlie only speaks because Gordon seems to be expecting it, but he doesn't really want to, because Gordon's being weird. He looks like someone just told him he's living in the matrix. Clearly that date means something to Gordon. "Ibrahim told me to set that as the password."

For a second, Gordon continues to stare. Then he shakes himself and types it into his phone. After a minute, he says, "I'm on. Thanks."

The atmosphere in the room stays strange, but Gordon doesn't offer more, and Charlie isn't going to ask. Gordon looks around the room, something sad and baffled in his eyes, which makes Charlie *want* to ask. Or maybe just take Gordon's hand while he says, *Talk to me. Prove that I'm not imagining that we seem like we're becoming friends.*

The intensity of the feeling surprises him and scares him a little.

Gordon snaps out of it. Plopping down on the couch, he looks up at Charlie and smiles, weirdness gone. Mostly gone. Something lurks in his eyes. "Okay, hit me. I'm ready to learn."

Charlie rubs the elbow of his denim shearling jacket before he slips it off and lays it on the back of one of the armchairs. He's wearing a Hole T-shirt, which means the white lines of his old cutting scars are visible on his ropey arms. For a long time, he hid them under long sleeves, but

Ibrahim taught him not to be ashamed of the things he's survived and the marks they left. He always said everyone has scars, whether you can see them or not.

As he kneels on the floor next to the tote and pops it open, he sees Gordon's eyes take in the scars. Gordon doesn't say anything. If he did, Charlie isn't sure what he'd say. He's not ashamed, but he's definitely not ready to tell Gordon about when he was at his lowest.

There's a stuffed owl toy at the top of the tote, about the size of a saw-whet. Charlie presents it to Gordon. "If you're going to help me handle owls, you have to know how to hold them. Oh. By the way, are you up-to-date on your tetanus shot?"

"Yeah," Gordon says. "Why, are there rusty nails out there?"

"No, no, for when the owls foot you." Maybe he should have said *if* instead of *when*, even though it's definitely a matter of when and not if. "You can get tetanus from raptor claws."

"Yikes. Okay, good to know. But yeah, I'm up-to-date. I actually *have* stepped on a rusty nail, so I keep up with that shit."

Brandishing the owl toy again, Charlie says, "So, there's two grips you'll use. When you're getting them out of the net, mainly you'll hold them by the legs"—he demonstrates with the toy's not-exactly-anatomically-correct feet—"between the body and above the ankle. For saw-whets, their ankle is in the position we think of as knees, so about halfway down the leg."

"Hold the leg between the body and above the ankle," Gordon repeats. "Got it." When Charlie holds out the toy owl for him to practice on, Gordon takes it without so much as a smile. His eyes are serious and there's a little notch of concentration between his eyebrows. "Like this?" he asks, imitating what Charlie did.

It isn't anything like holding a real owl, but it's better than nothing. "Yeah. Good. The other hold is called the bander's grip. So what you do is"—he takes the toy back and positions it in his hand—"you hold its neck between your index and middle fingers, then sort of cradle its body in your palm."

As he demonstrates, Gordon asks, "That doesn't strangle them?"

"Well, you don't want to do it super tight, but birds' necks are actually pretty small. They have more feathers than you think." Handing off the toy, he adds, "You try."

Gordon carefully gets the stuffed toy into a bander's grip and Charlie smiles. If Gordon picks up things this quickly when they're in the field, it's going to suck that he's leaving next weekend. Charlie doesn't *need* help, in the sense that he's physically capable of doing everything on his own, but he'd very much *like* help.

And he won't mind the company, either, even if he himself isn't great company. He especially won't mind that the company is Gordon.

"I'll have you practice on some real owls later too," Charlie says. "The laid-back ones. That way you can feel how they move and everything."

Finally, the furrow of concentration in Gordon's forehead smooths away as he grins. "Cool. I'm passing so far?"

"With flying colors," Charlie assures him. Their fingers brush when he takes the toy back to put it back in the tote. An electric frisson travels up Charlie's spine, and goose pimples rise on his arms. He prays Gordon doesn't notice.

Next, they move on to data scribing. Charlie doesn't expect Gordon to memorize what each space on the spreadsheet is for right away. There's a lot of data to collect. It took Charlie several days out in the field with Ibrahim before he got the hang of it.

Charlie opens the tackle box he keeps his tools in and goes through each one, demonstrating as best he can on the toy owl and explaining what he does. Gordon makes small noises of recognition, like he actually remembers what Charlie did with each owl.

By the time Charlie's done lecturing, he's starving. Right on cue, Gordon's stomach gurgles loudly, which makes him laugh. "I promised you lunch, didn't I?" Gordon asks.

Shy suddenly without the buffer of teaching, Charlie nods and follows Gordon to the kitchen. Gordon gets out bread, grape jelly, peanut butter, and Nutella, along with a couple plates and knives. It makes Charlie smile.

"I hope this is okay," Gordon says, surveying the selection on the table. "Becky—my ex, sorry—always said I had the palate of a first grader."

"It's fine," Charlie assures him. "And I don't trust anyone who doesn't like Nutella."

"Right?" Gordon sweeps his hair off his forehead, and the way it refuses to stay swept and falls right back is terrifically distracting. "I should've known it wasn't going to work out."

As Charlie constructs his sandwich (peanut butter and Nutella, naturally), he chews over the mention of the ex. It's not any of his business, but he feels like he and Gordon might be… friends? Or getting there?

He eats half his sandwich before he blurts with no preamble, "Why did you break up with your ex?"

Gordon is mid-bite, but he pauses and puts down his sandwich. Charlie covers his face with his hands in horror that he actually *said* that. This is the moment Gordon makes up a reason to get Charlie out of the house, because he's awkward and his social skills are erratic at best.

When Gordon says, "She dumped me, actually." Charlie peeks through his fingers to see if he looks mad. There's a blob of grape jelly on the corner of his mouth, and Charlie wants very badly to wipe it away. Or possibly lick it away?

Something Charlie can't define exactly crosses Gordon's face. A cousin to shame, tinged with sadness. "It was when I told her I was bi. Well, a few weeks later. She said I was just gay and in denial."

Charlie removes his hands from his face with a snap of his wrists. "She said *what*?"

For the first time since Charlie spotted him in town on Friday, Gordon looks small. "Yeah. We were actually supposed to get married. So, bullet dodged, I guess."

A brave impulse propels Charlie out of his chair and over to Gordon's side, where he kneels. Grabbing Gordon's hand, he says fiercely, "It *was*. You shouldn't be with someone who's so—so—dismissive. Of you. And who you are."

Gordon's eyes are round, and the light slanting in through the mini blinds brings out amber and glints of tigers-eye in his irises. What is Charlie doing? Gordon doesn't need him of all people giving him the Just Be Yourself! pep talk. But when he tries to tug his hand away, Gordon holds on, curling his fingers around Charlie's.

"Thanks," he says quietly. "I know that. Most of the time, at least. It still, like, makes me doubt my own convictions about myself, though. Maybe she's right, you know? I thought I was straight for a long time, but I wasn't…."

Since they're still holding hands, Charlie squeezes Gordon's. "Well, maybe you'll identify as gay someday, but you identify as bi now. That's all that matters."

"You don't think I'll go back to being straight?" Gordon asks, a teasing note in his voice.

"That would be a tragedy," Charlie says before he can stop himself.

The look of surprise on Gordon's face fades quickly to a crooked little quirk on one side of his mouth. Charlie decides this is a good moment to disentangle their hands and get off his knees. He's here to teach Gordon how to help him band owls. Gordon's leaving in a week. Charlie needs to not be stupid.

When they finish their lunch, Charlie decides he wants to work on nets. He accidentally-on-purpose lets slip that there's an old farm track that goes out to the woods, hoping Gordon will say they can drive out there. He does, for this time at least. Charlie will have to think of a way to broach the idea of using it all the time.

They take Charlie's car, which embarrassingly has fast food wrappers stashed in a Walmart bag in the back seat. There's a vague smell of grease. Charlie barely notices it anymore—he didn't notice it at two in the morning when he drove Gordon home last night—but now that Gordon's in the passenger seat in daylight, it seems overpowering.

The Crown Vic really isn't built for bumping over a farm track that hasn't been maintained for decades, but it manages. Though Gordon does rub his tailbone and wince once they arrive at the woods and he gets out of the car.

Charlie grabs Net Two from the trunk, and the two of them trek to the net lanes. It's barely a minute walk.

"Why didn't you park here last night?" Gordon asks. "You wouldn't have had to spend all that time walking back and forth with all your stuff!"

"I d-didn't know if you were okay with me being here," Charlie points out. "I didn't think I should drive my car through your p-property."

"True. Well, you definitely can park out here." Gordon thinks for a second. "You might have to pick me up in exchange, though."

Charlie laughs. "Okay. Fair trade." He heads to Net Two's lane and picks up one of the poles from where he's stashed them in some underbrush. The ground pole, a piece of rebar with a flange on one end to anchor it, is where he left it last night. As he was tearing the nets down, Gordon watched him carefully, but Charlie doesn't expect him to remember anything.

That means he has to start from the beginning. Tapping the aluminum net pole he's holding against the ground pole, he says, "Each net has six poles keeping it up. This is a ground pole. There's one on the other side too. The lighter poles are hollow"—he shows Gordon—"and go on the ground pole."

"And the net goes around the longer poles, right?" Gordon asks.

"Right. The aluminum ones screw together." Charlie takes a breath. "I'll put one up, and you can watch? I'll go slow."

Gordon's eyes flick up to meet his, a gleam of amusement, or possibly mischief, lighting them up for a second. Charlie realizes what he said and feels heat rise from his chest to his neck and up his face. With a noise that's supposed to be a throat-clear but sounds more like he swallowed a bony piece of fish, he says, "Uh. Er. Okay. So, yeah. First thing is, you just slide the pole onto the ground pole."

Charlie inserts the ground pole into the net pole's hollow entrance, and god he's never thought of putting up nets as being full of innuendo, but *here he is* watching the ground pole disappear into the net pole's insides thinking about how he wouldn't mind Gordon being that deep inside him.

His face gets hotter and probably even more bright red. And there's some movement inside his jeans, which is the last thing he needs. Gordon doesn't seem to notice anything. He's watching studiously.

Charlie grabs the canvas bag containing the net and takes hold of five of the net's nylon loops. Showing them to Gordon, he says, "I always start with looping these around one pole. Then I let the net out slowly between here and the other end."

When he's doing this by himself, he goes a lot faster, but he wants Gordon to see how he keeps tension in the net and off the ground, so he takes it slow. On the other side, he starts to reach for a net pole propped against a tree, but Gordon grabs it for him and holds it out, smiling uncertainly.

"Is that the right one?" Gordon asks.

"Yeah! Thanks." Charlie puts it on the ground pole and grabs the second net pole. This is the part where skill enters the picture. "Now we get this side of the net set up. Everyone does this part a little different because it depends on your nets. But I like to do three loops on the top pole and two on the bottom." He plants the pole firmly in the ground and unknots the other set of five nylon loops on the net. "See how there's a little blue strip around this loop? This is the top."

Gordon peers at it and asks, "Does it matter if you put it upside down?"

"Yeah. I mean, not the end of the world, but they have a top and bottom."

"I don't know much about that kind of thing yet," Gordon says innocently.

Which doesn't help Charlie's blushing situation or what's happening in his jeans. He coughs. "So, um. Three loops on top and two on the bottom." The two that he puts on the bottom pole stay near the top. After he gets the three others on the top pole, he moves them so they're about equidistant from each other, with a little space at the top and bottom of the pole. Then he attaches the top pole to the bottom before moving the bottom loops into place.

He repeats the process on the other side, and then they have a fully set-up net. "Any questions?" Charlie asks.

Studying the net, Gordon says, "No. Seems pretty straightforward."

"Good, you can try now." Charlie's going for brisk, but these words come out bright instead. He makes quick work of tearing the net down.

Gordon looks vaguely freaked out as Charlie hands the net bag to him. "Oh wow. Um, okay. So, I start with wrapping these around the pole...."

Impressively, he gets all the way to positioning the loops on the poles before he looks to Charlie for help. "Like this," Charlie says, moving to help. Right when he gets a hand on the pole, Gordon moves his hand too. Their fingers fumble together and Charlie's stomach turns over at the feel of Gordon's warm skin against his own.

His mind goes blank and smooth as glass. What comes next in this process? And why hasn't Gordon moved his hand away?

"I didn't mess something up, did I?" Gordon asks.

Charlie snaps out of it. "N-no! Sorry." He shows Gordon what to do, then undoes it and has Gordon try it himself. Haltingly, Gordon gets the net up. It's a little saggy in the middle, but that's fine—Charlie still has to fix saggy nets all the time because a line got stretched too much, or the ground poles shifted, or some mysterious reason he can't account for.

Plus, Gordon has a big, proud smile on his face, and it makes Charlie a little weak in the knees.

Next, they do the whole thing in reverse, Charlie showing Gordon how to tear down the net, having Gordon set it up by himself again, then tear it down on his own. There's already a growing confidence to his movements. It's a funny feeling, losing Ibrahim and then having Gordon show up and have so much interest in banding. Charlie hopes he isn't clinging to Ibrahim's grandson because he misses Ibrahim.

Ibrahim's smile never did a thing to Charlie's knees, though, so there's that. And when Charlie accidentally bumped Ibrahim's hand, he just mumbled "sorry" and forgot about it, if he noticed it at all. Ibrahim was like a father to him. Gordon is….

Gordon isn't *anything* to him, not really. Someone who seems interested, someone who wants to help. Someone who's being nice enough to let Charlie use his property every night for a couple months.

Someone who's been very clear he's going to leave in a week, which means catching feelings is stupid. Plus, Gordon just came out and just broke up with his fiancée. Hooking up feels vaguely like taking advantage. So no catching feelings and no casual sex. That's fine. Charlie can manage that.

Gordon finishes tearing down the net for the third time, and the lopsided grin on his face makes Charlie's heart thrum just underneath the surface of his skin.

Yeah. Charlie can manage this. It's fine.

Chapter Nine

IT'S BEEN so long since Gordon was excited about something that he doesn't quite know what to do with the bubbly feeling welling up through his chest and coursing through his bloodstream. Everything has been the same for years. For forever. Get up, go to work, come home.

And now there's *this*—this huge disruption to his life, and in the middle of it, a cute, lanky guy devoting his free time to owls. It's the coolest thing Gordon's done since who knows how long ago. He sort of wants to run into the middle of the weedy, overgrown field next to the house and yell at the top of his lungs.

After they're done with Charlie's Intro to Owl Banding, Charlie drops Gordon off at the house and says he'll be back around seven. There's a half-formed invitation to hang around sitting behind Gordon's teeth, but Charlie seems fidgety and shy again, so Gordon lets him go.

There aren't that many hours left until seven, but there are enough that Gordon doesn't know how to fill them. Now that he has Wi-Fi, he could log on to work and check what he missed on Friday… but, ugh. He's a project manager. No one's going to die if he doesn't check his email until Monday.

He could watch something, but he'd have to stream it on his phone, and he hates doing that. Anyway, there's really nothing he's watching. He and Becky were watching a period drama that neither of them was really enjoying, which is a slightly too-on-the-nose metaphor for their relationship. Ever since they broke up, the only reason he puts anything on is for background noise.

Maybe he should call Jennifer? His best friend texted him Thursday night to tell him to drive safely, and Gordon texted her on Friday to let her know he was here, but other than that, they haven't talked.

If he calls her, he'll start talking about owls and Charlie, and he feels weirdly possessive about both. This is something that's all his right now—something he doesn't have to explain to anyone or justify why he's spending his time on it. He doesn't feel ready to talk about the fact that his grandfather's Wi-Fi password was apparently *his* birthday. He doesn't even feel ready to think about that.

He puts a hand in his pocket and feels a piece of paper crumpled at the bottom. Right, it's Steph's farm. Well, he didn't buy eggs at the grocery store, and it's something to do. Funny, if you'd suggested he go to a local farm to buy eggs on Friday, he would have scoffed.

When he plugs the address into his phone, the map tells him it's a fifteen-minute drive. It's coming back to him how pretty much everything here is a fifteen-minute drive. Lake Street? Fifteen-minute drive. Lakeside Tavern? Fifteen-minute drive. Neighbor? Fifteen-minute drive.

Steph's family's farm is apparently called Haugen Dairy, which probably makes her Steph Haugen? Maybe? There's a big steel livestock gate standing open and a small gravel lot inside. Gordon avoids the deepest tire ruts and parks near a building that's somewhere between a barn and a shed. A square piece of plywood is propped next to the door and reads OPEN in hand-painted white letters.

As Gordon gets out of the car and shuts the door, a dog starts barking excitedly. Within a few seconds, it comes tearing around the side of the building, a brown blur as it races toward Gordon.

"Winnie!" a woman hollers. The dog freezes about five feet in front of Gordon, tongue lolling out of its mouth as it pants and gives Gordon the doggiest grin he's ever seen. "She's all worked up today because Gary's kids were here—oh!" the woman continues, stepping through the door to the building and shading her eyes with a hand. It's Steph, out of her Edna's uniform and instead in jeans and flannel.

Gordon pats his knee at Winnie, inviting her closer. Immediately, she trots to him, tail wagging violently. Not that Gordon knows much about dogs, but she looks like pure mutt. When she reaches him, she licks his hand happily, then rears up to swipe her tongue across his cheek.

"Hello to you too," he says, patting her on her soft head. She yips, twirls a couple times, and bounds over to Steph. Gordon straightens and feels weirdly shy suddenly. The awareness of this kind of thing being the epitome of what he wanted to escape from presses against his chest. But he's here now, so: "I figured I'd come by and get some eggs."

"Great!" Steph beams. "Come on in. Winnie, get *down*. You don't have to put up with her."

"No, it's fine. I like dogs." Gordon follows her through the door, Winnie crowding through alongside him, keeping her eye on him to make sure he's keeping up. Inside is the kind of farm store that he's spent most of his adult life avoiding, if not outright disdaining. Utilitarian wooden shelving houses jars of preserves and honey, their labels clearly homemade and printed on the home inkjet printer. A big chest freezer takes up one corner and a refrigerator that might be older than him sits next to it.

"If you bring an old egg carton, you get a discount," Steph says, going to the ancient fridge.

"Hey, I thought I was getting a discount anyway," Gordon protests good-naturedly.

She grins and pulls a battered supermarket carton from the refrigerator. "On the house, just this once. You decide to stick around?"

"I'm staying for the week." Winnie butts her head against his hand, and he scratches behind her ears. There's a twinge of something in his stomach, which echoes like hollowness behind his sternum. A week seemed like forever on Friday—a slow drag of days that would make sorting through his grandfather's possessions a welcome way to pass the time.

Now, it occurs to him that the next five days—seven, if he doesn't leave until next Sunday—is hardly any time to learn about owls and banding from Charlie. It's also hardly any time to learn about Charlie. That makes the twinge bloom into an all-out twist of regret.

"A week for sure," he amends. "Who knows, though."

With a smile, she hands him the eggs. "Cool. This town needs some new blood now and then."

"I'm not sure I qualify." It surprises him how nice it is to hear—that he might be welcome, even appreciated, around here. "Hey, I don't think I've even introduced myself? My name's Gordon."

"You never did, but small town. I got your name."

He scoffs a little. "Right. No secrets here." Except whatever went down between his mom and grandfather.

She shrugs. "Not really. It's not all bad, though, you know? There's plenty of good when everyone knows everyone else."

"I'll take your word for it." Plus, he can't figure out how his grandfather and Charlie fit into this town where everyone knows everyone's business. He shifts his hold on the eggs to pet Winnie again, who licks his hand before she wanders off. "Do you know Charlie Gustafson?"

"Yeah, of course." Tilting her head, she adds, "Quiet, keeps to himself. He has that stammer. I always figured that's why he doesn't say much."

Of course Gordon noticed Charlie's stutter, including how it comes and goes. For some reason, he finds himself excavating Steph's tone, looking for judgment or mockery. She sounds matter-of-fact, though. "People kind of make fun of him, right?" Gordon pushes.

Steph rolls her eyes. "Told you, we need new blood around here. People make fun because they only see one way to be and they start thinking that's the *only* way to be. Charlie Gustafson's been through it. All he's ever been is respectful." She pauses. "Plus he leaves good tips."

"Charlie's been through it?" Gordon repeats. "What do you mean?"

Fixing him with a penetrating look, she says, "I somehow got the idea you don't care for everyone knowing everyone else's business?"

Gordon flushes. "You're right."

The look in her eyes gets sharper. "If Jason Miller's been stirring shit up about Charlie, the first thing you're gonna do is stop listening to him, and the second thing you're gonna do is tell me what he's saying."

"No, no!" Gordon almost drops the eggs and his heart does something scrambly. It's really important that Steph doesn't think Gordon would make fun of Charlie. "I mean, Jason was saying stuff about Charlie on Friday, but I've been... kind of getting to know him, I guess. He was friends with my grandfather, apparently."

The sharpness in her face fades. "Good. Jason sometimes forgets this isn't high school anymore."

In his pocket, Gordon's phone buzzes. When he checks it quickly, there's a text from Jason lighting up the screen. Speak of the devil. *Haven't heard from you all weekend. Need help moving shit?* the text reads.

Gordon slips it back in his pocket without responding. "I like Charlie," he says simply. The memory of standing there and letting Jason make homophobic comments stings even worse now.

Nodding approvingly, Steph says, "I bet he could use a friend." Winnie returns to his side and looks up at him with big brown eyes. Steph laughs. "I think Winnie's volunteering."

"She'd be the best friend of all, wouldn't you, girl?" Gordon gives Winnie's head a vigorous rub and her tongue spills out of her mouth in joy. The truth, obviously, is that Gordon has no idea if Charlie likes dogs. He doesn't know much about Charlie at all. And he only has a week to get to know him better.

At least a week. He has a place to stay, doesn't he? And he works from home, anyway. There's nothing pressing to return to, certainly not his depressing, mall parking lot apartment building with his bare-walled and still half-furnished apartment.

For a few minutes more, Gordon and Steph chat before Steph sends him on his way with another carton of eggs for Charlie. As he returns to the house with too many hours to go until meeting Charlie, his phone buzzes again. It's another text from Jason. *Yooo I'm driving around, got my truck cleared out and ready to haul some shit to the dump. Send me the address and I'll swing by*

The dump. Jesus. When he was in high school, kids used to sneak in there to smoke pot. He tore a pair of jeans on the rusty chain-link fence one time and his mom let him have it—not for ruining the clothes, but for hanging out somewhere he shouldn't have been. He remembers her snapping, "Do you think you don't smell like pot right now?" as he tried to sneakily take the jeans off and toss them in the washing machine before anyone saw him with a rip down the length of one leg.

Gordon tosses his phone in the cupholder and stares out the windshield. Thanks but no thanks, and not just because he's barely touched his grandfather's stuff. Just the bird banding totes, which, now that Gordon's thinking about it, don't even make any sense for him to keep. It definitely doesn't make any sense for him to toss them in the back of Jason's pickup so they can be trashed.

It's weird that his grandfather didn't give them to Charlie.

Maybe it's not so weird. From the things people have said, his grandfather's decline in health came on fast. No one was expecting him to get so bad so quickly, so probably he just never thought to tell Charlie to take the bird banding equipment.

Charlie could have taken it himself, though. He's been in the house. Bringing in the mail. Watering plants. Surely he knows where all the bird banding things are?

It's a level of honesty that Gordon isn't quite prepared to internalize. It's also funny that while Charlie couldn't bring himself to take any of those totes out of the house, he had no problem setting his nets up on land that wasn't his.

A small smile tugs at Gordon's mouth, which he can't really explain. He'll give the totes to Charlie tonight.

Tonight finally comes, and when he hears Foo Fighters blasting from car speakers along with tires crunching on gravel, he's off the couch and at the door like a shot. Like a guy with a crush, heart rabbiting, running a hand through unruly hair. He's probably projecting or something, because Charlie's the first person he came out to who reacted the way Gordon thought people were supposed to react. And because Charlie's gay. And because Charlie's attractive, all sharp Nordic angles with that mop of shaggy hair the color of pale yellow sweetcorn.

Right. Projecting.

As Charlie opens the car door and swings his long legs out, Gordon is already lugging the totes, one stacked on another. There are two bigger ones sitting just inside that seem to have bird stuff in them too, but Gordon doesn't recognize it from anything Charlie has shown him.

Charlie stops abruptly, his gaze flipping between the totes and Gordon's face. "Figured you should have these," Gordon says, holding them at the end of outstretched arms. They're heavy, and Charlie doesn't immediately reach for them, which means Gordon's left straining to keep them up for about ten extra seconds that he hadn't planned on.

Charlie's eyes snag on Gordon's shoulders and run slowly over his arms, still bared in his T-shirt. The hot swell of pleasure at the attention is definitely just more of Gordon projecting.

Awareness seems to snap at Charlie all of a sudden, like a rubber band against skin. He grabs the totes, hands brushing over Gordon's. "This is Ibrahim's banding stuff," he says, like he thinks Gordon might just be giving away random boxes.

"I know. It doesn't make any sense for them to sit around in the basement. And if you don't need any of it, you'll have a way better idea of where it should go than I will." Gordon peers into the back seat of the car to make sure it's clear and opens the door. The hinges squeal.

Charlie is still staring at him. Gordon hasn't been able to see until now—but his eyes are a clear, pale blue, a shade too delicate for comparison to the sky.

Gordon makes himself look away before something shakes loose inside him from the clean purity of that color. "Unless you don't want it. There's two more. Sorry, maybe I shouldn't have assumed."

"No, I do! I do want it. I just—I—" Charlie looks down at the totes in his arms before he shoves them in the back seat. "I wasn't expecting that." He puts a hand on the lid and smiles shyly at Gordon. "Thanks."

"It's nothing." That smile makes it feel like everything. "I'll get the other two."

"I can get one."

Maneuvering through the doorway and getting the totes out brings them into contact again, arms and hips brushing. Charlie has his shearling jacket on and his body heat clings to it, and Gordon feels it curling up his limbs.

Once everything is loaded, Gordon grabs a jacket from inside, just in case he gets cold sitting outside tonight, and the carton of eggs that Steph sent along for Charlie. Charlie doesn't seem to know how to react to that.

They drive out to the banding site and Gordon puts his newly minted net skills to the test. He only manages to get one up while Charlie does the other three, but when he's finished, Charlie wiggles one of the poles and says it looks good.

There are more owls in the nets tonight. Each net run results in at least one, sometimes two. Gordon carefully watches Charlie extract each one, not feeling ready to try it himself. Instead, he takes up the duty of writing down the data they take off each owl. At first he's slow at it, but after a few owls, he gets into the rhythm. Charlie does everything in the same order each time, which helps.

There's a lot of sitting in silence, but they talk too. The next night, they talk a little more. Not about anything important—not about Gordon's grandfather or what Gordon's going to do about the house. Though Gordon can't remember if he ever mentioned to Charlie that he's not going to keep the house, and now he feels a strange reluctance to bring it up.

Charlie talks about birds, about all their adaptations and how smart owls are and how there's so much still to learn about them. Gordon thinks it's pretty amazing that a lot of the people doing the research are just… people. People like Charlie, who love birds enough to give up hours and hours of their lives to catch them and collect all this data.

Every night when Charlie drops Gordon off back at the house, Gordon almost says that. But spending time with Charlie is creating some kind of bizarre inverse social effect where Gordon, who's never been shy, keeps finding himself bashful. They seem like they have a good thing going, and he's afraid he'll start gushing. They haven't even known each other a week. If Gordon starts gushing, Charlie might decide knowing each other for a week is still too long.

Suddenly, it's Friday and Gordon can't imagine leaving today to drive back to Minneapolis. Sunday's still on the table. Probably. Maybe. If not Sunday, then sometime next week.

As Gordon waits on the porch for Charlie, he yawns and rubs his eyes. He's a night owl, but staying up so late and getting up early for work has him pining for Saturday morning. Sweet, sweet sleeping in.

Headlights cut through the gloaming on the road, turning into the driveway. Alanis Morissette is howling out the open windows. Charlie's arm is slung over the door.

Gordon stands, hopping into the Crown Vic when Charlie rolls to a stop. Charlie smiles that same shy smile he's offered Gordon every night this week. It might be getting infinitesimally less shy, which is a thought that sends a little flutter through Gordon's stomach.

Charlie shifts the car back into drive and announces, "You should extract an owl from a net tonight."

"What? No. Seriously? I can't. Can I?" Gordon realizes he's literally sitting on the edge of his seat and attempts to dial it back. "You really trust me to do that?"

In the fading light, Gordon sees the sidelong half-glance Charlie throws his way. It seems like Charlie's asking himself the same question. "I'll be right there," he says. "And the only way to learn is to do it. Er, unless you d-don't want to learn? You don't have to."

"I do." Charlie's let him touch the owls a few times. They're so soft. "And it would help you, right? You'd be able to band them faster."

Last night, on their second-to-last net run, there were five owls caught. Even though Charlie obviously knows what he's doing, it still took him a while to get all five owls out, during which all Gordon could do was stand there and hold the owls once they were in their bags.

"Yeah, it would help a lot." They roll to a stop at the edge of the woods and get out of the car. By now, carrying everything to the picnic table in the clearing is an easy routine. Even the nets are getting easier to put up. Gordon still isn't as fast as Charlie, but on Wednesday he was able to start on his second one before Charlie could get it.

While he stretches the second net from pole to pole, it occurs to him that he'll never be as fast at setting them up as Charlie if he leaves on Sunday. Or Monday. Or even any time next week. And only getting to handle the owls for a few days would be a bummer too.

He lingers over the far end of the net, catching flashes of blond hair through the twilight and the trees. Charlie hasn't brought up the subject of Gordon being gone after this week, and Gordon isn't sure if that's because he knows Gordon's leaving—or because he's secretly hoping Gordon will stay.

He should probably feel that out before he invites himself to be Charlie's research partner for another few days. Week? Weeks? Wouldn't it be kind of a shame to learn how to do all this stuff just to bounce next week? On the other hand, that means staying here, in Sawmill Lake, the place he couldn't wait to get out of when he was a teenager.

It's a nice night. Warm for the beginning of October, especially in northern Minnesota. Charlie shucks his jacket off and swipes a hand across his forehead. The motion draws Gordon's attention to the way his hair has darkened, just the tiniest bit, with sweat. The flutter he gets from Charlie's smile returns, turning to a hot squirm low in his body.

Gordon leans back, closes his eyes, and listens to the lure, counting each high fluting pipe until he's sure the hot feeling in his hips isn't going to turn into anything else.

"Tired?" Charlie asks, breaking the silence.

Smiling, his eyes still shut, Gordon says, "Aren't you?"

"Yeah. I guess I'm used to it. I catch up on sleep in the winter."

Gordon straightens up and searches for signs of tiredness in Charlie's face. Besides a hint of purple smudged under his eyes, you'd never know he's spent every night for the past week up until the small hours of the morning. "I don't even know if you have a day job. Sorry, that's shitty. I should've asked."

With a little breath of self-deprecating laughter, Charlie says, "I have one. It's boring. I can work from home, though. Sometimes"—there's a mischievous crackle to his voice—"I just sit in my pajamas all day."

Gordon laughs. "Same."

Suddenly, a notch appears between Charlie's eyebrows and his spine locks upright, tension stiff across his shoulders. When he doesn't say anything, Gordon asks, "Everything okay?"

The notch between Charlie's eyebrows gets deeper. "Do you hear that? The lure," he clarifies. Obediently, Gordon listens to the lure piping away by the nets. It doesn't sound quite the way it normally does, but he's not sure he would have noticed without Charlie saying something first.

Charlie's fingers flex on his legs. Despite himself, Gordon's attention catches for a few seconds too long, staring at the way Charlie's fingers dimple into the muscle of his thighs. He makes himself look away and focuses harder on the sound of the lure, trying to pinpoint what sounds different. It's fainter, maybe? There might be a little bit of a crackle to it that wasn't there before?

With a quiet breath, Charlie swivels to open one of the totes, grabbing something from inside. "It's almost time for a net run," he says. "I'm going to change the lure's batteries."

"Okay." Gordon pushes to his feet and snugs his newly acquired headlamp around his forehead, flicking it on as he follows Charlie into the trees.

At the net lanes, it's easier to tell the lure is crackling. Charlie turns it off and heads for it, moving past Nets Four and Two, which Gordon sees are empty. He goes to check the other two and sees the dark form of an owl hanging from Net One.

"There's an owl," he calls.

"Good! That's why we're here," Charlie calls back.

Gordon grins. There have been flashes of that all week—a looser, more at-ease Charlie, who's kind of biting and snarky.

The owl stares at him upside down as he shines his light down on it. Charlie told him he should extract an owl tonight, and this one doesn't look too tangled. Does it? Does he actually have a clue? He's watched Charlie do this a bunch of times now and he always makes it look really easy.

Gordon tentatively puts a hand to the trammel line to open the net pocket wider. The owl squirms around and he hastily lets go. "Should I try to get it out?" he asks, turning his head toward the light bobbing close to the ground through the trees.

"Yeah, I'll be there in a second. But you can start! Control the feet."

"Control the feet," Gordon repeats in a mumble, reaching for the net again. The feet look a lot scarier now that it's his hand descending toward the curved talons that taper to needle-sharp points.

Just get under the talons and get his fingers on the legs. He can do that. He takes a deep breath—

And then Charlie's there next to him. Gordon forgets about his headlamp and shines it right in Charlie's eyes. The light makes Charlie look pale and washed-out. "I don't have it yet," he says, stating the very obvious.

Charlie smiles at him, even though Gordon has made no progress on extracting this owl *and* blinded him. "That's okay. Just bring your hand in under the feet and get the legs between your fingers—like that! Perfect!"

Gordon's holding an owl. Well, sort of. He has an owl's legs locked between two fingers. They're soft with downy feathers, but underneath, feel bony and surprisingly sturdy. The owl's feathers brush against his hand and heat radiates from its small body.

Peering over Gordon's shoulder, Charlie says, "She doesn't have any of the net in her talons. She must know she's your first."

Gordon glances at him. There's a little smirk hovering around Charlie's lips. Which are... very close to Gordon's. His skin prickles with that awareness. This close, Charlie smells like woodsmoke and something fresh and oceany.

With a nod at the owl, Charlie says, "I start with the wings."

"Okay." Gordon keeps a firm grip on the owl's legs and uses his fingers to find where the net loops are tangled around one of the wings. Carefully—and much more slowly than Charlie does this—he untangles loop after loop, working the thin nylon strands out of the owl's feathers and over the joint of the wing.

When he frees the first wing, he looks at Charlie. Charlie gives him an encouraging smile. "Perfect. Same thing on the other side."

After getting one wing untangled, Gordon feels like he can do anything. That overconfidence is probably what makes him take so much longer with the other wing. Charlie just watches, nodding every time Gordon looks to him to make sure he's not doing something wrong.

Finally, he gets the wing out. Like he's seen Charlie do, he flips the owl upright. There's still some net tangled around its head, trailing back like a veil. Its big yellow eyes fix on him. "She looks like she's thinking, 'What the fuck,'" Gordon says.

Charlie's breath of laughter puffs against Gordon's neck. "I know. They're funny."

To get the net off the owl's head, Gordon slowly works it back and forth in a side-to-side motion, the way Charlie does. It comes free feather by feather, fluffy brown and white down puffing out like bedhead with each loop that loosens.

The final loop comes off and for a second, Gordon just stands there, the owl in one hand and the net clutched in the other. Realization kicks in and he grins. "I got her out!"

There's an answering grin on Charlie's face. "That was perfect! You just have to get her in the bag now."

A bag is ready and waiting in Charlie's hands. With a little coaching, Gordon transfers his hold on the owl from the legs to the bird-bander's grip, where her back and wings are fitted snugly into his palm so she can't flap around. Gordon lowers the owl into it and lets her go.

Immediately, she squirms, flapping her wings. Gordon feels the tip of a talon graze his finger and he pulls out his hand swiftly, tying the bag shut the way he's seen Charlie do.

He's beaming, not even caring if the owl scratched him. He actually did it! He actually did this really cool thing. People won't believe him when he tells them he held an owl.

Charlie's beaming too, which finds Gordon's pride and happiness and splits it into prismed joy, like light through angled glass.

It's not until Charlie bands the owl and they release it that Gordon realizes something's different. Giving Charlie a puzzled look, he asks, "How come the lure isn't on?"

Charlie sighs. "It's dead."

Chapter Ten

IT'S A MIRACLE the lure lasted as long as it did, which doesn't stop Charlie from being sad and anxious that he's losing most of tonight and who knows how many more days if he can't get a replacement quickly.

He and Gordon take down the nets, pack up, and bring everything to the car. The drive back to Gordon's house is quiet. Charlie is so used to his own silence that he doesn't realize until he stops the car that his silence probably seems like anger.

"You did great with the extraction," he says before Gordon can get out of the car. "That was really good. S-sorry the lure crapped out."

A bright, pleased smile flashes across Gordon's face. Charlie's glad he's not standing up, because it's the kind of smile that makes your knees buckle. "Thanks. Hey, do you want...." He stops, not exactly a hesitation, like it would be if Charlie were talking, but a thoughtful pause, like he knows what he wants to ask but is thinking through how to say it. "Do you want to come in and have a cup of tea or hot chocolate or something?"

No. Don't do it. Gordon's leaving and getting closer to him is just a recipe for sadness. It's bad enough that Charlie's high school crush reignited the moment he saw Gordon outside Edna's last week. The very last thing he needs is to accept offers to share hot drinks in the close, warm light of Gordon's kitchen.

So he says, "Sure."

The kettle is the same one Ibrahim used—cobalt blue, sitting on the stove's back burner, waiting for the moment it was needed. He used to make thick, strong Arabic coffee for the days Charlie came over to discuss findings and possible papers.

Gordon fills the kettle with water and turns the burner on before he pulls a box of store-bought tea from the cabinet. "Um, I hope Sleepytime tea's okay," he says, his olive complexion turning ruddy. "That's all I bought when I went grocery shopping."

"That's good." Charlie clasps his hands in front of his hips, then lets them fall to his sides. His shearling jacket is still on, even though the house is warm.

Like Gordon can hear his thoughts, he asks, "Do you want me to hang your jacket up?"

"Oh—um." He doesn't care about keeping the jacket on, but he likes the idea of Gordon wanting him to be comfortable in this house.

He pulls off the jacket. Gordon takes it and hangs it on a coat hook by the door, which Charlie obviously could have done. There's a zingy feeling in his chest that doesn't seem in keeping with his sensible self's admonitions not to catch feelings for a guy that's already turned his back on this town once.

"Is it weird for you to be here?" Gordon asks suddenly, leaning against the counter next to the stove. "Like, in this house? When you and my grandfather were so close?"

Charlie looks around the kitchen. It looks mostly the same, but it... feels different. Ibrahim was a presence, and the force of his personality imbued this entire house.

There's something about Gordon that changes the mood of this space. Charlie can't articulate it and is pretty sure he doesn't want to. *You make it feel like something new* doesn't seem like the thing to say to a man who's going to leave later this weekend.

"It was weird when it was empty," Charlie finally says. "Before you got here." His face is going red. Even that admission seems too far.

But Gordon looks relieved. Maybe even happy. "Good. I didn't even think about it until I invited you in that maybe this is something you used to do." He looks toward the kettle, where steam is beginning to curl from the spigot. "I'm sorry you lost my grandfather. Now that I've... I don't know. Being here, seeing what you do. Seeing how cool it is, and you teaching me the way he taught you. I'm just... sorry. That you lost him."

A lump moves up Charlie's throat, but he swallows and it sinks back down. "I'm glad I can teach you some of the things he taught me."

The kettle starts to hiss, then whistle. Gordon prepares mugs of tea for both of them and Charlie crosses the kitchen to retrieve his. The herby smell of chamomile unwinds some of the tension in his brain. "You really like it? Owl banding?"

Gordon's face lights up. "It's *so* cool. I still can't believe I held an owl tonight. And you're amazing at it. I love watching you."

Charlie meets his eyes, startled. And pleased. And full of butterflies from a sentence that included the words *I* and *love* and *you*.

So yeah, he's doing a great job over here of not catching feelings.

"I have to go buy a new lure tomorrow in Duluth," he says, which is a non sequitur but not too mortifying—unlike the next thing that comes out of his mouth, which is: "Do you want to come with me? We c-could go up to Hawk Ridge and get lunch at Canal Park and have a beer or something and hang out and—um, I should… stop. I should stop talking."

He takes a mouthful of tea. Which is scalding. But the alternative to choking down too-hot tea is spitting it all over Gordon's kitchen floor, so obviously he chooses choking it down and third-degree burns on his esophagus.

There's a slow, disbelieving smile creeping over Gordon's face. "Really?"

"Sorry, it was stupid. I was being stupid. You have better things to do."

"That sounds really fun. Like, that sounds pretty much like the best thing I could be doing tomorrow."

Gordon's looking at him, something in his eyes sparking like a campfire trying to catch light, and Charlie's stomach feels hot—not just from the tea. He reminds himself of all the reasons he shouldn't get involved with Gordon specifically, and for good measure throws in his general unsuitability for romantic relationships. They boil down to him being a freak and a weirdo, and Gordon is obviously the opposite of that.

Charlie smiles tentatively, then more easily. "I can pick you up at ten?"

IT'S ABOUT an hour and a half from Sawmill Lake to Duluth, right at the tip of Lake Superior's westernmost point. They're on the least interesting approach to the city, from the northwest. If you're coming from the south, you crest a hill and see Lake Superior and Duluth laid out below you, the gray of the water, barges cutting through the waves, bridges picked out like stitching. The elevated freeway brings you slowly from the top of ancient mountains, to roof level with early-twentieth-century brick buildings, then dips beneath the looming profiles of those built in the late twentieth century. Eventually you reach the end of the freeway and the lakeshore winks between mansions and manicured lawns.

The route they take just gives them a good view of Miller Hill, the ugliest part of Duluth. It's all big box stores and traffic congestion around the mall. It probably doesn't seem like very much traffic to Gordon, so Charlie doesn't complain about it.

Anyway, the traffic seems less annoying than it usually does. The drive has been full of music and conversation and laughter. Charlie's pretty sure he can be funny, because he's funny in his head—but he's not used to being funny out loud. Every time he tries it with Gordon, saying the dry things he'd normally keep to himself like he's tossing pebbles one at a time into water, Gordon laughs.

They go to a sporting goods and hunting store first for the lure. Technically it's made for hunters, so Charlie will load his collection of owl calls onto it when he sets it up. The store is full of hunters with deer hunting season approaching. Once Charlie hooked up with a guy from Duluth who was a big hunter, and every time he comes in here, he's nervous about running into him. Usually he's in and out, but today, Gordon distracts him with the gear in the camping section.

"Look at all this freeze-dried food you can get!" Gordon says gleefully. "This is like, a culinary journey around the world. Beef stew, chicken curry, pad thai, biscuits and gravy… stroopwafels! What a time to be alive."

Charlie bites his lip to keep from laughing too loudly. "I did invite you out to lunch, didn't I?"

Another laugh. Charlie is no longer trying very hard to remember why he shouldn't catch feelings for Gordon. In fact, it might be a good idea. If Charlie wants it enough, he's sure he can figure out how to make it a good idea.

Impulsively, he grabs a couple stroopwafels. "Dessert," he says, and Gordon gives him a huge, gorgeous smile.

Yeah, Charlie definitely wants it enough to figure out how to make this a good idea.

With the lure taken care of, they have the whole day to hang out. Charlie keeps looking at Gordon to remind himself that yes, Gordon said this sounded fun, and yes, he's actually here with Charlie.

The day is perfect northern Minnesota fall, mild sun warm enough to go without a jacket, but enough crispness in the air that there's no danger of getting too hot. Charlie drives them to Hawk Ridge, a park high above the city. There are cars lining both sides of the road near the entrance—birders, here to try to catch a glimpse of the fall migration of thousands of birds of prey.

There's a good chance that some of the banders Charlie knows online will be here today. Normally he'd convince himself to try to find them and have an IRL conversation, but shy away before approaching any of them and instead sit alone on the exposed basalt, watching hawks float on thermals and the tiny white dots of sailboats on the lake far below.

Today, he's not alone. Today, Gordon's here, and the backs of their hands brush lightly as they walk the remaining distance up the hill to the park. The edges of the road are thronged with people. Most of them have binoculars or spotting scopes; many are bristling with cameras and huge lenses.

"Was I supposed to bring binoculars?" Gordon asks uncertainly.

Charlie shakes his head, realizes Gordon is still looking nervously at the crowd, and says, "No. I didn't. It's nice to bird here, but it's nice to just sit too."

Gordon gives him a relieved look. It's so strange to think about Gordon being nervous about doing the wrong thing. The Gordon who Charlie had a crush on in high school always seemed so confident. Sometimes it seems like nothing's changed since high school—the same people are still jerks to Charlie and Charlie's still an outsider.

But maybe people do change? Or maybe Charlie's so used to being the one who feels like he's doing everything wrong that it never occurred to him that other people felt the same way.

They pick their way across the flat planes of rock until they reach Charlie's favorite bench. Even when the park is crowded like today, this bench is off the beaten path enough that it's usually unoccupied.

"I forget sometimes how pretty it is around here," Gordon says, surveying the landscape. Bright paint smears of red, orange, and yellow blaze amongst the trees, more of them turning bejeweled with fall foliage than remain green. They're far enough from the crowds that the only sound is the light breeze shushing through the leaves and birdsong.

"Yeah. That's a g-good thing about it." Charlie crosses his ankles and props his feet under the bench. He looks sidelong at Gordon, wondering if it's okay to ask questions about his life.

This is the part Charlie really sucks at. Some part of him craves not being so alone all the time, and he just wants to rush through the getting-to-know-you conversations. People think he's weird if he opens up about himself, and they think he's weird if he tries to get them to. Either that or they're the kind of people who share their life story with everyone, and he's just a random person they're going to forget.

He takes a deep breath and decides to try. "When you left Sawmill Lake. After high school. Did you go to the University of Minnesota?"

Considering he's seen Gordon wear U of M T-shirts, it seems like a good guess. But it's an easy start.

"Yeah, Twin Cities," Gordon says. He rests an arm on the back of the bench behind Charlie's shoulders. If Charlie leaned back, his shoulders would be right in the curve of Gordon's arm.

"What did you major in?" Charlie realizes he doesn't know what Gordon does for a living, only that he has a job that allows him to telecommute.

With a good-natured grin, Gordon says, "I majored in Oh Shit I Have To Pick A Major. Marketing, technically. I already had most of the pre-reqs."

"Is that what you do?"

"Nah. I'm a project manager for a company that sells website design software. Basically, I just make color-coded spreadsheets and set up meetings for the people actually doing the work."

Which doesn't sound so bad. Except for the meetings part. Charlie hates meetings. They're a last resort for him at work.

"What about you?" Gordon asks. His arm is still on the back of the bench.

"Oh." Charlie shrugs awkwardly and looks at his boots. Obviously Gordon would reciprocate the Q and A. Normally if he gets into this conversation with people, it's not anyone from Sawmill Lake and he can sidestep the college conversation. It was stupid to bring it up with Gordon if he didn't want to talk about it.

Except he's not sure that he doesn't want to talk about it. He thinks he does, because he wants to get closer to Gordon.

Watching a bird flit from one treetop to another, Charlie says, "Well, I got into Stanford. With a full ride."

When he chances a look at Gordon, Gordon's eyebrows are up. "Wow. I knew you were smart, but I didn't realize you were like... *smart* smart. You lived in California and you came back here?"

"I didn't go," Charlie says. "My mom was sick and sh-she finally got a diagnosis right after graduation. So I pulled my acceptance to Stanford and went to the University of Minnesota Duluth instead." Gordon remains silent. Charlie chews his bottom lip before going on. "I only did a semester, though, because my mom's health got so bad."

The breeze blows hair into Charlie's face. It looks pretty awful, he realizes abruptly. The last time he had a haircut was.... He can't remember. Summer. The beginning of summer?

Hesitantly, Gordon asks, "Did she get better?" It sounds like he already knows the answer.

"No." Charlie glances at Gordon, gauging through his eyelashes if he can maintain eye contact. What he sees on Gordon's face makes him brave enough to. There's sadness and empathy, none of the awkward discomfort he's normally faced with when he shares his history. "It was lung cancer. It spread really fast. So she—no. She didn't get better."

Gordon puts his hand on Charlie's leg. It rests there, warm and steady. "That's shitty. And unfair."

Charlie almost laughs, he's so surprised. People usually pull an exaggeratedly sad face and say *I'm sorry*, before they change the subject. Either that or they ask if his mom smoked, and if he tells them yes, they can't quite hide that they're thinking, *Well, what do you expect?* "It was. It is." He pushes his hair behind his ears. "My mom would have fucking *loved* Taylor Swift's pivot to pop, for one thing."

Gordon lets out a bark of laughter and claps a hand over his mouth, though he lets his smile peek through his fingers. "Was your mom a Swiftie before Swifties were a thing?"

"God. Gordon. You have no idea." A pleased little smile startles across Gordon's face, like seeing a shooting star out of the corner of your eye. Has Charlie never said his name to him? When Gordon shifts on the bench, angling his body toward Charlie, Charlie lets out a puff of breath. "She raised my sister and me alone. I never gave her enough credit. And then she was gone. And I was...."

"Mad," Gordon supplies when Charlie trails off. Charlie nods. He's not surprised when Gordon says, "My mom died in a car accident when I was twenty-five."

Taking a chance, Charlie lets their legs press together. Gordon pushes his knee into Charlie's a little. Enough to tell it's on purpose.

Dark specks in the sky make Charlie point. "Look. Hawks."

Gordon straightens and leans forward, like the couple extra inches are going to give him super vision. The hawks look like a color-inverted night sky—black stars suspended in the daylight. "There's no way you can tell those are hawks."

Charlie raises an eyebrow and Gordon stares him down, though there's a tiny smile twitching at his full lips. After a second, Charlie relents, "Okay, fine. They're too far away. But I still bet they're hawks."

"You're on," Gordon says. "Bet you a beer they're not."

"We're literally at *Hawk* Ridge."

"So this should be an easy bet to win." Gordon's knee is still pressing against Charlie's. "I'll throw in dinner too."

"You can just ask me out," Charlie says, his mouth running away with the words before his brain has the chance to vet them.

A bright red blush creeps across Gordon's cheeks. Charlie finds it breathtakingly charming, though he regrets blurting that out. Gordon will probably rescind the bet now.

But Gordon says, "It might just be a bet. Also I might need to test the waters. Or. I don't know. Am I getting shot down? Sorry, I don't— this is like, new. I do want to buy you a drink."

The birds are drawing closer and are almost certainly hawks, judging by the reactions of the birders back on the road. A shiver of excitement, the thrill of something *happening*, runs up Charlie's spine. He takes a moment to make sure he doesn't word vomit or, on the opposite side of the spectrum, stutter so much that he loses the thread of what he's saying and Gordon can't understand him.

"Okay," he says.

Somehow, Gordon's blush gets deeper, but a bright smile flashes across his face. "Yeah?"

"A drink," Charlie says. Then, "You really want to buy me dinner?"

Gordon's knee presses harder into Charlie's, a hot, steady point of contact between them. "Yeah."

The smart part of Charlie's brain is still fully aware that Gordon isn't sticking around, and that maybe letting him buy dinner—letting him take Charlie on a date—isn't the best plan. He shuts it behind a door, locks the door, and throws away the key.

As the first bird coalesces into an identifiable form, Charlie smiles. He points to it. "Sharp-shinned hawk."

"Guess you win," Gordon says. His fingertips brush the back of Charlie's hand.

Chapter Eleven

THEY GO down to Canal Park, the bottom of the spit of land that separates Saint Louis Bay from Lake Superior. The area is touristy, full of stores catering to people from the Cities here for a long weekend or stopping on their way to the North Shore. Expensive outdoor outfitters, boutique-y women's clothing stores, that place every town along the North Shore has that sells decorative housewares made of driftwood and sea glass.

Charlie hasn't been down here in forever. It's so nice today that it's busy, kids running around, couples holding hands, seagulls wheeling and watching beadily for unwary tourists who aren't guarding their food carefully enough.

By unspoken agreement, Charlie and Gordon head for the shipping canal that gives the park its name. The Aerial Lift Bridge looms above them, spidery steel girders and cars thumping over the road surface. Canal Park posts the shipping schedule on their website, but Charlie didn't think to check it before coming. There's something about watching the huge barges come through the canal, looking close enough to touch, that finds the childlike glee inside even the most jaded adults.

Gordon leans his elbows on the concrete wall, staring up at the lift bridge. When ships come through, or even tall sailboats, the whole thing rises, stopping traffic to and from Park Point. Only smaller craft ply the waters of the canal today, though.

"You probably want to have an early dinner so we can get back and put the nets up?" Gordon asks.

Charlie leans against the wall too, close enough to Gordon that their arms touch. The contact sends a teenage thrill zinging to the base of Charlie's spine. "We can take the night off. I have to figure out the new lure, anyway."

That's kind of overstating it—they aren't rocket science. But just in case Gordon thinks Charlie is too eager and uncool, it sounds like a good hedge.

A bright, surprised smile appears on Gordon's face, which he seems to forcibly wipe away. "Are you sure?" he asks. When Charlie nods, the smile reappears. "Cool. We can take our time."

A gull lands on the wall nearby, blinking one orange eye at them. "We don't have anything," Charlie informs it. "And you shouldn't eat french fries, anyway. They're bad for you."

The gull cocks its head. Gordon looks at Charlie, a smile on his face that Charlie can't categorize. All he knows is that no one has ever smiled at him quite like that, and his neurons are firing at a million miles per hour, telling him to be mortified about conversing with a herring (he thinks) gull but also insisting that Something Is Happening because Gordon's smiling and his eyes look soft and he hasn't moved his arm away, so warm skin is pressed to warm skin.

Adrenaline makes him push off the wall and ask, "Want to walk out to the lighthouse?"

He's barely stuttered in hours. Has Gordon noticed? Does he realize how significant that is?

"Let's do it," Gordon says cheerfully.

The concrete pier stretches less than a thousand feet into the lake, where a lighthouse sits. Walking out there is an exercise in avoiding everyone else taking advantage of the nice weather. Normally it would make Charlie twitchy being around so many other people, but with Gordon at his side, tolerating it is easier.

No, it's not that, exactly. It's more like being with Gordon has Charlie in a bubble of happiness, so even when people bump into him, it doesn't matter. Like the two of them are a complete world on their own, and nothing else is real.

If he thinks about it too long, it sounds too improbable. Gordon Schumacher and him! Thinking about it is inviting something to come along and break this impossible, wonderful turn of events.

The breeze is stronger at the lighthouse, bringing the smell of cold water. Several kids are chasing each other around and around while their parents pretend not to see it happening. Charlie and Gordon tuck themselves against the curve of the lighthouse. The wall is warm against Charlie's spine.

"If you could do anything you wanted, what would it be?" Gordon asks suddenly. "Someone just handed you a blank check. Where do you go? What do you do?"

Charlie doesn't even have to think about it. "I'd buy radio transmitters so I could fit owls with them. I'd follow them to where they nest and observe them there. And I'd finally try to research whether or not the males I catch—"

Abruptly, he stops, a flush creeping up his neck to his face. He got too caught up in the question, dreaming about what he could do with unlimited money. His dream is to research whether the male owls he catches are attracted to the audio lure because of, not in spite of, it being the mating call of a male saw-whet. He wants to observe same-sex sexual behavior in northern saw-whet owls, and he can only do that by observing the birds he bands over a period of time.

But he hasn't told anyone about that, not even Ibrahim. It will probably sound stupid to Gordon. Or he'll make it into a joke or like some cutesy thing to teach kids that love is love or whatever, like the gay penguins at the New York Zoo.

Gordon is watching him expectantly, like he thinks Charlie is considering the question instead of berating himself for dreaming. There's no blank check and there isn't going to be. Not that Charlie ever would have expected it, but Ibrahim didn't leave him anything.

When Charlie stays silent, Gordon's eyebrows draw together. Charlie wants to run his fingers over the notch in his forehead. "You'd try to research the males you catch...?" Gordon prompts. "Research whether they what?"

Shaking his head, Charlie mumbles, "N-never mind. Just something I daydream about."

It seems like Gordon might press him, but then he nods, which Charlie appreciates more than he knows how to say. He hates being forced to talk.

"I don't know what I would do," Gordon says. "So I think it's pretty cool you do."

"You don't know?" Charlie asks, surprised. "But you're so...."

When he trails off, Gordon looks at him, his mouth and an eyebrow quirked up. "Impulsive?"

"Confident," Charlie says. "I was going to say confident."

Gordon's mouth opens soundlessly, then closes. There's befuddled surprise on his face, like that's the last word he'd ever use to describe himself.

Feeling like he may have put his foot in his mouth, Charlie rushes on, "You were so confident in high school. Y-you knew you wanted to leave Sawmill Lake and go to the Cities. You went to a big school and didn't get overwhelmed, and you live there and have a life, and—"

Wait, ha, no. This isn't making anything better. He's making an ass of himself.

His face must be bright red. He needs to say something to make this less embarrassing, but his brain goes entirely blank.

"You noticed me in high school?" Gordon asks. When Charlie nods, Gordon looks even more befuddled. "Was I being a dick?"

He sounds worried and Charlie shakes his head. "You were—" *Hot. The boy I dreamed about.* "Confident," Charlie repeats. "You knew what you wanted."

"When I was eighteen," Gordon snorts. "I'm in my mid-thirties, my fiancée dumped me, and I just realized I can't think of a single thing I really want to do. Oh god, is this why dudes have midlife crises and buy sports cars?"

Even though Gordon looks genuinely distressed, a tiny laugh escapes Charlie. It's partly relief that Gordon didn't say, *Hold up, weirdo, remind me why I'm hanging out with you when you're obviously so bad at human interaction?* "It would have to be a pretty major midlife crisis for you to go from your current car to a Ferrari."

"Toyotas are very reliable," Gordon says, then cracks a smile. "I'm serious, though. Yeah, I knew what I wanted when I was a teenager. It was easy. Get out of Sawmill Lake. Once I did that, I just kind of… drifted."

Charlie takes a chance and puts his hand on Gordon's shoulder. Through the fabric of Gordon's T-shirt, body heat radiates, sinking into Charlie's skin and veins. When Gordon leans into his touch, Charlie's breath catches. A slight shift and they're facing each other, Gordon's face tilted up toward Charlie's.

The moment cracks down the middle as Gordon clears his throat and scuffs a toe against the ground. His shoulder slips out from under Charlie's palm. Gordon puts his hands in his pockets and says, "Helping you with owls is the only thing I've been excited about doing in like… a really long time. A depressingly long time, probably."

Neither of them speaks for a minute or two. The family with the rambunctious kids is leaving, both parents trying to wrangle the kids like they're border collies herding sheep into a paddock. Charlie's conceptions about people and the way they live their lives are realigning themselves. The idea that anyone could envy him for having it all figured out has never crossed his mind. His whole life, he's felt like he's missing something that everyone else just gets.

He's always felt there's something *not enough* about him, and now Gordon is saying the same thing about himself.

"Maybe," Charlie says slowly, tasting the words to feel out their truthfulness, "everyone puts too much pressure on themselves to figure it out by a certain time? But why would we figure everything out when we've barely lived any of our lives?"

Gordon stares at him. Charlie feels his face getting hot again. He's not good at being profound and he's now made that abundantly, painfully obvious.

"So," Gordon says, "you're super smart, super funny, *and* you're wise?"

Charlie puts his hands over his face because he can't think of anything else to do. He thinks he's blushing and smiling like an idiot, maybe laughing a little too. A touch ghosts over the ledge of his hip— Gordon, hesitantly laying his hand there, and then hooking his fingers into Charlie's to pull his hand away from his face.

"You are," Gordon says, a note in his voice that Charlie doesn't understand. "You know you're all of those things, right?"

When Charlie shakes his head, it's less, *No, I don't know*, than, *It never occurred to me to think of myself like that.* Whatever Charlie heard in Gordon's voice bleeds over to his face, and Charlie still can't read it exactly. "Hasn't anyone ever told you any of that?" Gordon asks. He sounds fierce.

"Why would they?" Charlie asks. He fiddles with a hole along the seam of his jeans. "My coworker told me I'm really good at trivia once."

Gordon's other hand comes up to grip Charlie's hip on the other side. "I'm sorry I didn't notice you in high school," he says. He sounds like he means it. "I'm sorry I was too self-involved."

Their faces are distractingly close. Charlie could count the hairs in Gordon's eyebrows that don't align neatly with the rest. He could put a hand to Gordon's face and brush his thumb across the thick, black fringe of his eyelashes. He could get lost in the warm, dark depths of Gordon's eyes and close his own, until their lips brushed.

"It's okay," Charlie says softly. "I never expected you to notice me."

A flicker of sadness crosses Gordon's face. Again, he stops what's happening between them from spooling out to its natural end. He drops his hands and steps back. It's almost enough to make Charlie wonder if he's imagining it. But no—Gordon's hands were on his hips, pressing down, palms hot and wanting.

"I just wish I had," Gordon says. He lets out a whoosh of air and smiles more easily, amiable and easygoing again. "Can't change the past, I guess."

They walk back along the pier to the park, where they buy a basket of fries from a stand to share. The bench they find facing the lake is quiet at first, but soon a group of ring-billed gulls has gathered, staring up hopefully.

"Please can I give them a fry?" Gordon asks, his eyes big as he dangles one. Every time he moves it, the gulls follow it with twitches of their heads.

"It's bad for them!" Charlie objects, but he's laughing.

"It's bad for *us*!" Gordon grins and Charlie wants to preserve that. It's very important suddenly that Gordon not be sad or down on himself or otherwise unhappy. Did Charlie feel this way when they got in the car this morning? God, he thinks he did.

Plucking a fry from the basket, Charlie tosses it to the gulls, who scramble for it, wings flapping. Gordon gasps, feigning shock. "You said it was bad for them!"

"Toss one to that little guy in the back," Charlie says.

Gordon's smile gets brighter and he bumps his shoulder against Charlie's.

They end up walking all the way back to downtown from Canal Park, where they spend the waning afternoon poking into stores up and down Superior Street. They stop in a craft brewery for a few beers. Gordon pulls an ancient box of Connect Four from the game shelf, which Charlie proceeds to repeatedly slaughter him at.

After the fifth game, Gordon says, "Man, I used to win against my ex's niece every time we played this."

"How old is she?" Charlie asks, tipsy and happy.

"Ouch! Wow! Gustafson coming in with the slapshot!" Gordon drains the rest of his beer. "She's five."

Charlie rests his cheek on his hand and just smiles, stupid and infatuated and obvious about it. He's having more than butterflies—this is like fireflies, wings and flashes in the dark lighting him up inside. Blaming the beer is tempting, so all his gazing and laughing and flirting can be hand-waved once he's sober. It's not the beer, though, and he knows it.

Though the alcohol makes it easier to get out the words bouncing around in his brain. Like they're on a Slip 'N Slide to his mouth. Haha, that's totally a drunk thought! This is nice, though, giving his inhibitions a break for the night. With his anxiety gone, his stutter mostly disappears. It's such a *relief*. Is this how other people feel all the time? Words just coming out easily? Saying what you want to say without having to rehearse it in your head first? The only person he's ever felt at ease with was Ibrahim, and that didn't happen right away.

Blaming the beer is *really* tempting. It would be easier if it was the beer's fault, rather than the fact that he's definitely falling for Gordon.

They walk back to Canal Park for dinner at a Mexican restaurant. Charlie finds himself telling Gordon about going to community college after his mom was gone; how he has an associate's degree in accounting and works for a small commercial real estate company in Duluth that's allowed him to telecommute ever since he was hired; how he'd love to work with wildlife somehow but that his job is enough to financially support his banding in his free time, so it's okay that it's not his passion.

Gordon opens up about his family: how when he went to the Cities for college, his parents moved away from Sawmill Lake, too, and divorced during his sophomore year; how his dad brought his new wife and baby to his mother's funeral and Gordon lost it on him; how he essentially has no relationship with his half sister, let alone the woman his father is married to.

And they just… talk. About nothing, and about anything and everything. They keep touching each other's hands across the table. Gordon's foot taps Charlie's, then comes to rest next to it. Neither of them moves away.

The clatter of dishes in the kitchen is loud by the time they leave, sound bouncing around the mostly empty restaurant. Even though it's late, their server still breaks off from her conversation with her coworkers to wish them good night.

The alcohol has had plenty of time to metabolize, so Charlie knows he isn't impaired as they get in the car. Still, there's something about the two of them in the Crown Vic, cutting through the night, that makes him feel like he's in an altered state. The orange highway lights feel syrupy, and when they fade into the rearview mirrors, soft darkness folds itself around them.

The green glow of the digital clock on the dashboard isn't enough to illuminate either of them but paints a suggestion of features. The arc of a curl falling over a forehead, the tip of a nose, the bow of lips as they curve in a smile and dimple under the pressure of a front tooth.

By the time Charlie pulls his car into Gordon's driveway and turns it off, it's past midnight, just like a regular night in October. Except this hasn't been a regular night.

Gordon puts a hand on the door but doesn't make any other move to open it. "Thanks for letting me tag along today."

"Thanks for coming with," Charlie replies. "It was a lot more fun than it would've been. Otherwise, I mean, if I just went to get the lure alone."

"A lot more fun, but still a chore?" Gordon asks, obviously teasing.

"It wasn't a chore," Charlie shoots back, smiling. "Because of you."

He realizes what he said, how it sounds. When he turns it around in his head to study its different angles, though, it's exactly what he means.

There's enough light to see the way Gordon smiles back. His eyes hold Charlie's. "I had fun too," he says. "A lot of fun."

They look at each other, quiet unspooling like gold between them. The car creaks as it cools and settles.

And Charlie leans across the car to kiss Gordon.

It's soft at first, a tentative press of lips. It's sweet. And it feels *right*.

It feels even more right when Gordon makes a tiny sound and puts his hand to the back of Charlie's neck to pull him closer. His tongue finds the seam of Charlie's lips and Charlie opens them. Their tongues slide together. Gordon makes another noise, a tortured groan, like he's been waiting for this forever.

Charlie puts a hand to Gordon's chest and feels his pounding heart—or maybe that's Charlie's heart, keeping the same wild rhythm.

Abruptly, Gordon yanks himself backward, leaving Charlie halfway over the center console. Gordon's eyes are wide and his shoulders are heaving. "I—" he says, his voice strangled. "Sorry, I—sorry." His hand, scrabbling for the door handle, finally finds it and pulls it open.

He practically falls out of the car and slams the door shut behind him while Charlie's still processing that the kiss is over. By the time his body and brain are both in agreement that the kiss is over and *why the hell is the kiss over?*, Gordon has fled up the porch steps and into the house. None of the lights turn on.

Charlie sits there for another minute before his hands start shaking and a hard chunk of iron lodges itself in his chest.

Stupid. He did something wrong. He misread things or missed a signal or—something. He fucked up, and he ruined everything.

Chapter Twelve

GORDON STAYED In Sawmill Lake too long; that's all he can think as he stumbles through his grandfather's house in the dark. His heart careens through his chest as his body does the same thing, from front door to the living room, where he grabs his work laptop and shoves it in his duffel. Clothes are spread around the room; some are in the dryer. Fuck it. He has to get out of here.

It's an hour later and he's flooring it down I-35, following the signs for Minneapolis/St. Paul, before he lets himself think the words, *Charlie kissed me.* It's a good thing he's the only person on the road because it makes him swerve into the other lane. The part of his mind responsible for higher thinking breaks into his lizard brain's panic for a second to ask, *Why am I running when that's what I wanted?*

But actually, it's scary to think about that too. It's terrifying how much he wanted it, terrifying how good it felt to have Charlie's skin under his hand, Charlie's mouth against his, Charlie's tongue in his mouth.

He concentrates on driving through the night, and by the time he parks in his assigned place at his apartment building, he's so tired that it's all he can do to drag himself upstairs to his apartment and fall into bed.

HE DOESN'T get out of bed until three in the afternoon on Sunday, waking to a sick haze of regret and anxiety. Last night he acted like a child, not a thirty-six-year-old man. What the fuck is his problem?

He wasn't ready for that. That's what his problem is. Sure, he wanted to kiss Charlie. Like, theoretically. He just wanted to kiss A Guy, and maybe it didn't exactly matter what guy it was? It was never supposed to be anyone in Sawmill Lake, that's for fucking sure. Didn't he think about how he wasn't going to come out to anyone there? And he goes and comes out to the first queer person he meets there. In a place he hates. A place he's not staying. A place he one hundred percent does *not* want to develop any ties to.

Because what's going to happen? Charlie, super smart, interesting, funny Charlie, who knows what he wants and is confident in who he is, is going to realize that Gordon isn't worth kissing. Gordon's interests include: playing match 3 games on his phone, watching whatever Hulu recommends, and scrolling mindlessly through Instagram. He might be the world's most boring man. And he's so out of tune with who he is at his core that he's nearing forty and just figured out for sure that he's bi.

When he retrieves his duffel bag from the car, which he was too tired to do when he got back last night, he finds one of Charlie's hoodies inside. For a second his mind just spins blankly, as he holds the hoodie in his hands and wonders how it got here. Is Charlie here? Did Charlie follow him because he wants to fight for him?

Gordon laughs at himself, a harsh, guttural sound that startles him with its volume.

Then he starts crying.

Just for a minute. He remembers that he grabbed the hoodie from the banding site, thinking it was his in the dark, only realizing when he was doing laundry that it was Charlie's. Somehow, even though Gordon washed it, it still smells like Charlie.

He doesn't know if he's surprised or not that Charlie hasn't texted. If their positions were reversed, would Gordon text? Gordon should text right now. If he wasn't a complete fucking coward, he would. But what would he say? *Sorry I ran away when you kissed me, are we cool? Btw I have your Hooo cooks for y'all hoodie.*

Maybe it goes without saying that he doesn't text at all.

Even though Charlie has maintained radio silence all day, Gordon's still a nervous wreck in the hour leading up to the time they normally meet for banding. The time comes and goes without a message. When his phone buzzes, he leaps for it, but it's just a text from Jason giving him the phone number for his cousin who does commercial real estate. That's something to deal with later. Tomorrow. Instead of replying, Gordon stress eats and paces for another two hours before it becomes clear that Charlie isn't going to text.

Well, that's… good. Charlie got the message Gordon sent when he got kissed and bolted.

He goes to bed at nine, exhausted, and cries a little bit more.

THE NEXT day, he logs off work early and heads straight to his favorite Northeast Minneapolis bar to meet Jennifer, his best friend.

Even the kitschy tiki decor doesn't cheer him up as he threads his way through tables to find Jennifer already seated in a booth.

She takes one look at him, ties her straight black hair into a ponytail, and says, "Shit, dude, this calls for a scorpion bowl."

He waves away the suggestion as he slides into the booth and leans his elbows on the table. His whole body aches. Why does his body ache? He hasn't done anything. "You don't like large-batch cocktails."

"Yeah, you look like you need the whole thing." She slaps the table. "Stay here, I've got your first drink."

His protest is very weak, and while she's at the bar, he just stares blankly at the opposite side of the booth. The leather of the high back is cracked and worn.

Jennifer returns and plonks down a foamy white cocktail with an umbrella in it. "Painkiller. Four ounces of rum. You're welcome. You want to talk about it?"

"Blergh," Gordon says around the straw he immediately starts sucking liquor from. Good thing he's been depression-eating all day to give the liquor something to soak into.

A minute goes by while he drinks too much too quickly and gives himself brain freeze. As he pinches the bridge of his nose, Jennifer asks, "Was Bumfuck, Middle of Nowhere that bad?"

"Don't call it that" comes out of his mouth completely without his consent. What the hell?

Jennifer looks taken aback. "Okay, sorry. What's going on? When you texted that you needed a drink, I thought it was just a really Monday Monday."

He looks at her across the table: this woman whom he met at his very first real job, when they bonded over doing data entry all day, all the bizarre people they worked with, and the fact that they were the only two people of color in their department. She's Korean American, one of the wave of Korean adoptees in the eighties. They made a game out of how confused white Minnesotans got about an Asian woman and an Arab man with names like Carlson and Schumacher.

When he quit the job, they stayed friends. They've been there for each other through new jobs and job searches, moves, new significant others and breakups, and everything in between. When Becky dumped him, he cried on her shoulder. Would she really judge him for being bi?

He stirs his drink with the straw. "I fucked up, Jen," he says.

"Did you sink your entire savings into NFTs?"

"What savings?"

She lets out a snort of laughter. "As long as it's not that, it's fixable. What's up? I've barely heard from you ever since you went up to B—uh. What's the place called that you're from, again?"

"Sawmill Lake," he says miserably. Where is he supposed to start?

For a moment she studies him intently. Then her eyebrows go up. "You met someone." His face obviously gives him away, because she yells, "You *did*! You met a simple, small-town girl when you went back to your hometown, who's going to show you all the charms you gave up when you went to the big city—"

"Guy," he says quietly.

She stops her Hallmark holiday movie synopsis and stares. His heart rate climbs, and his armpits get damp. Shit. He hadn't planned how he was going to come out to her, but that definitely wasn't going to be it.

"You met a… guy?" Jennifer says. Gordon nods, his throat too tight with nerves to speak. If Jen rejects him after he screwed things up so spectacularly with Charlie, he doesn't know what he'll do. "Just to be clear, you met a guy in a romantic sense?"

Gordon nods and makes himself say, "I'm bi."

With a slow nod, Jennifer says, "Okay. Like, always? No, dumb question, obviously always. Is this a new-to-you thing?"

There's no judgment on her face, which gives Gordon the courage to say, "Yeah. Sort of. I guess I've suspected for a long time, but I just didn't want to admit it to myself. Until recently. I think the first time I was for sure like, *I'm bi* was in the spring." There's something else he has to tell her, which he glossed over initially, blaming the breakup on growing apart. "Becky dumped me after I came out to her."

Immediately, Jennifer's face gets thunderous. "She *what*?"

Downing another strawful of his drink, Gordon explains, "We were having some stupid fight when we were packing the apartment, and she said the real reason she broke up with me was because bi guys are just gay guys who haven't admitted it to themselves yet."

"Bullshit!" Jennifer somehow looks more enraged. "That is the *biggest* load of *fucking bullshit* I've ever heard." Abruptly, her face crumples, and she moves to his side of the booth, squishing in next to him so she can put her arms around him. "Oh Gordon. Gordon, honey, that's not right. Thank you for telling me. Thank you for trusting me enough to tell me after she said that to you."

Tears sting Gordon's eyes. He has to stop crying; this is getting ridiculous. "I was really nervous about telling you."

Her arms tighten around him. "I know. I can't even imagine. Thank you."

They stay that way for a minute or two, Jennifer gently rubbing his back, before Gordon pulls away. "So um, yeah. I met this guy in Sawmill Lake...."

It takes a while to explain about everything, especially because Jennifer interrupts frequently to make him clarify things. When he finally gets to the end, with the kiss and him running like Charlie's car was on fire, she looks at him thoughtfully.

"So," she says. "It sounds like you were freaked out by the kiss? Things were moving too fast?"

"Yes? No?" Gordon's drink has been empty for a long time but he doesn't feel like another, so he just keeps drinking the melting ice. "I wanted to kiss him. I've just never kissed a guy. I guess maybe I got scared I was going to do something wrong." When she raises her eyebrows, he says, "Okay, I totally did something wrong by bolting."

"Yup." Drumming her fingers on the table, she adds, "It sounds to me like you really like him. So you should tell him."

He lets out a surprised laugh. "Sure. I'll just show up and tell him, 'Hey, I got scared about kissing dudes when we kissed, but actually I really do want to kiss you.'"

"Yeah. That. Say that."

"I can't say that!"

She throws up her hands. "Why not? Especially if you're thinking about staying up there—"

"Whoa, whoa." Gordon stares at her, baffled. "I never said that."

Jennifer's lips purse. "You didn't exactly have to."

"No, you don't understand." He laughs again and runs his fingers through his hair. "I'm definitely not thinking of moving up there. I'm selling the house and the land."

Now Jennifer's lips are pursed and her eyebrows are raised sky-high. "The land where the guy you like is studying owls?"

The way she says it feels like a sucker punch. "Well—yeah, but—"

"Have you told him that?"

"Aren't you supposed to be on my side?" he demands.

Her expression doesn't change at all. "Yeah, I'm on your side. I think you should go back to Sawmill Lake, admit to Charlie that you like him and that you fucked up, and then admit to yourself that you don't want to sell your grandfather's property."

Gordon opens his mouth to deny the last part, but then he realizes she's right. At least, his certainty that he's going to sell the property has been trickling away steadily over the past week. He hasn't actually decided not to sell it, but he's no longer as committed to the idea.

"Yeah, see? I'm right," Jennifer says.

"You're not completely wrong," Gordon concedes. "Maybe I'm not as jazzed about unloading the place as I was. That doesn't mean I'm going to keep it."

"You better tell your guy, then."

"He's not—I'm not—" How can such a tiny collection of words contain so much to refute? "First I have to get him to talk to me again."

Jennifer unlocks her phone and types something, then pushes it over to him. It's Google Maps, showing a route from their current location to Sawmill Lake. *3 hr 2 min*, it informs him. The implication is clear—if he gets in the car right now, he can be back in Sawmill Lake before nine o'clock tonight.

"Won't know unless you try," she says.

If he's in Sawmill Lake tonight, he'll be able to catch Charlie at the banding site. "You're the worst and best influence, Jen," he says. "Do you mind if I get out of here early?"

With a huge grin, she stands to let him out of the booth. "I think that's exactly what I was suggesting. Get it, man. Or don't! Whatever you're ready for."

He laughs and hugs her. "Thanks, Very Special Episode. And thanks for"—he motions vaguely—"being so cool. With me. And the coming out stuff. You know. Let me buy your drink?"

"Nah, I got it. It's your coming out present." She folds him in another quick hug before letting go. As Gordon heads for the door, Jennifer calls, "Hey! Just in case I didn't say! Becky can go fuck herself with that biphobic BS!"

Gordon shoots a grin over his shoulder and strides out the door. This isn't quite confidence, but it's motivation, and that might be even better.

Chapter Thirteen

CHARLIE HAS chosen to pretend that the entire Gordon episode was a dream. A week and change of a wonderful man who didn't think he was a freak, wanted to sit in the dark with him every night for hours to catch owls, who said nice things about him, and who seemed to be falling for Charlie like Charlie was falling for him.

Yeah, if he thinks about all of that and how he fucked it up by going in for a kiss that was clearly unwanted, he'll shut himself in his house for at least a week. Which would maybe be fine at any other time of the year, but he can't afford to lose an entire week of banding, especially not when he's already lost one day to the broken lure and the wonderful magical totally normal and uninteresting trip to Duluth to buy the replacement.

For all of Sunday, after the Kiss of Death, Charlie allowed a faint flame of hope to burn deep in his heart. When he arrived at Gordon's house on schedule and didn't see Gordon's car parked there, the flame guttered. When Charlie sat there, waiting as the sky darkened from twilight to night, and the house remained completely dark and silent, the flame died.

There hadn't been a single text from Gordon all day. With Gordon's car gone and the house silent and dark, obviously empty, Charlie takes the hint. As though it wasn't enough of a hint when Gordon fled after they kissed.

Now it's Monday night, and Charlie's blasting "Disarm" by the Smashing Pumpkins as he turns into Gordon's driveway. The fact that it's Gordon's driveway means nothing to him. Nothing. Nope. It just happens to be the way to his preferred parking spot for the site. Ibrahim's dead; Gordon's gone. There's no one here to tell him not to park on the property.

Except there are two cars sitting in the driveway when Charlie pulls in.

He's so surprised that he jams his foot down on the brake, drawing a complaining squeal from the tires. It's not dark yet, so he can see two figures standing in the driveway, now turned toward him with their hands in front of their eyes to shield them from his headlights.

A protective instinct surges in Charlie's stomach, even though it shouldn't, because there's nothing special about Gordon Schumacher or this house or this driveway where he kissed Gordon and ruined things. He puts his car in Park and throws open the door, ready to confront whoever is trespassing on Gordon's property.

Er. The way he's also planning on doing tonight.

When he gets closer, someone yells, "Speak of the devil! It's Charlie Manson!"

Charlie freezes, recognizing the speaker by voice the moment he's also close enough to do so visually. It's Jason Miller, whose emotional intelligence topped out around age fifteen. The man with him looks familiar, but Charlie can't place him.

"W-what are y-you doing here?" Charlie manages.

"What are *you* doing here?" Jason shoots back. He takes Charlie in, from his messy blond hair to his hiking boots, from his denim shearling jacket to his worn jeans. "I was just telling Joel about how this place is haunted. Are you here for the nightly satanic ritual?"

Charlie clenches his fists but can't make any words come out. They're rattling around his brain, retorts like, *It's a sacrifice, actually, and it's a good thing you're here because we need a victim!* Or even just, *That joke was old before either of us graduated.*

"Seriously, Chucky, what are you doing here?" Jason asks casually, like Charlie should just accept his juvenile name-calling.

If he's not going to get back in his car and drive away, Charlie has to answer. Obviously, he's not going to tell the truth. "I was… coming b-by to… to talk to G-Gordon."

He scrambles for what he could possibly want to talk to Gordon about that isn't kissing and running-away-from-kissing related, but Jason already has another shitty line ready. "I hope you weren't coming over to ask him out, dude. I don't think you're his type." As he says *type*, he cups his hands in front of his chest like he's holding up DD cups.

The other man—Joel—finally speaks up. "Do you know where Gordon is? My dumbass cousin insisted he'd be around to talk about putting this property up for sale."

Ice slides all the way down Charlie's spine. No. Gordon would have mentioned he was thinking about that, wouldn't he?

It hits him where he's seen Joel's face before: He has a billboard in Hibbing advertising his commercial real estate office. Charlie has even heard his name brought up during meetings at work once or twice—Joel Miller, who's trying to break into the Duluth market.

Joel is still waiting for an answer and Jason is doing something on his phone. "Um," Charlie tries, then swallows convulsively and chokes a little. Deep breath, hold, exhale. "I don't. Know wh-where he is."

"I've been texting him all night, man," Jason says when Joel gives him an aggrieved look. "You didn't chop him up and hide him in the woods, did you, Charlie?"

Charlie digs his fingernails into his palms. As obnoxious as Jason is, as much as Charlie wants to yell at him to shut up, the words he really, really wants to get out are for Joel. He digs his fingernails harder into his skin. This isn't the way to manage his stutter—this is why he has white scars up and down his arms—but he just needs to ask one question. "Is Gordon sss-selling the house?"

"That's what I was here to find out," Joel says, still glaring at Jason.

"He said he was interested in talking to you," Jason says, sounding like a sulky teenager.

"Yeah? Did he follow up?"

Jason's sullen silence gives Charlie hope. Maybe Jason brought up his cousin's company and Gordon was just being polite saying he'd talk to Joel. That's what people do here, after all. It's rude and uncomfortable to say no outright, so you show vague interest instead and never follow through.

"I'll ask him again," Jason says. "I'll get something set up."

"Sure, Jase." Joel heads for his car. "I want to talk to him before you drag me out here, though." He's barely closed his car door before the engine roars to life and he's accelerating out of the driveway.

When his headlights fade into the distance, Jason turns to Charlie. It's too dark to make out his facial expression, but Charlie doesn't need to see it to know that Jason is either smiling cruelly or scowling. "Why are you still hanging around?"

There's no good answer, so Charlie doesn't try to say anything.

Jason takes a step closer. "You have a crush on Gordy or something? Is that what this is all about? You came out here because you're into him?"

"Why do you care if I do?" Charlie asks, his voice low. The pads of both thumbs are burning; he's pretty sure his fingernails have broken the skin on both of them, but it's worth it to get this sentence out free of a stutter.

With a mean laugh, Jason says, "I don't. Actually, I think it's funny. Go ahead. Chase after him. Ask him out on a little gay date. Me and him will laugh about it."

You're an asshole, Charlie wants to say, but he'll probably stutter, or his voice will shake. Anyway, Charlie learned long ago that the best strategy for dealing with bullies like Jason Miller is to walk away.

So he does, turning his back on Jason and returning to his car. He'll park along the side of the road and lug his gear through the dark to the site. It will take him extra time to set up, but he's not going to prolong this standoff with Jason.

As he opens his car, Jason yells, "Maybe I'll hang out here awhile, and when Gordy gets back, I'll tell him you've got a gay boner for him!"

"I don't think he'll be surprised," Charlie mutters under his breath, where there's no chance of Jason hearing him. He'd like to inform Jason that queer guys' boners are the same as straight guys'. It would probably give him a crisis of sexuality.

If Jason's going to wait around here just to be spiteful, though, Charlie can't band. The lure will draw Jason's attention instantly, and he'd probably trash the site and Charlie's stuff just to be a creep. Especially if he knew it was Charlie's site.

There's nothing he can do but leave, his frustration and heartbreak and anger sloshing sourly in his stomach. He feels like he's crawling out of his skin and his hands hurt. His throat hurts from the weight of all the things he wanted to say to Jason and all the things he can't say to Gordon because Gordon's gone.

Maybe Gordon *would* sit around with Jason and laugh at Charlie. Stupid homo, thinking a guy like Gordon would ever be interested in him.

The bright glow of Edna's draws his eye as he drives through town on his way home. His routine is already fucked, why not do something really crazy and have pie for dinner? The decision feels made before Charlie has time to consider it. Decisively, he turns the car into a parking spot in front of Edna's. The dinner rush will be over by now. All the good pie might be gone. He doesn't care. He'll eat sour cream raisin pie if that's all they have left.

The sour cream raisin is actually pretty good, he has to admit when it's exactly what he ends up with. He eats it too fast, sitting alone in a booth, feeling alternately self-righteous and sorry for himself under the harsh lights of the diner. He has to blot his bleeding palms with a napkin.

Steph swings by with another glass of water. Noting his empty plate, she asks, "You want to bring the rest home, hon?"

He looks up at her, blinking in surprise. Steph has always been nice to him. He's even heard her tell people to knock it off when they're making fun of him.

Giving him a conspiratorial wink, she says, "I'll pack it up for you."

As she turns to walk away, Charlie gets out, "But doesn't someone else w-want it? Who… works here?"

"It's my night to take home the leftover pie," she says. "Sometimes you need to eat half a pie out of the tin, and that's not me tonight."

Charlie snorts with laughter. There's nothing but kindness in her voice. And she's not wrong. "Thanks," he says softly.

"Don't mention it, hon." Her gaze finds the bloody napkins, then the ragged cuts on his palms that he made with his fingernails. "You need a bandage for that."

"It's okay—" he begins, but she gives him a stern look and moves off, heading for the kitchen. When she returns a few minutes later, she has half of a sour cream raisin pie with plastic wrap over the top in one hand, with the check and some bandages in the other. He mumbles another thank-you and puts the bandages on right away.

When he walks up to the register to pay, Steph is furiously texting. She looks up at him consideringly and asks, "You're still at your place on Mesabi, right?"

"Yes?"

She nods and rings him up. He thanks her again and leaves for home, driving slowly in case a rabbit or fox darts into the road. The whole of Sawmill Lake's "downtown" is about half a square mile, so even driving slowly, it's a short drive.

The rambler he's lived his entire life in, aside from half a semester in the dorm at UMD, looks lonely in the dark. He pulls up to the curb and shuts off the car. When he gets out and closes the door, he stands still, holding the pie while his hands throb. He shouldn't have turned to self-harm to beat back the stutter. He knows better.

Inside, he flips on lights and puts the pie in the refrigerator. A barred owl calls outside and Charlie stands in the doorway between the kitchen and the living room, letting his forehead thunk against the frame. He should have gone back to the site after enough time had passed for Jason to get bored and leave. Waiting there for Gordon probably got boring really fast, especially because Charlie's almost certain that Gordon left Sawmill Lake and went back to the Cities.

Charlie could be doing something he loves right now, but instead he's standing alone in his house and absolutely not succeeding in pretending the last week and a half with Gordon never happened.

Maybe he should have texted. He just didn't want to make it worse. Usually he has a million things to say and no way to get them from his brain to his mouth, but this is the inverse. Texting is easy, but he doesn't know where to start.

With a sigh, he pushes off from the door frame and sits on the couch, opening his laptop. Maybe the universe is telling him to catch up on entering all his banding data on the Bird Banding Lab's website. If so, it's a very out-of-proportion message. The universe could have just sent a couple rainy nights to keep him inside.

The barred owl calls again outside. Charlie puts on Veruca Salt's first album quietly, so he can still hear the owl hooting over the music. Halfway through "Number One Blind," a car pulls up outside and stops. Charlie glances over his shoulder out the living room window, which faces the street. His neighbors are both in their sixties and usually aren't out this late. Kurt must have had a VFW thing in Hibbing.

He goes back to entering data. Only five more lines, and then he can pat himself on the back for getting this uploaded so early in the season, when usually he waits until the first night he gets snowed out.

The doorbell rings.

Charlie's spine snaps straight and his computer almost topples off his lap. He cranes his neck to try to see from the window who's at the door, but he's not sitting at the right angle. Why would anyone be ringing his doorbell at almost ten o'clock at night?

Confusion keeps him frozen with indecision, but the person at the door doesn't move away. Fleetingly, Charlie wonders if it's Jason coming by to start trouble, but that wasn't ever Jason's MO, even in high school.

Slowly, he rises to his feet and goes to the door, flipping on the front stoop light to increase the chances of witnesses in case he's about to get assaulted. He swings the door open.

Gordon is standing there, hands shoved deep in his jean pockets and trepidation on his face.

Chapter Fourteen

NOTHING HORRIBLE happens when Charlie opens the door, so Gordon made it over one hurdle. Unfortunately, nothing is continuing to happen. Charlie is standing in his doorway, dim, warm light behind him while Gordon is spotlighted in my-neighbors-can-see-this brightness, and he's not saying a word. He looks shocked more than anything, and Gordon searches his expression desperately for something to give him a clue about how this is going to go down.

Gordon shouldn't expect Charlie to say anything—not when Gordon was the one who acted like a coward and an asshole. "Hi," he starts, but that's wrong and inadequate. "I'm sorry," he adds, and there. That's a start.

Some of the shock trickles from Charlie's face, and something that looks, incredibly, like hope takes its place.

"I'm sorry about how I acted Saturday night," Gordon says, his hands clenched into tight, nervous fists in his pockets. "I know you don't owe me anything, especially not the chance to explain why I was a complete dick. But I'd, um. Like to? If you're okay with that."

Charlie steps back into the house. "Come in."

Gordon's heart thrums nervously as he steps across the threshold and slips his shoes off. This isn't going better than his wildest dreams, because in those, Charlie threw himself into Gordon's arms immediately and kissed him stupid—but it *is* going better than how he thought it would. The fact that Charlie invited him in is more than he deserves.

There's another long silence while Charlie watches Gordon from under a fall of messy blond hair. "Can I get you anything?"

First Gordon shakes his head, but then he amends, "Actually, I really have to go to the bathroom. I didn't stop on the way here. If that's okay."

Charlie shows him where the bathroom is, darting tiny glances at him the whole time. Gordon can't believe he actually said, *I'm sorry I was a jerk; do you mind if I take a piss?*

It sucks that this is the thing that brought him to Charlie's house for the first time—facing up to his own shitty behavior and the possibility that Charlie might reject him. He owes Steph a drink for texting him the address. Gordon didn't know what he'd do if Charlie wasn't at the banding site. Turns out it was a good thing to worry about, because when Gordon drove out there to check, Charlie's Crown Vic wasn't there.

When he's done, he makes sure to straighten the towel hanging on the rack after he dries his hands. It's fluffy and emerald green. The detail pricks him in the heart.

Quietly, he turns off the light in the bathroom and steps out into the hallway, following the spill of light on the floor to Charlie. The light leads to the kitchen, where Charlie is waiting, leaning against the sink with his arms folded over his chest.

The silence thickens between them. Gordon practiced what he'd say as he made the drive from Minneapolis, talking out loud to the windshield and miles of dark Minnesota freeway. Now that he's here, he can't remember any of it.

"What did I do wrong?" Charlie asks, his voice soft and fragile as a bird's wing.

The question jolts Gordon into taking several steps closer. He shakes his head, and even though he can't remember the perfect way he was going to say everything he needs to, he knows what he *wants* to say.

"I was the one who screwed up," Gordon says. "Not you. You didn't do anything wrong. I'm so sorry, Charlie." Being in the same room with Charlie again makes the memory of being pressed against him glow. He takes a deep breath. He wants that again. He needs that again. "I got overwhelmed. And scared. Because I've never done anything with a guy. That probably sounds really stupid, but I—I don't know, maybe I hadn't totally come to terms with being bi, and the more time we spent together, the more I like—well—yeah, and I wanted to be close to you. I wanted to kiss you. And then you kissed me, and I don't even know what happened. I just… panicked. And I was really stupid. And I'm sorry."

Charlie's arms are at his sides now, his shoulders straighter. "You didn't stop once while you drove?" he asks.

Gordon blinks. "I—no? I shouldn't have left in the first place. I just had to get back as fast as possible."

A hesitant, hopeful smile is trying to crest on Charlie's face. "You kissed me back," he points out.

"Yeah," Gordon agrees. "Was I bad at it?"

The smile breaks the horizon. Charlie ducks his head, and when he brings it back up, hair is in his eyes. "You weren't bad at it. But I wondered if you left because I was the worst kisser ever."

Against all Gordon's fears—maybe even expectations—this is going well. Charlie is smiling. Gordon's skin hums and he takes a step closer. "You aren't a bad kisser. At all. Like, really at all."

"Aren't?" Charlie repeats. "Does that mean you might want to do it again?"

"*Might* isn't the right word."

Charlie pushes off the edge of the sink and closes the distance between them. When he's close enough for Gordon to feel his body heat, he says, "Just tell me if you're overwhelmed instead of driving all the way back to Minneapolis. We can—slow down. Or stop. Or—"

Gordon puts his hands on Charlie's chest. He's so warm. It's like all his passion and intelligence is simmering inside him. "I'm not overwhelmed," Gordon says, Charlie's heat and scent curling around him. His heart is pounding.

One of Charlie's hands cups Gordon's elbow, then moves to lay on his back, drawing Gordon closer. His eyes are the wide, clear blue of the autumn sky. His lips are parted like he's still not sure this is happening.

Gordon surges up and kisses him.

Charlie kisses back, soft and achingly sweet. Gordon's hands slide up to his shoulders, then loop around his neck as he moves closer. This is—easy. It's easy, and it's right, and Gordon can't believe this scared him. His mind is quiet, because nothing in his mind matters. All that matters is the soft press of Charlie's lips against his, the warm hum of his body in Gordon's arms, and their breath mingling between them.

As Charlie pulls him further into his body, Gordon licks at the seam of his lips. For a second, Charlie eases back, but Gordon chases his mouth, catching it again more insistently. Charlie makes a noise and then Gordon is licking into his mouth, breath hot, tongues hotter.

Their bodies press flush against each other. Gordon experiments with moving his hands, exploring Charlie's shoulders, the flex of tendon and muscle familiar and not. His collarbone under the hem of his T-shirt wings wide and comes together in a perfect divot at the base of his throat. Gordon lets a hand fall down over Charlie's chest. Charlie's breath hitches when Gordon's fingers brush his pec, whispering close to his nipple but not quite there.

He stops at Charlie's stomach, letting it all sink in. Charlie's hand strokes up Gordon's neck and into his hair, the heel of his hand imprinting its shape on the bones of Gordon's skull. The hand Gordon has on Charlie's stomach finds its way to the small of Charlie's back.

They kiss, and Gordon doesn't see any need to ever stop.

As they learn the shape of each other's mouths, the kissing gets heavier and hotter, and the space between them feels like too much, even though it's just clothes. Gordon nips Charlie's bottom lip, which makes Charlie groan, and then he lets his hand slip lower, from the small of Charlie's back to the swell of his ass.

Gordon's slow-building desire explodes the minute he feels the curve of it under his palm. He's half-hard already, but the feel of Charlie's ass gets him the rest of the way there.

Charlie pulls away a little. Gordon stares glazily into his eyes, which are all pupil. His lips are swollen. It's a good look. Gordon could get used to causing that.

Shifting his hips, Charlie says, "You can ignore what's, um. Going on down there."

For a second, Gordon thinks Charlie means Gordon's hard-on, which he's not going to ignore, not in the slightest. But then he peeks between their bodies and sees the bulge at the front of Charlie's jeans.

"Oh," Gordon says. His eyes feel round as saucers. His hips ache and his cock throbs.

"We can stop," Charlie says.

Gordon looks up at him. "So I can't touch you?"

Charlie's mouth opens. His pulse is hammering in his neck. "You want to?"

"I might die if I don't," Gordon says completely seriously. The arc of Charlie's throat draws him in, the curve where neck meets shoulder begging to be kissed. Gordon nuzzles there first, breathing the salt and sea scent of Charlie's skin. Then he kisses, languid and slow, sipping at his taste. "Can I?" he whispers between kisses. His hand brushes Charlie's stomach again.

The rumble of assent in Charlie's throat is somehow one of the most erotic things Gordon's ever felt. He dips his fingers under the hem of Charlie's T-shirt and finds the button on his jeans. The metal is the hot blaze of a star and when Gordon pops it open, need burns through him like a solar flare.

He draws the zipper down and slips his hand inside, denim rough on the back of his hand and the cotton of Charlie's underwear skin-warm and soft. An inch down and—

Oh. His breath catches. Charlie lets out a tiny groan and twitches his hips forward. That's encouragement if Gordon ever heard it, so he presses his hand down, molding his palm to the shape of Charlie's hard dick.

There was a fear lurking in the back of his mind that he'd get to this point with a guy and feel nothing—that what he thought was attraction to men was just admiration, or even envy. It didn't matter that when they kissed the other night, Gordon was turned on as hell. Maybe it wasn't real. Maybe he was just having a midlife crisis.

The feel of Charlie's cock in his hand makes that fear evaporate once and for all. He lets out an animal noise and kisses Charlie again, hard and openmouthed, while he strokes Charlie through his boxer briefs.

Charlie yanks him closer by his belt loops and Gordon crowds him back against the sink again, needing to get closer, needing skin on skin. "You're big," Gordon says experimentally, which is true and somehow sexier than Gordon has ever anticipated. The long, thick cock in his hand makes him think of having it in his mouth, or his ass, and until this moment Gordon hasn't been sure about bottoming, but now he knows he wants to. Sometime, it's happening, and it's happening with Charlie.

If Charlie's into it, of course. Charlie's definitely into what's going on right now, his kissing assured and devastating. His hands slip under the hem of Gordon's shirt and every place his fingers touch leaves sparking trails of gold.

"Are you really, really sure you want to do this?" Charlie breathes.

In answer, Gordon moves his hand from over Charlie's underwear to inside Charlie's underwear. It's not like Gordon's never touched a dick before—he has one of his own!—but the feel of Charlie's somehow still takes him by surprise. It's velvet soft and hard at the same time. Smooth, delicate skin over steel. And it's furnace hot, so hot in Gordon's palm.

Charlie groans and Gordon jacks him slowly. The idea of stopping feels like the worst possible thing that could happen, so for good measure, he adds, "Yeah. I want you. I'm not gonna bolt again."

With a helpless sound, Charlie kisses him hard and grabs Gordon's ass, cupping those strong, steady hands around both cheeks. One slips inside Gordon's jeans and underwear, and the feel of those callused fingers and palm on his skin is a revelation.

Gordon swipes his thumb over Charlie's cockhead. It's wet and slick with pre-cum. Gordon's knees wobble at the surge of lust that goes through him. He pushes his thumb into the slit and Charlie whimpers, clutching Gordon tighter and grinding against him.

There's enough precum leaking out for Gordon to slick Charlie's cock with it. As he does, Charlie moans and shudders, his hips rocking. Even though somewhere in the back of Gordon's mind there's a faint sense of wanting this to last, his body takes over, revving to get Charlie to the finish line.

His fist moves faster, gripped around a rock-hard cock that for the first time isn't his own. It doesn't feel strange or unfamiliar the way he thought it might. It feels like the most natural thing in the world to touch Charlie, to lean in to kiss him, to let their tongues tangle.

"I'm gonna come," Charlie gasps out against Gordon's lips.

His hips shift away but Gordon keeps his hand where it is, pumping faster. "Good."

"No, but—I'm going to—it will get on you—"

"*Good*," Gordon repeats before he kisses Charlie harder. One of Charlie's hands squeezes Gordon's ass harder; the other comes up to clutch his hair. Charlie makes a desperate sound, shudders, and then Gordon feels it: the hot, sticky spread of another man's cum on his hand.

It's incredibly fucking hot.

"Gordon," Charlie mumbles. "Gordon, Gordon, I want—can I please—"

Gordon shoves his pants and underwear down his legs. Helpful. Just being helpful.

His cock bounces against his stomach and the brush of his shirt against it is almost too much feeling. Then Charlie's hand wraps around him, and Gordon's brain whites out.

It's over quickly. Gordon thinks he yells when he comes, all his nerves a swirl of fire centered on his dick and what Charlie's doing to it.

He only stops kissing Charlie so he can breathe. When they separate, Charlie's forehead dips to lean against Gordon's. Gordon opens his eyes to the warm blur of skin and fall of gold that's Charlie's shaggy hair.

"Wow," Gordon says articulately.

"I guess you like my kissing," Charlie replies.

The laugh that rolls out of Gordon takes him by surprise. Four hours ago he was struggling not to cry in a tiki bar, and now he's pressed up against a guy he really, really likes, cum sticking them together.

"Told you," he says.

They smile at each other. Stupidly. At least, Gordon's pretty sure he's smiling stupidly, and Charlie's smile looks stupid, but in the most endearing way imaginable.

Ducking his head, Charlie says, "We should clean up." He seems reluctant as he moves away from Gordon, turning around to grab a fistful of paper towels.

"Millennial napkins," Gordon says vaguely, wiping his hands and stomach when Charlie hands him a couple paper towels.

Charlie swipes at himself before holding out a hand to take Gordon's balled-up paper towel. "Maybe if the Brawny lumberjack was on napkins, I'd buy those."

Gordon laughs again. Charlie's got jokes tonight. It's one of the things Gordon loves about him—that quiet exterior that's quite clearly hiding a sharply hilarious sense of humor.

It's not the only thing his shyness is hiding. Even through the first-time-with-a-guy haze, Charlie's hunger was obvious. What would he be like if Gordon got him horizontal?

Things stir a tiny bit, but Gordon's going to table that thought for another time. "So," he says. A flash of alarm goes across Charlie's face and Gordon doesn't even think—he just reaches for him. Charlie's hand slides into Gordon's and his expression eases, though he still looks nervous. "I said I wouldn't bolt again," Gordon says.

"I know." Charlie stares at their joined hands before he looks up to meet Gordon's gaze. His hair is falling into his eyes.

"I meant it." Somewhere in the back of Gordon's mind, probably next to the part of him that wanted to make that hand job last, a little voice reminds him that the plan is to sell his grandfather's property and never come back to Sawmill Lake. Regardless of what Jennifer thinks, that's what Gordon needs to do. He left this town for a reason.

It's easy to push aside, firstly because Charlie's hand is in his, secondly because he can feel Charlie's body heat and see his shoulders and chest rising with each breath, and thirdly because he's not even going to worry about any of that until after Charlie's banding season is over. Selling the property is a problem for Future Gordon.

Present Gordon just wants to kiss Charlie and not think about a future in which he needs to make difficult choices.

"You really like me?" Charlie asks, his voice like light trying to burn through fog.

Gordon pushes himself up to kiss Charlie softly. "I really, really like you," he says. "So much. I don't understand why you're single when you're so amazing."

Red floods Charlie's face, but his eyes look bright and he smiles wonderingly. "I'm going to stop questioning this before you change your mind." He plays with Gordon's fingers. "Kissing doesn't mean this has to be… you know. Permanent."

"What do hand jobs mean?" Gordon teases.

Charlie huffs out a quiet laugh. "You know what I mean."

Neither of them says anything for a minute. Gordon could happily look at Charlie for hours, but it's been a long, emotional few days, and they both have to work in the morning. Though going to bed before midnight will be an early night in comparison to the hours Gordon has been keeping.

He brings Charlie's hand to his mouth and kisses the back of it softly. "Can I keep banding with you?" he asks. "Or is it against the rules to mix research and pleasure?"

"Of course you can," Charlie says immediately. He still looks amazed. Without warning, Charlie kisses Gordon hard, curling his fingers into the hair at the nape of Gordon's neck. "Of course. Tomorrow."

"Tomorrow," Gordon agrees, more complicated things like sentences or words he didn't just hear Charlie say fleeing in the wake of Charlie's mouth on his. And Charlie's body against his, still hard and firm but simultaneously soft and pliant. And Charlie's smell, body wash and sweat and sex. Gordon could mold himself into a shape where Charlie fits permanently if he's not careful.

"I should go," Gordon murmurs. "While I still have the willpower."

This is a revelation, is what he means, and if he doesn't walk out the door now, he might not be able to make himself step away from the warm, luminous circle of Charlie's arms and the hot press of his lips.

"Okay," Charlie says, but his hand fists Gordon's hair tighter.

After a second, he lets go. Gordon forces his legs to move him backward. Unfortunately, removing himself from Charlie's embrace doesn't actually make it any easier to leave.

Charlie gestures and says, "Your jeans are still undone."

"Oh! Whoops."

"Marlene next door wouldn't be mad about the view."

It takes until a sly sliver of a smile creeps over Charlie's face for Gordon to understand that Charlie is teasing him. "Are you pimping me out to your neighbors? Wait, is Marlene old?"

The smile gets wider. "A sexagenarian."

"You're fucking with me."

"She turned sixty-nine in July."

A laugh bursts out of Gordon. "Stop! You're fucking with me!"

Charlie's smile turns to a grin, and it gets so irrepressible that he has to bite his lip. That does things to Gordon, the way blood rushes to fill the surrounding skin, making Charlie's bottom lip look redder and plusher and kissable... er.

And Gordon's never going to get out of here if he keeps staring at Charlie's lips. "I'm going now for real," he says. "Even though I apparently have to fend off the skeevy stares of the elderly."

Charlie walks him to the door. Once Gordon gets his shoes on and pulls the door open, it's impossible for him not to kiss Charlie one more time. He can see them like he's an outside observer—two men standing in a doorway, light spilling into the dark around the edges of their joined forms.

Finally, he forces his feet to move him out of the doorway, down the sidewalk to the street, and to his car. There, he turns around, because of course he does. Charlie is still standing in the door, one shoulder leaned against the frame and his arms wrapped around himself.

Gordon sucks in a deep breath, gets in his car, and immediately opens the window so he can stick his arm out and wave. Charlie waves back.

When Gordon gets home, there's a text on his phone from Charlie: *I'm really glad you came back*

Something like a livewire spits sparks in Gordon's chest. He texts back, *I am too*

Chapter Fifteen

CONCENTRATING AT work the next day is pretty much impossible for Charlie, which is unfortunate, because he gets a bunch of forecasting stuff dumped on him by one of the directors. He doesn't have a background in forecasting and it's not really his job, but the minute it got out that he knows his way around an Excel spreadsheet, he became the forecasting guy.

It means he has to spend a ton of time googling how to do everything he needs to know to put it together. That's frustrating because all he wants to do is answer emails on autopilot and think about what happened last night.

If he had his way, he'd only be thinking about what happened last night.

Obviously Gordon's going to be a huge distraction at the banding site tonight. Luckily, they have thirty minutes to fill between each net check.

Midafternoon, Charlie's phone rings. It's a number he doesn't recognize, which isn't unusual, but it's a local area code without the Potential Spam label, which is. Charlie despises answering the phone, so he lets it go to voicemail.

The caller leaves one. It's Daniel Klein from Kristofferson & Klein Law, which immediately makes Charlie sweaty. There's no reason for a lawyer to call him, and yet there's a voicemail from a lawyer on his phone, requesting that Charlie call back. He listens to the message at least ten times, trying to discern something from the tone or words.

How is he supposed to daydream about Gordon *or* work if this is hanging over his head? It's the thought of being able to think freely about Gordon again without also thinking, *Shit I need to call the lawyer back* that makes Charlie finally pick up the phone and do it.

He doesn't breathe until someone picks up, which means in addition to stuttering his way through the reason he's calling, he also gasps the first few words.

The receptionist transfers him politely anyway.

Hold music crackles in his ear and Charlie puts the phone on speaker, then takes it off speaker. Both are horrible in their own ways. Also, the hold music is an instrumental version of Adele, but he can't place the song, and it's going to bug him.

There's a click, and then a voice says, "This is Daniel."

"H-hi, this is Ch-Ch-Charlie.... Charlie Gustafson."

"Yeah, Charlie, hi. Thanks for getting back to me so fast." Nothing in Daniel Klein's voice suggests he's particularly happy to have to talk to Charlie, which makes the feeling mutual. Charlie knows Daniel, of course, the way he knows everyone in Sawmill Lake. They went to high school together, though Daniel was a senior when Charlie was a freshman, and Daniel was still going by Danny.

Daniel is one of Sawmill Lake's golden children—one of the people who left, got an education, and came back. People would like him even more if he'd get married and have kids to shore up the dwindling population.

Charlie waits, trying to make himself say something anodyne. Something to move the conversation along. He knows exactly what to say! *Yeah, of course, Daniel!* Or, *Sure, sorry I missed your call!* He hates this, that in his head he's perfectly capable of interacting with people, but that same brain won't let him say the words.

The pause goes on a little too long before Daniel says, "This is probably going to sound out of the blue, but did Gordon Schumacher give Ibrahim Yassin's banding equipment to you?"

"Huh?"

"Did Gordon Schumacher give Ibrahim Yassin's—"

"I heard you," Charlie interrupts. It's just bizarre to hear Daniel asking about banding equipment. Or saying Ibrahim's name, even though Charlie knows Daniel has to have been Ibrahim's lawyer. For that matter, it's bizarre to hear Daniel ask about Gordon. Why the hell is he asking?

It takes a couple deep breaths before he can make the words come out. "Why d-do y-you... want... t-t-to know?"

"I'm tying up some loose ends with Mr. Yassin's will," Daniel replies, his tone clipped. That's how most people talk to Charlie. The fact that most of his interactions for the last couple weeks have been with Gordon has made him forget that this is the way it is usually.

It stings more than it should after all these years. People find him frustrating to deal with and they have no problem with letting it show.

He can't really blame them. He finds his stutter frustrating too. The irony is that the more people let their irritation show, the more anxious and uncomfortable he gets, and the worse the stutter gets.

"If you could just let me know?" Daniel prompts impatiently.

"Um, y-yeah. He d-d-d-did."

"He did. Okay. Thanks." There's a silence, but Daniel doesn't hang up. "As it turns out, Charlie, Mr. Yassin left you a sum of money."

Soundlessly, Charlie's mouth opens, which is even less helpful in a phone conversation than it is in a face-to-face one. His mind spins. Money? From Ibrahim? Who's been gone for almost two months now? Whose will was executed weeks ago? Why is Charlie only hearing about this now? And why did Daniel want to know about Gordon giving Charlie the banding gear?

"M-money?" is what comes out.

"About two million dollars," Daniel says.

Charlie's brain stops spinning. He's amazed his heart is still beating. He's definitely not breathing, which only becomes apparent when he coughs and gasps in a breath. "What" is all he manages.

"You'll have to come into the office for some paperwork. And there will be taxes, obviously."

"Two million," Charlie repeats. "Dollars."

"I have some time on Thursday if that works for you?"

Dazed, Charlie says, "Yes."

"Eleven? It shouldn't take too long."

Charlie says, "Sure."

"Great." Charlie hears typing. "I've got you down for eleven. Make sure you bring your driver's license and your banking information."

Charlie says, "Uh-huh."

More typing, then, "See you on Thursday."

The line goes dead. Charlie doesn't move. The number is still scrolling through his head. His brain is a nineties Windows screensaver, 3D text that says TWO MILLION DOLLARS, running across his mind in an endless loop.

It vaguely occurs to him he should make sure he doesn't have a conflict at eleven on Thursday. He does—a meeting with the director who wants him to do the forecasting stuff. Without a single moment of agonizing, he declines the invitation and asks if they can meet later on Thursday.

Two *million* dollars.

Now there's no chance at all that he'll be able to concentrate on work.

EVEN A SURPRISE Two million can't keep him from being nervous about seeing Gordon that evening. All day, he couldn't wait to lay eyes on him again. Eyes and hands. And lips. And, you know. Whatever body parts happened to get involved. The moment he got in his car to drive over to Gordon's house, though, his pulse rocketed to I-have-to-talk-on-the-phone levels. Maybe higher. He got sweaty. His stomach even cramped a little.

Deep breathing and Elastica turned up high gets him to a calmer place by the time he's pulling into the driveway. It's cold today, hovering in the low thirties, but Gordon is sitting on the porch steps waiting.

Something crazed rises through Charlie's chest and throat as Gordon beams and jumps to his feet. This can't be happening. Gordon can't actually be interested in him. *Want* him. And yet here he is, bounding toward the car, his words from last night pinging around Charlie's skull. *I want you. I won't bolt again.*

Gordon opens the door and slides into the passenger seat, leaning across the center console into Charlie's space. Right before their mouths make contact, he freezes. "Hey. I should've asked if it's okay for me to kiss you before I just went for it."

Charlie pulls him in until the remaining distance disappears. "God, yes, of course," he says, and then they're kissing. Even with the evidence right in front of him—and in his mouth—it still seems like this can't be happening. Not to him. The handsome, confident boy who Charlie crushed on from afar in high school can't possibly have come back after all these years and noticed him. That's not the kind of fairy tale Charlie gets to inhabit.

Except Gordon keeps saying nice things about him, saying he admires *Charlie's* confidence, of all people. And his hands are sliding up and down Charlie's back while they kiss.

When they reluctantly separate, Gordon has a lopsided grin on his face. He looks almost drunk on happiness and pleasure. "Hey," he says.

"Hi," Charlie replies shyly. They've been texting all day, but texting is different than talking. Charlie's good at texting. What if he can't be as quick in person and Gordon gets annoyed or disappointed?

And then there's the two million dollars. What will Gordon think about that? Charlie's pretty sure Gordon didn't get two million dollars. Charlie's pretty sure, in fact, that two million dollars was probably all of Ibrahim's money, which he left to Charlie, not his grandson.

He says none of this, instead leaning in to kiss Gordon again quickly. "Ready to g-get some more owls out of nets?"

"Absolutely." Gordon pumps his fist and settles back into his seat. "You'll probably have to help me again. Probably, like, by standing right up behind me and guiding my hands."

Charlie laughs. "I don't know if the owls will appreciate the romantic moment."

"Hey, they're the pervs looking for sex out of season and flying toward that male owl that won't shut up. The least they can do is put up with me shamelessly flirting with you."

With another laugh, Charlie says, "That's the best way I've ever heard anyone describe using an audio lure to catch birds."

Gordon shrugs. "What can I say, I'm a poet."

They drive out to the site and unload the car, then head out to the net lanes to set up. Charlie shows Gordon how to select the right call on the lure and turn it on before they walk back through the dark trees to the picnic table.

Since it's so much colder tonight, Charlie threw his collection of banding blankets in the car before coming out. They're in a big tote bag he slung on the ground. The temperature has already dropped enough with the coming of night that he pulls one out and offers it to Gordon. Gordon takes it, his fingers brushing Charlie's. The way Gordon holds Charlie's eyes makes it clear it's on purpose.

They settle next to each other on the picnic bench, at first with space between them. Gordon shifts. "Can I ask you something? But it might be offensive, so if it is, tell me, and I'm sorry I asked."

"Okay...," Charlie says cautiously. His brain provides him with a million possibilities, but for some reason the one that sticks out is that Gordon's going to ask him why his dick is such a bizarre shape. Which would be weird, because Charlie's fairly confident that his dick is a completely normal shape, if slightly larger than average.

Gordon fidgets. It's cute. Charlie wouldn't have pegged him for a fidgety guy. "I was wondering. Your—stutter? Is that the right word for it, or is there a better word that I don't know?"

"Stutter is fine. Unless you want to call it alalia syllabaris."

"Alaly…. Yeah, no. I think I have to stick with stutter. Anyway." Gordon pauses. "It seems to be, like, a lot less. I noticed the more we hung out the less you seemed to do it. And now it's pretty much gone."

This is actually a much easier question to answer than, *Why is your dick such a bizarre shape?* which, god, Gordon was never going to ask that. "It's always better when I'm comfortable with people. I have"—he waves vaguely—"pretty bad social anxiety? If that's not obvious. But that was from the stutter, probably. It's like a feedback loop."

"Yeah, I get that." Gordon looks at him. "Should I not have asked?"

"I don't mind. I know you're not making fun of me."

Tonight's half moon means it's light enough for Charlie to see the way Gordon's face hardens. "People are assholes. They shouldn't make fun of you."

Charlie shrugs. "It's not that bad. I'm used to it."

"You shouldn't have to be used to it."

There's anger in Gordon's tone, but not just that. There's guilt too. Charlie scoots closer to him until their hips touch. Gordon moves the blanket to cover Charlie's legs as well as his. The desire to take Gordon's hand prickles in Charlie's palm. "People really don't mock me about it much," he says truthfully. "They just think I'm… weird. I am, I guess."

"Maybe people need more weird in their lives."

It's a surprisingly nice thing to hear. There's no denial that Charlie *is* weird, which would be disingenuous. Weirdness is who Charlie is, and sure, maybe people here don't have a high tolerance for it, but there also aren't that many of them. He'd rather spend his time with people who like him *for* it rather than despite it. That was one of the things that drew him to Ibrahim.

There's something nice about the fact that Ibrahim's grandson is as accepting of Charlie's particular brand of weirdness as Ibrahim was. It would make Ibrahim happy, Charlie's sure of that, even though Ibrahim never talked about Gordon.

The prickle in Charlie's fingers gets too insistent to fight, and he brushes his pinkie against Gordon's hand where it's resting on top of the blanket. Gordon folds his fingers around Charlie's. His smile casts more light than the moon.

Every time there's a period of non-kissing, Charlie can't quite believe kissing is something he can, in theory, just do. But Gordon is holding his hand, fingers gently rubbing Charlie's, and his skin is so warm. Sitting next to him is like cuddling up beside a furnace. A thick, really nice-smelling furnace with great hair that Charlie wants to sink his fingers into again—so in fact, nothing like a furnace at all!

"You're like a furnace," he says, because of course he does.

Gordon laughs and wraps his arms around Charlie, nuzzling into the crook of his neck. That means Charlie can get a hand in his soft hair, waves of silky black falling across his fingers. "I'll keep you warm out here."

"I handed that to you," Charlie says. His dick likes what Gordon's doing to his neck—kissing slowly with an occasional delicious scrape of teeth and stubble.

The net check alarm goes off. Awful! But probably good, since Charlie's out here to catch owls, not to make out.

The nets are empty so they tromp back to their picnic table. Their breath fogs, sparkling in the moonlight. When they sit again, Gordon says, "So there's some research you want to do besides this?" Charlie gives him a puzzled look. Gordon must catch the confusion, because he clarifies, "You said something when we were in Duluth on Saturday. Sorry. Random. I meant to ask you more about it then, but I got… distracted."

"Distracted?"

Bumping a shoulder into Charlie, Gordon says, "Um, yeah. Distracted by you."

"Oh." Charlie's face heats, which is silly, considering he can still feel the tingle of stubble on his neck. Also, kitchen hand jobs. "Well, it's…." He's never told anyone about this, even Ibrahim, but he's been thinking about it for a while. "You know how we use the male saw-whet mating call to lure the birds?"

"Sure. I've flipped through your data. You catch mostly females."

"Right. Mostly." Charlie glances at Gordon. He looks excited to hear about this. "I catch some males, and some that I can't reliably sex but are probably males. I want to try to observe same-sex sexual behavior in saw-whets. If I could put GPS transmitters on the males, I could go to where they nest in the summer and observe them. I could set up cameras so I wouldn't have to sit out in the woods twenty-four seven. I could even observe multiple males in one season, you know, if I had the cameras...."

He pauses, but Gordon still looks rapt. "What do you think?" he adds, unaccountably nervous.

"I think it's cool and you should do it." Gordon puts a hand on Charlie's thigh and squeezes. "Queer owls. Hell yeah."

Ducking his head to hide his smile, Charlie says, "It's been observed in a couple owl species. Barn owls—we don't really have them around here but they're in central and southern Minnesota. Well, okay, actually they've been spotted in Duluth and a few other places up here, but—"

The moon illuminates the grin on Gordon's face. When Charlie stops talking, he says, "Hey, wait, keep going."

"I'm babbling about owls," Charlie says, suddenly feeling the accumulated weight of *all* the times he's babbled about owls since they met.

"It's not babbling! It's your passion. I love listening to you." Gordon's mouth opens but no sound comes out for a second. Charlie wonders if it was the *love* part of that sentence and wants to reassure him that it's okay, it's not like Charlie would think Gordon loves *him*. He's not delusional. "So you think you'd actually see gay owls?"

"They're not technically gay...." Charlie stops. "Now I'm lecturing you."

"No, teach me." Squeezing Charlie's leg again, Gordon asks, "What's the right way to talk about it?"

Something swells in Charlie's chest—gratitude that someone wants to hear about this, dizzying, joyful disbelief that it's someone he's romantically interested in. "Usually biologists say 'same-sex sexual behavior.' Because it doesn't just mean sex. It can also be, like, raising young together, or pair bonding."

Gordon nods. "Okay. So, you think you'd see same-sex sexual behavior?"

"Maybe," Charlie hedges. "Focusing on males that respond to another male's mating call is a decent place to start. I mean, there are other reasons they might fly toward the lure." Which is true, but he really wants it to be that they're looking for another male owl to get it on with.

The expression on Gordon's face makes him feel like he could and should try to make this happen someday. It's pure encouragement, edged with interest. "Money's the problem, though, right?" Gordon asks, sounding like he regrets saying it as soon as the words leave his mouth. "Sorry! Jesus. I wasn't trying to tear you down."

"No, it is. You're right."

"Is it the travel?"

Charlie shakes his head. "The GPS transmitters. They run about four thousand dollars."

Gordon's eyes widen. "Four *thousand* dollars? *Each?*"

"Yeah." Realization slams into him. With the two million dollars Ibrahim apparently left him, money *isn't* an issue. Maybe…?

He almost drops that tidbit into the conversation—*Hey, turns out your grandfather left me money!*—but at the last minute, the words hit the brakes and won't come out. For once, he's not annoyed at his stutter imposing itself. Maybe it's weird to bring up. Maybe it will bother Gordon that Charlie got so much money. In fact, Charlie doesn't see how it *won't* bother him. It's so much money, and Gordon hasn't mentioned getting anything except the house and land.

If it's going to bother Gordon, then Charlie would rather not know. It's impossible to conceive of this thing between them lasting forever anyway, so why court disaster? Even in Charlie's most optimistic imaginings, there's no possibility of anything real and long-term between them.

Real and long-term would require him to mention the two million dollars from Ibrahim. Doing… whatever it is they're doing right now: Gordon's shoulder against Charlie's, their thighs pressed together in a body-heat warm length, Gordon's hand seeping the hot-furnace of himself into Charlie's leg—it's just not something Charlie will get to keep forever.

Gordon's been silent for a minute, but finally he lets out a huff of breath. "Damn. Who knew looking for same-sex sexual owls was so expensive?"

He sounds so aggrieved that Charlie can't help but laugh, his half-formed worries about the money and what Gordon will think dissipating like clouds of breath in cold air. "It's homophobic," Charlie agrees.

"Exactly!" Gordon leans into him and Charlie feels a pang. This can't possibly last forever, but it would be nice if Charlie could pretend that the chance was there.

Chapter Sixteen

GORDON INVITES Charlie in for a cup of Sleepytime tea that night, which turns into making out, which then turns into rubbing off on each other. It could be embarrassing—Charlie hasn't come from doing that since he was nineteen and desperate—but instead it's hot. And oddly sweet. After he comes, Gordon gets soft and tender, his kisses making Charlie ache.

His boxer briefs are full of jizz, but it's his emotions that feel gooey. Gross, but true.

The next day they do it all again. Banding, that is, though there's also a nightcap of Sleepytime tea and orgasms. When Charlie first agreed to let Gordon help him, he assumed that he'd mostly rely on Gordon to take down data for him. Gordon's been a huge help there, but he's also a quick study with extractions. On Tuesday night, Charlie helped him, then just supervised. On Wednesday night, Gordon asks Charlie to watch him to make sure he's doing everything right, but Charlie doesn't intervene once.

By the end of the night (total owls: eleven), Gordon is extracting birds on his own, which frees Charlie up to extract any others at the same time. On the last net run, he was even able to get started on banding his owl while Gordon finished extracting his own.

A really bad, dangerous thought creeps into Charlie's head as he drives home on Wednesday night—technically, Thursday morning. His brain is fuzzy from lack of sleep and an abundance of sex, and his body feels hazy and warm, and what he thinks is that Gordon is such a natural at owl banding, maybe it's something he'd want to do more than just this fall. Maybe it's something he'd want to keep working on with Charlie. Maybe he'd be interested in camping out in Canada's boreal forests in the spring and summer, setting up cameras and trying to document saw-whet owls engaging in same-sex sexual behavior.

In the morning, he wakes up nervous about his meeting with Daniel Klein. The morning goes by in drips and torrents, mind numblingly slow for fifteen minutes that feel like an hour, then too fast for an hour that feels like fifteen minutes. He processes some payments and picks at his daily financial reporting before the dreaded hour arrives and he has to leave.

He doesn't bother driving because downtown Sawmill Lake is a seven-minute walk from his house, plus walking helps him manage his nerves better. When he arrives at Kristofferson & Klein, the receptionist, Bonnie, says, "You can go on in. Daniel's expecting you."

"Th-thanks," he forces himself to say.

Kristofferson & Klein's offices are a few rooms on the building's second floor, and Daniel's office has his name on the open door. Charlie knocks anyway, clutching his messenger bag to his stomach, because Daniel is engrossed in his laptop.

Daniel's eyes lift to take in Charlie and he motions to him to enter. "Hi, Charlie. Thanks for coming. You can sit anywhere."

There's a loveseat shoved into the corner of the office with a distinctly '70s coffee table in front of it. A rattan chair is on the other side of the coffee table but angled toward Daniel's desk, like the last person he met with had chosen to sit there. There are also a couple waiting-room chairs against the wall next to the desk.

After a few seconds, he chooses the loveseat, pressing his knees together and tucking his legs against the upholstery. His palms are sweaty as he clasps them in his lap in front of his bag, which is still over his midsection like a shield. Daniel pushes back from his desk, picks up some papers, and comes to sit in the rattan chair.

Daniel has dishwater blond hair and a crooked nose, like it's been broken. As he adjusts his glasses, he says, "This should be pretty quick. I just need to get a copy of your ID. Do you want us to cut a check or transfer the money directly into a bank account? You bank at Security State?"

Doesn't everyone in Sawmill Lake? It's the only one in town. Getting his ID out is easy, so Charlie concentrates on that. "Yeah. A t-t-transfer is. Is. Is fine." He thrusts his driver's license at Daniel, who takes it and scans it.

"You know this expires this year?" Daniel says, pushing his glasses up his nose, even though they don't seem to have moved since he sat down. When Charlie just nods mutely, Daniel puts the papers on the table. "That's the relevant page from the will with the bequest, and some information about the estate planning process if you're interested in having a will made. I'll be right back."

Daniel leaves the office with swift, contained movements, while Charlie contemplates who he'd even leave anything to in a will. His sister? They're not close. He doesn't have anyone.

That's... depressing.

Pushing the thought aside, he picks up the top paper and finds the highlighted portion. Not that Daniel needed to highlight it, because everything else is redacted. Seeing it in stark black and white—well, yellow—on the page makes his insides ring like a gong. "I give the sum of Two Million Dollars ($2,000,000) to Charles Gustafson in the event that my Grandson, Gordon Omar Schumacher, bequeaths to him my Bird Banding Equipment."

That answers the question of why Daniel asked if Gordon had given Charlie the bird banding stuff. Seeing it feels diminishing, somehow. Why was Charlie's two million dollars contingent on Gordon giving him Ibrahim's bird banding gear? If Ibrahim wanted him to have that two million, why would he leave it in Gordon's hands? The grandson he had no contact with and had no reason to expect that Charlie would have contact with?

A tiny spark of anger spits deep in him like a slow-burning fuse. He snuffs it immediately. He's getting two million dollars, plus he already has the bird banding equipment, which is worth plenty in its own right.

Still, it hurts a little. It's that same acidic malcontent from Gordon's first day in town, that little voice inside Charlie asking, *Why not me?*

Daniel returns, several copies of Charlie's driver's license in hand. He gives back Charlie's ID and says, "If you have a voided check, that's the easiest way to take care of the transfer."

People in general make Charlie nervous, but Daniel's curt, all-business tone is making him spiral. His heart is palpitating and his hairline feels damp. His mouth is so dry that he can't swallow. Talking will be even harder if he can manage to get the words to come out.

He dives into his messenger bag to find his checkbook. Somehow on the short walk over here, it got buried beneath crumpled tissues, Salted Nut Roll wrappers and several battered envelopes that look like bills. God, he hopes he paid those.

When he reemerges and holds out the entire checkbook to Daniel, Daniel is already dangling a pen at the end of immaculate fingers. His nails are weirdly distracting—they look manicured. "I just need one. Voided, please."

"R-right." Good, excellent, he just tried to hand his entire checkbook to someone. Good thing it's Danny Klein, who Charlie can't imagine doing anything with even a whiff of illegality to it. Charlie scrawls a messy VOID across the front of the check. It's fitting that he's using a check to get his inheritance from Ibrahim, since the only reason Charlie's written a check for the past fifteen years has been to pay Ibrahim back for stuff. Ibrahim refused to use PayPal or Venmo, let alone any of the sketchier money transferring options in other apps.

Daniel takes the check and paperclips it to the copies of Charlie's driver's license. He picks up another piece of paper from his desk and says, "This is just a form for our office's records to say that I went over this information with you. You can sign and date at the bottom."

When Charlie does that and hands back the form, Daniel says, "That's it. Easy. Thanks again for coming in. You should see that money transfer into your account within the next ten days, but if you don't, let me know."

Charlie tries to mumble something as he leaves. He's happy to get out of there, disliking the ugly emotions the money stirred in him as much as the social interaction keeping his tongue knotted with anxiety. Why would Ibrahim make Charlie's bequest contingent on Gordon being nice to him? It seems—flighty. Impetuous. Like Ibrahim wanted to play with him—and Gordon—after he was gone.

It just doesn't seem like him. Ibrahim liked word puzzles and sudoku. Riddles too. Not toying with people and their actual, real lives.

This calls for a Salted Nut Roll from Ben Franklin if anything ever did.

When he walks into the store, Donna is ringing up another customer, talking with her about grandchildren. Donna has six, none of whom live closer than the Cities. Whenever one of them does something noteworthy, or even just cute, Charlie gets to see pictures.

Once Donna's done chatting, Charlie sidles up to the counter with a candy bar. "Charlie!" Donna puts her hands on her hips and gives him a mock-scolding look. "Where have you been with my owl pictures?"

Some people have photos of their grandchildren; he has photos of owls. When he obligingly opens the photos on his phone so she can flip through all the recents, he settles in for her to coo over them. For the first time, it occurs to him that Donna might like to come out and actually watch him band. Before Gordon, he never considered it. She already likes seeing his pictures, and Gordon proved that people can be interested in watching him work.

Maybe. Something to think about, at least.

Donna gets to one picture and flips the phone around so Charlie can see it. "And who's this?" she asks archly.

The photo is of Gordon holding one of the owls he extracted. Lighting pictures with headlamps never makes for good photos, but Gordon being Gordon, he looks good in this one. He's beaming, black hair falling across his forehead while he holds the owl in a confident grip. The owl looks mildly disgruntled.

"That's Gordon," Charlie says, feeling a completely stupid smile spread over his face.

"*Oh*, I see." Donna looks like the cat that got the cream. "And who is Gordon, exactly?"

"Ibrahim's grandson," Charlie replies, like he doesn't know what she's asking.

She leans her elbows on the counter, and for a second Charlie has no trouble imagining her sixteen years old instead of seventy-six. "Just Ibrahim's grandson, hm? I recognize that look, you know."

"He's just helping m-me," Charlie says, still smiling like an idiot.

"Mm-hm." She flips through a few more photos before coming upon another of Gordon. There's no owl in this one; it's just Gordon, smiling at the camera, an expression in his eyes that lodges between Charlie's ribs. "Well, I hope you use one of those late nights to get some."

Charlie feels himself turn bright red. "D-Donna!"

She's laughing. "He's much too handsome to not, Charlie. He got Ibrahim's good looks, that's for sure."

"Well now I feel weird."

Looking utterly unapologetic, Donna says, "You need to seduce this man."

"Can I pay for this?" Charlie asks, brandishing the Salted Nut Roll.

She laughs again. "If you haven't gone for a roll in the hay with him by the next time you're in here, I'm going to have words for both of you."

It's possible that Charlie's face is never going to return to its normal color, but at least Donna relents and rings up the candy bar. When he hands over the money to pay, he says, "I sh-should take him out on a date, shouldn't I?"

"Do you want to?"

Charlie nods. He didn't realize how much he wants to until this moment. So much of their friendship and whatever they are now has been in the dark. That afternoon at Gordon's house and the day in Duluth are more sun-drenched in Charlie's memory than they probably were in real life, simply because they're the times he's gotten to see Gordon in daylight.

"You should bring him to the supper club in Chisholm," she says definitively. At the doubtful look Charlie gives her, she says, "It's a classic date spot. My sons both took their wives there for first dates."

He takes his phone back before she gets any other ideas—though telling him to hit it is probably enough for one day. "I thought we were just talking about... you know. Not marriage."

"Well, I do think you should have sex before you get married to him," she says, like he's being silly. "You want to make sure you're sexually compatible, don't you?"

Charlie puts his hands over his face.

Donna's hand pats his shoulder. "I'm sorry, I'm sorry. You take things at your own pace. But take him on a date. That would be nice."

"Okay," he says, ready to agree to pretty much anything. Between the two million dollars and this conversation, this conversation is more shocking.

As he leaves Ben Franklin and walks home, eating the Salted Nut Roll, he thinks about taking Gordon on a date and bringing him home at the end of the night. If that happened, Charlie inviting Gordon in, Charlie would want the night. And the morning too. It would mean losing a night of banding.

It might be worth it.

Chapter Seventeen

EVEN THOUGH the nights are getting noticeably colder, Gordon likes waiting on the porch for Charlie to arrive. He likes how darkness takes hold of the landscape, how the sky changes colors and how each sunset is different.

Now that he spends every night outside in the woods, he's learning to listen too. Sitting out on the porch as night falls, he hears geese and ducks, their calls carrying in the still air. There's a sound that scared the hell out of him the first time he heard it, but Charlie told him it was a barred owl. After that, Gordon looked up other barred owl calls, and he's pretty sure there's a pair nesting somewhere near the house, because they hoot and cackle back and forth to each other most evenings.

He hears the saw-whets too. They make piping little sounds and sometimes they scream like something out of a haunted house. If Gordon didn't know what they were, they would scare the shit out of him. Maybe those noises are part of the reason people think it's haunted out here.

Headlights swing into view and a smile spreads involuntarily across Gordon's face. His dumb bi panic from the weekend feels a million miles away. Even though he knows, in theory, what he was thinking (or not thinking), and why he did it, he can't understand it now. He really likes Charlie. Like, a lot. Maybe an unwise amount.

And it turns out that damn, he was really right about being bi, because he loves Charlie's body. The hard planes of muscle, the ropey sinew of arms and legs, his Adam's apple and stubble, his smell. His cock and the low, wanton gravel of his moans.

Gordon lets his head thunk back against the railing. Now he's getting hard, and Charlie's almost here. He's not sure if they're at a stage yet where he can casually drop that he's thinking dirty stuff and having the appropriate erection. Er, reaction.

When Charlie pulls into the driveway, Gordon stands and adjusts himself before crossing the gravel to get in the car. As usual, the music playing in the Crown Vic sounds like something off the soundtrack to a '90s teen movie. "Is this Semisonic?" Gordon asks.

"F.N.T.," Charlie says. "From the album before the one with 'Closing Time.'"

"Whatever happened to these guys, anyway?"

"They're still around."

"Really?"

Charlie gives him a look that Gordon wants to misconstrue as fond, the kind of fond you don't get of a person in only a few weeks. "They play at First Avenue sometimes. In Minneapolis! You could see them."

First Avenue, sure—only Minneapolis's most famous music venue, immortalized by Prince in *Purple Rain* and a place Gordon's never been. Sheepishly, he admits, "The only concerts I've seen are at the State Fair."

Charlie blinks. "You've never seen a show at First Avenue?"

With a wince, Gordon says, "No. Is that lame?"

"No!" The car bumps over a pothole Gordon has come to know and love/hate. As Charlie parks in the deep, bruised-purple shadows of the trees, he adds, "I haven't either. I just… just. I thought everyone in the Cities went there."

"I don't think it's that big," Gordon says, then cringes. He sounds like an idiot. Like he thinks Charlie meant everyone in the Cities goes there at the same time. But Charlie gives him that fond look again, and Gordon's sternum doesn't feel strong enough to withstand the ache behind it.

He tells himself to get a grip and gets out of the car.

"I'd like to go," Charlie volunteers wistfully as they're carrying stuff to the picnic table. "To First Ave. I've always wanted to."

"Yeah?" Gordon slides the plastic tote he's holding onto the picnic table bench and pops it open, unpacking everything and putting things in their place. "How come you've never been?"

"Oh." Charlie shrugs as he unpacks his tote. "I don't really, um… I've never really spent much time? In the Cities. Pretty much the farthest I go is Duluth."

Gordon puts both totes on the other side of picnic table. "I'll take you. What band do you want to see?"

"I—" A funny look crosses Charlie's face. "Really?"

Reaching for Charlie's hand, Gordon says, "Sure. Maybe after we're done banding, though?"

It's not until the words are out of his mouth that he realizes the full extent of what he just said. In his head, there's always been an expiration date on his relationship with Charlie, whether friendship or more-than-friendship. But now he's suggesting—imagining—that they'll have something beyond the next month or so. Like there's something here for real.

Like they can survive Gordon selling the property and going back to his depressing apartment where he can't sleep at night because the floodlights illuminating the mall parking lot are too bright. Back to a life that made sense when he was running away from something. But he's thirty-six years old now, and what does he have to show for his exciting life in the big city? What does he do there that's so wonderful? What has he achieved?

What's there that's better than here? Than Charlie and his owl research?

Gordon's stomach lurches sickeningly and his brain does something that feels like a ninety-degree rotation, like his entire perspective is shifting into a different alignment.

No. He's not doing this. He's not thinking about how the small town he fled the minute he could is actually, maybe just what he's been searching for all this time.

Putting a hand on his chest brings him back to himself. Charlie's giving him a concerned look. "Are you okay?" he asks.

"Yeah! Yeah, sorry. Just thinking." Gordon pauses. "Sorry, did you say you'd want to go to see a concert after we're done banding?"

The casual way he says *we* is really not the tone of a man who's going to walk away from all of this in a month or so. The way his heart gilds itself at the flash of unrestrained happiness on Charlie's face isn't, either.

"I'd like that," Charlie says, shy but not stuttering.

A distant part of Gordon's brain is panicking, but his body is grounded right here in this moment, one of Charlie's hands in his. Charlie leans down and gives him a swift, chaste kiss before stepping away.

Setting up the nets feels like a dance Gordon mastered. There's something deeply satisfying in slotting the poles into place and stretching the net taut between them, in raising it until it sways, invisible against the black night, over his head. It makes him understand why people learn how to dance or play instruments or build stuff. The only moves he's ever known were button combos on Xbox controllers.

It takes a few net checks tonight to catch any owls, but they finally get a couple just after ten o'clock. Gordon then gets the privilege of learning the one thing so far that he doesn't love about banding owls: flat flies.

The first flat fly launches itself from the owl Charlie is measuring, straight toward Gordon's face. Gordon lets out a yell that's half battle cry and half horror movie scream queen, vaguely aware that Charlie is letting out a feral hiss and growling, "Kill that fucking thing!"

One of Gordon's violent flails squishes the gross little thing against his chest. It leaves a smear of blood on his hands. Meanwhile, Charlie is talking in a soft, soothing voice to the owl in his hand: "It's okay, sweetie, it won't bother you anymore. Do you have any more of those horrible things?"

He brushes through the owl's feathers before smoothing them back into place. An involuntary shudder goes through Gordon as he settles back down to take data. After both owls are released, Charlie says, "Hippoboscid flies. Disgusting. I hate them. They're parasitic. Live on bird blood. Ugh."

"I hate them too," Gordon says, because the flat fly was gross, but also because it feels like the loyal thing to say, both to the owls and Charlie. With a smile, Charlie tries to take Gordon's hand, but Gordon pulls it back.

When Charlie freezes, Gordon realizes how he just came across. "Sorry—I have blood on my hand from the fly. I don't want to get it on you."

Before he's even done speaking, Charlie is rooting in one of the plastic totes. He emerges with a container of hand wipes, but instead of giving them to Gordon, he pulls out one himself and reaches for Gordon's hand.

This time, Gordon lets him take it. Carefully, exactingly, Charlie wipes blood from Gordon's palm, making sure none is caked in the creases of his skin. Charlie's hand is warm, his fingers curled loosely around Gordon's. His breath puffs in the space between them, smelling sweet and minty, like toothpaste. Somehow, knowing Charlie brushed his teeth before coming out here tonight makes Gordon's heart race almost as much as his nearness does.

It's one of the most romantic things that's ever happened to Gordon. No one has ever taken such care with him. Especially over something minor, something that he's totally capable of doing by himself. That it's Charlie, who as far as Gordon can tell hasn't had anyone look after him for a long time, makes him ache all over again.

Charlie stops and looks up at him, faltering when he meets Gordon's eyes. "What?" he asks.

Gordon shakes his head. "Nothing."

It's not nothing. It's the furthest thing from nothing Gordon thinks it's possible to be.

WHEN GORDON wakes up on Friday, he has to confront a stark truth. He's going to spend the next month, month and a half, whatever, in this house. He's going to finish out the banding season with Charlie, because every night he gets pulled deeper into this world of people sitting in the dark for hours in the hope they'll get to put a little aluminum band on an owl's leg. If you'd told him a year ago that he was going to get excited about something called a molt pattern, he'd have looked at you like you were crazy.

Of course, it's not just the owls. It's Charlie too. Sweet, quiet Charlie, who whispers to owls not to be scared and who cleaned Gordon's hand like it was something precious. Like Gordon was something precious.

He came to Sawmill Lake preemptively hating every minute he'd have to spend here and chomping at the bit to sell the property and house he never wanted. Now he has to face up to an inescapable fact.

There's no way he can sell the house or the land.

It's not just that Charlie will hate him if he does, though that's a huge part of it. It's that Charlie's project is important, and he's established here. There's habitat for the saw-whets on this land. If Gordon sells it, a developer will slap down some asphalt and a big box store.

Then there will be no more owls. No saw-whets migrating through, no barred owls calling to each other across the fields. There will be no rabbits watching him warily as he crosses from Charlie's car to the porch every night, no squirrels building leaf nests for the winter in the trees around the house. No deer walking like ghosts through the grass as the light fades every night.

And there's this thing, this tenuous connection, spiderweb thin, to his grandfather. Gordon doesn't know if it's real memories or things his brain is cobbling together to give him warm fuzzies, but blurry recollections are coming back to him of standing outside in bright, golden autumn light, holding a hawk on his arm.

There's no one to ask, no way to know for sure if it's a real thing that happened. But Gordon decides, deep down, that he wants it to be real. He didn't know his grandfather, but it's like he's coming to know part of him through Charlie and through working with owls.

Something settles in him once he makes the decision to keep the property. It's more like *admitting* he's going to keep the property. The decision feels like it was made as soon as he started helping Charlie band.

As usual, Gordon spends the entire day looking forward to evening. Work is work, tolerable but hardly thrilling. There's a team happy hour scheduled for tonight at one of the gazillion craft breweries that's popped up in the Cities in the last fifteen years, so Gordon finally fesses up to the fact that he's in Sawmill Lake. No one cares, they just want to know if he has a boat up here.

It's a good day, plus it's Friday, which means he gets to sleep in tomorrow. And then, right after five o'clock, Jason shows up.

"Hey, Gordy!" Jason claps him on the shoulder when Gordon opens the door. "You're a hard guy to pin down for a drink!"

Yeah, mostly because Gordon's been sending noncommittal responses to Jason's texts suggesting they hang out. "Yeah, you know. Work," Gordon says vaguely.

"It's quittin' time, isn't it?" Jason grins. "C'mon, I'll buy you a couple."

"A couple...?"

"Beers, dude! Lakeside! It's been too long!"

Gordon almost points out that prior to a month ago, it had been almost twenty years since they'd seen each other. Instead, he musters up a smile and says, "Yeah, sure. I can hang out for a little bit." He's not exactly sure what the future holds for him in Sawmill Lake, but if Jason's going to be, like, a neighbor, then Gordon's probably going to have a we-get-beers-sometimes relationship with him, anyway.

They drive over to Lakeside Tavern separately. Inside, Gordon's stuck drinking Surly again. He orders some wings too. Might as well eat dinner here.

"How's it going, man?" Jason asks once they're seated at a table near the pull tabs. "What've you been up to?"

With a shrug, Gordon says, "Just working. Going through my grandfather's stuff."

Taking a swig of beer, Jason says, "I'm kinda surprised you're still here. You seemed pretty pumped to get rid of that old place."

"Yeah." Gordon considers dropping twenty bucks on pull tabs just to have something to do with his hands besides lifting his beer to his mouth. If he relies on that to avoid engaging fully with Jason, he's going to get trashed, even on Surly. "I don't know. I'm thinking about hanging on to it, actually."

"What? Really?"

Gordon draws lines in the condensation on his glass. "I haven't made any decisions about anything yet. But it's a nice house. Probably needs a little work"—like he knows—"but my grandfather seems like he kept it in good shape. And the land. I like the idea of it staying the way it is. I see a lot of animals. It's pretty cool."

"You should charge people to hunt on it." Jason mimes firing a rifle. "Bros from the Cities will pay big money to come up here and get their five-point buck for their man cave."

"Uh-huh." Obviously Gordon isn't going to do that. "That's a thought."

Jason drinks again. His beer is half gone already. "I still think you should talk to my cousin. There's a lot of interest in getting some chain stores in town. He could get you a real good price."

"Maybe." Saying "maybe" is the equivalent of responding to someone's movie recommendation with, "I'll add it to my list."

The wings arrive, along with a burger and fries and another beer for Jason, who fist-bumps their server and says, "Thanks, man."

Apparently Jason is unable or unwilling to understand that Gordon's *maybe* means *no*, because he says, "I'll set up a meeting for you and my cousin. His name's Joel, by the way. He's on a billboard in Duluth."

"Cool."

Jason pulls out his phone and taps out a text. "There. I sent him your deets. He'll probably give you a call next week."

Gordon stuffs a wing in his mouth to avoid responding. Future Gordon can deal with it next week. If he has to meet with Joel The Cousin to say no, he doesn't want to sell, so be it.

"I actually swung by your place with Joel on Monday," Jason says, taking a bite of his burger. "You weren't around."

For a second, Gordon's afraid he's going to choke on his mouthful of chicken. When he swallows, he's overambitious, and he has to gulp his beer to get everything down. Eyes watering, he says, "You should've texted."

"I did! I asked if you were home."

Wait—now Gordon remembers. He didn't see Jason's text until Tuesday morning, because on Monday night he was frantically driving back up here after his freakout over The Kiss. His focus was lasered on how to get to Charlie as fast as possible, and afterward, he didn't care about who was texting him if it wasn't Charlie.

"Oh, yeah—sorry. I had stuff going on that night." But Gordon doesn't remember the text saying Jason was at his *house*.

Jason shrugs. "Yeah, I figured, when you didn't text back. But Joel really wanted to see the place, so I brought him around anyway." He jams a couple fries in his mouth. "So, I actually wanted to warn you about something."

Gordon sits up straighter, unease threading through his stomach. "Warn me? About what?"

There's a disapproving expression on Jason's face. "When we were there, Charlie showed up. You know, Charlie Manson? So I don't know, man. He might have a crush on you or something. It might be a stalker thing. Like he's obsessed with you. Like that movie."

The unease in Gordon's stomach turns to something else—a thin line of molten anger. "That's not his name."

"Huh?"

"That's not his name," Gordon repeats, his words bitten off. "You shouldn't call him that."

Jason waves a dismissive hand. "Sure. Charlie Gustafson, whatever. It's just a joke. Did you hear the rest? I don't want you to get freaked out by his creepy gay crush."

Gordon shoves his chair back and stands, anger pulling him up like he's a marionette. "You can't say shit like that, man. Jesus. Are you actually homophobic or just ignorant?"

The older lady selling pull tabs is definitely listening to this. A couple people at nearby tables glance at them too. Gordon's trembling, his heart pounding. Confrontation isn't his thing, but he cannot, he *will* not, sit here while Jason insults Charlie.

It takes a second before Jason's mouth closes, which was possibly an interval that Gordon should have used to just walk away. "What the hell, Gordy?"

"Charlie's my friend," Gordon says. His throat jumps like his voice wants to break, but he buckles down and forces the words out. "That's why he was at my house. He's my friend. Even if he wasn't, the shit you say about him isn't right. And you're not just saying it about him. You're saying it about all queer people. Are you serious with that 'creepy gay crush' stuff? What's so creepy about it? Maybe I'd be flattered if Charlie had a crush on me!"

People are definitely staring now. Even the women playing pool on the other side of the bar have stopped their game to watch the excitement.

"Christ, man, calm down!" Jason looks vaguely frantic. "It was a joke! I'm sorry! Sorry, I didn't mean anything by it. Can you just sit down?"

Gordon shouldn't. He really, really shouldn't. He should walk out of here to prove a point. *It was a joke* is what people who get called out for being assholes fall back on because they don't want to face consequences for being dicks.

Except now Gordon is thinking about actually living permanently in Sawmill Lake, and having a very public blow-up maybe isn't the way to introduce himself to everyone. Reintroduce himself. He half recognizes a bunch of people in this place and they probably half recognize him too.

Grudgingly, he sits, scooting his chair in and glowering at his basket of wings. Jason leans across the table. "Hey, I really am sorry, okay? I didn't know you guys were friends."

"You shouldn't say that stuff about him anyway." Thank god there's still some beer left in his glass. He downs most of it and wipes his mouth with the back of his hand.

Jason looks guilty. "Yeah, I know." When Gordon gives him a doubtful look, he adds, "No, seriously, I know. I know I shouldn't make fun of him. I just—it's habit, you know?"

"Habit," Gordon repeats scathingly. "Really?"

"A bad habit!" Jason rubs the back of his neck. "I'll cut it out."

Gradually, the other bar patrons go back to what they were doing, conversation swelling from a few isolated words to a dull murmur of background noise. Gordon moves his glass back and forth between his hands, smears of condensation following it across the pitted, scratched wood tabletop.

After a minute or two of silence, Jason asks, "You'd really be flattered if Charlie had a crush on you?"

Gordon raises his eyebrows. "Why, jealous?"

"Naw man, sorry. You're not my type." Jason rubs the back of his neck again. His face looks a little red. God, is it possible that he's actually embarrassed? Gordon's going to put that in the W column. "So wait, are you…?"

The urge to put Jason out of his misery and fill in the blank for him jumps up and down, waving its arms wildly, but Gordon forcibly ignores it. He's pretty sure he knows what Jason wants to ask, and he's going to make him ask it.

Jason takes a big bite of his burger, takes his time chewing, but finally swallows, looks at the ceiling, the table, and back to Gordon. "…Gay?"

"It's not contagious," Gordon says.

"I wasn't saying that!"

Gordon can't help a little snort of laughter. "Yeah, okay." The days when he swore he wouldn't come out to anyone in Sawmill Lake seem like another lifetime. "I'm bi."

Even though Jason looks a little like a deer caught in the headlights, he's nodding. Progress, probably. No chance that Jason's going to go from *creepy gay crush* to marching in a Pride parade, but this is, in some ways, better than Gordon expected.

"Is Charlie hot?" Jason asks. Which, it has to be said, is also not something Gordon expected.

"Yeah," Gordon replies, a touch of defiance in his voice and a flicker of exactly how hot Charlie is flashing through his brain: a memory of how they jacked each other off last night, Charlie's back against his car as he gasped Gordon's name into the crook of his neck.

"Huh."

Focus. "What's that supposed to mean?"

"No, I'm just, I don't know. I never thought about it." Bizarrely, Jason really looks like he *is* thinking about it. "I mean, sure, *you're* obviously a good-looking guy."

Gordon blinks. "Thanks?"

The expression on Jason's face suggests he's working through a complex algebraic formula in his head. "I just never would've thought— you and him."

"Who says there's a me and him?" Gordon says, though it sounds weak. Hopefully Charlie doesn't have a problem with the town knowing they're some form of together, because at this point even flat-out denying it probably won't convince Jason.

Anyway, Gordon doesn't want to deny it. He's not just flattered that Charlie likes him; he's proud. He's never known anyone like Charlie. Someone so interesting and smart liking him is still mind-boggling.

And yeah. Jason gives him an incredulous look. "You're kidding me, right? Every time you say his name your face does a thing."

His face does a thing? Actually—yeah, that checks out.

"He's a really cool guy," Gordon says. "So if there was a me and him—I'm not saying there is—but if there was, it would probably be pretty great."

Jason looks like he's trying hard to look either supportive or happy for Gordon. Or possibly just not uncomfortable. He's not totally nailing it, but Gordon, grudgingly, gives him credit for trying.

The clock above the bar says it's almost six-thirty, which means Gordon can get out of here. Weirdly, the awkwardness of the conversation made this outing not the worst? Gordon definitely is feeling more kindly disposed toward Jason right now than he was when Jason showed up at his door.

Getting to his feet, he says, "I have to head out. I'm meeting Charlie soon."

As Gordon pulls out his wallet, Jason says, "I got this, man."

"No, it's fine—"

"Hey, let me get it, okay?" Jason gives him a determined look. "Because of the stuff I said. I guess me getting you a beer and some wings doesn't really make up for it."

It doesn't, but Gordon nods and pockets his wallet again. "Thanks."

His heart beats faster as he leaves Lakeside Tavern and gets in his car, just in case there was any doubt how he feels about Charlie. No wonder his face does a thing. His veins fizz and pop, and the sizzle of adrenaline hasn't quite left him. And now he can't stop thinking about how hot Charlie is—all his rangy, lean muscles and how he feels when Gordon presses up against him.

He puts his head back against the seat with a tiny groan, a hot ache spiraling in his hips. Good thing he's seeing Charlie soon, because his face isn't the only thing doing a thing.

Chapter Eighteen

WHEN CHARLIE gets to Gordon's house, Gordon is standing in front of the porch, his hands in his jacket pockets. He opens the door before Charlie even puts the car in park and slams it shut. "Mockingbird Girl" by The Magnificent Bastards is playing, and Gordon turns it down just a little.

"Does your seat go all the way back?" Gordon asks. Is Charlie imagining the growl in his voice?

"I think so?" Heat stirs low in Charlie's belly when he gets a good look at Gordon's face. He doesn't think he imagined the growl at all.

He pulls the lever on the seat to make it go back, and Gordon is on him in a second, clambering over the center console to push Charlie down. His body covers Charlie's as their mouths crash together. Charlie groans right away at the rough way Gordon's tongue enters his mouth. There are teeth on his lips, on his chin and jaw, and Gordon breathing hard as he kisses bruisingly.

Charlie grabs his ass and rocks his hips up, finding Gordon already hard. Maybe he's been hard. Maybe he's been standing outside the house, waiting for Charlie to get here and thinking about doing this?

The thought makes Charlie whimper.

Tearing his mouth away from Charlie's with a suck and a string of saliva that catches light from the headlights, Gordon pants, "I really— fuck. I want you. Now."

Before Charlie has time to explore in what way, exactly, Gordon wants him, Gordon makes it extremely clear by unbuttoning Charlie's jeans, drawing the zipper down, and shifting until his face is level with Charlie's cock.

The obvious implications of Gordon's face right there robs Charlie of the ability to speak for a pulsing hot moment. As Gordon drags Charlie's pants and underwear over his hips, he gets out, "Gordon, you don't—if you're not ready—" All he can think is *yes yes god yes* he wants Gordon's plush, soft lips on his cock, wants the wet heat of his mouth to swallow him down, but on the obverse of the thought is, *Gordon's never been with a man; Gordon's never had a dick in his mouth.*

"I wouldn't be about to suck your cock if I wasn't ready," Gordon says. He doesn't move. "Do you want me to?"

Charlie slides his fingers into Gordon's hair, so thick and soft and grippable. "Yes," he whispers. "God yes."

Gordon's eyes are discs of black that he keeps focused on Charlie as he lowers his face. He kisses Charlie's cockhead, his lips parted and moving over the slit. Every nerve in Charlie's body lights up in a white blaze, pleasure and sensation like an overexposed photo. He throws his head back and fists Gordon's hair harder, using every ounce of willpower he has to force his hips still.

"So that's what a guy tastes like," Gordon says, gravel and sex rumbling up his throat.

"Good?" Charlie somehow says.

"Mm." Gordon licks him slowly, tonguing all around the tip of Charlie's cock, under the glans, up and down the frenulum, which makes Charlie's legs jerk. "So fuckin' good."

The need to see Gordon grabs Charlie and he props himself up on his elbows. Gordon is watching him, mouth open, tongue tracing slick, hot circles over Charlie's tip. Muscles all across Charlie's belly tighten with spreading heat. It's been a while, and Gordon is. So sexy. So ridiculously sexy.

One of Gordon's hands finds its way under Charlie's jacket and sweatshirt, stroking his stomach, caressing his way down but not touching Charlie's cock.

Sweat dampens Charlie's hairline, the small of his back, between his pecs. His need builds and he bites his lip, clenches down to keep himself off the brink for a few more minutes. This is heaven; this is paradise. He doesn't want it to end.

Gordon flicks his tongue in Charlie's slit, licking his lips and swallowing. A crooked, wicked little smile tips one side of his lips up. And he takes Charlie's cock in his mouth.

Charlie cries out, unable to stop his hips hitching up. Oh god oh god Gordon's mouth is so slick and wet, so hot.

For a second Gordon seems at a loss, like he knew he needed to get Charlie's dick in his mouth but isn't sure where to go from there. His lips tighten around Charlie's shaft and Charlie makes an embarrassing noise. Gordon's eyes light up.

Slowly, he bobs up and down, lips a tight ring, cheeks hollowed as he sucks. Voice hoarse, Charlie says like a prayer, "Fuck, Gordon. You're so hot. You're so so fucking hot oh my *god*."

Gordon moans, eyes fluttering shut, dark lashes fanning across his skin. His hand massages Charlie's stomach, the crease between hip and leg, the inside of his thigh. His other hand moves to grip Charlie's base, the touch of fingers a shock of contrast.

He pops off and gasps, "I love this" before painting stripes up and down Charlie's cock with his tongue. His hand slips along wet skin, pumping Charlie while he dives back down with his mouth. He's letting out a constant soundtrack of thick, throaty moans, hand and mouth both moving faster.

Charlie's pulling his hair too hard. He makes himself loosen his grip, but Gordon shakes his head, taking Charlie's cock deeper. When he inevitably gags and coughs, his reflexes kick him back enough to speak. "Pull my hair. Fuck my face. I fucking want you—"

And Charlie would love to do that, really really love to do that, except the pure wanton filth of Gordon's voice pulls everything in him taut, tighter and tighter until it releases and he's flying over the edge.

"I'm coming," he gasps, expecting Gordon to pull back.

Instead, Gordon takes Charlie back into his mouth, sucking, licking, as Charlie shudders and twitches, hips hitching, balls and cock pulsing. Gordon's hand splays on his stomach, holding him steady through it.

His limbs don't feel attached to his body. His brain is nothing but cottony buzz.

His dick spurts one last time as Gordon pumps it. Somehow, it's clear in the motion how immensely satisfied Gordon is with himself.

"Damn, baby." Gordon crawls up Charlie's body, kisses his neck, his chin, and then his mouth. Charlie tastes himself on Gordon's tongue and something stirs in his balls. "That was amazing," Gordon whispers against Charlie's lips. "How'd I do?"

It seems to take a long time for Charlie to remember how to use words, but when he does, they come out hoarse again. "I'm pretty sure you know."

There's a purr in Gordon's voice as he replies, "Never hurts to do some positive reinforcement."

"I haven't come that hard possibly ever," Charlie says. "Are you sure you've never sucked a dick before?"

With a laugh, Gordon kisses him again. "Good, and yes. Beginner's luck, I guess."

"I can't move because of your beginner's luck," Charlie says very sincerely. Feeling is returning to his body in bits and pieces, which means he can feel Gordon's erection pressing into his stomach. "Unless I get to return the favor. I can move for that."

Gordon makes a throaty little noise, desperate and helpless, and rolls his hips. Yes, that's an urgent hard-on that Charlie definitely needs to help with.

Before he can wiggle into position, Gordon stops him with a kiss, sweet and soft. "Later," he says.

"Later?" This doesn't compute. Charlie wants to suck Gordon off right now, not later.

There's a tightness to Gordon's voice as he answers, but he says, "Yeah. I wanna think about it. How it felt to do it for you. And how it's going to feel when you do it for me."

"Oh my god," Charlie whispers. "Who are you?"

Waiting? Taking your time? Delaying your orgasm to heighten it? Most of Charlie's romantic encounters have taken place in under an hour, and that's generous. So is calling them romantic, really.

With a pleased and sultry little smile, Gordon kisses Charlie's neck. Charlie melts.

When Gordon raises his head, Charlie blurts, "I want to take you out."

"Out?"

Gordon looks confused. Has Charlie done such a bad job of showing how much he likes this man that it's a confusing sentence? "Out," Charlie repeats. "Like a date. Out on a date. Do you want to go on a date with me?"

Perfect, now he sounds like he's in high school. Which is maybe appropriate in a weird way, since he first developed a crush on Gordon when he was fifteen.

The confusion on Gordon's face melts to something more like surprise. Charlie scrambles to do damage control. "Sorry, that was stupid. You're not out to anyone up here, right? Or... anyone? I don't know what I was thinking. Ignore me. We don't have to go on a date, we can just—"

Gordon's mouth lands on his, silencing the torrent of words. Mostly. The kiss surprises him, so he makes a *mmph* sort of noise before losing himself to the feel of Gordon's lips.

"Of course I want to go on a date with you," Gordon says like it's the most obvious thing in the world. A foregone conclusion! Obviously Gordon wants to not only be seen in public with Charlie, he wants to be seen in public in a romantic way. "Where are we going? Should I dress up?" He makes a face. "I don't have anything very nice up here, but I can figure something out."

Shaking his head, Charlie says, "No, it's okay. It's nothing fancy. Do you know the supper club in Chisholm?"

Gordon looks politely baffled for a second; then his face lights with recognition. "Yeah! Wow, that place is still here? I took my prom date there."

"Alissa Jensen."

As soon as the name is out of his mouth, Charlie wants to die. Could he be any more lame? Gordon's going out with him and now Charlie goes and reveals he remembers who Gordon took to prom.

But somehow, Gordon looks amused, and maybe a little flattered. "You remember who I went to prom with," he says, his voice teasing.

"I think we have owls to band."

"Oh, no. Hold on a second." Gordon catches Charlie's wrist and pins it over his head. Oh. Oh no. That's really hot. "Did you have a crush on me in high school?"

"You were in the yearbook with her." Which is true, but the main reason Charlie remembers is because that summer between his junior and senior year of high school, after Gordon graduated, Charlie had looked at the picture of Gordon in a tux, dancing, more times than was probably reasonable.

"Charlie." Gordon kisses his jaw, then down his neck. It would definitely be illegal under the Geneva Conventions if the UN knew about it. "Did you have a crush on me in high school?"

At this point, no matter what he says, Gordon's going to think he did. He might as well tell the truth. "Yeah," he admits sheepishly. "You can laugh at me. It's fine."

Gordon's face is still nestled in the crook of Charlie's neck. There's a silence before he says, "I'm not laughing at you." Another silence. "Remember when I said I'm sorry I didn't notice you back then? I meant that."

"I'd rather have you now than high school you." Charlie realizes what he said and feels his face get hot. "Not that I have you now. I mean—I don't know what I mean—"

Gordon pushes himself up and looks straight into Charlie's eyes. "You have me now. If you really want me. I'm not that interesting. Not like you. I don't even have money to make up for a boring personality."

The mention of money reminds Charlie of the two million dollars. His decision not to tell Gordon pokes at him. Yesterday, as far as Charlie knew, Gordon wasn't going to stay here. Now he's talking like maybe he is.

"You're not boring." Charlie brushes his fingertips through Gordon's hair. "You're wonderful. And funny. And smart."

With a snort of laughter, Gordon says, "I'm not smart."

"Of course you are! Look how fast you picked up all the banding stuff! You're good at it. You understand it." He pushes hair behind Gordon's ear. "Don't ever say you're not smart."

There's another silence while Gordon stares at him. Charlie wonders if he said something wrong. It seemed okay in his head. For once it felt like the right thing.

Suddenly, Gordon hugs him, wrapping his arms all the way around Charlie's back and holding him tight. Charlie hugs him back. It's funny, but he feels like Gordon wants to say something—like the air between them is vibrating with the possibility of unsaid words.

In the end, he lets go of Charlie without saying anything. They look at each other for a moment before Gordon says, "Owls."

"Owls," Charlie agrees.

Chapter Nineteen

So, YESTERDAY Gordon almost told Charlie that he loves him. That's a thing that almost happened.

He didn't even realize it until the words nearly popped out of his mouth. There he was, on top of Charlie in the Crown Vic, and Charlie said that thing about how Gordon shouldn't ever say he isn't smart, a look on his face like he'd fight anyone who disagreed with him. And Gordon got so full up of feeling and that tender ache behind his sternum that he had to hug Charlie.

Which was when he almost said it. *I love you.*

He didn't, thank god. Charlie probably wouldn't want to go on that date tonight if Gordon dropped the L word right now. He probably would have been like, *Oh, guy gives his first blow job, thinks he's in love.*

Maybe that's all it is. Maybe Gordon was just full of hormones. Yeah. That's probably it. That fucked-out, post-sex haze. Even though he didn't orgasm until later, when Charlie blew him in the kitchen. Which was. Wow. Charlie's good at that. Maybe it has something to do with having access to the equipment all the time, because Charlie claims he doesn't have much experience.

Gordon almost said it then too. The L word. *I* and *love* and *you*. He's afraid Charlie could tell. He's afraid Charlie couldn't tell. He doesn't know what to do or what to think or feel. Isn't it too soon for this? He just got out of a serious relationship. He was engaged! And he hasn't known Charlie that long. And is it normal to fall in love with the first person of the same sex you're with?

They aren't even dating officially. Or are they? They're going on a date tonight, does that mean they are? Do they need to talk about it? Will Gordon be able to have that conversation without blurting out that apparently he's in love?

He doesn't get anything done all day, even though there's plenty to do. Now that he decided to keep the house, he needs to actually make it into a place he lives, instead of a place he's just staying. It's time to stop crashing on the couch, in other words, and make one of the bedrooms his.

The biggest one was his grandfather's, but Gordon still can't bring himself to spend time in there. The room has a presence. Not like it's haunted, but like the room hasn't let go of his grandfather. Like there's still a chance he might come back and pick up the book sitting on the nightstand.

Instead, he kills most of the afternoon looking at bed frames and mattresses online, because obviously whatever room he chooses, he's definitely not using his grandfather's old bed. It's not worth moving his own up here, since it's the cheapest frame and mattress from IKEA. He learned his lesson after a couple nights on that thing—a good mattress is worth splurging on. Especially when you're thirty-six years old, not twenty-two.

Is he imagining Charlie on every single one of the beds? Obviously. Instead of having the option to use augmented reality to see it in your space, furniture websites should give you the option to see your boyfriend sprawling on the mattress. Maybe allowing you to see your boyfriend writhing on the mattress is going too far.

Not boyfriend. Shit. Not boyfriend.

Gordon doesn't think boyfriend, at least.

But he does think about Charlie writhing on a mattress. He thinks about that so hard that he has to jack off to take the edge off before he explodes. Otherwise, if they go home together after their date, Gordon will probably embarrass himself by coming in his pants like a teenager. Every time he thinks about Charlie's cock in his mouth, he starts getting hard. He wants Charlie's cock inside him every way he can get it. He wants everything. Every single act he's ever gotten off to in gay porn or in the privacy of his mind, he wants to do them all with Charlie.

At least he eventually accomplishes picking out and ordering a bed. The mattress is one of those kinds where you can adjust the firmness separately on both sides. Better and more spacious than the couch. Room for two people.

By the time evening rolls around, Gordon is wandering back and forth across the kitchen, peering out the window to look for headlights and rearranging things in the drawers, guaranteeing that he won't be able to find the can opener when he needs it. He texted Jennifer to let her know he's going on a date with Charlie. She responded with party emojis and asked what he's planning to wear.

He hopes he looks okay—he's wearing a pair of dark-wash slim jeans and a maroon Henley with his charcoal Vans slip-ons. It's the nicest outfit he could put together. He ran down to the Ben Franklin on Lake Street to pick up some aftershave and styling mousse for his hair, so if nothing else, his hair looks good and he smells nice.

Finally, his restless pacing is rewarded. Charlie pulls into the driveway. Unlike every other night, he shuts the car off and gets out, which makes Gordon hesitate before going outside to meet him.

He gets halfway to the door, stops, starts again, and pauses again, by which time he hears Charlie's footsteps creaking on the porch stairs. Gordon splits the difference by opening the door before Charlie has a chance to knock.

"Oh!" Gordon feels like he's had the wind knocked out of him. Charlie looks gorgeous. He got a haircut, taming the worst of the shagginess but leaving some length so that it's long enough to swoop across the top of his eyebrows instead of in his eyes. The color looks somehow different and the same, which doesn't seem possible for a haircut to accomplish. It looks like sunlight, as though cleaning it up and putting a little product in it turned it from brass to gold.

His clothes aren't any fancier than Gordon's, which is a relief. Except he's wearing the hell out of them: navy blue corduroy pants and a sweater the color of homemade oatmeal, dotted with tiny flecks of blue. He's still wearing his boots, though. They look clean, like he spent part of his day scraping mud off them and buffing them so they look well-worn but nice.

Also, he's holding flowers—a cheerful, bright bouquet of red carnations and baby's breath. Nervously, he offers them to Gordon, cellophane wrapper crinkling. "I thought they were roses," he says, a flush rising to his cheeks that makes them the same color as the flowers. "The label says 'carnations,' though."

"I love them," Gordon says. He puts a hand on Charlie's hip lightly. Part of him still half expects Charlie to move away or remove his hand every time Gordon touches him. Instead, Charlie leans into him, dipping his head, his lips parted slightly.

Enthusiastically, Gordon tilts his head up, meeting the kiss halfway. Charlie's hands cup Gordon's face, warm and callused, and Gordon's stomach swoops.

"I'll put them in some water and then we can go," Gordon says breathlessly once the kiss ends. Of course, he has no idea if his grandfather had vases. Maybe in the basement, but the last thing he's going to do with Charlie standing in the kitchen looking like a whole-ass meal is go rummaging around down there for one.

So, like the twenty-two-year-old that his back has recently reminded him he isn't, he grabs a glass from the cupboard, fills it with water, and puts the flowers in it. They all tilt to one side, making the bouquet look lopsided. He's not doing it justice and he hopes Charlie doesn't mind.

Charlie gets a goofy smile on his face at the sight of the flowers in the glass, so it seems like he doesn't.

On the drive, Charlie gives Gordon control of the aux. It occurs to Gordon for the first time that there's no way this car had one originally. When he asks, Charlie says, "I installed it."

"By yourself?"

"Yeah."

"Man, you know cars, too. You know how to do everything."

"No!" They happen to be passing under one of the few and far between streetlights out here, so Gordon sees that Charlie's face is red. "No, I just looked up how to install the aux input. I don't know how to do anything else."

Gordon scrolls through his playlists and chooses a '90s one. Salt 'n Pepa starts playing. "Okay, sure. Act like that's not impressive."

"It's not," Charlie mumbles, but he sneaks a look at Gordon, and there's a small, happy smile on his face. Gordon loves being the cause of those little smiles.

It's a short drive to Chisholm, around twenty minutes by the time they wait at what feels like every red light. Highway 169 bypasses Hibbing, sort of. Gordon always gets a flash of his kid self when he drives 169 in the Cities, which starts in nearby Virginia, Minnesota and ends in Tulsa, Oklahoma.

His family had gone on vacation and flown out of Duluth, but on the way home, they had to land at Minneapolis-St. Paul International for some reason—Gordon doesn't remember what anymore. Instead of getting a hotel for the night, his parents decided to rent a car and drive home. They drove through what felt to Gordon like the biggest city imaginable until they got on, lo and behold, Highway 169. How could the same highway from home also be here?

Weird how some things from childhood stay with you. Like that book he can hazily remember from being super young, with the boy and the hawk. It's popped into his head a few times since he's been up here. He wishes he'd asked his mom while she was alive.

He wishes he knew what made his mom and grandfather so angry at each other that they never spoke again.

The supper club in Chisholm is exactly the way Gordon remembers it. He can't help smiling. It's still the same low-ceilinged, wood-paneled space with the bar in the center. The parquet floors look a little more battered, but considering how many years they've been here, it's a miracle how well they're holding up. Big, deep booths line the walls, the benches upholstered in dark green vinyl. Brass light fixtures with bankers-lamp green glass shades are mounted in each booth, casting each one in a warm, mood lit glow. Tables fill the rest of the space.

There are a lot of occupied booths and tables, and that makes Gordon smile too. Weeks ago, he wouldn't have given a shit. Now it makes him really happy that this place is still in business and still an institution.

They're led to a booth. When Gordon sits across from Charlie, the vinyl sinks with a hiss of air. He catches Charlie's eye and Charlie lets out an undignified snort of laughter, which he then bites down hard on his lip to suppress while the hostess hands them menus.

"Oh my god." Gordon hefts his. "You could bench press with this thing. I swear it's three times the size of what I remember."

"I don't think they ever take anything off the menu," Charlie says. That goofy smile is on his face again. Goofy and maybe a little giddy.

No one has ever looked at Gordon like Charlie looks at him. His heart contracts and then swells against his ribs, and a feeling washes over him like a warm wave, frothing and bubbly and tugging everything in him as it recedes.

"Can I hold your hand?" Gordon asks.

Charlie offers it across the table, palm up. Gordon takes it, interlacing their fingers so their wrists rest on the wooden tabletop. Their hands look good together, Charlie's pale skin against Gordon's tan, Charlie's long, graceful fingers against Gordon's shorter, stronger proportions.

Gordon rubs circles with his thumb on Charlie's hand. Under the table, Charlie nudges Gordon's foot with his own, and Gordon nudges back. It's stupid how much Gordon feels like a teenager with his first crush, except Charlie's looking at Gordon like he feels the exact same way, and somehow that makes it feel less stupid.

"I'm glad we're doing this," Gordon says.

"Yeah?" Charlie's smile lights up their booth. "Me too."

"What can I get you two to drink?" someone chirps from the front of their table.

Gordon jerks but doesn't pull his hand away, despite the way Charlie tries to withdraw his. He flicks his eyes from their joined hands to Gordon, then to their waiter, a gangly young man, then back to Gordon. Gordon squeezes his hand and smiles, and the tense set of Charlie's shoulders fractionally relaxes.

"Can we let you know in a minute?" Gordon asks.

"Of course! I'll check on you in a few. Wine list is at the back, and we have a full bar."

When the waiter hurries off, Gordon flips the gargantuan menu open to the wine list at the back. "Want to get a bottle? Do you prefer red or white?"

"Either." Charlie looks sheepish. "I don't know anything about wine. I wasn't even sure if you drank."

It takes Gordon a second to puzzle through that one. "Oh, because I'm Arab? I don't really consider myself Muslim. My mom did a few things here and there when I was a kid. She always made these cookies for Eid, and this dried fish stew thing with okra. Shit, what was that called?"

He thinks for a second, picturing both stew and cookies, but can't come up with the name. It makes him miss his mom.

Charlie squeezes his hand. "We could try to track it down online. I bet we could find it."

Gordon's stomach swoops again. No kissing required, apparently. "Yeah, maybe. That's a good idea." When Charlie's face pinks, Gordon wants to wrap him up in his arms, hold him close, and start convincing him that he has good ideas, that most of his ideas are good, and everyone who made him think otherwise is wrong, wrong, wrong.

They decide on a white wine from Washington because they both like the name, which is bird-related, and order an appetizer to share and entrees when the waiter returns. The calamari appetizer comes suspiciously quickly, at which point Gordon wonders if maybe it wasn't the best idea to order seafood in Chisholm. It tastes good, though.

As they polish off the calamari and sip their wine, Gordon asks, "Was my grandfather religious?"

Charlie takes a moment to think before he answers. "A little. I never saw him praying, but some years he fasted during Ramadan."

"The longer I'm here, the more I wish I'd known him." This is the opposite of romantic first date conversation, but Charlie doesn't seem to mind. "Don't laugh, but… did he ever say anything about me?"

The answer is obviously going to be no, so when Charlie says "Yes," Gordon almost spits a mouthful of wine across the table. Charlie's thumb sweeps in slow arcs across Gordon's hand and his gaze settles on the table, unfocusing. "Not a lot. It obviously made him sad that he wasn't part of your life." He chews his lip, looking torn, before adding, "I think he might have checked up on you on Facebook sometimes. Maybe Instagram too. He asked me to help him set up accounts on both."

The thought gives Gordon a pang of regret. He wishes he'd known, or that his grandfather had left a comment. Anything. "The Wi-Fi password is my birthday. In my house. The house. My house," he settles on.

Surprise flits over Charlie's face, but not much, like he almost already knew that. "The last thing he said about you was that you were getting married." He makes a noise that's half cough, half throat-clear.

Gordon leans over the table, trying to catch his eyes. "And you felt how about that?" he asks, teasing just a tiny bit.

"Like it was none of my business!" Charlie's eyes dart up to meet Gordon's, flashing and endlessly blue. A smile tugs at one side of his mouth. Gordon would lean across this table and kiss that spot if he could reach. "But also, I might have found a bottle of vodka at the back of my fridge and drunk all of it the day he told me that."

Gordon snorts. "I wasn't worth getting drunk on back-of-the-fridge vodka."

"I actually have a lot of evidence to the contrary." Charlie hesitates before he pulls Gordon's hand to his mouth to kiss it.

Of course, their food has to come right at that moment, and Charlie makes a squeaking noise and releases Gordon's hand, turning red. Their waiter smiles as he sets both entrees down. "How long have you guys been together?" he asks.

The two of them look at each other, the question Gordon feels on his face reflecting back to him on Charlie's. Are they together? Are they not just on a date, but dating?

Like. Gordon knows what he'd say. *This is our first date of many. I'm actually kind of crazy about him, and it's turning my life upside down.*

Charlie licks his lips nervously, opening his mouth to speak, but Gordon answers before he can get there. "This is our first date."

So yeah, that's part of what he really wants to say, which is almost as good as saying all of it, right? He hopes Charlie doesn't mind that he spoke up, like he doesn't think Gordon is babying him or patronizing him.

The waiter looks surprised. "I figured you'd been together longer. Well." He rests his fingers lightly on the edge of the table. "You're adorable. Enjoy the date."

Gordon and Charlie's eyes meet over the table as the waiter leaves. The question is still on Charlie's face, so Gordon pulls up his big boy pants and says, "I'd like to. If you want. You know, be together."

"Yes!" Charlie answers immediately, possibly a bit too loudly. He ducks his head and hunches his shoulders, but there's a grin on his face he's trying to bite back. "Yes. I really like you. Um. If that wasn't obvious."

Gordon feels like he might float away. "Yeah? I mean, I figured you liked me. Because of all the…."

"Orgasms?" Charlie asks innocently.

The wine Gordon was about to drink splutters back into his glass. "Those too."

If Charlie really likes him, then maybe someday that will turn into more? Obviously he's an amazing guy who can do way better than Gordon, but it's not impossible like could turn to love, is it? That's usually how it goes. That's how it went for Gordon. It just happened to go that way for Gordon really fast. Faster than he's ever fallen for anyone.

Maybe that should make him pump the brakes, but he doesn't think he can. He doesn't think he wants to.

They've talked so much during their hours sitting in the dark that talking across the table on their first date feels like a simple continuation of that. Charlie has always been easy to talk to, and it hasn't escaped Gordon's notice that Charlie almost never stutters around him anymore.

It makes him happy—the fact that Charlie feels comfortable with him. That Gordon doesn't make him feel stressed or anxious or nervous.

They eat dinner, they drink their bottle of wine, and Charlie makes Gordon laugh so hard that he almost snorts eggplant parmesan out his nose. They linger over dessert, letting the wine filter through them. Even though half a bottle of wine paired with a huge dinner isn't enough to get him drunk, Gordon feels more and more intoxicated with each minute that goes by sitting across from Charlie.

It's not hormones or afterglow or horniness making Gordon think he's in love with Charlie. Gordon *is* in love with Charlie, period.

A bright, shooting star arc of feeling swoops through him, spiraling up through his rib cage to soar around his heart. He never in a million years expected something like this to happen the day he drove back into Sawmill Lake, but it might be the best thing that's ever happened to him.

Chapter Twenty

CHARLIE IS so far from wanting the night to be done when they leave the restaurant that he invites Gordon over to do something. Watch a movie. Play a game. Have a drink. Cuddle and keep talking. Anything, anything at all, just as long as Charlie can keep being close to him—his warm skin, his warmer eyes, and the smile that makes Charlie want to curl up and purr like a cat in a patch of sun.

He's never felt this way about anyone. It's half terrifying, half exhilarating, but comfortable too. Gordon makes it easy to fall for him. There's no other way to put it and no point in pretending otherwise— Charlie is falling for Gordon, hard and fast. He's never had a real boyfriend, only casual hookups, and now this.

This. Terrifying and exhilarating, and Charlie wouldn't change that it's happening for the world.

At some point they'll have to talk about making the distance work, but the Cities aren't that far from Sawmill Lake. They'll figure it out. Tonight, he just wants to enjoy their first date.

Normally during banding season, Charlie's house gets to be a disaster—kind of like a combination of a plane crash debris field and something from Hoarder House Flippers. Possibly not that bad. Possibly he's just embarrassed that it was a mess when Gordon showed up on his doorstep on Monday.

Today, hoping very much that Gordon would come home with him, he cleaned everything. Every room, every surface. He vacuumed. He cleaned the toilet and both sinks. He changed the bedsheets, optimistically. Also optimistically, he ran up to Ben Franklin and bought condoms and lube. There may be nothing more uncomfortable on the planet than buying condoms and lube in a small town, but Charlie didn't have time to go farther afield like he usually would.

When they step inside Charlie's house, Charlie can't stop himself from crowding Gordon against the door and kissing him slowly. Gordon twines his arms around Charlie's neck and kisses back, deep as the ocean, and makes a low, helpless sound. Want goes straight through Charlie's body and settles heavily in his balls.

"Movie," he murmurs before he abandons propriety and fucks Gordon against the door. Gordon makes that noise again while he slips a hand under the collar of Charlie's shirt to dig his fingers into one of Charlie's traps.

That doesn't help with the whole attempt to not abandon propriety thing. Especially when Gordon's hips press into Charlie's, and Charlie can feel how hard he is.

The hot press of Gordon's cock against Charlie's makes heat rise to the surface of his skin. His hips roll like he has no control over them, and the kiss goes from a kiss to that blazing drag of lips and tongue against each other that's all prelude to sex.

Wrenching himself back from that is one of the hardest things Charlie's ever done (insert sex joke here), but he does, taking a step back. His face feels hot, and he makes no attempt to hide how hard he is.

Neither does Gordon, who—sweet Jesus—looks fuckable and half-wrecked right now. His lips are red and slick, eyes wide and black, skin flushed like sin, and there's just a hint of sweat in the dip of his collarbone.

"I can't believe you want to watch a movie," Gordon says, a rasp in his voice that makes Charlie's knees weak.

"It seems gentlemanly," Charlie says while his dick catalogues how Gordon's shirt clings to his shoulders and his jeans seem designed to accentuate his erection.

Gordon regards him, a softness creeping into his blown-pupil gaze. "Gentlemanly?"

"Yeah."

Gordon looks like he wants to say something but can't find the words. "Sometimes I can't get over how sweet you are. But Charlie"—he steps back into Charlie's space—"what if I don't want you to be gentlemanly?"

Charlie's mouth is dry. "I think…. Don't I… um, possibly have even more of an obligation to be a gentleman?"

"You have an obligation to start taking clothes off so I can suck your cock." When Charlie makes a strangled noise, Gordon falters. "Do you like dirty talk? I'm kind of talkative during sex, but if you're not into it, I'll stop."

"I'm incredibly fucking into it," Charlie says.

A grin that splits the difference between amused and carnal flashes over Gordon's face. "Good. Now, where's your bedroom? Uh, unless you really want to watch a movie. I'm horny, but I don't want to be pushy."

Why is Charlie fighting this? He never even wanted to watch a movie; he only wanted to be close to Gordon. So he hooks a finger into Gordon's belt and walks backward down the hall, towing Gordon with him. The intensity of his desire beats in his fingertips, spiraling tighter with the way Gordon keeps his eyes locked on Charlie's as they make their way through the house.

Charlie's bedroom is dark, and he makes no move to change that. Not until Gordon says, "Is it okay if we put the light on? I want to see you."

Which isn't a request Charlie's wired to ignore.

He lets go of Gordon and switches on the bedside lamp, since it's more than enough light to see by but still qualifies as romantic. When he turns back to Gordon, the look Gordon is giving him makes Charlie's balls throb.

"I want to do everything with you," Gordon whispers.

Charlie swallows. "I'll do anything you want."

Gordon closes the distance between them and presses against Charlie, pulling him down into a kiss. He nudges Charlie back with a leg, moving in time with him as Charlie steps back. The backs of his thighs bump the bed and Charlie lets himself tumble backward, bringing Gordon down with him.

Now Charlie's back is flat on the mattress, his comfortable, worn old comforter pillowing around him, and Gordon's weight presses him down as they kiss. The desire in Charlie's fingertips burns through the rest of his body, setting him buzzing like a live wire.

Gripping Gordon's hair, Charlie shoves his hips into Gordon's and kisses harder, nipping at his lip, tonguing into his mouth, sucking Gordon's tongue until Gordon gasps.

"Clothes. Off. Right now." The desperate, needy command in Gordon's voice is a huge fucking turn-on. Being in this bed is a big fucking turn-on. Charlie almost never has sex in a bed, especially not his own. Gordon runs a hand down Charlie's side to ruck up his shirt, brushing warm fingers over the ledge of Charlie's hip, before pulling his mouth from Charlie's. "I wanna be naked with you," Gordon says, scraping teeth across Charlie's jaw before sucking at the back of it, then Charlie's earlobe.

Some kind of guttural sound gathers deep in Charlie's chest, the kind of sound he can't ever remember making. He hooks his fingers under the hem of Gordon's shirt and pulls up, chasing the fabric with his hand so he can run his palm over Gordon's gorgeous, thick stomach and chest and body hair the second it's exposed.

Gordon helps Charlie pull the shirt over his head and straightens up, straddling Charlie's hips. Charlie takes him in for a moment: the broadness of his chest, the solid heft of him, the strength in his body. The pelt of fur covering his pecs and stomach, thicker at his belly button as it trails down under his waistband.

There's a flicker of self-consciousness on Gordon's face. "I'm not super cut, obviously."

"You're the sexiest thing I've ever seen," Charlie says. He puts both hands on Gordon's stomach, running them up his body, hair scratching against his palms. Gordon's stomach is soft and his pecs are hard, and his nipples stand at attention when Charlie rubs and flicks them.

Gordon tilts his head back, which makes Charlie want to suck his Adam's apple. Instead he keeps playing with Gordon's nipples, rolling them between his finger and thumb. Gordon's hips are twitching, little involuntary movements that make his bulge bump against Charlie's balls. Charlie decides he needs to see what Gordon will do if he adds some spit to the nipple-play.

What happens is Gordon groans, "Fuuuuck," and then, "Yeah, twist them. *Fuck*. Harder."

"You like it rough?" Charlie manages to get out, both because he's terrible at dirty talk and because he's so turned on he can hardly speak.

Gordon grinds on him, head still thrown back. "I think I do." He puts a hand over Charlie's, where Charlie is working a nipple into a hard, swollen little peak, and follows Charlie's hand back to his wrist, where he abruptly stops. "Why is your shirt still on?"

"Maybe I want you to take it off me," Charlie says.

Gordon obliges immediately, pushing Charlie's shirt up to his chin and pulling it over his head and arms. If Charlie didn't have a million other things to be self-conscious about, he'd probably add his body to the list. He's nothing special, just wiry, with patchy blond hair on his chest. His pasty chest, which looks like lutefisk compared to the rich, warm brown of Gordon's skin.

But Gordon makes a sound, and his gaze is hungrily cataloging every part of Charlie's exposed upper body, so he must like what he sees. "More," Gordon says, popping the button on Charlie's jeans. Charlie arches his hips and Gordon yanks his jeans down over his thighs, working them off one leg at a time. If Charlie's upper body is wiry, his legs are knobbly.

Gordon catalogues those too, this time with his hands. As he runs them up and down Charlie's calves and thighs, goose bumps rise all over Charlie's body. It's like Gordon is worshipping him, touching each part of him in turn like there's something holy about his body.

Reverently, Gordon leans in to place a kiss at the inside of Charlie's knee, then works his way up Charlie's thigh as Charlie's toes curl tighter. When Gordon gets to the hem of Charlie's boxer briefs, he lifts his eyes to meet Charlie's. His hands slide across Charlie's hips and he hooks his fingers into the waistband. "Yes," Charlie huffs out, skin buzzing.

When Gordon pulls the boxer briefs off, the elastic catches Charlie's cock, pulling it down only for it to bounce back heavily on his stomach, leaving a spot of precum. Gordon makes a noise that goes straight to Charlie's very hard, leaking dick and licks a slow, wet stripe from root to tip. Charlie gasps, back arching.

"You're so sexy," Gordon says, his voice all sexed-up gravel. He swirls his tongue over the head of Charlie's cock, then closes his mouth over it with a moan that vibrates through his lips and ratchets up Charlie's need that much more.

Lifting off with a wet pop, he stands back up. Charlie props himself on his elbows to see what he's doing and is rewarded with the sight of Gordon unzipping his jeans, pushing his pants and his underwear down together, and stepping out of them to crawl, naked, onto the bed.

"Scoot back," he says.

Charlie does, unable to tear his eyes away from Gordon for a single second. His legs are hairy like his chest, and his cock is perfect. It's not the first time Charlie's seen it, obviously, but it feels like it, because it's the first time he's seen all of Gordon.

They fall into a tangle of limbs, of skin and skin and skin, of sweat and the scratch of body hair and stubble. Their kissing is urgent, creeping toward desperate. Charlie wants to feel all of Gordon, wants to be closer than close. The way their cocks are grinding together has him racing up the side of a mountain, climbing into clouds he can't see past. He has a feeling there are stars beyond those clouds. His body definitely thinks so.

"Wait—wait," Charlie gasps. He lays a hand on Gordon's shoulder, fingers curling over his slick skin and pressing into a plane of muscle.

Gordon stops, raising his head to look Charlie in the eyes. "What's wrong?"

"Oh god. Nothing. Nothing." He hooks a leg over Gordon's and Gordon's face eases into a relieved smile as he brushes Charlie's hair off his forehead. Charlie traces the line of Gordon's collarbone, urging his body to a lower altitude. No stars yet. "I was getting too, um. Excited."

Gordon's smile gets rougher. Sexier, *somehow*. "Oh yeah? That's an ego boost. But I definitely want you to last a little longer."

His hips rock to punctuate the point, and Charlie runs his hands down the broad expanse of Gordon's back to his gorgeous round ass. There's enough there for two big handfuls, which Charlie squeezes, guiding the movement of Gordon's hips. When he digs his fingers in, Gordon moans and drops his head, burying it in the crook of Charlie's neck.

He sucks so hard that Charlie's sure he'll leave a mark. The thought makes him feel crazy with desire, with the need for more, more, *more*. Restlessness thrums through him, his body looking for a way to get closer.

Gordon nuzzles into the side of Charlie's face, runs his tongue along the shell of his ear, and growls, "Fuck me."

With an enthusiastic twitch, Charlie's dick says, *Yes please*. On the other hand, his brain, even if it's not the head he's making decisions with right now, reminds him that Gordon's new to being with men. Bottoming might be too much too soon.

"Are you sure?" Charlie asks. His voice is hoarse and his brain is unhelpfully supplying images of how Gordon would look underneath him. "I don't want to rush you into something. Or hurt you."

"I've played around. I have a dildo and a butt plug."

Charlie's dick gets painfully hard at the image of Gordon fucking himself on a dildo. "Oh," he says, completely incapable of making his tongue form other words. It's thick and useless in his mouth, picturing Gordon. Maybe bouncing up and down on it in a chair? Suction-cupped to the shower wall so he could push back on it, thrusting his hips to take it?

"You like that idea?" Gordon purrs, looking immensely pleased with himself.

"Uh," Charlie manages.

With a grin, Gordon rolls off Charlie to lie back on the bed. "Tell me how you want me."

Charlie gets up to retrieve the condoms and lube from his dresser, tossing them on the bed next to Gordon before he kneels on the comforter himself. "On your knees," Charlie says.

For a second, Gordon doesn't move. Instead, he gives his fat cock a few slow strokes, eyes hooded as he watches Charlie. "Do you normally top?"

"Whatever," Charlie says, watching the leak of precum from Gordon's dick. "Both." He's done very little of either, but he loves both.

Stroking himself again, Gordon says, "So you want this dick?"

Charlie bites his lip. "Yeah. But." He reaches for the condoms and opens the box. "You first."

Judging by the way Gordon's eyes blow out to all pupil, this was the right thing to say. Before Charlie can open a condom, Gordon says, "I don't have anything, just so you know. I got tested just to be safe after Becky broke up with me."

"I don't either." Charlie looks at the box of condoms and tosses them over his shoulder, reaching for the lube instead.

With that roughened, sexy smile again, Gordon gets on his hands and knees. Heat flushes Charlie's body as Gordon presents his gorgeous ass. It's covered in dark hair like the rest of him. Heart galloping, Charlie spreads his cheeks and laves his tongue up and down Gordon's crease.

Gordon swears explosively, his hole twitching, and Charlie teases it with the tip of his tongue to hear Gordon reduced to incoherence again. Circling Gordon's hole with his thumb, he asks, "Is this okay?"

"More," Gordon groans.

Lubing up a finger, Charlie pushes against Gordon's entrance. He's about to tell him to relax, but then Gordon does it without being told, beautifully. Charlie's finger breaches him and slides right in, drawing another groan from Gordon, this one throaty and filthy. "Good?" Charlie whispers.

Gordon rocks back on Charlie's finger. "So fucking good. Give me more."

Two fingers, which only makes Gordon's rhythm stutter for a second, and then three, which he needs to pause for. Charlie waits, giving him time to adjust. When Gordon moves again, slowly and torturously, he asks, "When are you going to put that big dick in me?"

Charlie has to lean over and bite the swell of Gordon's ass where it meets his back. "You're going to kill me if you keep talking like that."

Gordon's hips swivel. "Give me that big, thick cock, baby. I wanna feel you in me."

Charlie bites down harder while his dick spasms. Then he straightens and shuffles closer into the furnace-hot radius of Gordon's body. Their legs press together, Gordon's bracketing Charlie's as he spreads wide.

Slowly, Charlie runs his hand up and down Gordon's spine while he lines himself up with the other. The sound of lube dribbling out of the bottle and coating his dick is obscene. At the touch of his cockhead to Gordon's rim, Gordon shudders and breathes harder. Sweat gathers at the small of his back under Charlie's palm.

There's a bit of resistance as Charlie pushes in slowly; then Gordon's entrance yields and Charlie slides in. Gordon lets out a long, low moan as Charlie makes some kind of noise. He's hardly aware of what he sounds like, because the feel of Gordon tight and slick and hot around him is the only thing his brain can process.

"Okay?" he makes himself ask.

Gordon's hands are fisting the comforter, his head dropped so his forehead is resting on the bed. "Unnn," he answers, which is difficult for Charlie to parse in his current state. He adds, "Feels good. Fuck me. 'M not made of glass."

Charlie grips Gordon's hips, rocking his dick in and out a little. When he looks down, the sight of himself sunk in Gordon makes his vision blacken at the edges and a hot flush rise to the surface of every inch of his skin. "You look perfect like this," he murmurs.

Pushing back into him, Gordon repeats, "Fuck me. C'mon, fuck me. Give it to me."

His body has had it with holding back, especially when Gordon keeps telling him not to. So Charlie draws out almost all the way and snaps his hips, ramming Gordon hard. Gordon yells, and moans, and throws his head back. His mouth is hanging open, and his eyes are shut tight, and Charlie's never seen someone so lost in the sensations of sex before. It shouldn't be possible to get more turned on, since he's more turned on than he's ever been in his life, but Gordon is so—unfettered. Free.

Charlie wants to make him fly.

He changes his angle and he swears he can see lights flare under Gordon's skin. "Holy *fuck*. Charlie. Charlie oh my god yeah, that's it, right there, *right* there—fuck, fuck, fuck—" Gordon's legs are shaking, the tremor moving up into his hips. Sweat drips off both of them, coating Charlie's hands and making it hard to keep his hold on Gordon's hips.

With each slamming thrust, Gordon's babbling devolves into incoherence, then wanton moaning. His elbows shake and give out, leaving him with his face mashed into the comforter. Charlie wraps an arm around his stomach and pulls him upright, so his back is pressed to Charlie's front.

In this position, he doesn't have the leverage to fuck Gordon as hard, but the angle slides his cock against Gordon's prostate in long drags. Gordon tightens around Charlie and the back of his head drops onto Charlie's shoulder. He stretches his arms back to cage them around Charlie's head. "Feels so good," Gordon groans. "So good."

The ability to speak has entirely deserted Charlie. Everything in his brain and body is devoted to fucking Gordon, to holding him in place, to breathing in the thick perfume of sweat and sex. He's not going to last much longer.

Make Gordon fly. Charlie wraps a hand around Gordon's cock. It's hard as steel, hot and dripping, and Charlie has to bury his face in Gordon's neck, gasping against his skin, to try to stave off his orgasm.

"Oh—fuck—yeah. Fuck, baby. Yeah, Charlie." Gordon's cock twitches and he grabs a handful of Charlie's hair. "I'm gonna come."

"Wanna see that," Charlie says, but his face is pressed so tight against Gordon's skin that he's probably impossible to understand. "Gor, oh my god." He jacks Gordon in time with his thrusts at first, long and slower, but speeds up his hand as he senses Gordon getting closer.

"You too," Gordon gets out, his breath coming in short, sharp pants. "Come inside me. I want it. I wanna be full of your cum—"

Charlie's grand plan to make Gordon come first falls apart in starbursts, the sun burning across all his nerve endings as he lets go, shattering into a million bright pieces.

Awareness yanks him back to himself as Gordon shudders, tightens impossibly around Charlie's cock, and comes.

The first shot hits Charlie in the eye, and it's deeply unsanitary and deeply, *deeply* hot, especially when Gordon keeps coming, spurts of thick white cum painting his pecs and stomach. He's whining, keening almost, with each pulse from his cock, until finally he sags, dead weight in Charlie's arms.

Charlie's muscles give out and he lets them both tumble to the bed. For a minute or two, neither of them move. All Charlie can hear is the pounding of his own heart.

With a deep groan of exertion, Gordon rolls over, flinging a leg, an arm, and half of his torso onto Charlie. "Oh my god," Gordon says, his voice hoarse.

"Yeah," Charlie agrees, feeling floaty. The cum on his face is getting sticky, but he can't make himself care enough to wipe it off. "I've never come that hard."

"I've definitely never come that hard. Holy shit." Gordon laughs shakily. "Wow."

With effort, Charlie grabs at the comforter to wipe it across his face. "You liked it?"

"Um, hell yeah. We're doing that again tomorrow."

A warmth spreads through Charlie—not the fevered hot flush of his body responding to Gordon's, but the sunlight of what's dawning between them. It's brilliant like the sparkle of frost at sunrise, like the glitter of light across water.

"Is that your way of asking if you can spend the night?" Charlie teases.

A lazy, sated grin spreads over Gordon's face. He looks completely wrecked and completely beautiful, hair a sweaty, tousled mess, bedroom eyes whiskey brown and satisfied. "Well, I was hoping you'd say I might as well stay if we're doing this again tomorrow."

"Want to spend the night?" Charlie obligingly offers.

Gordon lets out a happy sigh. "Thought you'd never ask." He gazes at Charlie like Charlie is the best thing he's ever seen. "You called me 'Gor' at the end there."

"I did?" At another time, Charlie might be embarrassed. No, he'd definitely be embarrassed. Bestowing nicknames on people isn't a thing he does. Now, though, he's too boneless and content to worry about it.

"Yep."

Charlie traces his fingers lightly down the line of Gordon's spine. "Is that something you'd like if I kept doing it? Or do you hate nicknames?"

A little shiver goes through Gordon's body when Charlie's fingers reach the small of his back. "I like it. Especially if you call me that."

Smiling, Charlie kisses Gordon, whose mouth is sweet and soft, and he realizes he isn't fall*ing* for Gordon. He's fallen. He's in love.

His brain offers him a buffet of reasons he should freak out. He closes the door on it, kisses Gordon again, and decides to worry about it tomorrow.

Chapter Twenty-One

IT FEELS like some kind of karmic rebalancing is in effect. Last weekend was one of the worst of Charlie's life, and this weekend is one of the best. Waking up with Gordon in his bed is a huge, mind-blowing thing, the sum of a bunch of smaller, joyful things. The way the sheets soak up Gordon's heat. The solidity of his arm around Charlie's body. How he buries his face in Charlie's hair, still mostly asleep. His slow, drowsy smile as he wakes up, blinking sleep and what looks like happy surprise from his eyes.

When Gordon says, "I was having the best dream about sleeping next to you," and Charlie replies, "Well, good news."

It takes a while, but eventually they get out of bed. They try to shower together, but the shower isn't big enough, so after they fool around with slippery hand jobs—and a lot of laughing when Gordon keeps knocking the shampoo bottle over—Charlie gets out of the bathtub to let Gordon finish washing while he waits his turn to do the same.

Gordon offhandedly suggests they walk over to Edna's for breakfast. Normally, Charlie wouldn't want to. Breakfast is the busiest time at Edna's, and more people means an increased possibility that someone will think it's funny to loudly mock him. This morning, the idea doesn't bother him.

A big part of that is Gordon, obviously. Charlie's not proud of this, but there's an element of gloating to it. People will probably make assumptions about the two of them and why they're eating breakfast together. Mostly, though, he just wants to be out with Gordon. He wants to do things together, and he's sick and tired of his resignation to being treated like the town freak.

What does he gain by hiding? He's been hiding his whole life, trying not to remind people of his presence and his quirks—all the things that make him weird and mockable.

And he's realized something in the past few weeks. Charlie always thought that hiding was sometimes what you had to do so you'd be left in peace to do the things that were important to you. That's what Ibrahim taught him—not intentionally, but it's the lesson he passed on by keeping to himself, by living in this town for decades and decades and forming so few connections.

At the end of his life, Charlie doesn't want to die alone in the ICU. He doesn't want there to be one person on the entire planet who cares whether he lived or died. He doesn't want a funeral that no one attends. When Ibrahim was taken to the hospital to die, the only reason Charlie knew was because they had plans that day and he pulled into the driveway as his friend was being loaded into the ambulance.

Anyway, having breakfast with Gordon at Edna's seems like a good step in preventing a sad and lonely outcome to his life.

On the walk there, Gordon catches Charlie's hand and interlaces their fingers. He looks at Charlie with a question in his eyes, and Charlie answers by squeezing his hand.

People look at them in Edna's, but it's easier to ignore today. He's sitting across the table from Gordon, their feet resting against each other's. Maybe Gordon's insistence that Charlie's really impressive and interesting is starting to rub off on him, too.

Their waitress—not Steph, who must not work the morning shift—compliments his haircut, which is the first time it occurs to him that anyone would notice or care. He smiles at her shyly and says, "Th-thanks, Chloe."

After she takes their food order and refills the coffee cups they've already drained, Gordon leans across the table. "Do you know who she looks exactly like? Skyler Johnson. Do you remember her? She was a grade ahead of me but she was always getting busted for smoking on school grounds."

"That's because she's Skyler's daughter," Charlie says.

The look of horror on Gordon's face makes Charlie laugh into his coffee, to which Gordon says, "I saw that. And Jesus Christ, how can Skyler have a daughter old enough to work? Am *I* old? Oh god. I'm old, aren't I, Charlie?"

"You're older than me," Charlie points out. Gordon kicks him lightly, and Charlie kicks him back, a stupid smile taking up residence on his face.

Gordon leans back in the booth and rests an arm along the top. The position does nice things to his shoulders and chest. "Pretty sure you didn't think I was old last night," he says, his voice pitched just loudly enough to carry across the table and no farther.

Charlie's heart stutters, his cock twitches, and an ache goes through his hips, while Gordon looks extremely pleased with himself. "I need more data points," Charlie says mildly. At least, he's going for mild. His hands and face feel hot, so it's entirely possible that what he's actually projecting is horniness. "Maybe later we should have a repeat, but switch things around."

"For science," Gordon agrees while his throat jags and his pupils get wider.

After breakfast, they walk around town. Most of the leaves have fallen from the trees by now, but there are a few spots of faded red and yellow clinging stubbornly to the branches. The sun is out, but it's cold. It will definitely be a blanket night at the banding site later.

Gordon leads Charlie to the park a block off Lake Street, though from the look on Gordon's face when they get there, it's not clear if he consciously thought about it or just found himself walking in that direction.

"This is still here, huh?" Gordon says, a wry note in his voice. When Charlie makes an affirmative noise, Gordon cuts across the fading, dormant grass to the playground. Well, Charlie thinks of it as a playground, but it's just a swing set and a jungle gym in a dome shape.

All of it has seen better days. It's been here since they were kids. Now, kids hardly play here. Partly because there are hardly any kids in Sawmill Lake anymore, and partly, Charlie has to assume, because who wants to play on a rusty old playground when there are tablets?

Gordon leans against the jungle gym, surveying the park. A maple that's been here for as long as Charlie's been alive casts a long, grasping shadow across the playground. "Do you remember that summer they tried to do music concerts here?"

Wow, that's digging deep. The last time Charlie thought about that was probably when it was happening. "Didn't it get rained out a bunch of times?"

"Oh yeah, it did." Gordon laughs a little. "I was in band that year and we had to play a couple times for that. I was so mad."

Intrigued, Charlie leans next to him and says, "You've been keeping that close to your chest. You play an instrument?"

With a louder laugh, Gordon says, "I *played* an instrument, if you can even call it that. I was pretty questionable." Charlie looks at him expectantly, and Gordon adds, "What?"

"What instrument did you play? Obviously!" Charlie nudges him. "You have to tell me."

Gordon looks long-suffering. "Trumpet." He groans. "God, the blowing jokes tell themselves, don't they?"

"Yeah," Charlie agrees, laughing when Gordon punches his shoulder lightly. "It could be worse! If you played oboe, you would have been blowing wood."

The undignified snort of laughter Gordon lets out is incredibly endearing. "Okay, well, yeah. When you put it like that, I guess that's a silver lining? Though." He gives Charlie a slow once-over and Charlie feels something rev and heat under his skin. He's never been eye-fucked quite so obviously. "I discovered recently that I like blowing wood a whole lot."

"You're a natural," Charlie says, positive his face is red. Flirting isn't going to save Gordon from this conversation, though. Charlie needs to know more about him playing trumpet. "Why did you quit playing?"

"Because I sucked. Seriously. Trumpet wasn't my calling. And I never liked band, anyway."

"Why'd you join?" Charlie asks curiously.

"A girl." Gordon rolls his eyes at himself. "I'm pretty sure school bands count on padding their numbers with hormonal idiots who can't play an instrument to save their life."

"I bet you weren't that bad."

"No, I definitely was."

Charlie considers. "Who was the girl?"

"Kelsey Berglund. She never looked twice at me. Well, actually, she did, but only because I was playing too out of tune."

Charlie laughs and slips an arm around Gordon's waist. Gordon leans into him. It's comfortable and a little bit wonderful. Maybe a lot wonderful. Maybe Charlie's starting to wonder how long he can stand long distance, because he wants to be around Gordon all the time. He's just not sure how to bring it up.

Instead, he asks, "What made you think of those concerts?"

"Oh." Gordon blows out a breath. "My grandfather came to one of them."

The mention of Ibrahim makes Charlie feel off-balance. "I thought you never had any contact with him."

Gordon shakes his head. "I didn't. I just saw him standing at the back of the crowd. I remember I played a bunch of wrong notes when I realized who he was. Not that anyone would've been able to tell the difference, since I was always playing wrong notes." He's silent for a moment. "It was weird, because we didn't have any pictures of him in the house. At least I never saw any. But I saw him standing there, and it was like I was three years old again. I knew exactly who he was."

Charlie doesn't know what to say, but he thinks maybe staying quiet is better. When Gordon speaks again, he sounds sad. "I wish I knew what was so bad that my mom needed to cut him out of our lives."

"It might have been the other way around," Charlie says, trying to be fair. "He was pretty stubborn when he thought he was right about something."

"Yeah, I guess." Gordon leans his head against Charlie's.

On the street, a car drives by slowly, but Gordon doesn't pull away. There's no mistaking that they're two men holding each other, and a thrill goes through Charlie. He didn't think he still had hang-ups about being seen showing affection to another man in public. He's been out in Sawmill Lake for a long time. But part of him never thought there would be a man who could be both in Sawmill Lake and interested in Charlie for more than an hour or two.

"I wish she would've given me a choice." Gordon's voice is soft. "Like, whatever happened, I should've been able to decide if I wanted to have a relationship with him."

This time Charlie knows the right thing to say is nothing. He holds Gordon tighter.

The car circles the park again, the driver staring out the window at them as she goes by. The expression on her face is hard to see, but it looks disapproving.

Gordon sees it too. "What's her problem?"

"Us."

Out of the corner of his eye, Charlie sees a scowl darken Gordon's face. "She can join this century. Jesus. Do you get a lot of that here?"

"No," Charlie answers honestly. "But I also usually don't hang out in Elm Park cuddling with my boyfr—" He stops, mortified. They haven't used that word. There he goes again, letting stuff just spew out of his mouth.

Gordon straightens up. Fuck. Is this going to scare him off again? But when Charlie makes himself look at Gordon, Gordon's grinning. "You were going to call me your boyfriend."

"I'm sorry," Charlie says quickly.

"I'm not." Gordon cups a hand around the back of Charlie's neck to pull him into a kiss. If that woman is still driving around shooting hate rays at them from her eyes, she's probably extra crotchety now.

Gordon pulls away, his hand lingering on Charlie's shoulder. "Full disclosure, I'm sure I have some baggage from breaking up with Becky. And like. This town, if I'm being totally real. Coming back here is gonna be an adjustment, but—"

"Sorry, what?" Charlie interrupts. "What do you mean, coming back here?"

"I'm staying," Gordon says, like this is obvious and something they already talked about. "There's stuff about the Cities I'll miss, but being back here made me realize there's good things in Sawmill Lake too."

"You're staying," Charlie repeats.

Worry flashes over Gordon's face. "Uh, that doesn't bother you, does it?"

"You're *staying*." The near future is realigning in Charlie's mind. Half-formed considerations he hasn't had time to stress about, like whether his Crown Vic can survive repeated, frequent trips down 169. The farther away future goes from a blurry haze to something with a shape, with edges he can just about trace.

He's smiling, he realizes. He can see it reflected back at him from the pleasure in Gordon's eyes. "That's really good," he says. More advanced vocabulary has deserted him. All he can see is that future. All he can feel is Gordon's warmth next to him, curling around him, and Gordon's hand that's still resting on the back of his neck.

"Yeah?" Gordon's smiling too. "Cool."

A puff of a breeze rattles the few leaves clinging to the maple's branches above them. The man Charlie's in love with is going to make a life here. Cool hardly begins to describe it, but he nods, his smile getting stupid, because he can't think of a better word. "I thought I'd have to drive down to visit you all the time," he says instead of anything befitting the occasion.

Gordon kisses him again. Charlie sinks into it: the assured way Gordon kisses, the way he can go from tender to scorching and back again, the way he lets out a tiny, helpless huff of air that makes Charlie feel like he's something precious.

"I've never chosen a place because I wanted to be there." Gordon tangles his fingers in Charlie's hair. "I only ever left the place I was before and landed wherever was convenient. And it sounds kind of crazy, even to me, but I want to be here."

Words that Charlie isn't ready to say out loud crowd his mouth, pushing to the tip of his tongue, and he buries his face in the crook of Gordon's neck to keep them inside. Gordon puts both arms around Charlie, and that's nice too.

"This is really good," he says again, his words so muffled by Gordon's skin that they're probably not coherent. He could probably say *I love you* and Gordon would be none the wiser, except Charlie doesn't know how he could say those words and not have them come out as a physical manifestation of his feelings, an infusion of gold filigree that would kiss and spiral across Gordon's skin until he was as lit up, as gilt and glowing as Charlie feels inside.

Chapter Twenty-Two

THEY HAVE an awesome owl banding night, their best of the season so far. Gordon feels like he's being baptized by fire when, on their third net check, there are ten owls caught in the nets.

For a second they stare, before Charlie says, "You want to start at Net Three, and we'll meet in the middle?"

One of the owls is so tangled that Gordon panics a little. If he hurts an owl, especially because he barely knows what he's doing, he'll never forgive himself. When he gets Charlie to help him, Charlie spends a minute or two working on the tangled knot keeping the owl trapped, then shakes his head and pulls out a pocketknife.

"He's stressed," Charlie says, cutting strands of the net like it's nothing.

Gordon watches. "You don't mind just cutting it like that?" He doesn't know what a new net costs, but he has a feeling they aren't cheap.

"We should always put the health of the bird first. Nets are just nets, they can be fixed." Charlie's movements stutter and he pauses. The light from Gordon's headlamp catches on the ends of his pale eyelashes as he blinks rapidly. They're so light at that moment that they remind Gordon of frost glittering on glass.

One more cut and Charlie is able to finally slip the tangled knot of net over the owl's head. Gordon has a bag ready. "We'll band this one first," Charlie says as he ties the bag shut.

They extract the rest of the owls and Charlie gets to work banding the one that got itself so knotted up in the net. Sneakily, Gordon names him Tangle, even though he's one hundred percent sure Charlie would say he shouldn't name the owls. It doesn't stop him from writing it down in the Notes section of the data sheet.

Tangle is a hatch-year owl (aka, born earlier this year) and male by weight and wing chord length. After he's banded, spends time adjusting back to darkness in his little box, and flies away, Gordon says, "Maybe he got so tangled in the net because he's a teenager figuring out he likes boy owls better than girl owls."

Charlie gives him a shy but pleased little smile over the fluffy head of the next owl. "Thanks for not thinking my project idea sounds stupid."

Nothing Charlie does is stupid, and Gordon wishes with all his might that Charlie would see that. He'd like to personally arrange a parade where all the people who ever made Charlie feel less-than or stupid or too weird or defective have to go by and give him a sincere, personal apology. Except obviously, Charlie would hate that. "Of course it's not stupid."

Even in the cold light of the headlamps, Charlie's blush is obvious. He avoids responding by reading out numbers, which Gordon writes down on the data sheet. When it's time for the next net run, Charlie isn't quite done banding the ten owls they got from the last one, so Gordon walks over by himself. There are more owls—three this time instead of ten—and luckily for Gordon's jangling nerves, none as tangled as Tangle.

The night goes on like that, Charlie banding as fast as possible to catch up while Gordon keeps bringing him more owls. It's after two in the morning when they finally tear down the nets. The night is frigid, turning Gordon's fingers and toes numb. The tip of his nose is icy and he's used more Kleenex than he's proud of to wipe his runny nose.

He's exhausted and cold, but there's something bright and sparkling about the night. Their final total is twenty-three owls. Two are owls they banded a couple days ago, but one has a band that Charlie didn't put on. A "foreign retrap," Charlie calls it. They'll have to wait until he enters it into the Bird Banding Lab's website and hears back from the BBL about who originally banded it.

Gordon wonders if they can enter it tonight, then has to laugh at how invested he is in this work, when two months ago, he had no idea about any of it.

When Charlie notes down the stats, closes the data book, and meets Gordon's gaze, his eyes are bloodshot and shadowed with purple, but he's grinning tiredly. "This is my best banding night ever. My previous high was seventeen."

"Hell yeah, we beat that by six owls. New high score!" Clearly, Gordon's reached that stage of tiredness where you just start saying stuff. He decides to go with it and pulls Charlie to his feet, wrapping his arms around him and pulling him off the ground to swing him around in a circle. "Twenty-three saw-whets, baby!"

Charlie lets out a loud, startled laugh but submits to being twirled. He's heavier than he looks, but Gordon loves the solid weight of him in his arms. The idea of holding him up through everything hits Gordon like an uppercut. What if he was here for Charlie through the twenty-three owl nights and the zero owl nights? The good stuff and the bad stuff and everything in between?

Is this a forever kind of thing? Is he holding his future in his arms right now? Or is he getting a little loopy from being up until after two in the morning?

As Gordon sets Charlie back on his feet, Charlie pulls him in for a fierce kiss. When it ends, Charlie doesn't pull away. His lips rest against Gordon's, and they part on an inhale like he wants to say something.

It would be really good if he would, because Gordon's about to blurt out that he's crazy in love with him, and even though twenty-four hours was enough for him to interrogate his feelings and determine that he trusts them, he has no idea how Charlie will react. Charlie is probably smarter with his feelings than Gordon. There's no question that Gordon isn't being smart with his. He was in love with Becky, so ready to spend his life with her that he proposed. Look how that turned out.

Thinking about Becky, even if it's just for a second, smothers the urge to tell Charlie he loves him. When he does, it's not going to be with his ex on his mind.

Charlie leans back and puts both of his big, steady hands on either side of Gordon's face. His thumbs stroke Gordon's cheekbones, and after a second, he kisses Gordon's temple. "Do you maybe want to spend the night at my house again?" he asks, that sweet, shy note in his voice.

"Yeah, I do." Gordon slips his hands into the back pockets of Charlie's jeans and kisses him on the chin. It's bristly, even though Charlie's facial hair is too pale for him to have much of a five o'clock shadow. Or two o'clock shadow, whatever. Either way, it's sexy. Finding out all these new things turn him on is like an anti-midlife crisis. Like, yeah, he knew he found facial hair sexy, but he had no idea how hot it made him until he felt Charlie rub his scruff all over his body.

"Mind if I run into the house on the way out to grab a change of clothes?" Gordon adds.

"What happens if I say no?"

"I guess I can't put any clothes on tomorrow." Gordon shrugs, which is shameless flirting, considering he wore one of Charlie's shirts today.

"Oh no," Charlie says. "No clothes, you say?"

Gordon laughs and squeezes his butt.

Once Gordon retrieves clean clothes from his house, he slumps back into Charlie's car. The heat is on full blast, but there's no chance it will thaw Gordon out before they get back to Charlie's house. It's not a long enough drive.

Gordon yawns, feeling his eyes droop now that he's sitting somewhere comfy and warm. "Was Tangle the only male tonight?" he asks.

Glancing over at him, Charlie asks, "Tangle?"

"You know." Gordon waves a hand. Obviously Charlie doesn't know. "The owl that was really tangled. I named him Tangle."

"We really shouldn't—"

"Name the owls, I know. But I did." Gordon lets his eyes fall shut, but somehow he knows Charlie is smiling. It makes the air move differently, somehow. "I'm pretty sure he was the only male."

"He was, yeah. There was that one we couldn't sex, but I think it was a small female."

Gordon yawns again. "I wish you had your radio transmitter tags. You could've put one on Tangle and gone to find him next spring. See if he shacks up with another boy owl. I'd go with you and help out. Whatever you need me to do. Pretty sure I can start a campfire. I learned how to drive stick."

"Why would we need to drive stick?" Charlie asks. He sounds like he's about to laugh.

"I dunno. I'm just saying things I can do. I wanna be useful."

For a minute or two, Charlie doesn't say anything, and the only noise is the sound of the heater blasting and the tires on the road. Maybe it's more than a minute or two. Time gets weird and stretchy when you're right on the edge of sleep, and Gordon's definitely right on the edge of sleep. The warmth took him out faster than he thought it would.

"You're helping me so much, Gor," comes Charlie's voice, almost too quiet for Gordon to hear over the heater. "Even if you weren't, I'd want you to come with me."

Gordon smiles, and in his head, he says, *Awesome, I want to go, let's do it.* Then he remembers he needs to actually open his mouth and make words, since Charlie can't read his mind. "It's dumb that my grandpa didn't leave you money when you were so close with him. Then you'd have money for radio tags, and you could find all the gay owls."

Another silence. Then: "Probably not all of them."

"Okay, some of them."

Getting back to Charlie's house and waking up enough to walk inside reminds Gordon of being a kid and staying somewhere way past his bedtime. The car would stop and suddenly everything would be quiet, and his parents would whisper that they were home and help him out of the car. It always felt like time had stopped and like they were the only people in the world.

A memory swims just below the surface of his mind: a rough, callused hand ruffling his hair and a gruff voice saying, "He'll be a falconer, you wait and see," and his mom whispering, "When he's older, Dad."

It pings some other synapse in his brain, some deeply buried echo of yelling and something pressing on his lungs. He can't hold on to it as he wakes up, though, and it sinks back down into the murky depths of his memory.

He has to be careful not to trip as he gets out of the car, which he thinks he does a pretty good job of. Charlie's still waiting there to catch him in case he goes down, though, which is sweet.

"Season's catching up with you," Charlie says quietly, being respectful of his neighbors. That's sweet too. That he cares about things like that when he never felt accepted by those same neighbors.

"How is it not catching up with you?" Gordon mumbles. "Are you part vampire?"

"Is it possible to be part vampire?" Charlie muses philosophically, which is how Gordon knows that the late nights are catching up with him too. *Is it possible to be part vampire* is one of the most two-in-the-morning conversation topics he's ever heard. "I'm just an insomniac," Charlie adds.

Gordon stretches his arms over his head with a yawn and tips his head back. The stars are so bright here, even though there are lights glowing on the front steps of some of the houses on the street. So many stars, and he just never looked up when he lived here to see them.

Charlie touches his elbow, and that's enough to get Gordon moving toward the house. When they crawl into bed together, Gordon pulls Charlie close. He's spent too much of his life not looking up. Not noticing his parents' marriage was so unhappy. Not wondering more about his grandfather. Not running toward something, just running away from Sawmill Lake, looking back until he decided there were enough miles between him and his hometown. His willingness to mire himself in a relationship that didn't make him or his partner happy. Not examining his sexuality.

"You're thinking about something," Charlie murmurs sleepily, nuzzling into Gordon's hair, then the side of his face, before he kisses his temple and rests his lips there.

"Just about buying new furniture," he replies. If *is it possible to be part vampire* is a two-in-the-morning question, then *I'm having an epiphany about how I've lived my life* blows it out of the water.

"Hm," Charlie says, before his breathing deepens and evens out. Maybe he's not really an insomniac.

Maybe he feels as safe and happy in Gordon's arms as Gordon feels in his.

Chapter Twenty-Three

THE DAYS get steadily colder, the nights more so, and when snowflakes start catching in the wind that never seems to stop blowing from the north, Charlie gets a clenched-jaw look on his face. They keep going out, night after night, sitting in the frigid cold and hardly catching any owls. Sometimes, they don't even hear any. Just when Gordon thinks all the owls have definitely gone south, though, one will show up in the net.

As much as Gordon loves being at the site, when there's a string of ten nights in the twenties, with no end in sight in the forecast, he's kind of ready to rediscover evenings inside. Central heating is something he always thought he had a healthy appreciation for as a born-and-bred Minnesotan. He's discovered a new love for it this fall.

With Thanksgiving on the horizon, Gordon finally asks Charlie how long he usually bands.

It's a Sunday afternoon, and the low tonight is supposed to be in the teens. It will be twenty-two degrees by ten o'clock, and Gordon's fingers are already numb thinking about it. Charlie sighs and hangs his head. "As long as I can stand it."

"Okay," Gordon says stoically. "Just wondering."

Combing his hair back from his face, Charlie goes back to stirring the slow cooker chili they're having for dinner tonight. "It's getting kind of cold out there," he admits.

"Yeah, but if it's not too cold for you to band, you should keep going."

"Mm."

Gordon's leaning against the counter, in theory getting ingredients out for corn bread, but in practice just watching the play and movement of Charlie's shoulder blades under his shirt as he stirs. "What does 'mm' mean?"

Charlie replaces the lid on the slow cooker and glances at Gordon. "It means since we've only gotten three owls in the last seven days, and we're both freezing our balls off out there, maybe we should call it."

"Hey, speak for yourself. My balls are warm and toasty." Gordon waggles his eyebrows. "But they'd be much happier if they were getting cozy with yours."

Charlie smiles and bites his lip. "See, normally I don't have an offer like that to make me quit banding. Usually I just keep at it until I'm googling what frostbite looks like."

"Oh my god. Babe." Every time Gordon says that, he feels like he has a little power generator inside him making him glow so bright that Charlie reflects it back at him. "The owls don't want you to do that. Tangle doesn't want you to get frostbite. Think of him. And what about Elton, Lance, Ricky, and Boy George?"

"You really should stop naming all the male owls after gay musicians." The admonition would hit harder if Charlie wasn't giggling a little.

With a shrug, Gordon says, "Okay, I'll switch to actors."

The way Charlie laughs, bright and unburdened, makes Gordon willing to do anything for him. If Charlie wants to sit outside until it's sub-zero, Gordon will do it. But Charlie comes up behind him when he turns to the cupboard and reaches for the Jiffy corn bread mix, and then Gordon has a pair of warm, wiry arms wrapped around him.

As Charlie nuzzles into the crook of Gordon's neck, warm breath sending shivery awareness across his skin, he says, "I think I'll officially call it. Season over."

Gordon's core temperature cheers, but out loud he asks, "Are you sure? If you're saying that because I asked when you usually stop, you should keep going out." This relationship is too new for that kind of resentment to take root. Anyway, it's kind of sad knowing that he held his last saw-whet for the season and didn't even realize it.

On the other hand, Charlie's lean body pressed against his is giving him a lot of ideas about how they could spend the evening. If there's one thing about banding owls that Gordon would criticize, it's that it takes place at night, every night. Spending all that time with Charlie is amazing, and the emotional side of their relationship is flourishing. Gordon just really, *really* wants to spend more time naked together.

To be fair, weekends have had lots of naked time. But Gordon's horny, and he could spend the rest of his life worshipping Charlie's gorgeous body. Every time he gets to see those miles of smooth white skin, the pale gold hair on his legs and chest and stomach, the gilt curls of hair in his crotch, he doesn't want to blink. His long cock with the vein Gordon loves following with his tongue, his velvety balls with their masculine musk, his tight, hot hole—the Gordon who thought he was straight seems like he lived on a different planet. How did Gordon ever, ever convince himself he was straight?

Gordon lifts his arms to backwards-hug Charlie, the Jiffy box still in one hand. "I'm sure," Charlie says, kissing Gordon's neck. Gordon's insides turn molten, and he turns in Charlie's arms, wrapping his own around Charlie's neck and capturing his mouth in a slow, sultry kiss. He drops the Jiffy box, which thunks to the floor.

Charlie laughs into his mouth, which turns to a groan as he slips his hands inside Gordon's clothes. "Hey, babe," Gordon gets out between kisses.

"Mm?" This isn't a confusing *mm*, since Charlie backs him into the counter and unbuttons his jeans.

"There's something I wanna try." Gordon rucks Charlie's sweatshirt up over his pecs so he can play with his nipples. They're already red and abused from a weekend of sex, but Charlie whimpers and presses closer.

As Charlie unzips Gordon's jeans and palms his cock, he says, "Okay. Yes. Anything."

"Anything? What if it's weird?"

Charlie huffs a laugh and bites the hinge of Gordon's jaw. "Is it weird?"

When Charlie slips those magical fingers of his into the fly of Gordon's boxer briefs, Gordon tips his head back and lets his eyes close. "Pretty sure it's not weird. It's in my favorite porn."

Abruptly, Charlie draws back. Shit, did Gordon say something wrong? Does Charlie hate porn? But no, there's a smile twitching at his mouth.

"You have a favorite porn?" Charlie asks.

"Uh." Maybe he just made himself sound like an idiot. "I mean… it always gets the job done."

Charlie presses his lips together hard in the way Gordon knows means he's fighting not to laugh. Even though Gordon's now totally sure he made himself sound like an idiot, he doesn't feel like Charlie's laughing at him. There's no mockery in Charlie's lit-up eyes and barely suppressed laughter, just delighted glee.

"Not to like, try to convince you about the artistic merit of two guys fucking on camera for people to jack off to, but it's very tender," Gordon says.

The lip-pressing has turned to lip-biting. "I'm sure," Charlie says, right before he cracks and lets out a guffaw.

Gordon lets him laugh for a second, then leans in and says in a gravelly voice, "I wanna eat out your hole."

The way Charlie's eyes snap wide and his pupils flare out until his irises are only a thin strip of blue is one of the biggest power trips Gordon can imagine. "Yeah," he says, running his hand up and down over Charlie's chest and stomach. "I wanna get you so soaking wet that my cock slides right in that hole."

"Okay." Charlie's voice sounds strangled and his pulse is hammering in his neck. It might be Gordon's imagination, but he's pretty sure he can smell pheromones and arousal coming off Charlie in waves. "Oh my god. *Okay*. Yes, I mean. Fuck yes, please, let's do that."

They surge into a kiss again, both of them moving toward each other at the same time. The press of Charlie's slick tongue against his makes Gordon achingly hard, and then thinking about having his own tongue inside Charlie's ass somehow makes him even harder. God, he's wanted to do this forever, first just with a man, any man, and then with Charlie specifically.

And he hasn't fucked Charlie yet either, because getting fucked by him is mind-wipe, astral-plane good, and Charlie's started panting about how beautiful Gordon looks with Charlie's dick inside him. For him, that's pretty serious dirty talk. After he says that, the floodgates open, and he lavishes praise on Gordon. It's addicting. No one ever praised Gordon during sex before or told him how gorgeous he is.

Gordon gives Charlie a gentle push backward, encouraging him toward the kitchen door and his bedroom beyond. When Charlie moves, he lets out a surprised yelp and stumbles. Something crunches and *womps*, which is when Gordon remembers he dropped the box of Jiffy corn bread mix on the floor.

Now the box is crumpled, courtesy of Charlie's foot, and corn bread mix is settling on the linoleum like snow. "Damn, sorry," Gordon says with a wince. "Should we clean that up?"

"Absolutely not," Charlie declares, corn bread mix clinging to one leg of his jeans. His pupils still look blown out, and Gordon's not going to argue.

With a grin, Gordon kisses Charlie while he walks him backward to Charlie's bedroom. On the way, his phone buzzes, which he obviously ignores. Charlie's shoulder bumps the bedroom doorframe as Gordon steers him in, and Gordon decides to take the opportunity to pin him against a hard surface and grind against him.

As Charlie moans, Gordon pushes his shirt over his head. Having it shoved up to Charlie's armpits before was fine and good, except it didn't take much movement to fall and cover Charlie's body again. Totally unacceptable. Now it's gone, and Gordon touches Charlie, squeezing a pec, flicking a nipple, tracing ribs, stroking his fingers through the fine, gold hair on Charlie's belly.

He bends his head to suck one of Charlie's nipples and his phone buzzes again. He ignores it, but it goes off once more, and then a further three times in rapid succession. As if that's not enough, it starts ringing.

"Jesus Christ." Gordon steps back from Charlie with an apologetic grimace. His own shirt is only half on, so he pulls it off the rest of the way, a motion which Charlie tracks hungrily. The two hundred texts on Gordon's phone are from Jason, as is the missed call.

When the phone starts ringing again, Gordon rolls his eyes. Of course it's Jason. What the hell does he want?

"Are you going to get that?" Charlie asks, clearly hoping the answer is no.

"I shouldn't." Until forty-five seconds ago, Gordon was so hard he was almost in pain, and only a few short minutes (maybe seconds!) from having his tongue inside Charlie's asshole. But Jason's texts seem frantic. They include: *Are you around*, *I need to talk to you*, and *I need your help!* That last one preceded the phone calls.

Scrubbing a hand over his face, Gordon says, "It's Jason Miller. I better see why he's calling. If he's in trouble or something, I'll hate myself if I ignored him."

Charlie's expression, which twisted in dislike at Jason's name, softens at the last part. The look he gives Gordon is full of tenderness, and Gordon's stomach fills with butterflies like he's back in high school. "I'll be here," he says, leaning back against the doorframe and crossing his arms over his chest.

For a second, Gordon hesitates. The bedroom is dim, the curtains half-drawn and sunk in blue shadow, while the light from the kitchen reaches warm yellow fingers down the hall. Charlie is a chiaroscuro masterpiece, his body lit up like white gold on one side and shaded on the other the same color as the sky at twilight.

He's beautiful. And Gordon's an idiot for walking away to talk to Jason. "I'll go outside to call him back," he says.

"Why? It's cold."

Giving Charlie a lopsided smile, Gordon replies, "Because I know you and Jason aren't exactly BFFs, and I figured you wouldn't want to hear any part of a conversation involving him before I take you apart with my tongue."

The sharp bob of Charlie's throat makes Gordon's pulse beat against his veins. "Wear a jacket" is all he says.

Gordon doesn't bother, instead stepping outside shirtless, with his jeans hanging low on his hips. Whoops, they're unzipped. He pulls up the zipper one-handed but doesn't bother buttoning them as he taps Jason's number to call him back.

Jason answers on the first ring. "Dude, I'm so glad you called back. I'm in trouble."

Unconsciously, Gordon's spine straightens. It's going a little far to call Jason his friend, but he doesn't want anything bad to happen to the guy. "What's wrong? Do you need help?"

"Yeah. I'm fucked, and you're the only person who can help me."

Now Gordon wishes he'd put a shirt on. Or grabbed his keys in case he needs to get in the car right now and—what? Bail Jason out of jail or something? Except no, he has to tell Charlie where he's going first.

He turns around, reaching for the doorknob. "Where are you, man? I'm at Charlie's place on Mesabi, so if you're in town, I can get there pretty fast—"

"I'm gonna lose my job, Gordy," Jason interrupts, his tone wobbly.

Gordon freezes, his hand on the doorknob, halfway through turning it. "What?"

"My job. I'm gonna lose my job. I've been promising Joel you're going to sell that land you're sitting on. He has big developers lined up, and he's breathing down my neck. They're gonna put a Walmart in!"

Slowly, Gordon withdraws his hand from the doorknob. "Why would you promise that?"

"Because you told me you were selling!" Jason sounds like he's crying. "Now Joel's saying you're not returning his calls or texts, and he's going to look unreliable and like a cocktease because of all these developers ready to grab that land—Gordy, you gotta meet with him. I can't lose my job, man. I have credit card bills; shit costs so much lately—"

"Jason—slow down. Stop. Just—take a breath, okay?" Queasy unease roils Gordon's stomach, with an oil slick layer of guilt on top of it. He *did* tell Jason he was selling. Pretty categorically. And he *has* been ignoring his realtor cousin, Joel's, attempts to contact him. Which is maybe not the most adult thing to do, but Gordon hates awkward conversations.

His heart is beating nervously fast, and he decides to take his own advice about breathing. "He's probably not going to fire you."

"He already told me he's going to if I can't make you talk to him. He said this week's my last unless he gets you to sign with him."

Jesus. Fuck. Gordon rubs his forehead. He's not going to sell the house or the land, and he's distantly pissed as hell that a bunch of developers are salivating over the chance to turn all of it into giant discount store and an even more giant parking lot. Joel Miller is fucking shady, getting them all lined up in the wings just waiting for Gordon to sign a contract with him. Probably salivating over the big, fat commission he'd get.

But he doesn't want Jason to lose his job, either. They're never going to be real friends, not with the way Jason's treated Charlie all these years, but when they were at the bar, Jason tried a little, and that's worth something.

Also, he just doesn't want to be responsible for someone losing their job, even if they're an asshole who brought it on themselves. Karma would for sure come back and kick him in the balls.

"Jason, look. I don't know how to say this…." A car goes by on the street, the driver staring at him. Gordon lifts a hand in a sheepish wave.

"Please don't say you already sold the place with a different real estate agent," Jason begs.

Looking to the pale, November afternoon sky helplessly, Gordon replies, "No. I decided not to sell."

There's silence on the other end, finally broken by sniffling. So yeah, Jason's definitely crying. That really doesn't make Gordon feel good, even though he didn't do anything wrong.

"Shit," Jason finally says. "Shit. Shit. *Fuck.* Gordy, man. What am I gonna do?"

"I'll talk to him," Gordon says. His voice comes out much more confident than he feels. "He was probably just having a bad day. C'mon, I'm sure he's not going to fire you because you had a lead that didn't work out. That's not a fireable offense." Maybe it is. He has no idea. "I'll text him as soon as I'm off the phone with you."

"He can do what he wants," Jason says miserably. "Everyone does what he says at the office. If he wants me gone, I'm gone."

"I'll talk to him," Gordon repeats.

"You can't tell him I called you!"

"No, man, of course." Based on what he's hearing, Joel doesn't sound like the kind of guy to be moved by a story of his cousin sobbing into a phone over the fear of losing his job. "I'll figure something out. I'll make it sound like... I don't know, like I have some doubts about him. Unless I should say I'm working with someone else?"

"No! No, don't say you're working with someone else." Jason doesn't speak for a second, just sniffing now and then. "Yeah, the other one, though. Maybe. Fuck, I'm sorry for putting you in the middle of this."

Which he should be, but Gordon feels kind of responsible too. If he'd met with Joel weeks ago like he said he would, maybe Joel wouldn't be threatening Jason's job. "Don't worry about it. I'll do what I can, okay?"

"Okay." A tiny ray of hope makes its way into Jason's voice. "Thanks, Gordy. You're the best."

It takes another minute to extricate himself from the call, and once he does, Gordon makes himself send a text to Joel asking if he's still interested in listing Gordon's property. He goes back inside to wait for the response and finds Charlie in the kitchen cleaning up the cornbread mix that exploded all over the floor earlier.

"You should've let me do that," Gordon says, his Jason-guilt close enough to the surface that this only adds to it. He's batting zero on making people's lives easier this weekend.

Charlie looks up from where he's kneeling on the linoleum and brushes his hair out of his eyes, leaving a swipe of cornbread mix across his forehead. "It's okay. What did Jason want?"

A lizard brain urge slams shut a fire door between Gordon's brain and mouth. He never told Charlie that he planned to sell the property, and now it doesn't seem like anything good would come of it. Since he's definitely not selling, what's the point in bringing it up at all?

"Uh," he says, scrambling for something else. "He made some bad fantasy football trades and lost a bunch of money."

He's a horrible liar, and Charlie looks unimpressed. After a second, though, he says, "I guess that's the kind of emergency Jason has."

Gordon chuckles in a totally real and not lying liar way. "Yeah. First-world problems."

While Charlie sweeps up the rest of the cornmeal mix, Gordon's phone buzzes with a text. It's Joel, asking if he wants to get lunch at Edna's to "talk shop" on Tuesday.

Sounds good! Gordon texts back, with a smiley face for good measure.

By the time he pockets his phone, Charlie's done cleaning up. After he washes his hands, he slips his arms around Gordon's neck. "So, where were we?"

Between Jason's desperation, the impending meeting with Joel, and the gnawing feeling that he's doing something wrong by not telling Charlie, Gordon's libido has been extinguished. He attempts a casual smile as he rests his hands on Charlie's hips. "I'm not sure how I feel about going from talking to Jason to sex."

Charlie makes a face. "When you put it like that."

Gordon laughs, worried he sounds weird. Is Charlie giving him a strange look? "You want to finally watch that robot movie?" A movie about giant robots punching each other is a poor substitute for his mouth on Charlie's ass, but he doesn't want to have any of this stuff on his mind when he sends Charlie into low-Earth orbit with his tongue. Gordon's never been one of those people who uses sex to escape his worries—his worries just creep into the sex.

"Okay." Charlie gives him a searching look, like he knows there was more to the phone conversation than what Gordon is saying. Probably imagines Jason poured his heart out to Gordon about something, and now Gordon's adhering to some kind of bro code and refusing to share Jason's secrets. Which… isn't far off.

Everything will be fine. They'll watch a dumb action movie, the stuff with Jason and his job will fade into the background, and Gordon and Charlie will fuck, because Gordon's probably making this into a bigger deal than it is, and in a couple hours, that will be obvious.

Yeah, definitely. He's overthinking this. It's going to be fine.

Chapter Twenty-Four

THE GOOD News is that Jason doesn't call Gordon again on Sunday or Monday. The bad news is that he texts. A lot. From his text bombardment, Gordon's pretty sure that Jason's doing a speed-run of the five stages of grief.

On Tuesday, though, all he gets from Jason is a terse request to let him know how the meeting goes. Gordon blocks off an hour for lunch on his work calendar, then changes it to an hour and a half, in case of disaster. He has a bad feeling about this lunch. Every time he thinks about the fact that he lied to Charlie, guilt squirms through his insides.

When he gets to Edna's, Steph waves from behind the counter. He chooses a booth in her section after surveying the diner and not spotting Joel Miller. Less than a minute goes by before she's at the table with a mug and a coffee carafe, plus a couple menus.

"So, you and Charlie," she says as the coffee pours in a smooth stream into the cup.

"I figured everyone in town knew weeks ago," Gordon says, grabbing his customary two sugars and two creams.

She winks. "Everyone did. I just didn't say anything until I knew it was for real."

Raising his eyebrows, he asks, "We get the Steph seal of approval?"

"Are you kidding?" She digs out a couple extra creamer pods from her apron to replenish the ones he's dumping into his coffee. "You two are adorable. Makes my teeth hurt whenever I see you together."

Gordon laughs and rubs the back of his neck. "Is that your way of saying we should tone it down?"

"Nope." She gives him a pointed look. "And if anyone makes you feel like you should? Screw 'em. Charlie deserves someone who's crazy about him. Why shouldn't you show it in public?"

Gordon's face gets warm, but he's not going to deny that he's crazy about Charlie. "I can't believe he was single," he says instead. "The men up here let him get away? Bananas."

"I told you, sometimes people think there's only one way to be." Someone waves at her and she shoots him a smile before going to help them.

So his feelings for Charlie are so obvious that other people can see how he feels. That's comforting and terrifying at the same time. Does Charlie realize Gordon's in love with him?

One of these days, he's going to have to man up and tell Charlie. It's getting stupid that he hasn't. He's moving back to Sawmill Lake, for fuck's sake. Pretending that Charlie's not a huge part of that is silly.

Before he can sink fully into a lunchtime crisis re: to confess or not to confess, the door swings open and Joel Miller strides in. Gordon recognizes him from the light internet stalking he did last night.

There's a slight resemblance between Joel and Jason. They both have the same light brown hair and brown eyes, small nose, and round face. Joel gives off I'm On A Billboard vibes, though, and his features are more appealing in a way Gordon can't put his finger on. He looks like he could model dad polos in a Kohl's catalogue.

When Gordon waves, Joel comes over. There's a glossy folder under one of his arms. Gordon stands to greet him and gets assaulted with a handshake so firm that's he's pretty sure something pops out of alignment in his shoulder.

"Hi, Gordon, Joel Miller. So great to finally connect with you!" Joel flashes him a salesperson smile and Gordon returns it weakly.

"Um, yeah. Sorry it took me so long to get in touch." Gordon looks at his coffee cup and wonders if he can sit back down. "It's been a busy couple months."

"Sure, sure. Don't worry about it." Joel slides into the booth and Gordon sits across from him. The glossy folder ends up in the middle of the table, facing Gordon. Nodding toward the coffee, Joel asks, "You haven't ordered yet, have you?"

"No, just coffee."

"Perfect. Lunch is on me."

They both take a minute to study the menus, even though Gordon knows what he's getting, since he always gets the same thing. Joel waves to Steph, who returns, snagging the coffee carafe on the way. Gordon downs the rest of his coffee to make room for more in his cup.

Joel smiles at Steph. "Can I substitute the protein in the Cobb salad?"

There's a tiny twitch at one corner of her mouth. "I can do chicken or steak."

"Let's do the steak," Joel says. "Dressing on the side, please."

When she nods, Gordon says, "I'll have the same thing I always do."

"Grilled cheese and tomato soup with fries coming right up," Steph says, giving him a look he can't exactly read. He knows it was meant for him, though, and that Joel wasn't supposed to see it.

"So, Gordon, Jason says you guys were friends back in high school?" Joel asks.

Ugh, Gordon was really hoping they could get right to the point of this meeting, but of course Joel wants to chat first. It's nice in theory, because sure, you want the person selling your house to take an interest in you as a person (or at least pretend to), but it's just dragging out this whole thing.

Gordon decides after this is over, he'll ask Charlie if he wants to get dinner somewhere tonight. With banding done, they didn't see each other last night, and Gordon missed him with a stubborn insistence that refused to be ignored.

"Yeah, we had the same friend group," Gordon says vaguely.

"And you live in the Cities now?"

Gordon hesitates. "Well—I moved down there to go to college and stayed, yeah. I have an apartment there for now."

"Cool, cool. There's so much to do down there." Joel turns on his billboard smile. "And now you have this huge piece of land up here! You didn't expect to inherit it, right?"

"No...."

"I have a lot of clients just like you. They move where the jobs are, and when an elderly parent or relative passes, they have to decide what to do with it." Joel opens the glossy folder, which is filled with more glossiness. Gordon's eyes refuse to focus on any of it. "I'll be straight with you, Gordon. I've got some buyers real interested in your property. If we play this right, we could be looking at a bidding war, and I don't need to tell you what a great deal that is for you—"

"I'm not sure about selling," Gordon interrupts. He wants to smack himself. He's not sure? Bullshit! He's totally sure! He's definitely not selling! Why is he trying to soften it?

He opens his mouth to clarify that in fact he *is* sure, but Joel asks, "What's the sticking point? Are you concerned about the house being torn down?"

"No. I mean, yeah, I would be—"

"I understand completely. There are probably a lot of memories tied up in that house. It was your grandfather's, right? You must have been close. We can ask the buyer to leave it as-is." Joel smiles. "It's a big decision. Tell me what else is on your mind. I know we're just meeting each other, but I want you to feel like we'll have a partnership if we work together."

"That's—it's—" Joel would give a used car salesman a run for his money, but there's something weirdly compelling about his fakey pathos. When he leans forward over the table and draws his eyebrows together, it transforms his Just-A-Guy handsomeness into a quality that's hard to look away from.

It's also hard to disagree or contradict him, let alone tell him no. Plus, he managed to cram so many wrong things into one monologue that Gordon doesn't even know where to start. Curiosity makes him ask, "A developer would really leave the house there?"

"Sure, if it was a condition of you selling," Joel says.

Yeah right. Gordon doesn't believe it for a second. *That's* what he's going to say. You're a liar, buddy, and you're not turning my grandpa's land into a parking lot.

Except his food hasn't come yet, so… that would be awkward. Plus, he still needs to thread the needle of turning Joel down but not putting Jason out of a job. He takes a slow sip of coffee to buy himself time to respond.

"Okay," he says, which makes him sound like a genius. Great. Master negotiator. He knows how to do this—he's a project manager, for Christ's sake. Most of the job is getting people to do what you need them to while being nice about it. "You said something about a bidding war?"

He doesn't care about a bidding war, but maybe if he seems like he cares, it will be enough to get Jason out of hot water.

Steph drops off their food and makes a face at him, which he takes to be sympathy for having this meeting. He tries to convey some gratitude for feeling seen, but probably doesn't pull it off.

It's appropriate that Joel has a bunch of steak strips sitting in front of him now, since his eyes lit up kind of like a cartoon wolf when Gordon asked about the bidding war. As Joel dumps the entire cup of dressing onto his salad, he says, "Yeah, you've got a really nice piece of land there. I've seen bidding wars over way less desirable real estate. With that lake on the property?" Joel whistles. "It's got resort written all over it."

"Lake," Gordon repeats blankly. At Joel's strange look, he amends, "Lake! Right. Yeah." Jesus. He had no idea there was a lake on the land. His grandpa had lakefront property and didn't even have his house on it?

Something that's not firm enough to be a memory bubbles up from the depths of his unconscious. There's a heavy green sensation of tight airlessness, a sense of light glittering too far above him.

He shakes himself out of the—memory?—because Joel is talking again. "There's a developer I know who built a beautiful resort up in Grand Marais. Luxury cabins, glamping, great restaurant on site. I've definitely got him interested in your property for his next project. And there are a few others I mentioned it to, just to gauge their interest. It's high, Gordon. I'm telling you, you could really clean up if you go about this the right way."

"How much are we talking?" Gordon asks before taking a bite of his grilled cheese.

Joel looks smug, like he knows he's going to close the deal. "I think we could push it up to three quarters of a million. Maybe even eight hundred grand."

Gordon almost chokes on his grilled cheese. Joel looks even more smug. "Wow," Gordon coughs. "That's… a lot."

It *is* a lot. And for a second, Gordon's almost tempted. With that kind of money, he could pay off his student loans. He could sell the land and buy something cheaper in town. And if a developer is interested in turning it into a high-end resort, Gordon could demand that they leave Charlie's net lanes alone. It could be a condition of the sale.

Something catches Joel's eye behind Gordon and he whips out his Just-A-Guy smile again. "Hey—I met you when I was taking a look at a property! It's Charlie, right?"

Gordon whirls in the booth. His back protests with a series of pops and cracks, which he'll pay for later. Standing frozen right behind the booth is Charlie. His face is bloodless and his jaw is clenched, while his normally clear blue eyes look bruised.

"Hey," Gordon says, reaching for him, because Gordon can't be in Charlie's presence without wanting to touch him. Plus, something looks wrong, and Gordon's instinct has always been for physical comfort.

Charlie jerks away. "D-don't," he says.

It occurs to Gordon at that moment that the look on Charlie's face might be because of something Gordon did.

He wracks his brain, glances at Joel, who's watching this with interest, and asks in a quieter voice, "Are you okay?"

Which is like, maybe the dumbest question he's ever asked, because Charlie is *definitely* not okay. His shoulders are rising and falling as he breathes in quick, short gasps, and Gordon can see his pulse hammering in his neck. He's used to seeing that when Charlie's hard at work fucking Gordon, so it gives him some confusing feelings to spot it now, when Charlie looks like he's barely holding it together. It's been long enough now that Gordon can tell—the level of distress Charlie's in right now would have other people crying and screaming.

For another moment, Charlie stares at him. He's fraying, Gordon can tell, unraveling as emotions roil him. But it's not enough to be able to tell there's something wrong. Gordon needs Charlie to *tell* him.

"Charlie?" he asks softly.

"We're just talking shop, Charlie," Joel pipes up. "You can join us as long as you don't mind listening to me yammer on about what we want to list Gordon's property at." His smile is a little less calculated, like he's genuinely trying to put Charlie at ease.

It doesn't work, which Gordon isn't even the tiniest bit surprised by. What does surprise him, though, is the way Charlie's eyes widen before he turns and storms out of Edna's.

Gordon almost calls after him, realizing at the last second how much Charlie would hate that. "I'll be right back," he says to Joel before jumping up and hurrying after Charlie.

Between the length of Charlie's legs and his furious pace, Gordon has to jog to catch up with him, which he finally does a block from the diner. Panting, he stops right in front of Charlie, only to have Charlie ignore him and keep walking. "Charlie, wait! What's wrong?"

Gordon tries again, scrambling to catch up, and grabs Charlie's arm. Charlie yanks it back so violently that Gordon stumbles, surprised. But at least it worked and Charlie isn't fleeing from him anymore.

"Wh-wh-what's *wrong?*" Charlie repeats, his voice strangled. "H-how c-c-can you even a-ask that?"

The fact that Charlie's stuttering so much is almost worse than the fact that he's furious. When Charlie stutters like this, it's because he's anxious and stressed—and that means Gordon's the one making him anxious and stressed.

And then it hits him. Of course Charlie's upset! He's right, how *can* Gordon even ask that? Is Gordon really this stupid?

"Oh god, I'm not actually selling!" he practically yells, wincing at the way his voice echoes off the surrounding buildings, including the Kristofferson & Klein offices. Lack of volume control is okay, though. He's just glad he figured it out.

Charlie's shoulders come down a little bit, so they're not hunched up around his ears quite as much. "Y-you're not?" he asks warily.

"No!" Gordon almost laughs, dizzy with relief. "Sorry, wow, I wasn't even thinking. Of course you thought that's what I was doing!"

"Yeah," Charlie says. He still sounds wary, but his posture is thawing little by little. "Why are you m-meeting with Joel Miller if you're not selling your house? He said he was going to talk about what you want to list the property at."

Gordon waves a hand. Just a misunderstanding! Explaining will barely take more effort than that hand wave. "I guess Joel is breathing down Jason's neck about me listing the land. That's why he called on Sunday, he was freaking out and saying Joel was going to fire him if I didn't list with him. So I'm meeting with him and, well, I guess kind of stringing him along. I'd feel bad if Jason lost his job because of me."

With a slow nod, Charlie says, "Okay. But. Um, why would Joel b-be mad at Jason?"

"Oh, because Jason told him I was going to sell."

"But why would Jason even th-think that?" Charlie asks.

"I told him I was. When I inherited the house and the land."

Charlie's quiet for a second. "So you just... never told him you changed your mind?"

"Right."

There's another moment of silence. Charlie seems to chew on his next words before he speaks. "I n-never told you, but after that weekend we went to Duluth. When you—um. Left. I went to band on Monday, but Jason and Joel were at your house."

"Yeah, I know." Gordon scowls, but there's no reason to bring up Jason's ugliness right now. It's not like Charlie doesn't know the kind of stuff Jason says. "He mentioned it to me."

"But you still didn't say you weren't selling?"

Too late, Gordon sees the cliff he's happily about to sail over. "Well, I hadn't really made up my mind at that point not to sell."

The silence that falls this time has the same quality of an anvil plummeting toward a Looney Toons character. The way Charlie looks at him makes Gordon feel like he just ran over someone's dog.

"I can't believe you." Charlie's voice is tight, raw, and devastated. Betrayed. "You were going to sell."

"Yeah, but I'm not," Gordon says quickly.

"But you *were*." The tension that had almost bled out of Charlie's body coils right back up in his shoulders. He's shaking. "You were going to sell Ibrahim's property. We were banding. I taught you how to do everything! How to set up nets and extract the owls… all those nights…. And we were *fucking*." The expression on his face has turned to pure horror. "All that time, you were going to sell."

"Yeah, maybe! I mean, I was thinking about it. But I'm not! Isn't that what matters?" Gordon asks. A hollow is excavating itself in his chest, right behind his heart.

Charlie takes a step backward. "No. You were going to. *That's* what matters. We were… we were together, and you still wanted to sell. Even though you knew how important it was."

"You can't be mad at me because of something I was thinking about doing but didn't actually do." Gordon steps toward him, but Charlie backs up again. The hollow in his chest floods with desperation, like water sloshing into a tide pool at high tide. "That's not fair, Charlie. C'mon."

With a bark of hard, unhappy laughter, Charlie repeats, "Not fair? It's not *fair* that I trusted you, and that I was fall—" Blood drains from his face and he shakes his head violently. His hair tumbles across his eyebrows. "I can't believe you. You're…." He struggles for words, makes an inarticulate sound, and finally forces out, "You're not… who I thought you w-were."

"I didn't *do* anything!" Gordon says again, just as uselessly as every other time he's said it. "What did you expect me to do, get a call about how I inherited a house in a town I never wanted to come back to, and just hold on to it out of the goodness of my heart?"

"I expected you to n-n-not sell it when you found out I w-was using it!" Charlie shoots back. "You pretended to care!"

The accusation, wildly unfair and totally untrue, hits Gordon like a punch to the solar plexus, and for a second he can't get a breath. When he can breathe again, he says, "Well, I guess if it was so important that you keep banding there, then my grandpa should have left the land to you, not me." A wounded, cornered-animal part of him lashes out cruelly, adding, "He didn't leave you anything, though."

Charlie's head snaps back like Gordon slapped him. His eyes go wide. "Ibrahim left me two million dollars," he says fiercely. "So actually he did think I was important."

"*What?*" Two *million* dollars? The wounded animal in Gordon decides it's not getting out alive, so it charges. "That's probably what you wanted the whole time, right? You got close to my grandpa because you knew he didn't have anyone else, so then he'd leave you all his money?"

"I had no idea he had that much money—"

"But you knew he had something—"

"No, I didn't!" Angry tears glitter in Charlie's eyes. "I didn't care about money! I just cared about not being lonely anymore!"

Wind gusts like it's shoving silence between them, stinging Gordon's ears and the tip of his nose. The cold knifes through him and he realizes he left his coat back in Edna's. Charlie dashes his hand across his eyes before he turns and walks away, long strides eating up the ground. His shoulders hunch as he puts distance between them.

Gordon doesn't want to watch Charlie walk away, and he can't help himself from watching Charlie walk away. His chest aches. He's angry and sad and indignant all at the same time, but mostly he thinks his heart is breaking, when he just got used to it being whole.

Chapter Twenty-Five

CHARLIE GETS all the way home, the biting wind freezing tears on his face, before he remembers that the entire reason he walked to Edna's was because he doesn't have anything in the house he feels like eating. That means now he's not only crying, he's still hungry.

There's a sick ache spreading through his body. His heart is nothing but a pummeled, bruised lump of pain. The revelation of Gordon's betrayal keeps almost receding, and Charlie's brain, jumping into some kind of self-protective mode, will nearly convince him to forget it happened. Then it comes surging back, worse than ever.

By the time he gets his shoes off, it's all he can do to fold himself onto the couch, where he curls into as tight a ball as someone who's six-three can. Except he realizes he can't just disappear from work, so he makes himself uncurl and log back on.

Emails swim in front of his eyes, and his next realization is that he can't face working for the rest of the day. He IMs his manager, whose blessing to take the afternoon off he receives.

He contemplates curling up again and wallowing in his hurt. His heart wants to crack into pieces and sieve through his ribs. It's like a drumbeat in his head: Gordon was going to sell his land. Gordon was going to sell his land. Gordon banded with him and loved the owls and was going to sell his land. Gordon kissed Charlie, and he was still going to sell his land.

Charlie was stupid enough to think they were a team, and now he's the idiot who didn't understand that Gordon was just bored and looking for something new. He probably would have changed his mind about staying. He's probably changing his mind right now about not selling. Joel Miller probably reeled him in by promising the land and the house will sell for a million dollars, and Gordon's probably thinking it's the least Ibrahim can do for him, since Charlie got double that in the will.

No, he's not going to wallow. He's going to go out and forget about Sawmill Lake for the rest of the day. He's going to go… get drunk.

Yeah. That sounds like an amazing plan.

THERE'S A MEXICAN restaurant on the outskirts of Hibbing that Charlie deems acceptable for getting drunk. He's eaten here before, a long time ago with his mom before the cancer and chemo made her lose her appetite. It's dim inside, with colorful papel picado banners strung thickly across the ceiling. Latin pop is playing with that too loud quality music has in restaurants where a big crowd has recently cleared out. There's a little terracotta fountain in one corner.

A tired-looking mother is sitting at a table, trying to get her toddler to eat while a baby in a high chair cries. Charlie wonders if the baby just found out the man he's in love with was going to betray him. Probably not.

He sits at the bar, mumbling hello to the bartender, a young Latino man. In a faint nod toward propriety, he orders chips and salsa to go with the three beers he downs too quickly.

The alcohol puts him in a fuzzier place where his chest doesn't throb so badly. Or maybe he just can't feel it as much. Maybe when the alcohol wears off, he'll start to feel it more.

That's unacceptable. He orders another beer. And some more chips. Because the chips are good. Maybe he'll get some guacamole too!

He whiles away the afternoon there, sometimes scrolling on his phone, sometimes contenting himself with a thousand-yard stare. The bartender tries to make conversation a few times, but even drunk, Charlie's no good at talking to other people.

Gordon was so easy to talk to. It took hardly any time at all for Charlie to lose all the anxiety that keeps his words trapped inside his head. But Gordon wasn't who he was pretending to be. He was just... he was... he was lying. That's what. If he was going to sell the land, he should have just said that right away!

And the fact that he got mad about Charlie getting money in the will is the cherry on top. Yeah, Charlie didn't mention it because he didn't want to change things between them! He didn't want a thing that had nothing to do with the two of them to get in the way of what was between them.

Oh. Wait.

Except no, it's not the same at all. Because Gordon was going to sell the land that Charlie bands on! All Charlie did was keep something to himself.

Granted, Gordon decided not to sell. But he decided not to sell because of owl banding, and Charlie, and them falling for each other. If they hadn't met, then the land would be for sale right now.

Charlie gets the bartender's attention. "C-can I have another beer?"

With a nod, the bartender grabs another Modelo, pops the cap off, then puts it down in front of Charlie. Quickly, so the buzz doesn't have a chance to dissipate, Charlie swallows a quarter of it. It sloshes in his stomach in a not entirely pleasant way.

Plus, four-and-a-quarter beers in, Charlie finds himself stepping back and studying this situation like he's a bystander to it. If he was a bystander, he'd think, well, does it matter why Gordon decided not to sell the land? Isn't there actually something kind of nice about the fact that it was Charlie, and something so important to Charlie, that changed Gordon's mind?

He should have said something. It was wrong of him to plan to do a thing that he knew would break Charlie's heart.

But, Bystander Charlie points out, he didn't do it in the end. Can he blame Gordon for wanting to get rid of some land he never wanted? Shouldn't he focus on what Gordon actually *did* instead of what he was going to do, but didn't?

"Shut up," Charlie mumbles to himself. The restaurant has grown steadily busier in the hours he's been sitting there, and someone a couple seats down at the bar looks at him with mild concern. Charlie swallows another mouthful of beer.

A plate with a steaming cheese quesadilla appears in front of him. Charlie looks up, meeting the eyes of the bartender, who smiles at him. "You should eat something. You want salsa?"

Blinking at him, wide-eyed and flummoxed, Charlie says, "Um. Sour cream?"

The bartender winks. "Coming right up, guapo." After a minute, he returns with two little plastic cups of sour cream, which he slides across the bar to Charlie. His nails are painted a deep plum purple. "Girl problems?" he asks. When Charlie shakes his head, he leans across the bar and asks in a lower, knowing tone, "Boy problems?"

Charlie's eyes snap up to his. There's a gentle smile on the bartender's face, which relaxes the worry that hadn't quite bloomed to fullness yet. "M-maybe. A little. Um. Yeah."

With a nod, the bartender says, "Eat. It's on the house. And you tell me if you need a car to get home, okay? My brother drives for Uber."

The care of this complete stranger lights a little ember in Charlie's chest. "Okay," he says softly.

Someone signals for the bartender's attention down at the other end of the bar, and with a last smile for Charlie, he goes to help them.

There's still half a bottle of Modelo left, but Charlie's starting to feel queasy. The quesadilla smells incredible, all cheesy and greasy, with perfectly crisped tortilla lending it that carbohydrate solidity. He picks up a triangle, dips it in the sour cream, and takes a big bite. It's probably the best thing he's ever tasted.

He demolishes the quesadilla and is wiping his hands on a napkin when a voice says next to him, "Hey, Charlie? Do you mind if I join you?"

Charlie's shoulders stiffen. He turns to look at the speaker. Jason Miller is standing there, looking uncharacteristically nervous.

The seat next to Charlie is empty, but part of him wants to say no. Jason is mean. He's a bully, and he doesn't care if Gordon's kind of friendly with him. Cordial with him, maybe. And oh no, thinking of Gordon makes him sad, because maybe they're over? Maybe there's no Charlie and Gordon anymore. Maybe Charlie has no reason at all to give Jason the time of day.

Minnesota nice wins out. Charlie nods and pushes out the neighboring barstool. Jason takes a seat, and when the bartender returns to take his order, he gives Charlie a questioning look—definitely a *is this the boy?* look. Charlie shakes his head mutely.

Once Jason has his beer, he clears his throat and purposefully turns to face Charlie. "I thought that was your car outside. That's the only reason I came in. I, uh, I owe you an apology, Charlie. Probably, I don't know, a lifetime of apologies. I've been an asshole to you for a long time."

By this point, Charlie is staring, his mouth hanging open slightly. "What?" he finally manages. He has more to add, like, are you Jason's nice twin? Is this an *Invasion of the Body Snatchers* situation? Did you suffer a traumatic brain injury?

Or maybe the explanation is more prosaic and Jason is pretending to be decent as a prank.

Charlie closes his mouth and gives Jason a suspicious look. "Wh-why are you ap-pologizing to m-me?"

"Because, man, I've been giving you shit since high school. Or middle school, I don't know. A long time." Jason's face is red.

Charlie listens to the dull murmur of voices in the restaurant, the music that's faded into the background with the swell of the crowd, the clatter of plates and silverware, and the bartender speaking Spanish to one of the waitresses as she comes to pick up her table's drink order.

"Is this a joke?" he asks slowly. "Is this... just... to make me look stupid?"

Jason looks ashamed. Jason! Ashamed! Charlie didn't think he even had the capacity for that emotion. "No. No, I've been thinking about stuff. How I treat you. Some of the stuff I say." He pauses. "A lot of the stuff I say. Like calling you Charlie Manson."

"And the homophobic stuff," Charlie says clearly and stutter-free. It goes straight from his brain and out his mouth, and after the words land, he's not quite sure how he made it happen.

The last thing Charlie expects is for Jason to take a deep breath and nod. "Yeah. That too. I don't even know why I say that shit, man."

"Maybe because you don't like gay people."

With a wince, Jason says, "I... maybe. I don't know. It's not that I don't like gay people. I don't even really know any. Just you, and I've always been a jerk to you. So I don't know. I guess it was just easy to rag on you for that too."

There's a silence. Jason swallows a mouthful of beer. Charlie watches the fountain trickle in the corner. "You just h-had a change of heart? J-just like that?"

With a frank honesty that Charlie grudgingly appreciates, Jason says, "Not 'just like that.' Gordy about ripped me a new one a few weeks ago. I thought he was going to throw a punch when I said something about you."

The mention of Gordon makes Charlie flinch, which luckily Jason doesn't seem to notice. It takes a second for the rest of what Jason said to seep through his brain. The part about Gordon defending him. "Gordon defended me?" Charlie asks, just because it seems possible that maybe Jason's not remembering right or that Charlie misheard.

"Yeah, in the middle of Lakeside during happy hour." He shakes his head, a rueful expression on his face. "It was kind of a wake-up call, I guess. Like, that was a thing he was willing to do, stand up in front of half the town and say how great you were. And he just announced he was, what do you call it, bi. Like him liking dudes didn't matter one way or the other, and the rest of us were stupid for thinking it did."

Charlie's beer is almost gone and he decides he won't have another. There's a part of him that's so, *so* tempted to tell Jason to fuck off, that he doesn't need an apology and he certainly doesn't need Jason's approval.

A bigger part of him knows it will make him feel good for a few minutes, or maybe an hour at most. After that he'll just remember that someone did the brave thing and admitted they were wrong, and he threw it back in their face for a temporary hit of dopamine.

"I guess... apology accepted," Charlie says. He can't get the image of Gordon defending him out of his head. That was brave too. He doesn't think Gordon understands how brave he is to interrogate his sexuality in his thirties, to take a chance that he'd blow up his life by coming out to people. To then find his life blown up but to not go back into the closet, content to pass as straight the way he'd been doing.

In fact, Gordon's been incredibly brave these past few months, not just coming out but also coming back to the town he hated and being open-minded enough to consider it with new eyes. To not hang on to that hate and to find that there were reasons now to stay.

Charlie grips the edge of the bar as a wave of lightheadedness and nausea goes through him. It was definitely wrong of Gordon not to tell Charlie from the start that he planned to sell the property. But Gordon's right too—in the end, he decided not to. He wants to stay in Sawmill Lake.

God, Charlie hopes he didn't fuck that up.

"You okay, man?" Jason asks with concern, putting a steadying hand on Charlie's shoulder.

"I—um—yeah." No, but he's not going to sob on Jason Miller's shoulder, of all people.

Understanding transforms Jason's face. "Oh, shit. I know that look. That's the 'I fucked up bad' look."

"No!" Charlie says. Then, miserably, "Yeah."

Bro-ily, Jason pats his shoulder. Charlie doesn't hate it. There's never been anyone to console him through things like this. Ibrahim was never into offering comfort—he always believed in throwing yourself into work until things didn't hurt so much. That's always worked for Charlie before. Or maybe all he was doing was deferring his need for comfort.

"Will flowers make it better?" Jason asks, playing flawlessly to the most clichéd version of the clueless straight man.

"They p-probably wouldn't hurt." Truthfully, Charlie has no idea how to go about fixing this. He's never been in a relationship, so he's never had a fight and he's never had to find a way to make up after one.

Patting his shoulder again, Jason says, "You'll be okay. I could tell how Gordy felt about you that night at Lakeside. He's crazy about you." He hesitates. "That's how I knew I was wrong about a shit-ton of stuff. 'Cause I didn't think anyone would look like that if there was something gross or wrong about it."

Why does every revelation about Gordon have to be wrapped up in the simultaneous revelation that Jason isn't a complete troglodyte? Gordon's crazy about him? Obviously, Charlie's crazy about Gordon, but the reverse being true seems so much less likely.

"This is a weird day," Charlie finally says.

"Yeah." Jason swirls his beer in his glass before taking another sip. "I think I'm gonna lose my job, so there's that."

"Oh. Sorry."

Jason shrugs, though it's obvious he's unhappy about it. "It was probably stupid to think I could be a realtor. Whatever. I didn't come in here to talk about myself." He turns on the stool to face Charlie again. "Are we good?"

Charlie feels his face twist. "Maybe eventually. If you put your m-money wh-where your mouth is."

For a few seconds, Jason looks stymied, like he really expected that after years—decades!—of targeted assholery, Charlie's going to forgive him with one conversation. But he nods slowly and finally says, "Yeah, okay. I get that."

Charlie nods in return, and the two of them sit in silence, both of their beers finished. "You having another one?" Jason asks, indicating Charlie's empty bottle with a jerk of his chin. When Charlie shakes his head, Jason adds, "Want a ride home? You look like you've had a few."

"You knew I was drunk and you s-still had that conversation with me?" Charlie asks accusingly.

With a shrug, Jason replies, "You're the most sober drunk person I've ever seen. Pretty sure you still shouldn't drive, though."

Ugh, Jason isn't a complete troglodyte, *and* he doesn't let people drive drunk? Is this real, or has Charlie crossed into a parallel dimension?

"Okay," Charlie acquiesces grudgingly.

Jason signals to the bartender, waving away Charlie's cash when he fumbles it out of his wallet. "I got this," Jason says, which leaves Charlie no choice but to mumble "Thanks."

As they both get up to leave, the bartender reaches across the bar to put a hand lightly on Charlie's wrist. "Hey. Do you know him?"

The affronted expression on Jason's face makes Charlie snort with laughter. "Yeah. He's a jerk. But he's harmless."

"I'm a jerk who just bought your five Modelos," Jason grouses.

The bartender nods. Impulsively, Charlie says, "What's your n-name?" before adding, "I'm Charlie. This is Jason. My boyfriend yelled at him and n-now he's not a homophobe anymore."

Maybe he's drunker than he thinks he is.

Giving Jason a speculative up-and-down, the bartender says, "I'm Sebastian. Here's my number just in case." He scribbles it on the back of beer-ringed cardboard coaster and pushes it into Charlie's hand. It's sweet. Where did all these sweet people come from? "You call me if you need help, okay?"

"Okay," Charlie says, holding it against his chest for a second before putting it in his pocket.

They head out to the parking lot. It's dark now, and cold. Charlie's breath fogs in the air, shot through with streaks of orange lights illuminating the asphalt and the cars. Windshields and windows are frosty and glittering.

"There's a parade, right?" Jason asks.

Charlie wrests his attention away from the weird beauty of the parking lot and back to Jason. "Parade?"

"Yeah. For Gay Pride? They have a big parade in the Cities, right?"

It takes Charlie a second to process this. "Pride. It's just Pride."

"Right, yeah. Sorry."

"Duluth has a festival too."

"And a parade!" Jason sounds really proud of himself. "I saw that while I was looking at stuff online. We could have one in Sawmill Lake, too."

"You were d-doing research… on queer stuff," Charlie says faintly.

Jason's car beeps as he unlocks it. "How else am I supposed to learn anything?" he asks like Charlie's the idiot. They get into the car, which smells like Scotchgard. It's clean inside. As Jason turns the key in the ignition, he says, "I watched some gay porn, too, which—"

"Oh my *god*." Charlie claps his hands over his ears and sinks down in the passenger seat. "No, nope, no, I don't want to hear about your porn habits."

"It's not a habit!" Jason protests. The heat comes on before they've even turned out of the parking lot. The blast of air doesn't quite drown out Jason's innocent, "Yet."

Charlie pretends to gag, Jason laughs, and they pull onto the highway, headlights cutting through the dark to illuminate the way back to Sawmill Lake.

Chapter Twenty-Six

GORDON WASN'T exactly at his best for the rest of the meeting with Joel. Forget saving Jason's job, it's all he can do to save himself the embarrassment of breaking down crying and mainlining an entire pumpkin pie by himself. He never got this emotional when he was with Becky. That probably should tell him something, but in the aftermath of the fight with Charlie, all he can think about is how unfair Charlie was and how Charlie *lied* about the *two million* freaking *dollars*.

So when he sat back down in the booth in Edna's and Joel said, "So, what are you thinking? Should I get the contract ready?" Gordon just looked at him blankly.

"I'm not going to sell," he said, because regardless of what just went down outside, selling to some developer who's going to tear down the woods and pave over the fields isn't something he's interested in. Gordon is leaving the land for the deer and the rabbits and the raccoons, the coyotes he's heard yipping and howling at night, the fox that noses around his yard.

He's leaving it for the owls, for the little saw-whets who made him realize he was good at something and that it wasn't too late to run toward a thing he wanted instead of away from the stuff he didn't.

Joel looked ticked off, though, which probably doesn't bode well for Jason. Gordon will call him.

After the meeting—after the fight—Gordon makes himself concentrate on work. He sets up meetings and takes notes, suggests timelines and pushes people to commit to deliverables.

A thought sneaks into his head as four o'clock approaches: If his grandfather had left two million dollars to him instead of Charlie, then he wouldn't have to do this stupid job that seems more pointless today than it ever has. Is this how the rest of his life goes? He logs into work and fills his day with tasks that add nothing meaningful to the world, and then he does it all over again the next day?

He doesn't even care about his grandpa leaving Charlie money. If he'd found out any other way except in the middle of a fight, he would have been thrilled! Charlie deserves two million dollars. Gordon can't think of anyone who deserves two million dollars more than Charlie. He'll have money for the GPS trackers he wants to put on the male saw-whets he catches. He'll be able to get the equipment he needs to follow them into Canada. That money will fund his dream, and that's a good thing.

Except it got all mixed up in anger and escalation, and now Gordon can't stop feeling this dumb twist of bitterness. All he wants is to call Charlie and ask if they can talk, to see if they can fix this (they have to be able to fix this, right?). But every time he starts to reach for his phone, he thinks, *Charlie knew that he got the money while I just got the house and the land, and he's probably been laughing at me this whole time.*

It doesn't even make any sense. Was his grandpa senile? Why give Gordon the land and Charlie the money, when the land means the most to Charlie and Gordon could have used the money to finally pay off his student loans?

He scrubs at his face and locks his computer a few minutes past four, unable to devote any more fraying concentration to work. There's an email notification on his phone from the company he ordered his new bed from letting him know the delivery will be two days from now. That gives him something to focus on besides the hole in his heart—he has to decide what room is going to be his bedroom and finally stop sleeping on the couch.

There are two rooms upstairs, an office and his grandpa's bedroom. The office is small and the ceiling slopes down with the gabled roof on one side. It's perfect for a kid's room, not so great for an adult.

It shouldn't make the hole in his heart gobble up more space in his chest to think about that room making a good kid's room. He and Charlie have been together for a month, if that. Kids have rightly not crossed Gordon's mind. Well, until now. And now he's thinking they blew it. They blew something great before it even got off the ground.

So yeah. He's going to face the creepiness factor of converting his grandpa's room to his own. It's fine—it's not like he died in there or anything.

Gordon closes his laptop and tosses it to the cushion next to him before he gets up and stretches. The stairs creak when he walks up them, his feet heavy. Standing in the door of the bedroom, surveying it, the idea of clearing it out seems as daunting as ever. Maybe more, because there was this assumption in the back of his head that Charlie would be here to help him.

Charlie would have wanted some of Gordon's grandpa's things because they would have meant something to him. And while they cleaned the room, they could have flirted about all the stuff they were going to do in the new bed. Now it's just going to be Gordon hauling this stuff out. He might have to call Jason to ask for help, after all.

Rubbing his face again, Gordon makes himself step across the threshold. When it feels like any other step into a room, he scoffs at himself. Did he think his grandpa was haunting this place?

The bed is a double, with metal head- and footboards, those ones that are supposed to look like wrought iron but are just hollow steel. Those are manageable on his own. The mattress and box spring, on the other hand, are a two-person job. Lifting them isn't the problem, it will be getting them down that narrow staircase.

Other than that, the room is sparsely furnished. A small dresser with nothing on the top. A nightstand with a drawer sitting next to the bed. There's a reading lamp on the nightstand and a book, but nothing else. The closet is open, with clothes hung neatly on hangers.

There are a few pieces of art on the walls—sketches of hawks and falcons that now Gordon wonders about. Did his grandpa draw them? There's a framed photo as well, which has gone muted and sepia-toned with age. Gordon draws closer to study it.

It's a young couple, a man and a woman, standing in front of a door with ornate metal scrollwork. To one side of the photo, cut off, is a window with more of the ornate metalwork, with what looks like a metal screen set into the center. The design on the screen is just as detailed as the metal, if not more. A palm tree is growing off to the other side of the photo. The building the couple is in front of looks like it's made out of concrete, and the thin strip of sky visible at the top of the photo is a hard, hot, desert blue.

Gordon looks more closely at the couple, unsurprised when it's a little like looking at a younger, more Middle Eastern version of himself. It must be his grandpa, and the way he and the woman are holding each other makes Gordon think she's his grandmother.

If his grandpa was a mystery, Gordon's grandmother is like the parents in fairy tales. You know they must have existed at one point, but they have no bearing on the story. Gordon's mom almost never talked about her. When Gordon asked once as a little kid, she just said that her mother had died a long time ago. She's short, probably just over five feet tall, and pretty, with a cheerful smile and curly black hair that she's wearing uncovered. She looks like his mom.

They look happy in the photo. Young and in love. Suddenly, Gordon is hit with fierce longing to know these people. Was this taken before they came to America? It doesn't look like America. It looks like Iraq, probably? Why did they leave? Were they running? Were they scared? Or were they just looking for a better life, the same as any of the other immigrants who came to America over the years? He'll never know, and it makes him sad.

Curiously, Gordon takes the frame off the wall and slides the photo out, hoping for something written on the back to identify when and where it was taken.

There's something written, but it's in Arabic: البصرة

Gordon makes a frustrated noise and sits on the bed, bringing the picture with him, while he figures out how to type Arabic letters on his phone. It takes so long that when he finally figures it out and gets it translated, his shoulders ache from hunching.

At least he has a straightforward answer. The writing means Basra. Is that where his grandparents were from?

There's no one left who knows. His dad is useless—Mom's Iraqi heritage was always more of a footnote to him than anything else, and it was very obvious that he'd never valued any kind of relationship with Mom's one remaining parent. Gordon never heard his dad push for a reconciliation between his mom and grandpa.

Charlie is his only connection to his grandfather. And now everything's fucked up with Charlie, because Charlie doesn't see the difference between something that might have happened and what *actually* happened. And because Charlie kept the two million from him.

What really bothers him is how Charlie doesn't trust him. That's what it comes down to, doesn't it? He doesn't trust him. Obviously he doesn't trust him, because if he did, he wouldn't have been so fast to think the worst of Gordon. If Charlie trusted him, he wouldn't have kept the two million dollars a secret all this time.

Gordon's grip on the photo tightens, crimping lines into the edges. He slides it back into the frame and hangs it on the wall again. He'll take it down later when he figures out how he wants to decorate the room. Or maybe he'll leave it there, who knows. It's a tether to his grandpa, even if it's a thin one.

With a deep breath, Gordon checks out the dresser. It's three drawers and comes up just past Gordon's waist. Opening the first drawer feels weird, but when all he sees are some flannel shirts folded in neat piles, smelling of nothing but laundry detergent and the faint wood smell of decent furniture, the other drawers are easier. There are jeans in one and boxers and undershirts in the other. Everything looks soft and worn, but still in good condition. He can donate it to a thrift store.

The closet is even more spare, just a few pieces of formal clothing. One suit with huge eighties shoulder pads, a couple blazers, and a couple pairs of slacks. None of it looks like it's been worn in at least two decades. That can go to a thrift store too. There's probably someone around here looking for a costume for an eighties party.

That just leaves the nightstand. The paperback is a tattered old John Grisham novel. The pages are dog-eared and there's a receipt stuck about two-thirds of the way through. A smile sneaks onto Gordon's face. He's not much of a reader, himself, but when he occasionally picks up a book, he does the same thing, grabbing whatever's laying around to use as a bookmark.

Maybe he'll try reading this one. It will tell him something else about his grandpa, even if it's a little thing. He'll know his grandpa liked this book.

Or maybe he was hate-reading it. That's a possibility too, Gordon guesses.

He opens the drawer and his heart stutters. Staring up at him from the top of a stack of papers is a children's book. There's a boy on the cover, a brown kid in a thawb with a desert landscape in the background and a falcon flying at his shoulder.

A memory barrels into him as he stands, bent at the waist, looking at the book like it's a magical relic. Like he's Indiana Fucking Jones and he just found the Arc of the Covenant, and it might incinerate him if he touches it. He's sitting on the porch of this house, his legs swinging free on a wooden bench, the boundary between the shade of the porch and the bright day sharp on the lawn. A kind voice with an accent reads to him slowly while a strong, weathered brown hand points out each word. There's a glossy bluish falcon on the railing in front of him, shaking its feathers every so often. Leather bands hang from both of its legs. One has a longer leather cord clipped on, which is tied securely around the railing.

His throat tightens as he finally reaches for the book. It's as eighties as the clothes hanging in the closet. Now Gordon knows where he saw this book and what happened to it. His grandpa kept it. Or maybe his mom wouldn't let Gordon have it, so she left it with her father on the last day they spoke.

Gordon sits on the bed as he holds the book in his hands. The springs creak and there's a faint dusty smell. Slowly, he opens the front cover.

An envelope slides into his lap. Gordon's heart clenches. Why is there an envelope in this book? Gordon doesn't want to have this kind of temptation dangled in front of him. Things were different that first time he drove up here, resentful of this town and his estranged grandfather. Now he's too hungry for connection to this man he'll only ever know in the past tense to possibly respect the privacy of either his grandpa or whoever he wrote this letter to.

He flips the envelope over and gets sucker punched by the name written in neat block letters on the front.

His name.

The envelope is shaking. No, those are his own hands. He's trembling. Even though it's a different language, a different alphabet entirely, it's clear that the writing on the back of the photo and on this envelope were written by the same hand. It's like a ghost is looking over his shoulder.

An urge grabs him to shove the envelope back in the book and shove the book back in the nightstand drawer, and close the drawer, get rid of the nightstand, never know what his grandpa wanted to say to him.

His hands are already opening the envelope, though, not giving his brain a chance to catch up and pump the brakes. Still shaking, he pulls out and opens the sheets of lined paper inside.

At first his eyes glaze over, unable to focus on or make sense of the small, neat writing covering the papers. He breathes slowly and smooths the sheets over his leg. He's afraid, he realizes. He's afraid that the only thing he'll ever hear from his grandfather is bad. What if the letter says he's glad he didn't have any contact with Gordon?

Only one way to find out. He takes another deep breath and reads.

Gordon,

If you find this note, it will be because I was as cowardly in my last days as I've been my entire life. I've told myself for many years that your mother's wish was for me not to intrude on your life, so I would respect that. Your mother has been gone for years now, الله يرحمها but I kept the promise I made her. I think I've always known, deep down, that it is really my fear of how you'd welcome, or not welcome, contact from me that kept me from reaching out. You don't know me. My memories of you are so clear, but I don't think you would remember me at all.

You were a sweet boy. Sensitive and curious, so interested in the world around you. We would sit on the porch together and watch insects, birds, and animals. You loved my birds. Zarqaa was your favorite because she was so interested in you, too.

I've never been brave enough to reach out to you, but I've tried to follow your life as well as I could on the internet. Charlie taught me how to use Facebook, even though he said no one uses it anymore except old people. I told him that I'm an old person, so it's the right place for me! I'll get to Charlie, though.

I wish I had gotten to see you grow up. You seem like a kind man who cares for his friends and family. I saw that you were engaged to be married, and then not engaged anymore, and that this happened recently. This is a terrible time for me to die and leave you this house, but leaving you the house was the best way I could think of to make you come back here.

Now I'll tell you about Charlie. Charlie is like a son, or maybe more like a grandson. You'll wonder if he was your replacement and I'll assure you he wasn't. He was family that I gained through happenstance and a shared love of this place. He's good and kind, with the best heart of anyone I've ever known. He's also shy, and you may think he doesn't have anything to say. He does, and once he trusts you, he'll make you think and make you laugh. I have a feeling you would like him very much. Maybe that's wishful thinking, but I prefer to think it's intuition.

I'm leaving all of my money to him. I hope that doesn't upset you. I know you have debts from college. If necessary, you can sell the house and land, but I hope you don't do that either. What I want is for you and Charlie to meet. I know that even if you only spent a small amount of time together, you would like him, and he would like you. Yes, I'm matchmaking. Maybe I'm making the wrong assumption about you, but I don't think I am.

There is a clause in my will that directs my money to only be given to Charlie once you pass my bird banding and falconry gear to him. If you don't know what that is, he'll show you. I'm sorry to play games, but this was the only way I could think of to make sure the two of you would meet. It will sound silly if I say I know that you'll make sure Charlie receives the money I'm leaving him, but I know. Intuition again, maybe. His address is enclosed.

I'm sorry that I didn't get to watch you grow up or see the man you've become except through the screen of my computer. I still treasured that I got even that much.

Go meet Charlie. You could make each other happy. That's what I want for both of you. Make each other happy.

With love,
Jiddi

Jiddi—Grandpa. Gordon remembers joyfully calling it out and running across the front yard to be scooped up in his grandfather's arms.

Tears sting his eyes and he reads the letter again from top to bottom, his mind quiet as he lets his grandpa's words wash over him.

There are things missing—like what happened between him and Gordon's mom, and how his grandpa figured out he was queer—but this is more than Gordon ever expected. It feels sort of silly and childish, but it's almost like he had a guardian angel watching over him all these years. His mom was gone and his dad stopped caring, but his grandpa never did.

Jiddi. It feels right to think of him as Jiddi.

And he feels like an asshole for getting mad at Charlie about the money. Not just the money. He feels like an asshole for not being up front with Charlie about his plans. From the start, he knew how important this land was. Even if he didn't understand the full emotional significance, he knew that selling it would be a blow, and maybe Charlie wouldn't have a logical response to finding out, even retroactively, what Gordon was planning.

You could make each other happy, Jiddi wrote. God, Charlie makes Gordon so happy. And he threw a tantrum about money? Or was it not about the money at all? Was it actually about the fact that Charlie got Ibrahim in his life and Gordon didn't? Maybe instead of getting defensive and bent out of shape, Gordon could have taken a breath. He and Charlie both have wounds, and some of them may be scars, but some are fresh. It's naive to think they'll never have disagreements with each other, but they can disagree without opening any more wounds.

Gordon looks up from the letter. It got dark while he was sitting here. His back twinges as he stands. Too long sitting hunched over on an old mattress. He fumbles for the light in the hallway, which illuminates the stairs enough for him to find his way down to the first floor. His phone buzzes in his pocket as he picks his way across the living room in the dark. Maybe it's Charlie—

Oh. Right. No, Charlie probably isn't texting him. Charlie's probably doing something fun and not thinking about Gordon at all. Of course, it's Charlie, so "something fun" is probably like, entering data into the Bird Banding Lab website.

A smile pulls at his lips as regret hitches in his chest. Regardless, he's probably not thinking about Gordon.

Gordon turns on the living room light and looks at his phone. Not entirely surprisingly, the text is from Jason. *Thx for meeting with Joel. Doesn't look good for my job but fingers crossed*

With a wince, Gordon texts back, *Sorry, man. I think I maybe just made things worse for you.* He hesitates, then adds, *Things kind of went to shit*

Yeah, I kind of figured, since I found your boyfriend sucking down Modelos in El Loro del Norte. Joel said he showed up during lunch and spooked you

For a second, Gordon can't entirely unpack the component parts of this message. There's the casual reference to Charlie as Gordon's boyfriend, which he wouldn't have expected Jason to do in… maybe not a million years, but a hundred, at least. There's the fact that Joel apparently thinks that Charlie had something to do with Gordon not signing on the dotted line with Joel.

And there's the part about Charlie drinking alone in El Loro del Norte, which a quick google shows is a Mexican restaurant in Hibbing. At least, Gordon assumes Charlie was drinking alone. He hopes Charlie was drinking alone. Oh god. What if he wasn't drinking alone? What if that wasn't just a fight? What if Charlie's so done with him that he's out trying to hook up?

He agonizes over his phone before forcing himself to type, *Was Charlie with someone?*

Not until I got there. I drove him home, btw. Dropped him off a few minutes ago

Down with paternalistic bullshit and everything, but Gordon sighs with relief to hear Charlie isn't drowning his sorrows in some other guy's body. He desperately wants to go over to Charlie's house, but if he's drunk, maybe it's a bad idea. He might be influenced by alcohol to make decisions that he wouldn't make sober.

His phone buzzes again with another text from Jason. *I'm not exactly Mr Good At Relationships, but I'd go over there if I were you*

Jason advising him to go to Charlie's house is exactly the thing that should make Gordon decide *not* to go, because yeah, he trusts Jason's relationship expertise about as far as he can throw the guy. But in the end, he grabs his keys and heads outside to his car.

Bad idea or not, he needs to see Charlie. He needs to apologize and maybe, *maybe*, if he's really lucky, he'll get to hold the man he loves again.

If he's really lucky, he'll get to tell Charlie that he loves him.

Chapter Twenty-Seven

FIVE MODELOS is too many. Charlie's very sure of that. He doesn't know where the cutoff is between pleasant drunk haze and I'm-going-to-puke misery, but he definitely crossed it at some point tonight. Does that make him a lightweight? What's a normal amount of beer to consume before throwing up?

Charlie squeezes his eyes shut and leans his forehead against the wall. He's standing in the hall between the kitchen and the living room, one arm braced over his head and the other curled over his stomach. Whether he's a lightweight or not, and how much beer is normal before you throw it up, is probably better pondered when his stomach isn't on the verge of revolting. His preference is to not vomit, so thinking this much about vomiting probably isn't helping him with that goal.

A headache is edging around the boundaries of his awareness, too—sharp prickling in his temples that doesn't linger more than a second or two. He'd head that off with ibuprofen if he thought he'd keep it down.

Dammit. Now he's thinking about puking again.

He clenches his teeth hard, hard enough to feel his jaw pop and his molars creak. Ever since his mom went through chemo, he's hated throwing up, probably to an irrational level. It reminds him of her being sick and how helpless he was. The smell of vomit is inextricably linked to death and his own failure to keep his mom alive.

Deep breath. In, then out. Another. It wasn't his fault. It's not his fault that Ibrahim died, either. He can't make the people he loves stay in his life through force of will and the strength of his want.

Gordon's proof of that. Charlie wanted him to stay so, so much. And now he might go because Charlie overreacted.

The nausea recedes a tiny bit, which doesn't make much sense, since the most sickening thing of all is the idea of losing Gordon.

Right then, the doorbell rings. Charlie pushes himself off the wall a little, keeping his forearm braced over his head. Who would come to his door at this time? Actually, he has no idea what time it is, but it's dark, and he's been wallowing in nausea for a while.

He should ignore it. He should lie down and hope he feels better in the morning. But a stupid little voice in his head whispers that maybe it's Gordon, and that's enough to make him drag himself to the door.

It's not going to be Gordon. It's probably a delivery, something he forgot he ordered. It's too much to hope that Gordon will show up at his door twice wanting to make amends.

But when he swings open the door, Gordon is standing there.

Charlie's heart surges in a way that doesn't do his stomach any favors, but he doesn't care. Gordon's here, and that means Charlie can say he's sorry for the way he acted.

"I'm sorry," he blurts at the same time Gordon says, "I love you."

For a rare moment, there's nothing in Charlie's brain. It's white noise. Television static. The silence at the end of an album.

"What?" is what finally comes out of his mouth.

When Charlie opened the door, Gordon looked determined, but his face flips to trepidation. Nonetheless, he repeats the words that Charlie's brain is insisting he said, even as his heart can't quite believe it: "I love you."

Neither of them moves. Charlie's mouth opens but nothing comes out.

Wait. No. Something is definitely about to come out.

He claps a hand over his mouth, turns around, and bolts for the bathroom, where he falls to his knees, hunching over the toilet, and heaves a good portion of the five Modelos and the quesadilla into the bowl.

Tears and snot run more with each convulsion of his stomach, and through the sheer physical misery, all he can think is how he couldn't have fucked up this moment much more spectacularly. Gordon probably left. Anyone would.

A hand soothes across his shoulders before rubbing between his shoulder blades. "Well, I got laughed at once for saying that, but no one's ever thrown up," Gordon says, sounding unfairly, impossibly fond.

Charlie tries to laugh, but it comes out as more of a gurgly cough. He cannot, he absolutely *cannot*, tell Gordon that he loves him when he's hanging over the toilet with a string of pukey saliva dangling from his lip.

He grabs for some toilet paper to wipe his mouth and nose, flushes the toilet, and straightens. Gordon's hand stays on his back, still rubbing small, comforting circles. "I love you too," Charlie says. He thinks about it. "Or maybe you want to take it back. In that case, it's just I love you."

Gordon's face breaks into a wide, bright smile. "Not taking it back." With his thumbs, he wipes the tears from Charlie's cheeks. The gesture almost makes Charlie cry for real, and it's only with effort that he forces down the lump in his throat.

At least it's not vomit.

"Did you get it all out, or do you need to…?" Gordon motions to the toilet.

Shaking his head, Charlie says, "I think that's it." Now that he threw up, he feels much better.

With a grunt, Gordon pushes himself to his feet before helping Charlie stand. He slips a hand behind Charlie's head to pull him closer, but Charlie puts his hand over his mouth again. "I can't kiss you right after I threw up!" Charlie says, the words a little muffled by his palm.

But Gordon laughs and kisses the back of Charlie's hand, then stands on his toes to kiss his cheek. "You totally can, but brush your teeth if it makes you feel better."

He does, Gordon's hands resting on his hips the entire time. When he's done, he barely has time to turn around before Gordon's there, crowding him back against the wall, his heat and bulk pressing Charlie's spine and shoulders to the cold tile. Gordon threads his fingers in Charlie's hair again, and this time Charlie lets him pull their faces close so their lips can meet in a kiss that's slow and soft, deep as the blue night sky and just as spangled with stars.

Charlie sinks into the kiss, letting their fight drift away like dandelion fluff. Eventually they'll stop kissing, and Gordon will stop gently tugging Charlie's hair between his fingers, and Charlie will rejoin the real world where everything isn't gilt and perfect.

The kiss ends, but instead of pulling back, Gordon brushes his lips against the corner of Charlie's, then along the line of his jaw, then on the sensitive spot below his ear. Only after he lingers there for several long seconds, his breath warm and gentle against Charlie's skin, does he tilt back to look Charlie in the eye. His throat moves as he swallows, and Charlie can see the thrum of his pulse.

"I'm sorry I wasn't up front with you about my plans." Gordon strokes the back of Charlie's head. "I lied to myself for a while that if I didn't sell until after you were done banding, you wouldn't hate me. But if I'm being really honest, I was lying to myself that I was going to sell at all after I met you."

Charlie slides his hands over Gordon's shoulders to loop them around his neck. Shaking his head, he says, "*I'm* sorry. I overreacted."

For some reason, that makes Gordon look fierce. "You didn't overreact. You reacted like someone who got blindsided. You don't have to downplay what you felt." When Charlie gives him a wry look, Gordon offers him a sheepish half smile. "But I'm not mad if you're going to forgive me."

Charlie hugs him tightly, and Gordon presses his face into the crook of his neck. "I'm sorry I didn't tell you about the money too. I swear, I was never trying to get anything. I loved Ibrahim—"

"I know. I know." Gordon sounds ashamed. "I can't believe I said that. I know he was family to you. You were to him too. You know that, right?"

A thick, hard knot of grief pushes against Charlie's sternum, the same knot of grief he's been trying to do something with ever since his mom died. Now, though, something different happens. Something threads through the grief—acceptance or healing or love—and it loosens and sinks away, dispersing through him.

"I shouldn't have said that when you're not feeling well," Gordon says, pulling back to look up at Charlie.

"No, no—thank you. I mean, I knew that. But it's nice to hear it." Charlie thinks for a second. "Are you just saying that? How do you know?"

"I found a letter." Amazement crosses Gordon's face, like even though he said the words, he can't quite believe them. God, Charlie will never get tired of watching him. His face is so expressive. It reminds Charlie of the play of light and shadow as clouds cross the sun. "He wrote me a letter before he died. I think I was supposed to find it right away, but I didn't until a few hours ago when I was cleaning out his bedroom. He talked about...." But he trails off, his gaze far away for a second. "A lot. He talked about a lot. You can read it. But he talked about you. And me. He wanted us to meet. That's why I got the house, to make me come back here."

"So we could meet?" Charlie asks, his breath catching.

Gordon nods. "He knew about me being bi somehow. Or about me not being straight, anyway. He wanted us to meet each other because he thought we'd make each other happy."

Charlie presses his lips to Gordon's forehead and squeezes shut his eyes, overcome by the magnitude of everything that's happened today. The fight, the bar, the conversation with Jason. Gordon coming here and being in love with him. A letter from Ibrahim, where he gives their relationship his blessing because he had a feeling they'd be good together.

It's like Gordon senses that Charlie's getting overwhelmed. His arms go around Charlie's waist, solid and strong, and he says, "C'mon. Let's get you to bed. You should sleep. Christ, I should've waited until tomorrow to tell you everything."

As he tugs Charlie away from the wall and steers him toward the bedroom, Charlie says, "I'm glad you told me. Also I love you, did I say that?"

"Yeah," Gordon says with a huff of laughter. "But I don't mind hearing it again."

"I'll say it as many times as you want," Charlie promises. Maybe it's just because bed is within spitting distance, but exhaustion drops around him like a heavy blanket. "As many times as you want and as long as you want."

The tender expression on Gordon's face nearly undoes Charlie. It's all he can do to get undressed and crawl into bed, and once he's under the covers, he reaches for Gordon. "Stay?"

"Yeah," Gordon says. There's a roughness to his voice, like water over pebbles washing away the hurts they inflicted on each other today. "Yeah, of course I'll stay."

He strips down to his boxer briefs, and even though it's a struggle to keep his eyes open, Charlie does his best so he can appreciate Gordon's body. When Gordon climbs into bed, Charlie gets to appreciate it against his own. Snuggling close, Charlie mumbles, "I'll be human again in the morning."

Gordon's chuckle is a low rumble in his chest, and it's so sexy that Charlie almost makes an attempt to not pass out. So instead he murmurs again, "I'll love you as long as you want."

Maybe it's just his brain conjuring things as he drops off into sleep, but he swears that Gordon murmurs back, "What if I want it for always?"

GRAY DAWN light, the color of a dove's wing, wakes Charlie. His mouth feels sticky and tastes like mint and garbage, and the ache in his temples is trying to decide if it wants to progress to full-blown headache. His stomach feels better, though.

More importantly, there's a warm, sleep-heavy body next to him, breathing deep and slow, which means that everything that happened last night was real and not drunk dreams conjured by his brain because it desperately wanted everything to be right.

Somehow, everything *is* right, no fantasizing necessary.

Charlie shifts onto his side and Gordon mumbles in his sleep, sliding his arm across Charlie's hip and drawing him possessively nearer. It's nice, this feeling of belonging to someone. This feeling that he matters so much to another person that their lives couldn't be untangled from each other, like they're two vines who crept in each other's direction over years and years and once they met, twined together and grew toward the sun.

The feeling is so good that he wonders if he should have tried harder to have it before, with someone else, because then he'd have some idea what he's doing. It's funny how they're both inexperienced in different ways. Of the two of them, Gordon's inexperience with gay sex is easier to remedy.

It will be okay, though. He just knows, somehow. Whenever he met someone in Duluth for a hookup, he never felt right about trying to see them again. There was never anything there except physical attraction. It's different with Gordon.

"You're thinking about stuff," Gordon murmurs, his eyes still closed.

Charlie moves closer to him, hooking a leg over Gordon's thigh. Not that there isn't plenty of physical attraction with Gordon. "Us," he says, loving the sound of it.

A slow smile blooms sleepily across Gordon's face. "So you're still okay with me being in love with you this morning?" He tightens his arm around Charlie's waist and tugs him closer. Morning wood presses into the crease of Charlie's thigh and crotch, making him shiver as blood rushes south.

"I should be asking you." Charlie wiggles closer, giving his hips a little twitch as his dick plumps. "Since I threw up after you said it to me." Not sexy. Why did he say that?

But Gordon laughs and opens his eyes. For a second, Charlie lets himself get lost in their warmth and the rich brown of his irises, flecked with amber and ringed by a thin band of hazel that's almost gray. Why don't people ever talk about how beautiful brown eyes are? Why doesn't anyone ever acknowledge the complexity and interplay of all the different shades of brown you can see in one person's eyes?

Gordon splays his hand at the small of Charlie's back, kneading. His fingers dip into the waistband of Charlie's boxer briefs and Charlie can't help a little exhale of pleasure. Gordon moves his fingers lower, finding the curve of Charlie's ass, while he keeps his eyes locked on Charlie's. "I love watching you," he says. "It's so sexy to watch you get turned on."

By now, his whole hand is inside Charlie's underwear, and he cups one side of Charlie's ass and squeezes. Charlie can't stop his moan or the way he hitches his arm around Gordon's neck, pulling their bodies together chest to chest, hip to hip, thigh to thigh.

"Yeah," Gordon whispers. "That's it, baby." He traces Charlie's cleft from top to bottom a few times, maddeningly slowly and pushing a little deeper inside each time, until he finally delves down to feather the tip of his finger over Charlie's rim. "So fucking sexy," Gordon says. He still hasn't taken his eyes off Charlie's face.

There's not space in Charlie's body to contain the heat Gordon's creating. It's rising to his chest and his face. His hips are moving, pushing into Gordon so their erections grind together.

With his free hand, Gordon pushes Charlie's boxer briefs down around his knees, then grips both their cocks to jack them together. His eyelids finally flutter as he lets out a throaty groan. "Fuck, Charlie. That big dick feels so good."

Charlie gasps with the pleasure and the hotness and Gordon's sheer shocking debauchery. He could probably come from listening to Gordon dirty talk into his ear alone.

He touches every part of Gordon's body he can get to, rolling down his underwear just far enough that they make a little shelf for his ass, which makes it even bouncier and fuller, so Charlie can get two really good handfuls. And there are shoulders and arms, lats and obliques and the ledges of Gordon's hips.

And Gordon's still teasing his hole, circling and massaging, until he breaches it up to his first knuckle. When Charlie makes a helpless sound, Gordon wriggles downward. "Lie on your stomach," Gordon says. Charlie does, feeling like he's floating in a pink and gold haze. Maybe he's still a little drunk.

Gordon flings the covers off them and the cool air curls against Charlie's skin, a scalding contrast to the heat between them. As Gordon kisses down Charlie's spine, across the small of his back and over the swell of his ass, Charlie fucks the sheets under him slowly, seeking friction and not wanting it at the same time.

When Gordon spreads him and licks his hole, it's not exactly a surprise. Gordon said he's always wanted to do this, and they didn't get the chance the other night. But the stardust fire of nerve endings all crackling to life—*that's* a surprise. He jerks and cries out and Gordon chuckles, the buzz against Charlie's hole defying his brain's ability to categorize.

Rimming is good. Charlie knows this. The superlatives haven't been invented to describe how it feels to have Gordon rimming him. Gordon spreads him wider and gets in deeper, and time gets floaty and disconnected from reality. Reality becomes the light and heat racing in spirals over Charlie's body, first outward from Gordon's tongue and fingers as he touches and strokes, tugs and squeezes, and then the opposite direction, curling and gathering in his hips as his muscles wind tighter and tighter.

He's about to tip over the edge when Gordon pulls away with a filthy, wet sucking sound. "Do you like getting fucked?"

It takes Charlie a second to remember how to talk. At first all that comes out is a groan, but then he manages, "Mm, yeah."

"Good, because your hole is begging to be fucked right now." A thick finger slides inside Charlie with no resistance, and he arches toward it—or—into it? It feels so good. "You're soaking. And so loose."

"Gor," Charlie pleads.

The grounding weight on Charlie's legs vanishes as Gordon scrambles off the bed for the bedside table, where lube is sitting comfortably beside a stack of books. When he returns, he nudges Charlie with a knee until Charlie rolls onto his back. The sight of Gordon slicking himself with lube makes him groan, and Gordon, who's watching Charlie, licks his lips.

"You want this cock?" Gordon closes his fist around himself and pumps slowly, letting out a grunt. Charlie can't make his mouth form the words to agree, so he just nods. "Say it," Gordon says, reaching down to smear lube over Charlie's ass.

For a second, all Charlie's throat will do is work soundlessly as Gordon looks down at him, a finger rubbing Charlie's hole. His eyes are dark with sex and his hairline is damp. His beard has been scraping against Charlie and he reaches out, his hand feeling weirdly disconnected from the rest of his body, to rub his palm over Gordon's face.

Gordon turns into Charlie's hand and kisses the center of his palm, his eyes closing and dark eyelashes fanning across his cheekbones before he opens them again to give Charlie a sly, sidelong look. A hitch of a crooked smile makes Charlie's heart stutter. How can he sound so filthy but look so mischievous?

"I want it," Charlie says, shuffling closer and raising a leg to rest on Gordon's shoulder.

Gordon lifts the other leg up and kisses Charlie's calf, tenderly stroking his ankle while his eyes rake over Charlie. Has there ever been a time where Charlie felt simultaneously so powerful and powerless during sex? He's completely at Gordon's mercy, but he can see the effect he has on him.

Then Gordon slides inside him in one powerful, long thrust, and Charlie doesn't feel anything but mindless pleasure and the desperate need for more. More closeness, more of Gordon's grip on his hips, more of his, "That's so good, baby. Look at you, fuck yeah, you're so perfect." More of their skin touching and coming together, more of Gordon filling Charlie, more of this. Them.

He just wants more of this, forever, because he'll never get enough.

When he comes, it doesn't feel like it originates from any one place, instead radiating out from his hips until he's shuddering and yelling, covering his chest and stomach in pulse after pulse from his cock.

Gordon lets out a breathless, happy laugh, tugs at Charlie's legs to change his angle slightly, and only pounds into him a few more times before he's coming too, his face suffused with the kind of ecstasy that Charlie knows he won't ever forget. Never mind that he's fucked-out and slack-brained. He's painting this into his memory because it would take paint to capture how gorgeous Gordon is.

After a few more lazy thrusts, Gordon carefully pulls out. Oversensitivity crackles like television static under Charlie's skin, the echoes of something cosmic. Then Charlie feels some of Gordon's cum trickle out, which is a lot less cosmic and a lot more wanton. Gordon eyes it before he gives Charlie a dirty grin, bends over, and licks a stripe across Charlie's sensitive hole.

Charlie bucks, shouting, and Gordon laughs before he pins Charlie to the bed with his body and kisses him. His mouth tastes like musk and cum and it's dirty but sweet at the same time, because he's smiling against Charlie's lips.

"I love you," Gordon says. "I love you, I love you, I love you."

Hugging Gordon tightly, Charlie gives him a hard kiss in return and replies fiercely, "I love you too."

Eventually, one of them remembers that it's a work day and they can't stay in bed all morning, kissing and touching lazily. Once they've showered, Charlie turns on the coffee maker. As it gurgles and rattles to life, Charlie remembers, "My car's still at El Loro del Norte."

"And my laptop's at home," Gordon says, peering hopefully at the coffee maker's first few drips. "I'll drive you up to Hibbing before I head back." He hesitates. "Sorry in advance for being not smooth, but do you want to do something after work? Dinner or something? I'd invite you to come work at my house, but that's probably overboard."

There's a hopeful look on his face even as he says that last part, though, and Charlie's chest feels light. "I could come over and work at your house," he says, trying to sound casual and knowing that he's completely failing.

Gordon shoots him a smile so bright that it easily outshines the pale November sunrise outside. "We're not smooth," he says. He looks thrilled about it.

"Not at all," Charlie agrees.

The coffee maker hisses and burbles, and Charlie knows this is the point you can pour yourself a perfect cup. On the way to pour it for Gordon, he gets distracted by the prospect of putting his hands on Gordon's shoulders and looping his arms around Gordon's neck, and when Gordon pulls him close for a slow kiss filled with promises, Charlie gives up on the perfect cup of coffee.

Chapter Twenty-Eight

OVER THE next few weeks, fall spins into winter. Frost turns to snow, the sparkling on brown grass, fallen leaves, and windshields turning to a clean white dusting It's not much yet, just the kind that reminds you you're in northern Minnesota and you'd better be prepared. It's crunchy underfoot when Charlie and Gordon take walks around the land.

Every time Charlie looks at the property now, a twangy snap of gratitude goes through him. It could be gone. It could have been turned into a Walmart. It doesn't take him long to realize he unwittingly sabotaged all of Ibrahim's plans—he was the one who cleaned up the house and tidied things before Gordon got there, hiding away the book that contained the letter in the nightstand.

After Charlie reads Ibrahim's letter—and cries over it—he confesses to Gordon that he nearly ruined everything. Gordon looks at him like he's crazy and says, "There was no way we weren't going to meet. It was pretty much fate."

Which is such a sweet, unexpected thing to say (so much about Gordon is sweet and unexpected), that Charlie pulls him into the bedroom. Gordon's fancy new bed has had plenty of breaking in since it was delivered, but there's always room for more. Fate can't expect them not to explore their compatibility to its fullest extent.

Over Thanksgiving, Gordon invites his friend Jennifer up for a couple days. The idea of meeting her puts Charlie on edge, but Gordon assures him he doesn't even have to come over if he doesn't feel comfortable. "I want to show you off," Gordon tells him like it's obvious, "but I don't want you to be miserable." Sweet and unexpected again. When Charlie goes over to Gordon's to meet her, his stutter is manageable.

Edna's puts up Christmas lights, it snows again (enough to require driveway shoveling and make Gordon vow to hire a plowing service so he never has to shovel his driveway again), and the lakes start to freeze over. One of Charlie's and Gordon's walks on Ibrahim's land takes them down to Sawmill Lake, the body of water the town is named for. As they stand on the shore, mud frozen into the shapes of whatever animals last walked there, Gordon stares out at the still surface, his breath fogging in front of him.

The remnants of a floating dock are half beached about thirty feet down the shoreline, where there's also a beach that's part sand and part mud. The dock is very DIY—rotting plywood over old plastic barrels that have been bleached so badly by the seasons that Charlie can only guess at their original color.

"I can't believe you never mentioned I own a lake," Gordon says. He's smiling, but there's a funny note in his voice.

Charlie shrugs and burrows deeper into his jacket, pulling the shearling collar up around his ears. The chill coming off the water is damp and wants to settle right in his bones. "Ibrahim hated it. I sort of forget it's here."

With a slow nod, Gordon exhales a plume of breath that glitters in the still, frigid air. "I have a weird memory," he says like he's not sure he should. When Charlie turns to look at him, his gaze is far away. "I think I might have almost drowned?"

Charlie's stomach clenches and he can't help but find Gordon's gloved hand, hooked by a thumb from his jeans pocket. Gordon curls his fingers around Charlie's and tucks both their hands into the pocket of his jacket. "Here?" Charlie asks, throat tighter than it should be, considering this must have been years ago. Decades. If Gordon isn't sure, he must have been a young child.

"I don't know." Gordon casts his eyes over the lake, like the mirrored water and creep of lacy ice might have an answer. Branches snick against each other in a slight breeze, that kind of winter wind that you can't see but can feel. He shakes himself. "You know what? I've never even wondered why this town is called Sawmill Lake. Was there actually a sawmill here?"

"On the other side of the lake," Charlie says. Gordon looks pleased and impressed he knows, which makes a little glitter bomb go off inside Charlie. "I've been over there once. There's not much to see. I think most of the stone got taken to use in other buildings when the mill stream stopped flowing."

His area history is a little hazy. The stream was deeper at one point? Or wider? And it got diverted or something. Or maybe the industry just moved on, which he's fine with, because he doesn't need logging so close to where he's banding.

"Gor," Charlie says quietly. Another thought has snuck in among the quiet of the December day, the bare branches and the still water. "Do you really think you almost drowned? Do you think… that maybe that's why your mom and Ibrahim stopped talking?"

The start of surprise that goes through Gordon looks like a shiver—which maybe it is. Maybe Charlie's projecting, thinking it's surprise, because his own surprise feels like a physical thing.

"Did he say something like that?" Gordon asks.

Charlie shakes his head. "He never said anything about it. Really. I just thought, if you remember something… and Ibrahim didn't like the lake. I don't think he ever came over here. When I realized the lake was on his property, I asked if he ever went out on it, and he got…."

It's a hazy half memory of his own: Charlie excited about cleaning up the old canoe they used when he was a kid—his mom, his sister, and him, after his dad walked out on them but before Hannah pulled up stakes and left at sixteen—so he could bring it out on old Sawmill Lake. He'd gotten way ahead of himself, which he can recognize now was because he'd lost his mom and was looking for someone to fill that role, and Ibrahim had stepped into it so naturally.

"He got annoyed," Charlie finishes. That doesn't really describe it. The way Ibrahim had gotten was like a brittle veneer of acceptable irritation over a deep, dark chasm of emotion that he was straining not to let loose. Charlie had felt like he was looking into an ocean trench, full of things he'd never understand, or like the depths of Lake Superior, rusty and corroded wrecks that won't ever see the light of day again. "It was obvious something happened here, but I never mentioned it again."

Gordon makes a little sound, thoughtful and maybe a little sad. "I guess it doesn't really matter, does it? My mom and Jiddi went to their deaths without ever getting over it. Maybe it's better if I don't know. It would be, like, perpetuating the cycle or something."

Charlie holds his breath to stop himself from blurting out anything. One, two, three, four, breathe. The words come out anyway: "But do you want to know?"

Making a face, Gordon says with exasperated interest, "*Yes*. It's such a mystery! Like, perfect letter, Jiddi, except why didn't you put that part in? Ugh. This is super petty, isn't it? This isn't the point of anything. Right?"

"Yeah, maybe." The tightness that seized Charlie's lungs at the thought of Gordon drowning is finally loosening, enough so that he can pull their hands out of Gordon's pocket and kiss the fuzzy, gloved back of Gordon's hand. "But if you want to know, maybe you should try asking your dad."

At the suggestion, Gordon rakes his free hand through his hair. "I haven't talked to my dad since Father's Day." He laughs. "Jesus—I haven't told him I'm bi. This is going to be a wild call. 'Hey Dad, did I almost drown when I was a kid and is that why Mom and Jiddi never talked to each other again? Also I like guys now, too, I have a boyfriend, and I'm moving back to Sawmill Lake.'"

The idea of being even obliquely introduced to someone's parents makes Charlie feel queasy. "That might be a lot for one call."

The magic powers Gordon uses to sense when Charlie starts having a social anxiety crisis kick in, and Gordon hugs him. "I don't have to say anything about you if I call."

"Will he want to talk to me if you do?" Charlie asks. His voice wants to crack, which is embarrassing.

Gordon scoffs. "No." Immediately, he looks upset. "That sounded horrible. It has nothing to do with you, sweetheart."

In addition to being absolutely filthy in bed, Gordon has turned out to have a full phalanx of pet names that he was just waiting to deploy. Charlie gets an urge to run around in circles like a happy puppy every time Gordon calls him any of them. "I'm not offended, I don't want to talk to him either." When Gordon laughs, Charlie adds, "Plus, if you're going to call him to ask about the… lake"—he can't bring himself to say *almost drowning*—"it should probably just be a conversation about you. Talking about me is a distraction."

Gordon tightens his arms around Charlie and hitches him closer. "You," he says in a low, purposeful voice, "are not a distraction."

"I was a distraction when I came over for lunch the other day," Charlie points out.

"You are occasionally a distraction," Gordon amends. "You can keep being that kind of occasional distraction."

"Occasional?" Charlie asks, mock affronted.

"Only because I can't take a long lunch every day," Gordon sighs. "I need a lot of time to make sure I eat you out as thoroughly as you deserve."

Charlie's face goes so hot that he's surprised vapor doesn't rise from it in the cold. Gordon grins. When a quick search for his voice yields nothing, Charlie leans down to kiss Gordon softly. Softer, probably, than most people would kiss their boyfriend after he says he likes to thoroughly eat them out. "I love you," he says when he remembers how to talk again.

Gordon threads his fingers through Charlie's hair and pulls him back down into a kiss.

On the walk back through the woods to the house, Gordon's phone rings from his pocket. Sometime in the past couple weeks, he changed his ringtone to a saw-whet call, which has made Charlie realize he has a powerful sense memory associated with it, and possibly a bit of a Pavlovian response.

When Gordon fishes it out of his pocket to look at the caller, a complicated series of emotions passes over his face. "It's Jason. Do you mind if I answer?"

Charlie waves a hand to indicate he doesn't and Gordon puts the phone to his ear. There's a seedling of a relationship between Charlie and Jason that started the night Jason came into El Loro del Norte just to talk to Charlie. Friendship is too strong a word to describe it, but they have a text conversation. Yesterday, Jason sent him a meme that actually made Charlie burst out laughing.

And his job is definitely in danger. Joel tried one more time to convince Gordon to list the property with him, which Gordon of course shot down. Jason told Gordon he had to go out to his car and cry after Joel shouted at him in front of half the office.

Since Charlie wouldn't have pegged Jason as a guy who would admit to crying in his car, he sent a sympathetic Ryan Gosling "Hey Girl" meme in solidarity. Jason sent back hugging gifs—plural, more than one, including one with a teddy bear—which Charlie still hasn't quite quantified into something that makes sense.

If you'd told him a few months ago he'd care at all about Jason Miller's emotional well-being, let alone care this much, he'd have asked what parallel universe you were visiting from.

Aside from pleasantries after he picked up, Gordon hasn't said much on the call. When he speaks, it's to murmur consolations. By the time he hangs up, beers with Jason have been arranged for the following day. "His cousin fired him," Gordon tells Charlie as they continue walking across dry, crunchy leaves. "That guy was a dick, but Jason thinks he'll never make it as a realtor without Joel helping him."

A squirrel climbs a tree in front of them, claws clicking and skittering on the bark. Something clicks in Charlie's brain, too, the same rapid tick of a thought that disappears into the branches. When he can't catch hold of it, he lets it go.

He reaches for Gordon's hand. They walk in silence for a few minutes, the sounds of the winter forest creaking and snapping around them. Nuthatches bleat overhead and chickadees scold.

Just before the house comes into sight, Gordon says, "I'm going to call my dad."

"Really?"

"Yeah." Gordon looks wryly at Charlie. "Not much good comes out of… I don't know, giving a family member so much power. My mom and my jiddi didn't speak for the rest of their lives after they fought. Jason staked all his ambition on his cousin. And I…." He pauses so long that Charlie's not sure he's going to go on, but then he says, "I could have asked my dad any time what happened between my mom and Jiddi, but I think I was afraid knowing would make me hate one of them."

Charlie squeezes Gordon's hand. "It won't."

Gordon's "Yeah" is more an exhaled cloud of breath than a word.

Chapter Twenty-Nine

GORDON DOESN'T let himself plan the call to his dad. If he thinks about it, he'll think too much and chicken out. His dad has a weird power over him too, even though they're barely involved in each other's lives. They're so uninvolved that Gordon can always hope that one day it will be better, and every time they talk on the phone it's obvious that if that's ever going to happen, it's not now.

They never talk about anything serious. They never talk about Mom, that's for sure.

While Charlie starts dinner, Gordon sits on the couch and calls his dad.

It rings so long that Gordon thinks his dad isn't going to answer. Just as he starts to formulate something to say in a voicemail, there's a click, and his dad's voice says, "Hey, Gordon. What's up? Everything okay?"

Which about sums it up. Why would he call unless something was wrong?

"I'm fine." Shit. Now that he's doing this, it feels weird to just launch into his question. "Um, how are you? How are Kim and Claire?" he tacks on, because it would be rude not to ask about his dad's wife and daughter. He's never thought of either of them as his stepmother and stepsister.

There's a heartbeat of a pause, like his dad's trying to decode what's going on. "They're good. Claire's doing hockey again this year. How's Becky? Did you guys set a date yet?"

He can't help laughing, which probably confuses his dad even more. "Becky and I broke up." And, yeah, that's not the kind of thing he'd tell his dad, at least not until the Christmas, birthday, or Father's Day call.

His dad is quiet again for a second before responding. "Are you joking?"

"No. Why would I be joking?"

"You laughed."

Gordon shakes his head, glad his dad can't see him. "Yeah, I—sorry. It's not funny. We broke up a few months ago. So yeah, the wedding's obviously off."

"I'm so sorry—"

"It's fine." He listens to the rhythmic thunk of a knife on a cutting board in the kitchen, a smoky desire to tell his dad he's seeing someone new drifting through him. More than drifting, maybe. Telling his dad would be some weird kind of satisfying. It might get a reaction, which is more than he's gotten out of his dad in years.

That's not fair to Charlie, though, who's so much more than a way to get a reaction out of his distant father. Gordon promised Charlie he wouldn't tell his dad about him yet, so he won't tell.

Shifting on the couch, Gordon asks, "You know how Mom and Jiddi cut each other out of their lives?"

"Jiddi?" The surprise in his dad's voice makes it easy to picture his face. Gordon has a bad feeling he gets the same expression of dumbfounded confusion when something comes out of left field to surprise him. "Wow. It's been a long time since I've heard you say that."

"Yeah." Gordon's throat hurt. "Probably since I was three, right?"

"Five. It was your fifth birthday."

The concrete proof that his dad remembers, that he in fact knows exactly what day it all went down, jolts Gordon unpleasantly. Does he really want to hear this?

Yes and no, and maybe that's something he's going to have to sit with. "What happened between them?"

There's such a long silence on the other end of the call that Gordon thinks it dropped. "Dad? Are you still there?"

His dad draws in a long breath. "Yeah. Sorry. Geez, Gordon. Where's this coming from? It's been a lot of years to dredge all that up again."

In the kitchen, the fridge opens and shuts, and a stove burner clicks, the gas tick-tick-ticking until the flame whomps on. They're having lemon and zucchini pasta for dinner with some zucchini they found in the back of Charlie's freezer the other day. Next summer, Gordon's going to try to get a garden growing in his yard. He has a sun-drenched, romantic vision of preparing home-cooked meals with vegetables from his own garden with Charlie.

"I'm back in Sawmill Lake," Gordon says. Of course his dad doesn't know about any of it. There was zero reason for him to be in Jiddi's will.

"*What?*"

"Jiddi passed away," Gordon goes on. "He left me his house and all the land."

"Are you pulling my leg?" His dad sounds like he can't decide if he should be laughing or not. "Sawmill Lake? You couldn't wait to get out of there!"

Gordon swivels so he can look over his shoulder into the kitchen. The stove isn't visible from this angle, but he can see the shutter of light and shadow as Charlie moves around. "Yeah, well. Things change, I guess."

"Guess so." His dad sighs. "You really want to hear all this? It's ancient history."

"I think I have to."

Another sigh gusts into the phone. "You probably don't even remember, but you spent a lot of time with Ibrahim. Your jiddi. You loved being over there, and he was really good with you. Always said you were his habibi." Gordon has no idea what that means, but he's assuming it's good. It sounds pretty too. "You loved the birds. Amira—sorry, your mom, she always worried about them hurting you, but Ibrahim said you had a connection to them."

Ever since Gordon found the letter, he's tried to remember Jiddi's hawks and falcons. Sometimes flashes come to him of slate-blue feathers and bright orange eyes, and he wonders if that's Zarqaa, who he apparently loved.

Even if he can't remember the hawks, though, he knows he has a connection to birds of prey, because of the way he fell head over heels for saw-whets. "I think he was right about that."

"Oh yeah? Well, he'd be happy." His dad actually sounds interested. He has no idea how happy Jiddi would be. "Especially after…. Damn. This is harder than I thought to talk about." He clears his throat. "We were going to have a party for you at our house, but your mom and I wanted to get things ready to surprise you, so we dropped you off at your jiddi's place for him to watch you. You wanted to go swimming at the big lake. That's what you always called it—"

"Sawmill Lake," Gordon interrupts. "Like, Sawmill *Lake* Lake. There was a floating dock?"

"Yeah," his dad says, clearly surprised and thinking Gordon remembers instead of that he stood there looking at the sad remains of that dock today, a memory vaporing around the edges of his mind. "When we came to pick you up, we went straight down to the lake. When we got there, Ibrahim was with one of his birds. It was fussing about something and he was trying to calm it down. You were....” There’s a silence. “You were in the water, not moving. Just floating there, not making any noise. You went under and didn’t come back up, and Ibrahim never noticed.”

“Jesus,” Gordon exhales.

“I’ve never seen your mom move so fast. She was in the water before I even figured out what was happening. Pulled you out, got you breathing again. And then she let her dad have it.” His dad pauses, and the silence stretches longer this time. “I thought she might kill him. The bird got loose and took off, and then he was yelling at her about that too. You were crying, I thought about almost drowning, or because of the screaming, but when I left with you, you kept howling about the bird getting lost. Your mom accused her dad of caring more about his birds than you. I agreed with her.”

The line goes quiet again. Suddenly, Gordon can picture his dad sitting in his favorite recliner, leaning forward so his shoulders hunch and his head droops. There’s not much hair left on his dad’s head to hang over his face, just some gray-blond wisps that he tries to arrange to look fuller. Gordon definitely takes after his mom.

He realizes he should say something, but his mouth is dry. It feels like he hasn’t taken a breath in minutes—like he’s back in the lake, sinking below the surface. “They never talked again after that?” Gordon asks, obviously. The entire arc of his life feels tied to that moment and that decision.

“I don’t know what they did after your mom and I got divorced.”

Gordon shakes his head, then remembers he’s on the phone. “Yeah, no. They didn’t talk after that.” For a second he expects his dad to say something about the divorce. An apology, maybe, for... what? Not breaking up the marriage. It was obvious how much happier his mom was after the divorce.

No, Gordon wants an apology for the fact that his parents got divorced and his dad checked out. And maybe it’s not the same thing, but that day on the lake made Jiddi check out of his life too. It’s not even abandonment issues, it’s something less interesting.

Which is always how Gordon’s felt, he realizes. Less interesting than everyone else.

A shape interrupts the light spilling in from the kitchen. Gordon looks over his shoulder to see Charlie standing there, forehead creased into furrows and teeth notched into his bottom lip.

He's never been less interesting to Charlie. And Charlie kept opening the door to him. Welcoming him and teaching him and making him feel—making him *realize*—that he has things to offer too. He holds out a hand, and Charlie stops biting his lip as he crosses the living room to slip his hand into Gordon's.

His dad's voice on the phone surprises him, because the rough warmth of Charlie's palm against his filled up all the corners of his attention. "Are you going to sell the old place?"

"No." Gordon brushes his thumb over the back of Charlie's hand, marveling at the delicacy of the bones when he knows how strong Charlie is. "I was going to sell when the lawyer first called me, but then I got up here and…." He meets Charlie's eyes. "And things are different now."

With a surprised sound, his dad says, "They must be."

Dinner is probably almost done, and Gordon found out what he wanted to know, so he can end this call. Calls with his dad never last more than ten minutes anyway, and even that would be pushing it. He thinks about how he just had to give this town a chance, though, and how it gave back to him once he did.

"Hey, Dad, I have to go, but maybe we could talk again when we both have some more time? Or—" Is he really going to suggest this? "—maybe we could get together sometime. Meet halfway or something."

"I'd like that, Gordy," his dad says with a surprising fragility, like maybe he wanted that too but was too afraid to ask.

Well, if you spend your whole life being afraid to act, how are you ever going to be happy?

The conversation only takes another few seconds to wrap up, and when Gordon puts down his phone, he pulls Charlie's hand to his mouth and kisses it, keeping his lips pressed to Charlie's skin after.

"Did you find out what you wanted?" Charlie asks.

"Yeah."

"Do you want to talk about it?"

Gordon's a verbal processor, so yeah, definitely, at some point. Right now, though, he says into Charlie's knuckles, "I think I have to let it settle for a while."

Charlie nods. "Okay." He leans over and plants a kiss in the center of Gordon's head, his breath moving Gordon's hair and tickling him a little. "Dinner's pretty much ready."

Getting to his feet, Gordon slips a hand around Charlie's waist and says, "Thanks, babe. Sorry you had to do it all yourself."

"No, no, it's fine." Charlie leads him into the kitchen and finishes cooking as Gordon gets plates and silverware for the counter. Every few seconds, Charlie darts a glance at Gordon, and it's been long enough now that Gordon recognizes Charlie's I-need-to-say-something face.

The pasta is really good, like everything Charlie makes. Get yourself a man who can cook, and everything. None of his recipes are complicated, but they're all delicious. Which means Gordon eats half his share before he says, "I can tell you're thinking about something." Charlie ducks his head, smiling a little at getting caught, and Gordon nudges him with his foot. "Go ahead. There's plenty to unpack from that call with my dad."

At that Charlie blinks, his eyes widening a little. "Oh! No, that's not—I was thinking about something else." He chews his lip for a second, but before Gordon has much time to wonder what *something else* is, Charlie says in a rush, "I think you should sell the land."

Chapter Thirty

CHARLIE WINCES, because as usual, he's just blurting things out. "Sorry, that's not—I should back up."

Gordon puts his fork down, looking somewhere between shocked, horrified, and amused. It's honestly not an expression Charlie thought was possible for a person to make. "Did I just get proof of an alien abduction?" Gordon asks.

Swiveling his chair so he can face Gordon, Charlie says, "I think you should sell the land to me."

The idea came to him when he heard Gordon tell his dad over the phone that when he first inherited the house, he was going to sell it. That made Charlie think about Jason needing Gordon to list with his fucker of a cousin, Joel, so he wouldn't lose his job, and how Jason *did* lose his job. And that made Charlie wish there was a solution that would keep the land and house intact and out of the hands of developers, but also didn't mean Jason needed to give up on his dream of being a realtor.

Again, what is this universe where he cares about Jason Miller's dreams, but this is where he is. That teddy bear hugging a heart that Jason sent might have jarred something loose in his brain.

Charlie hasn't really thought any of this through, but he's pretty sure it's a good idea and that it will work. "Jason wants to be a realtor but thinks he needs his cousin to do it. Hire him as your realtor, get him to list the land, and I'll buy it. It's worth two million dollars, right?"

"Uh." Gordon stares. "I think Joel said I could maybe get up to a million?"

Leaning forward, Charlie says, "Gor. I have two million dollars. Tell Jason you want to list for two million. I'll pay asking."

Now Gordon is shaking his head. "No. No way! Charlie, that's so much money."

It *is* so much money, and honestly, Charlie hasn't thought about this for more than ten minutes, but with each passing second, he becomes more wedded to it. "You have student loans to pay off," he says, which is playing dirty. But he wants this. He wants to give this to Gordon.

"Not *two millions dollars* worth!" Gordon looks appalled. "Anyway, you need that money for your project. You need to buy the radio transmitters to be able to track down the gay owls."

It's Charlie's responsibility as a researcher to remind Gordon that you really can't ascribe human sexual orientation to animals, but the words won't come. He's too taken aback by the fact that Gordon cares that much about his research. "I…." He shakes his head. "I want to give you a fair price for the land. If you want to sell." He adds the last part sheepishly. "Sorry. I'm getting ahead of myself. Would you want to sell it to me?" He stops to consider for a second. "Is this a stupid idea?"

Gordon finally picks up his fork again and takes a couple more bites of dinner. His expression goes from vaguely mulish to considering, and Charlie jiggles his knee, waiting.

"I'm not taking a million, and I'm especially not taking two million," Gordon says.

The victory of Gordon saying he'll do it gets swamped by Gordon being so stubborn about the amount. "But—"

"You'll need that money," Gordon says firmly. "You can't keep doing accounting if you're up in the woods in Canada somewhere. I mean, think about it. You'll need an RV, right? It's way more practical than staying at a motel or an Airbnb. And you'll probably want a generator. And I assume there's special equipment to track the radio transmitters? Plus, maybe you'd want a satellite phone because I bet the cell signal is shit. How long do you figure you'd be up there?"

Charlie doesn't realize how dumbly he's staring until Gordon addresses that last question. "Um. Well, breeding season is March to May, but the males start defending territory earlier. The spring migration isn't that well understood. Or their breeding range, actually."

"So you're going to make a huge contribution to saw-whet research," Gordon says like all of this is a done deal and not a pipe dream. "You should keep the money, baby. My jiddi wanted you to have it."

"He wanted us to be together," Charlie says. "So it will still be your money."

"Only if you're proposing marriage," Gordon points out like it's a joke.

Charlie opens his mouth to say, *No, of course not, it's much too early, that's crazy.* Without saying anything, though, he closes it, looking at his lap to gather his thoughts. This part, he's not going to blurt out. This part, he needs to think about, because he's so bad at talking, but some things are too important to mess up.

"Sweetheart?" Gordon says, sounding worried.

With a deep breath, Charlie slides off his chair to stand in front of Gordon, who looks at him with wide eyes. "I'm not proposing marriage," Charlie says carefully. "But I know myself, and I trust what I feel. And Gordon, the way I feel about you is... forever." There's a brightness to Gordon's eyes, and his throat bobs as he swallows.

Lightly, Charlie puts his hand on Gordon's leg, savoring the body heat soaking through the denim of Gordon's jeans into the tips of Charlie's fingers. "So this isn't a proposal. I don't ever need to get married. I don't know if you'd even want to get married—"

"I do," Gordon interrupts. His voice is fierce, edged in joy like a winter sunset edges itself in rose, glittering like fresh snowfall under moonlight. "I want to get married. To you. You could propose to me right now and I'd say yes."

Charlie's heart thuds so hard against his rib cage that he worries he pulled something. Stupidly, his mouth goes completely dry as Gordon's words cast everything in Charlie's life in bright, golden light. "You would?" he squeaks.

Gordon pushes his plate away from the edge of the counter in a clatter of cutlery and Corelle and stands, his body pressed right up against Charlie's. Dark hair falls in his eyes and licks curl under his ears, and Charlie imagines watching the black turn to gray and silver, and how he could be the luckiest person in the world to see that, and how the laugh lines in Gordon's face will get deeper, and the little crinkles at his eyes will fan out.

"Yeah," Gordon says. "Yeah, Charlie, of course I would. Of course I feel forever about you too, baby."

Charlie succumbs to the need to bury his fingers in Gordon hair, combing through his curls and tugging them until Gordon's face tilts up and Charlie can brush his lips over Gordon's. Then, because he's ridiculous, he murmurs, "So you'll let me buy the land?"

With a laugh, Gordon cups his hands around the back of Charlie's neck and pulls him into a hard kiss.

Epilogue

"IT SHOULD be right around here." Gordon pinches the tablet to zoom in on the map, hoping the radius of the transmitter they're tracking might shrink. No go. It stays stubbornly wide, which means they might still be as far as sixty feet from their goal.

Next to him, Charlie cranes his neck, peering up into the cedars towering over them. "Is the signal okay?"

"Yeah, good signal." The dot indicating the GPS tracker they affixed to an owl last October jogs a little. Maybe a satellite just passed overhead. "Let's try this way," Gordon adds, keeping his voice down. They're out here this afternoon to identify good spots for net lanes so they can get nets up in the next couple days, once they get approval from the park on their chosen locations.

They wind amidst the trees, fallen cedar needles carpeting the ground and deadening their footsteps. The thickness of the forest makes the late afternoon into more of a gloomy early evening, but finding saw-whets during the day is a million times harder, so failing light it is. Charlie gets ahead of Gordon, and for a second, Gordon gets distracted watching him and the graceful, long-limbed way he moves. Some things you never get tired of watching, and his boyfriend in his element is definitely one of those things.

Fiancé! Not just boyfriend anymore, fiancé. It's so new that he hasn't gotten used to it yet.

His toe catches on a root and he stumbles. His first reaction is to clutch the tablet to his chest to shield it. If he's going down, he's saving the tablet. The research! The research is more important than the structural integrity of his bones.

At Gordon's grunt of surprise, Charlie whirls and catches him, keeping him upright. "My hero," Gordon says, feeling ridiculous for tripping.

Charlie has one hand on Gordon's shoulder and the other on his chest, and he's looking at Gordon with concern. "Are you okay?"

248 LEE PINI

Shaking out his free arm, Gordon says, "I didn't drop the tablet."

"Gor, I care about you, not the tablet." Charlie pats him like he's looking for hidden injuries, and it's unbearably sweet.

"I'm okay, baby. Really." Gordon reaches up to pluck cedar needles out of Charlie's hair, taking the opportunity to brush a thumb over his cheekbone. "I just have to get used to the rugged terrain of the Canadian wilderness."

Charlie laughs. "You can literally see Thunder Bay from this park."

"Thunder Bay is basically wilderness," Gordon points out, which makes Charlie laugh again. Gordon loves making Charlie laugh. And he loves even more when Charlie makes him laugh, which shouldn't surprise him anymore but somehow still does. Living with Charlie, being engaged to Charlie, hasn't taken any of the edge from his sharp, funny, and sometimes wicked sense of humor.

Then, because Charlie's smiling and that's Gordon's favorite sight in the entire world, he fists his hand in Charlie's hair and pulls him into a kiss.

When they separate, Charlie's smile is bigger. "At least this park has road access. We could've—"

His eyes widen and he squeezes Gordon's shoulder hard. Gordon doesn't have to ask what's there. Slowly, he turns. On the tree behind him, the tree whose root he tripped over, about five and a half feet off the ground, a northern saw-whet owl sits on a branch staring at them. The GPS tracker they fitted it with last fall is visible, the antenna hanging down from the owl's back, where the tracker sits nestled in its feathers.

"Hi, Tangle," Gordon breathes.

It was perfect, really, when they re-caught Tangle (Charlie insists they call Tangle by the number on his band, which Gordon gets, but... it's just not as catchy). He ended up in their nets in early October, just as tangled up as he was the first time. It's clearly his thing. Charlie was vibrating with excitement when Gordon read the band and recognized one of their own, and the fact that they managed to recapture one of their owls made Tangle the perfect owl on which to install the first of their ten GPS trackers.

Even though Charlie still has plenty of money left over from buying the land, he didn't want to start with more than ten trackers. At close to five thousand dollars a pop, Gordon understood, even if he also kind of wanted to go crazy and get enough trackers to put on every owl they caught. Charlie pointed out that they have no idea if this project is going to work.

Gordon knows it's going to work. He knows it's going to work because Charlie designed it. He wrote up a proposal and he submitted it to an owl research organization, and they gave him a grant that's covering a bunch of the costs of living out of an RV for three weeks in a provincial park near Thunder Bay, Ontario.

On the branch in front of them, Tangle blinks his golden eyes. Gordon reminds himself not to anthropomorphize the adorable owl by wondering if it remembers them. But yeah, he totally hopes it remembers them.

With another blink, it shuffles sideways on the branch and takes off silently. It's immediately lost in the thick cedar stand, but the GPS trackers aren't almost five thousand dollars for nothing. The GPS data is instantaneous, and even if it's not exact down to the centimeter, it's still pretty close. They're able to follow Tangle's flight path to a dead cedar nearby, which is riddled with holes from woodpeckers.

Charlie taps Gordon on the shoulder and points. About ten feet off the ground is a hollow large enough for a saw-whet owl to fly in and out of, and below it is a large branch, where a saw-whet is sitting. It's obviously not Tangle, since this one doesn't have a tracker. Gordon squints but doesn't see a band, either.

"Is Tangle around here?" Charlie whispers. Gordon gives him a gleeful look. Charlie mumbles something that sounds like a bunch of numbers, and still grinning, Gordon shows him the tablet, which shows Tangle stationary somewhere in the vicinity.

Suddenly, the owl on the branch lets out a high-pitched *toot-toot-toot-toot*. Watching a saw-whet produce its mating call during breeding season hits harder than Gordon thought it would. He's so used to listening to that sound nonstop every night from the audio lure for a month and a half that it's bizarre to watch it happening.

Charlie grips Gordon's bicep. "That's a male," he breathes. Gordon knew that—he's learned something after two banding seasons—but hearing the breathless excitement in Charlie's voice is one of his favorite things in the world. He'd be happy to let Charlie teach him his colors and shapes if it made him excited like this.

The second owl goes silent before calling again. Gordon glances at the tablet, which is still showing Tangle nearby. The indicator judders a little and the altitude quickly drops to zero before climbing again. It takes Gordon a second to realize Tangle probably just tried to make a kill, swooping down to the ground for a mouse or vole.

He looks around the forest, squinting through the thickening dark. They'll have to switch on their headlamps to walk back to the trailhead, where the RV is parked. This seems like a good spot for the nets, but Charlie will be the one who decides. Tangle is hanging around here, though, and there's definitely at least one other male owl in the area, so hopefully they'll be able to band and get a few more GPS trackers on some males.

A silent, dark shape flits overhead, circling again and again. By the tenth circle, they've confirmed in hushed voices that it's definitely Tangle because they can see the GPS tracker on his back.

"What's he doing?" Gordon whispers.

There's a jump in Charlie's throat and his pulse is visibly thrumming in his neck. "Male owls circle a potential mate like this. With prey, usually. Can you see if he has something?"

Gordon has never wished harder to see a dead mouse in his entire life, but Tangle is flying too quickly, and the dark is coming on too fast.

After several more circles, Tangle slows and lands on the branch next to the male owl who's been calling. There's just enough light left to see that there's something in his talons and splashes of red on the white feathers covering his legs.

Charlie sucks in a sharp breath and fumbles for his phone, getting it into video mode and holding it up. "He's presenting prey. It's—he—I can't narrate, oh my god. Our confirmed male owl by weight and tail length, band number—um, Gor, what's the band number?"

"Can't remember," Gordon says, wanting to jump up and down and dance around Charlie yelling like an idiot. They're watching one male owl perform mating behavior toward another male owl.

"Tangle," Charlie says helplessly. "We're watching Tangle present a prey item to another male, confirmed by call."

The other male studies Tangle before moving closer and ripping at the prey with his beak. Charlie squeaks and Gordon puts a steadying hand on the back of his neck. His own smile is so wide that his cheeks hurt. "Breathe, sweetie. Don't pass out and miss this."

Leaning back into Gordon's touch, Charlie narrates for the video, "This is the first recorded instance of same-sex sexual behavior in northern saw-whet owls, and—this video is horrible and I'm going to get a much better one with the good camera, oh my god—"

Tangle feeds a piece of gristle to the other male and Gordon rubs Charlie's neck in lieu of jumping up and down and dancing around Charlie, yelling like an idiot. Within a few minutes, the owls finish eating. As silently as they both appeared, they take flight again, disappearing into the dark trees.

Charlie stops recording and flings himself into Gordon's arms. Even though Charlie has five inches on him, Gordon lifts him off his feet and spins him around. They're both laughing, and it sounds like Charlie also might be crying a little, but then laughing again. It's a lot. Gordon gets it. Emotions don't always come out the way they're supposed to when you're in the middle of a life-defining moment.

When Gordon puts Charlie back on his feet, Charlie grabs his face in both hands and kisses him hard. Gordon holds him close and kisses him back, and when they finally break apart, Charlie says, "I never would have done this if not for you."

"Yeah, you would've." Gordon hugs him tighter for a second. "But I'm glad if I helped you get here."

"You did." Charlie strokes Gordon's face before burying his fingers in Gordon's hair. Somewhere in the distance, a saw-whet calls. Gordon smiles and tilts his face up again to meet Charlie's kiss.

Acknowledgments:

Like Charlie (and now Gordon), I spend October and part of November sitting out in the dark woods listening to the lure and hoping to get northern saw-whet owls in the nets. My endless gratitude goes to Michelle, our project leader, for her enthusiasm and generosity in sharing her knowledge and training with us volunteers. Michelle and her husband, Mark, have taught me so much about birds and banding over the years. They both have an incredible amount of knowledge and experience, and I'm lucky that I get to learn from them. I'm also grateful to everyone else on the crew for their experience, knowledge, and company, as well as Kirk and the rest of the naturalists at LNC.

Thank you so much to the team at Dreamspinner! Publishing a book is a collaborative effort and I sometimes feel like I have the easiest job by writing it. From the editors to the art department to marketing, I couldn't be happier to have found a place there. Huge thanks also to my beta readers, Anke and Fuji.

My parents fostered a love of nature and wildlife in me from a young age, and it's one of the greatest gifts they've given me. Thanks, Mom and Dad!

Finally, as always, thank you to Laura, my favorite reader and my partner in everything.

Keep reading for an excerpt from
Six Places to Fall in Love
by Lee Pini!

Chapter One

June

THE RED of the sand against the blue of the reflected sky is so stark and bright it sears Percy's eyes. His camera shutter snaps as he takes a picture. It won't sell—who wants a picture of a puddle?—but it captures something about this place. The sky, the earth, the colors— maybe it's because he's from here, but there's nothing like an African sky to make him feel connected to everything. Everything that matters, at least.

The hum of an engine drifts in on the cool breeze. Percy's knees pop as he stands from his crouch in front of the puddle. He's feeling every one of his thirty-two years lately. It's going to be hell when he's actually old, but he'll keep coming to the bush until he literally can't. They'll have to drag him away.

No, scratch that—just let the hyenas and the jackals have him. Back to the land, or something. When he tells his friends he'd rather be eaten by scavengers, they either laugh like he's joking or look horrified. But if he says he wants to be part of the landscape he loves, that lives inside his soul, for eternity, then they look at him like he's mad. Maybe a bit happy clappy.

A Land Cruiser comes into view, bumping along the rutted road. Less road, more track. This is the part of the reserve set aside for conservation, so the roads are nearly nonexistent.

Percy shifts his camera and his rifle on his shoulder and watches the vehicle's approach. Its occupants resolve into two figures, driver and passenger. He hooks his fingers into his water bottle, pulls it out of his backpack, and twists the cap off to take a long drink.

The Land Cruiser pulls up in a cloud of dust and a man jumps out. It's one of those quintessential safari moments. Percy thinks about snapping a photo but doesn't. The man lifts out a pack and swings it onto his back, thumps the side of the Land Cruiser, and heads Percy's way.

Percy lifts his hand in a wave to the driver—it's Rhys, who cheerfully offers to sleep with Percy every time Percy's here (and just as cheerfully accepts the rejection)—then turns it to a thumbs-up. The Land Cruiser reverses, turns around, and is gone, leaving dust and the sound of its engine behind. Both settle to nothing as the man jogs across a gully with a trickle of water at the bottom.

Percy shoves his water bottle back into its pocket, considers smiling, and decides against it. Smiling doesn't come easily these days, and he's awkward enough without his weird hostage-situation rictus.

Midday sun glints off the silver in the man's hair. The contrast between the silver and the black of the rest of it is as stark as the sky against the ground. It would make a nice photo. The silver is premature—this man is surely around Percy's own age, maybe even a year or two younger. It's odd having seen someone's CV and knowing when they finished university, and by extension how old they are, but not having met the person yet.

As the man gets close, he extends a hand. "Hey there. I'm Rob. You must be Percy de Villiers."

Rob Hale's—he pronounces it Ha-lay, which is something Percy is determined to get right—easy grin makes it difficult not to like him immediately. The grin, plus the shadow of stubble on his jaw, plus his golden skin and the beachy wave to his salt-and-pepper hair, also makes it difficult not to find him attractive, which is sort of the last thing Percy needs.

"Yeah," Percy says, shaking Rob's hand. He watches for the flicker of reaction at his limp handshake. The bush is for the man's man, and Percy has been around enough men overflowing with misplaced machismo to last a lifetime.

Rob doesn't react. "It's great to finally meet you," he says in some indeterminate American drawl that might be Southern. There's a little gravel to his voice. He's shorter than Percy, but most people are. Some sort of Dutch gene for height was hiding in his mixed-up family tree and came out of hiding when he hit puberty. Rob is solid, too, almost stocky. Muscular. With a beard, he'd make a great bear. He's dressed appropriately for South Africa in late fall: brown khakis, gray T-shirt, green hoodie tied around his waist.

Percy casts a critical eye over Rob's pack, but it looks good. Compact, with the bedroll secured at the bottom. Percy has the tent—only one—strapped on his own pack. For safety's sake, he wanted them sleeping in the same tent, because that way Percy will wake up if Rob decides he wants to go on a late-night bush walk.

Hint: this is a bad idea.

"Listen," Rob says, "I want to start out by thanking you for letting me come with you. I know you had a lot of journalists submit applications, so it's really an honor to be selected."

God, Percy *hates* this sort of fawning. But Rob is right that a load of journos wanted this tag-along. What Rob doesn't know is that he only got the gig by the skin of his teeth. Percy's agent, Eunice, lobbied hard for a big-shot French nature writer, but Percy dug his heels in. He wanted Rob, and he's not sure he could even tell you why. His credentials aren't anything special, and he's never had a piece blow up. His blog does middling numbers. On the surface of things, he's an entirely average travel writer.

"Thank you for accepting the offer," Percy says. Can't go wrong with platitudes, yeah? "How was the trip in?"

"We had to stop and wait for elephants to cross the road!" The pure glee in Rob's voice makes Percy smile.

"Ellies are still hanging round the main fence, then, yeah?" The camera bumps against Percy's hip. "They were there when I drove up the other day too."

Percy could never be in the hospitality industry—and safari camps are a whole other level of hospitality. But the wonder on Rob's face gives Percy an inkling of why people do it. And he can tell that Rob is the kind of person who makes it worth it.

Something eases in his chest. This whole thing has been so stressful, even though it was his idea in the first place. The endless second-guessing about his choice has plagued Percy ever since Rob signed the contract. He hasn't had a solid six hours of sleep in months. Then again, he's got plenty to lose sleep over, so.

"I love it here already," Rob says.

"Your first time in Africa?"

"I went to Morocco once to write a piece on Moroccan leatherwork," he offers. "But sub-Saharan Africa, yeah. First time."

"You like it so far?"

Rob rakes his fingers through his shaggy black hair. "Honestly, I went straight from the airport to my hotel, and my transfer picked me up this morning and drove me up here. So I kind of feel like I've barely seen any of it so far."

Yeah, Americans don't tend to stop and play tourist in Joburg. Percy's usually torn between pride in his country and complete and total agreement on that score.

"Well," Percy says, "hopefully you got to stop at the lodge for some lunch before Rhys brought you out here."

Rob's eyes light up again—and again, Percy is struck by how good-looking he is. Obviously, Percy did some light online stalking of all the serious candidates, but he doesn't remember thinking Rob was anything special. Turns out he was very, very wrong about that, because Rob is dead fit.

"Yeah!" Rob replies. "Wow. It's gorgeous, isn't it? Have you stayed there?"

Percy nods. "The camp manager is a friend." Sort of an understatement. Katlego is the reason Percy made it out of childhood with his sanity intact. Intact-ish. She was his governess's daughter, and they were basically raised together. Katli is more like a sister than a friend. "You're staying a few nights after we're back from the bush, right?"

There's that easy grin again. "Are you kidding? That's definitely not the kind of place I can afford normally. I'm taking the chance to stay in the lap of luxury."

Percy's bankrolling this whole thing. He sees it as an excellent use of family funds. Doubtless his father would disagree, but his father has rather worn through his credibility when it comes to the proper use of money.

"Good," Percy says. He's itching to get out into the bush. His camera is loaded up with two blank memory cards, he has his other lenses snugged in the custom pocket in his pack, and he can tell the light's going to get better and better as the day goes on.

He clears his throat. "So. I know you signed all the waivers and release forms—"

"Yeah, if a lion eats me, my family won't sue."

With a snort, Percy goes on, "We have to go over some rules, though. Mainly one, really—the rest are all sub-rules of that." He pauses to make sure he has Rob's attention. "You must, at all times, do what I say. If I say stop, you stop. If I say go, you go. If I say climb that tree, you climb the tree. If I say run—and you better hope I don't say run—then you run. Also, my rifle is off-limits."

Rob nods. "Understood. You're the expert."

Sometimes people say that and they're patronizing him. It doesn't matter how many awards he's won, how many back country or bush or mountain treks he goes on. Some people hear de Villiers, and all they can see is a pampered, rich Cape Coloured kid. Never mind that he's got an Apprentice Field Guide qualification, and that includes the four hundred required hours. To plenty of South Africans, Percy is always going to be rooftop infinity pools, manicured gardens, eight beds/eight baths, and so far removed from the way most South Africans live that it's a joke.

Not that having the NQF2 is exactly a window into how most South Africans live, but, well—he did that on his own, and no amount of money or family connections could buy it. It's one of his proudest achievements.

It's also the only reason he can be out here in the bush with, as far as insurance is concerned, a tourist.

"My job isn't just taking nature photos this week." Percy gives Rob a serious look. "It's keeping you safe. Just because your family won't sue me if a lion eats you doesn't mean it's a good look."

Rob holds his hands up. "Sure. You have a reputation to consider. I get it."

Percy's shoulders tighten and he can't help the twitch of tension. "Yeah, right. My reputation. That's the idea behind all of this—get the focus back on my work, instead of"—he grimaces—"my personal life."

There's a sympathetic light in Rob's eyes, but Percy seriously doubts he has any real idea of what Percy's gone through the past few months. Which—ugh—sounds so whinging, so poor little rich boy. Other people have it worse. Obviously. So much worse. In fact, Percy feels responsible for a lot of that so-much-worse.

"I'm here to focus on your work," Rob says, before adding with a half smile, "And to not get eaten by a lion."

Oh *no*. He's this good-looking and he has a sense of humor?

Percy shifts his pack on his shoulders and steadies his camera and rifle. "Any questions before we start? Concerns I can alleviate?"

"Isn't bringing a healthy level of concern into the bush the right way to approach this?" That half smile flits across Rob's face again, a flash of crooked front teeth that Percy didn't think Americans were allowed to have.

It's impossible—literally impossible—not to return the smile. And that's red flags across the board, alarms and red alerts, all-hands-on-deck level *do not get this way with the journo you handpicked for this excursion.*

"I think we're going to get along," Percy says. He swigs from his water bottle and offers it to Rob, who takes it without any hesitation and drinks. "We walk single file. Keep your voice down and stay close to me so we don't look like something big and easy to pounce on."

Rob nods. Percy surveys their surroundings once more. There's nothing but birdsong and the occasional buzz of the insects that survive South Africa's fall and winter.

With a quick hand signal to indicate the direction they'll start off in, Percy takes the first long stride that will take them into the bush.

This had better all be worth it.

SCAN THE QR CODE
BELOW TO ORDER!

LEE PINI is a queer author who has been writing since they could pick up a pencil. They have lived in England, Northern Ireland, and Florida, and currently live in their home state of Minnesota with their wife and cat. Lee studied archaeology at the graduate level but currently uses their degree primarily to chuckle knowingly at classics memes. When they aren't at their day job or writing, they're reading vociferously, listening to music, enjoying nature, or nerding out. Their dream is for someone to one day write fanfiction about their characters.

Connect with Lee:
Website: www.leepini.com
Instagram: @leepiniwriting
Bluesky:@leepini.bsky.social
Facebook:http://www.facebook.com/lee.pini.is.writing

Follow me on BookBub

They say what happens in Vegas stays in Vegas, but when Lewis wakes up married after a wild, drunken night at his best friend's bachelorette party, he's worried he's affected the rest of his life. Tad might be sweet, drop-dead gorgeous, and so easy to be with, but the obvious solution is a speedy divorce. The fact that they both live in New York City should make the process easy… so why is it taking them so long to sign the papers? Or even take off their rings? And why do they keep ending up in bed?

Tad's anxiety and fear of coming out to his family has driven guys away before. Can he dare to believe Lewis is different? Lewis, his friends, and his loud, loving Italian family support Tad in a way he's never experienced, and it's easy to imagine a lifetime of that unconditional love. But life isn't a romcom…

Or is it?

SCAN THE QR CODE
BELOW TO ORDER!

The Boyfriend Fix

LEE PINI

Renowned surgeon Ben McNatt is up for the job of his dreams, and when he gets it, he'll be the youngest chief of neurosurgery in his hospital's history. His success rate is flawless, but his perceived lack of compassion is hurting his chances. He's always viewed relationships as a distraction, but a loving partner might change his colleagues' ideas about his heartlessness. He'll do whatever it takes for this promotion—even pretend to date. The natural choice for his fake boyfriend is the cute guy at the coffee shop.

Jamie Anderson is in student loan debt up to his eyeballs. He has three roommates, and not in a quirky found-family way. He works sixty hours a week as a barista, and his boss won't stop hitting on him. He's even given up on love. He makes do with fantasies about the hot doctor that comes in for coffee every day like clockwork.

A fake relationship might solve Jamie's handsy boss problem too. And there's no way it will lead to real feelings when that's the last thing either of them wants.

So why are they having so much trouble convincing themselves they aren't falling for each other?

Scan the QR Code
Below to Order!

In a last-ditch effort to finish a manuscript, Thomas Kovacs packs up his teenage daughter, Alexis, and relocates to a small town in northern England. Things have been strained between them for months, but the closer Thomas gets to the end of his book, the more distant Alexis becomes.

Krishna Singh came to Corbridge to open a bookstore and start a family. After two years, his business is thriving. His family? Well, he hasn't gotten around to that yet. Actually, he hasn't even dated. The closest he gets is bonding over books and music with an American teenager who comes into his shop.

When it turns out the teenager's dad is none other than Krishna's favorite author, he wastes no time in getting to know Thomas. But attempts at something more go about as well as Thomas's writing, or his relationship with Alexis. Can Krishna convince Thomas that they all deserve a happy-ever-after?

SCAN THE QR CODE
BELOW TO ORDER!

When We Finally Kiss Good Night

LEE PINI

Camp Bay Lake Holiday: Book One

Jake lost his Christmas spirit when his husband left him on December 26. This year, when a friend offers him her reservation at a resort in Florida, he jumps at the chance to get away. No snow, no Christmas trees, no problems.

Except the resort does a Christmas Golf Cart parade every year, and Alex, the man in the neighboring cabin, wants Jake's help with his.

Jake just wants to be left alone… until he spies Alex's design. Maybe working together won't be so bad. Can an unexpected friendship reawaken more than Jake's holiday spirit?

SCAN THE QR CODE
BELOW TO ORDER!

As Long As You Love Me So

Love Me So

LEE PINI

Camp Bay Lake Holiday: Book Two

Theo Stirling, a shy electrician at Camp Bay Lake Resort, has been secretly in love with his best friend and coworker, Adi Rodriguez, for years. Little does he know, Adi—a bubbly front desk worker and grad student—feels the same way about Theo. Neither has been brave enough to confess their feelings, but this Christmas, they both plan to use the resort's Golf Cart Parade as the perfect moment for a grand gesture.

Just when everything seems to be falling into place, Adi's sister is in a car accident, and he has to miss the parade. Determined not to lose his chance, Theo brings the holiday magic—and his heartfelt confession—directly to Adi and his family, proving that love is worth the wait.

A heartwarming rom-com about friendship, family, and the courage to take a leap, *"As Long As You Love Me So"* is full of holiday joy, humor, and romance.

SCAN THE QR CODE
BELOW TO ORDER!